MURDER BY COMMITTEE

A completely unputdownable cozy mystery

VERONICA HELEY

The Ellie Quicke Mysteries Book 6

JOFFE
Ostara
CLASSICS

Revised edition 2023
Joffe Books, London
www.joffebooks.com

First published by Severn House in Great Britain in 2005

This paperback edition was first published
in Great Britain in 2023

Cover art by Dee Dee Book Covers

ISBN: 978-1-83526-151-4

CHAPTER ONE

What woke her?

Was it the crash of glass being broken in the conservatory? No, that wasn't it. The digital clock on her bedside table said half past twelve. She listened. It appeared to be a quiet night. No cars in the street; not that there were usually many on this quiet side road. An owl hooting?

No, a man shouting in the distance.

Midge wasn't where he'd started the night, tucked up at her back. She turned on the bedside light. The cat was standing at the foot of the bed, ears pricked, looking at the door.

Ellie's mind went into overdrive, for she had good reason to be frightened.

The shouting was . . . where? Not at the front of the house, which was where she slept. Had he got into the garden? Perhaps he thought that Ellie slept in the back bedroom . . . now occupied by someone else?

Ellie groped for her mobile phone. Where had she left it? She searched through the clothes she'd taken off and then the pockets of the dressing gown hanging on the back of the door. Yes! The mobile was there. She hesitated. She didn't want to ring the police if it were just some stupid drunk yelling at the moon.

She opened her bedroom door. Midge poked his head out, and shot through the gap. She whispered, 'Come back, Midge!' He took no notice.

Well, the shouting had stopped. She'd over-reacted. There was no danger. She'd be jumping at shadows next.

Except she'd turned off all the lights before she came up to bed, and now there was a light on downstairs.

She could persuade herself that she'd forgotten to turn it off, and go back to bed. Or . . . she could go downstairs in the dark and see who had turned on the light in the kitchen.

Crack!

It sounded like a gunshot! Followed by the unmistakable sound of breaking glass.

And then someone swearing . . .

* * *

Ellie Quicke, widow, retrieved a plastic spaceman from under her dining table and sat back on her heels to scan her pretty green sitting room. Clearing up after her grandson's visit — much as she loved him — involved gymnastics and the occasional bout of furniture moving. She would be extremely glad when he outgrew his present habit of shredding paper and smashing plastic toys.

Ellie ran her fingers through her mop of short, silvery hair and pulled down her blue jumper, which had ridden up. She did not consider herself of an age when she could expose her midriff to view without embarrassment.

Her visitor was on the phone still, so Ellie lifted an empty coffee mug and mimed, 'Another?'

Kate was tall, dark and handsome; she was also a good friend and next-door neighbour. She was jiggling her delightful moppet of a baby against her shoulder, while holding her mobile phone to her ear with her free hand. Judging by her frown, Kate wasn't hearing good news.

Kate shook her head at Ellie's offer of another coffee and said into the phone, 'But . . . that's ridiculous! And very short-sighted of him.'

The phone quacked, and Ellie dived under the settee for a torn sheet of paper. This one was buff-coloured, and looked official. Oh dear! How on earth had little Frank got hold of that? She scrambled to her feet, still holding the scrap of paper. Where was the rest of it?

Kate said, 'Yes, of course I realize that there's a lot at stake, but you want me to do . . . what? Yes, of course, I see that discovering who had really done it might help, but it's not my field . . . Yes, yes. I have mentioned her in the past, but . . .'

She looked directly at Ellie, who mimed, 'Me?' and pointed at herself. How could she possibly be the subject of a conversation Kate was having with her boss? At least, Ellie assumed it was her boss.

Until the birth of little Catriona, Kate had held down an important job in the City, which had brought in far more money than her foxy-faced teacher husband would ever make. Before Catriona had been born, Kate had planned to put her into a crèche when she was six months old, and go back to work, but now the six months was up, Kate couldn't bear the thought of leaving her baby.

As she'd just been telling Ellie, Kate wanted to stop work altogether for a couple of years, because they could manage on Armand's salary for a while if they were careful. He was as besotted with Catriona as Kate, but it took him differently. He wanted her to have a private education — which neither of them had ever had — and he wanted to do a loft conversion, so that she might have her own big room for all the toys he wanted to give her. They'd need Kate's salary to pay for that.

They'd also discussed downsizing, selling their house and moving out of London, but it would have meant a long commute for him, and Kate didn't really want to do that because she loved her little house and garden and living next door to Ellie. They'd even wondered if they could employ an au pair or even a live-in nanny for a while, but it would have stretched their finances and not been a permanent solution.

Ellie sympathized, remembering how difficult it had been for her to leave her daughter after she was born. She'd been lucky enough to get some secretarial work to do at home, which had helped make ends meet, but then she'd never had Kate's sort of job.

At that point, Kate's mobile had rung, and it sounded as if she were being dragged back to work willy-nilly.

Kate said, 'All right, I'll ask her, and ring you back.' She switched off her phone, and stood up, with the baby still on her shoulder. She walked over to the back window with gliding steps. Catriona was almost asleep. Kate swung her hips, rocking the baby, patting her back.

Ellie waited while Kate organized her thoughts.

At last Kate was ready to speak. 'That was my boss, as you've probably gathered. I went up to see him on Monday because Armand's on half term, so he could look after Catriona. I rang Armand twice on the way up to the city, just to make sure she was all right. And once on the way back. As for concentrating on what Gwyn wanted . . .' She shrugged. 'What he was telling me was important, but it didn't seem real. I realize that in time, if I keep trying, I'll be able to leave Catriona in someone else's hands long enough to get back to a normal working day.'

Ellie jumped to the wrong conclusion. 'You want me to look after her in the daytime, so you could get back to work? I suppose I could now and then, but—'

'It's not that. He doesn't want a part-timer who clock-watches, and anyway you've got more than enough on your plate already.'

'By law,' said Ellie, 'doesn't he have to take you back?'

'Yes, but he can shift me sideways into a boring job no one else wants, or . . . ask me to use my friendship with you to solve a mystery for him.' She laid her sleeping baby in her expensive buggy and resumed her seat.

Ellie sank back into a chair, only to find herself sitting on yet another plastic toy — broken. She aimed it at the waste-paper basket, missed, and tried not to mutter a bad word under her breath.

Kate hadn't noticed. 'There's absolutely no reason why you should help me out. Your husband's left you very comfortably off, you've a nice little house in a good district near a parade of shops, you own another which you could sell for a large sum if your aunt didn't live in it, you've money in a trust fund, masses of friends and a lively grandson to remind you what it's like to play bears under the rug. Admittedly your daughter is . . .' Kate was a kindly girl, and she hesitated to describe Diana in acceptable language.

'Difficult? Impossible? A daughter from hell?' Ellie grinned. 'Go on. Say it!'

Kate grinned, banishing a frown. 'You may call her what you wish, but . . .'

Ellie's smiled faded. 'Diana has her good points, but if I've gone prematurely grey, I suppose I can blame it on her.'

She glanced at the telephone. When Diana wanted her mother to do something, she didn't ask; she demanded. At the moment, Ellie was unpopular with her daughter because she was refusing to answer the telephone. Diana could rant and rave at the answerphone instead.

'You look lovely,' said loyal Kate. 'If I look half as good as you when I reach fifty-something, and have half as many men hanging around me . . . not that I want any other man but Armand hanging around me, but . . . now you've made me lose the thread of what I was saying.'

'That's a very impressive build-up. Now, spit it out!'

Kate seated herself where she could keep one hand on the buggy and rock it gently to and fro. 'I want you to come with me to see a man about a dog.'

Ellie couldn't help laughing. 'You're not serious?'

Kate nodded, without a flicker of a smile. 'Apparently the dog had a pedigree going back to the original spaniels which frolicked round the heels of the Merry Monarch. I exaggerate, of course, but not much. Apparently his master was even going to have an oil painting done of the dog.'

'What, no cats?' Ellie had been adopted as provider-in-chief of food and bedding by a marauding ginger tom. She held Midge in the highest esteem, but would never have thought of having him painted.

'He probably thinks cats are inferior animals, lacking any intelligence. I hope Midge didn't hear me, or he might decide to stop chasing pigeons from my garden and then we'd get no more raspberries.'

'Get a fruit cage,' said Ellie, absently. 'So why do you want me to visit a man who doesn't like cats?'

'That's just it,' said Kate. 'I can't think of a single reason why you should.'

Ellie leaned back in her chair to consider what Kate had told her, which wasn't much, when she came to think about it. Kate was trying to look demure, which didn't suit her.

Ellie could think of several reasons why she should do what Kate wanted, chief of which was that Kate was a good neighbour, a good friend, and Ellie was very fond of her. There was also the small matter of the buff form which Frank had torn up that morning.

Ellie smoothed it out. In one corner it said 'page ten'. Where were the other pages, she wondered. Her eye went round the room. Ah, something beige had been stuffed into the DVD under the television.

'Looking for these?' Kate wrestled some more buff-coloured pieces of paper from down the side of her chair.

Ellie pulled a face. 'My tax return for last year. I daren't tell my accountant. That's the second form ruined. The first one I left on top of the day's newspaper and it got thrown out in the recycling box. I thought I'd put this one in my handbag out of Frank's way this morning, but . . .' Where was her handbag?

Under Kate's chair. Kate fished it out. It was open, and inside was Frank's cup, empty, a half-eaten biscuit and some more of his plastic spacemen. Ellie groaned. 'He must have stood on something to get it off the shelf when my back was turned. I did leave the room for a few minutes when the window cleaner came. Oh dear. What am I going to say to my accountant now? I feel such a fool!'

Kate dimpled. 'You give me an hour of your time this evening to talk to the man about his dog, and I'll deal with your tax return for you.'

'I am perfectly aware,' said Ellie, with dignity, 'that you are leading me up the garden path and there's something extremely nasty in the woodshed at the end of it, but what can I do? There's a meeting this evening that I ought to go to at church, but it would probably bore me rigid, so I accept.'

Kate stood up. 'Remind me to find little Frank something unimportant to tear up. Now Armand's at home all this week, so he can look after Catriona while we visit this man. Can you be ready at five? It's not far.'

'It's that urgent?'

Kate nodded. 'I'll get a meeting set up and ring Gwyn to say you've agreed to look at the problem.'

Ellie's misgivings were growing. 'Kate, it isn't something to do with high finance, is it? You know I'm hopeless at figures.'

'It's to do with people, which is what you're good at. And attempted murder.'

'What? Kate! I'm not tangling with—'

'It was the dog that got murdered. We need to find out who might have done it, and we start with the household. Right?'

'Start with . . . ? Kate, what are you dragging me into?'

Kate refused to say any more, but took Catriona away, leaving Ellie to wonder what she should wear to visit a man who despised cats. Something with a cat logo on it? Or should she go for something with a dog's head on it? She shook her head. Her wardrobe was sadly limited in that direction.

Her old pearl-grey dress with the cornflower-blue flowers on it would be best, possibly with a woollen jacket on top. October evenings could be chilly, and the weather forecast was not brilliant.

* * *

At a quarter past five Kate turned her car into the gravelled semicircular drive of an imposing piece of Gothic grandeur, and said, 'Welcome to Dracula's castle.'

Ellie surveyed the pepperpot turrets, the stained-glass windows, and the broad steps leading up to the imposing portico. 'I'd forgotten we still had a Millionaire's Row in Ealing. Most of these big old houses have been torn down to make way for blocks of flats. Rather splendid, isn't it? This one must be twice as large as my dear Aunt Drusilla's, and I thought that was pretty big. Is it a listed building?'

'You can't do as you like with listed buildings. The man we've come to see would pay good money to stop this place being listed.'

Was their appointment with a client of Kate's? Ellie was intrigued. Of course, she realized she was being manipulated, but so far she was amused rather than annoyed.

Kate spoke into an entryphone, and while waiting for someone to answer, Ellie noticed that she was currently being observed by a CCTV camera. There was also a camera focused on the huge double doors that must lead to garages and side buildings. The place reeked of money. Paintwork gleamed, windows sparkled. The only dissident note was a figure in threadbare T-shirt and jeans, who was trying to remove some graffiti from the garage doors.

Graffiti did appear on shops and garage doors now and again. It was usually a crime committed by loners who wanted to show off their 'tag'. It was nearly always done at night and at street level. This particular graffiti artist had taken a risk, coming right off the road and round the driveway to get to the garage doors. It argued a certain amount of planning — or hate. Or both. Ellie felt it was a pity she couldn't make out what he'd spray-painted on the garage doors. Had the security camera caught him?

Kate caught Ellie looking up at the camera again. 'Mm, he's worth burgling.'

'Yes? Who is it?' The threadbare figure had come round from the garage, cleaning rag in hand. It wasn't a 'he', but a 'she'. A droopy sort of female; possibly a cleaner? There were keys in her hand, with which she opened the front door.

Kate handed over her business card. 'We have an appointment.'

The girl nodded, and let them into the hall. She was possibly a genuine blonde but had taken so little care of her appearance that it was hard to tell. She treated them to a nervous smile. 'I'll take you through to the den.'

A well-educated voice. The girl was probably only in her early thirties, though she looked older. Was she a cleaner? Possibly not. Then who?

As she led them across the hall, Ellie reflected that the girl's clothes had been badly chosen; a T-shirt and jeans that were too baggy, no bra, aged flip-flops. It looked as though she bought her clothes in charity shops.

Ellie held back a sigh. She'd only learned how to dress recently, thanks mainly to the interest Kate had taken in her. Ellie knew what a difference it made to your outlook on life when you were dressed appropriately for the occasion.

There was a dog lead on the mahogany table in the middle of the tiled floor, but no dog in evidence. The place didn't smell of dog either. There were sporting prints of dogs on the walls, grouped around a huge Victorian still life in an ornate gilt frame.

A solid-looking staircase rose up through the first floor to the second, and thence to a cupola in the roof. This place must be difficult to heat in the winter, although — Ellie checked — there was a good modern central-heating system, tucked away behind ornamental grilles. Everything looked well cared for.

The girl led them along a panelled corridor and knocked on a door.

'Come!'

They entered what had once been a billiard room. The floor was laid with parquet and the walls were panelled. What light there was came by way of stained-glass windows at head height, and an enormous clear-glass lantern over the place where a full-sized billiard table had once stood.

Originally there would have been a large, hooded light fitment over the billiard table, to enable the master of the house and his guests to play at night. Now billiard table and light fitment had been banished, along with the scent of cigars and good brandy.

No, perhaps the brandy remained. The end of the room contained a fully stocked bar, with appropriate stools and a couple of wooden armchairs ranged in front of it. The largest television Ellie had ever seen — even in shop windows — took pride of place where the billiard table had once stood, with just one huge red leather armchair in front of it. The television was on, and from the back of the armchair curled the scent of — not a cigar — but a cigarette. The room was fusty with cigarette smoke, and Ellie's nose twitched.

The girl said, 'Will you tell Arthur they're here?'

The red chair swivelled around; it probably rose and fell at the touch of a button.

Ellie blinked. Did she know this man? He looked familiar in the way that you might recognize someone whose picture you'd seen recently in the papers. Then she realized that she was looking at a man whom any director would cast as an extra in a programme about organized crime. He was shortish and thin, in his late twenties, dark and mean-looking . . . possibly Italian? Albanian? Polish? His hands were calloused and there was dirt under his fingernails. As he swivelled to face them, one hand went searching inside his jacket . . . for a gun?

Ellie blinked, and took a half step back, but Kate threw up her eyes in annoyance. She said, 'He's expecting us.'

'I don't know that, do I?' said the man, his hand still rummaging inside his jacket.

The girl looked embarrassed. 'Give it a rest, Marco.' And to the visitors, 'I'm afraid Martinez — his PA — is working elsewhere. Marco has been helping out.' She went to a phone on the wall, pressed a number and spoke into it. 'They're here.'

A voice echoed around the room. 'Be right out.'

Ellie blinked again. The man in the chair was . . . could he really be . . . a minder? A bodyguard? He was definitely not a personal assistant or a secretary. Neither of those would sit in their boss's chair, smoking and watching television. Ellie's opinion of the man who would employ such a bodyguard was — tentatively — not high.

The girl gestured to Kate and Ellie to take a seat. 'He'll be right out. I just have to . . .' She faded from the scene, leaving them there with Marco, whom she hadn't bothered to introduce. The television was showing some sort of soap opera, with people screaming at one another. The man in the chair divided his attention between the screen and the newcomers.

Ellie felt his eyes on her, and shifted, checking that her skirt was covering her knees. Was he really interested in her legs? At her age? How dare he! Kate was staring into the distance, probably calculating to the minute how long it was going to be before she could get back to Catriona. Then the man's gaze seemed to get through to Kate too. She looked startled, sat upright, and checked that the buttons on her jacket were all done up. Which they were. Kate bit her lip. Checked her watch. Looked at Ellie.

Was Kate going to suggest that they leave without seeing the man about his dog? At that very moment, an inner door ground open and a large man made an entrance.

'Faugh!' He waved large hands before his face. 'Get that stinking cigarette out of here, Marco. Open a window! Shut that damned TV off. And *get out of my chair!*'

Marco sprang out of the chair, shut off the TV, and looked around for somewhere to deposit his cigarette. Kate shrugged and looked up at the windows. Ellie tried to reach the nearest one, but the newcomer got there first, towering over her. He wrenched it open, creating a draught. Did the same to the door. He bellowed, 'Felicity!'

The atmosphere in the room began to clear. Marco curved his hand to hide his cigarette and lurked, flexing his neck muscles, furious at being told off in front of the women.

'Well!' said his boss. He did not offer to introduce himself. He took the chair his minder had vacated, and stared at the two women.

Ellie revised her first estimate. The man was only of middling height, in his late forties. Solidly built in a series of curves. His nose, though, was thin and beaky, protruding from between fat cheeks like a parrot's beak. He looked as if he might be a candidate for an early heart attack. He wouldn't take much exercise, if any. Correction: he might play golf for social reasons.

His eyes were the coldest Ellie had ever seen, startlingly pale. He was wearing an expensive midnight-blue silk suit which did its best to disguise his paunch, a striped blue and white shirt and a maroon tie. His shoes were brilliantly polished. He probably wouldn't clean them himself, but get his unfortunate girl Friday to do it.

No, Ellie did not like him.

Perhaps — she allowed the thought to crystallize in her head — she even feared him.

The droopy girl appeared in the doorway, wiping wet hands on her jeans. He didn't even bother to look at her. 'Get Marco an ashtray.'

'I was just—'

'He's going to drop ash all over the floor.'

The girl found a brass ashtray on the bar and took it to Marco, who put his cigarette butt out in it. She disappeared with an inarticulate 'I was just getting . . .'

Kate said, 'Let me introduce myself. I'm Kate—'

He cut her off. 'I know who you are. You're the girl Gwyn spoke about.'

'And this is—'

'I know who she is too. I've heard about her, haven't I? Meddling old busybody, came into some money, thinks she's Lady Muck.'

Ellie flicked a glance at Kate to see if she was as embarrassed by this as she was herself. Kate was frowning. She had thick eyebrows and, though she was a handsome girl, when she frowned she could look forbidding. As she did now. 'This is Mrs Ellie Quicke, who's good at solving mysteries in the community, particularly where the police are not to be involved. You told Gwyn you didn't want the police involved, didn't you?'

He frowned. 'That's right. No police. But I don't need her to sort this out. I know who did it.'

Kate said, 'Ellie, let me introduce Sir Arthur Kingsley OBE. In line for a step up to the House of Lords, if gossip is correct. He's a developer on a large scale. He's on the board of five international companies, has a penthouse flat in Docklands and a Georgian manor house in the Cotswolds. Locally, he's chairman of the Rotary Club, on the committee of the local Community Association, plus every charitable foundation that will get him a mention in the newspapers.'

Kate crossed one knee over the other and sat back in the manner of one prepared to enjoy watching a boxing match. Ellie didn't know what was expected of her. She drummed her fingers on the arm of her chair. Not a very comfortable chair. Sir Arthur had the only comfortable chair in the room.

He switched his eyes from Ellie to Kate. 'I told you, I can sort this out by myself. Anyway, she's probably afraid of dogs.'

Ellie blinked. He was right, of course. She didn't like strange dogs.

'She's good with people,' said Kate, in an even tone which might or might not be hiding her dislike of the man.

He leaned back in his chair to look at Ellie down his nose. She flushed. She'd heard of him, of course, but never actually come across him before. His reputation was that of a hard man. She remembered a particularly nasty case recently when he'd tried to buy a site occupied by a local firm of builders. After he'd been turned down, fire had gutted their premises. They'd been under-insured and had gone out of business. Arson couldn't be proved, but the site was now occupied by private housing from which he'd made a fortune. The original owners of the site were on the dole.

He presented the picture of a successful, smiling man in public. A bully, of course. If he were a gardener, this man would take a chainsaw rather than secateurs to prune a bush.

Since her dear husband had died, Ellie had discovered the truth in the old adage that if you stood up to a bully, they caved in. Her aged Aunt Drusilla had responded well to this treatment and Ellie was now fond of the once-dreaded old dear.

Ellie's daughter Diana was a tougher proposition than Aunt Drusilla, and Ellie couldn't claim that she'd fully mastered the art of dealing with her, but she didn't need to take rudeness from a stranger.

An irreverent thought popped into her head and she smiled.

'What?' he barked at her.

She didn't like people shouting at her, but managed to give him a civil reply. 'You remind me of Pooh-Bah, or Lord High Everything, a character invented by W. S. Gilbert. You probably don't know *The Mikado*, though I expect your mother taught you manners when you were a child.' She stood up, signalling to Kate that she'd had enough. 'I don't think I can help you with . . . whatever it is you want.'

'Didn't you hear me say that I don't need you to sort this out?'

She nodded, eyebrows raised, making for the door.

He shouted after her, 'Tell Gwyn I'm not impressed!'

Ellie paused in the doorway. 'Neither am I.' She swept from the room, closely followed by Kate, who was having a choking fit into her handkerchief.

They continued on their way past the droopy girl, who appeared from a door at the back of the hall with flour on her hands, out through the front door into the calm of the afternoon sunshine.

CHAPTER TWO

'You'll be the death of me,' crowed Kate, mopping her eyes. 'I thought you might tell him to mind his manners, but I didn't think you'd actually walk out on him. Now what do we do?'

Ellie reddened, a little ashamed of herself. She inserted herself into Kate's car and pulled the seat belt across. Had she been too hard on Sir Arthur? No, she hadn't. 'If someone's killed his dog, then I'm sorry, but they hit the wrong target. They should have tried for him. And no, that's not a nice thing to say, and I'll probably be sorry about it tomorrow, but he's a thoroughly nasty piece of work.'

'Agreed,' said Kate, inserting her key into the ignition. 'I told his PA that he'd have to be polite to you. I said you were the only person I knew who could sort out the mess he's got himself into. I wonder how long it'll be before we're reading his obituary notice in the papers.'

She turned the key, letting the engine idle. Waiting for Ellie to calm down.

'Obituary?' Ellie repeated the word. 'You expect him to die?'

'To be killed, yes. I rather think I do.'

'I'd cheer his murderer on. What am I saying? I wouldn't do that, but I won't help him. Why should I? And what could I possibly do to help him, even if I wanted to?'

'You could talk to his wife, perhaps.'

'Wife?'

'Felicity.'

'That's *his wife?* Poor soul.'

Kate turned off the ignition. 'Shall we? It won't take ten minutes.'

Ellie was reluctant. 'How important is it to you, to keep this man as a client?'

'Oh, he isn't my client. I wouldn't touch him with the proverbial. You can meet the man he thinks is trying to murder him tomorrow. You'll like him.'

Ellie extricated herself from the car, feeling baffled. 'All this mystery! Who is your client, then? This man Gwyn that he was talking about? Kate, if your garden path is leading me into a bed of nettles . . .'

Kate laughed, and leaned on the doorbell again. Marco opened the door. 'He said I wasn't to let you in, even if you came crawling back, so you needn't waste your breath. Anyway, he's going out in ten minutes.'

Ellie was thoroughly riled by now. 'Oh, go away, do. You might frighten children at Halloween, but you don't frighten me.'

Kate said, 'Bravo,' in a soft voice. And aloud, she said, 'We just want a word with Lady Kingsley. In the kitchen, is she?'

The minder's blood pressure was up. He pointed his forefinger at Ellie as if it were a gun about to go off and then, finding himself out of repartee, stalked off.

Ellie was still feeling ruffled, but tried to calm herself down by summing up Marco's character. 'Second-generation Italian, a jobbing gardener and probably not particularly good at that either. Thrilled at being asked to stand in for the PA. What was his name, Martin something? Marco couldn't pass for a PA, so he's playing the part of a heavy and overdoing it. Not the real thing.'

'Agreed.' Kate led the way across the hall to the door from which Felicity had appeared earlier. 'I think the kitchen may be this way.'

The kitchen was large and contained the very latest stainless-steel fitments. Felicity was the one thing out of place in it. She was fumbling with the lid of a food mixer. Yes, she was wearing a plain gold wedding ring and a practical watch. Her complete outfit wouldn't have cost as much as the shirt her husband was wearing.

Her husband had spent money on his surroundings — to show off his wealth? — but his wife was going around looking like a refugee from the Balkans. Quite a contrast.

When Felicity saw them, she dropped the lid, blushed, reached for something on which to wipe her hands. 'Oh, I'm so sorry. Was he rude to you? I did hope . . . but I'm trying to get supper ready for . . .'

'It's perfectly all right,' said Ellie, feeling sorry for the girl. 'Could you spare a minute to talk to us?'

Felicity gestured at an ovenproof dish on the work surface. 'I can't stop, must get this into the oven, he likes his supper dead on six when he's got a committee meeting, and I'm all fingers and thumbs today.' She poured some stock from a saucepan on to the mixture in the dish.

'Not to worry,' said Ellie, in her comfortable way.

Felicity seemed on the verge of tears. 'Everything's almost ready. I just have to put the pastry on top. It's a lot easier to mix pastry by hand, I think, but Arthur says he's bought me all these machines and I . . .'

'I quite agree with you,' said Ellie. 'It saves the washing-up, too, if you do it by hand. What's that you've got there? Chicken with onions and mushrooms? Tasty.'

Kate had faded away to a stool by a breakfast bar, content to let Ellie take over.

'I'm all right, really,' said Felicity, trying to fit the lid on to the food mixer the wrong way. 'It's just . . . poor Rex dying that way . . . it was horrible! Then having him cut up to see why he died. Then having to bury him. I'm still shaking.'

'I don't think I could bury a dog,' said Ellie, with ready sympathy. 'How brave of you.'

'Well, Marco wouldn't do it,' said Felicity, adding a smear of flour to her cheekbone as she disposed of a tear. 'So I had to. Rex was so *heavy*! I wouldn't have thought such a little dog could be so heavy!'

'I know, I know,' said Ellie, who didn't know, but had the horrors at the thought of having to bury her beloved cat Midge, who was quite a weight in real life. Ellie didn't like to think about having to bury Midge if he died. 'Do tell me about it.'

She took the mixer off the girl, slotted the lid in the correct way, switched it on, watched the mix with care, added a drop more water, and switched it off.

Felicity sniffled, pulling a tissue from a box on the counter. 'Supper should have been on ten minutes ago. It's the only thing I had to do all afternoon, apart from getting the graffiti off the garage doors, and now it's going to be late.'

Ellie saw there were potatoes peeled and in water on the stove already, with a steamer for some broccoli beside it. She threw some flour on the work surface, scooped the ball of pastry out of the mixer, and floured that, too. 'You put the veg on, and I'll do the pastry, right? Can you cope with cooking vegetables in the microwave? I'm hopeless, get the timing all wrong. Hand me the rolling pin, will you?'

Felicity perked up, handing over the rolling pin. 'Potatoes, yes. But I haven't tried greens yet. I was all right with the old microwave, which was pretty straightforward, but this one's got so many controls I can't cope. I'm not very clever with machines, you see.'

'That makes two of us,' said Ellie. 'But I think you're very clever to keep a big house like this looking immaculate. Do you have any help?'

'Two mornings a week, but *he* likes to have the house quiet when he's at home. I can't even run the washing machine then. It is a bit of a problem. He's got a housekeeper at the manor in the country, of course, so he doesn't need me there much, and there's a cleaning firm does for the flat in the Barbican.'

Felicity was definitely calming down, her hands beginning to move competently across the work surface, testing, tasting, adding salt, laying a large tray with a cloth and utensils for one. Only for one?

Ellie used the tines of the fork to press a pattern all round the edge of the pastry and, unasked, Felicity handed Ellie a bottle of milk and a pastry brush to add a glaze.

'You've done that so prettily,' said Felicity. 'I've never seen a pie finished off that way before.'

'Ah well. I'm old enough to be your mother, my dear.'

What had she said wrong? Felicity went bright red, dropped the oven gloves she was holding and dived after them. Ellie exchanged a glance with Kate, who mimed bewilderment.

The pseudo-minder, Marco, banged through the door to say, 'He says he can't wait any longer and I'm to drive him tonight. He also says that if anyone rings, you're to take a message, and you're not to leave it for the answerphone.' Marco smirked, treating Felicity as if she were hired help. 'Oh, and you two . . .' he said to Ellie and Kate, 'he says he doesn't want you hanging around, so you'd better get going.'

'Oh, but supper's . . .' Felicity indicated the pie. 'It's just ready to . . .'

'*Marco!*' His master's voice.

Marco flashed his teeth at them and vanished, letting the door bang to behind him. Felicity found some cling film in a drawer and fitted it over the pie with hands that shook. 'I'll put it in the fridge and it'll do for another day.' She was avoiding their eyes. 'I'll show you out, shall I?'

Ellie said, 'I must wash my hands first.' She didn't wait for permission, but used some liquid soap and ran water at the sink. Felicity had picked up the pans containing the vegetables she'd been intending to cook, and stood there, gazing into space.

Ellie said, softly, 'You'd better cook them. You know potatoes shouldn't be kept for long in water once they've been peeled.'

Felicity put the pans down and led the way to the hall, without another word. Ellie and Kate followed her.

A silver Mercedes was just being driven away. Ellie could still see the marks where Felicity had been scrubbing the graffiti off the paintwork.

'What a pity,' said Ellie. 'That door's going to need repainting, isn't it? Unusual to get graffiti so far off the street.'

'Yes. No. I mean, we know who did it. At least, I think I know, but I don't want to get him into trouble. It was just a misunderstanding about his bill, really.' She seemed to regret even saying so much because she whisked herself back into the house and closed the door.

Ellie and Kate got into Kate's car and belted up. 'Much to think about,' observed Kate.

'I wonder if Felicity will bother to cook for herself tonight,' said Ellie. 'Somehow, I doubt it. Will you kindly tell me what's going on?'

Kate started the car. 'Did you notice that she seemed more distressed about the dog's death than the threat to her husband?'

'Is there really a threat?'

'Yes.' Kate concentrated on her driving, glancing at the clock on the dashboard now and then. 'I'll be back for Catriona's bath time, with luck.'

'Explanations can wait?'

Kate sighed. 'I was hoping Armand and I could take Catriona out into the country for the day tomorrow, as there's still so much colour in the trees, but I suppose I'd better help you sort this mess out. Tomorrow morning, ten o'clock, I'll introduce you to the chief suspect for the poisoning. We'll take the car to the tube and go up that way. It's quicker than driving all the way up to Canary Wharf, and avoids the congestion charge.'

Kate turned into their road and parked as neatly as she always did. In front of them was a flashy silver sports car with a registration number they both recognized. Diana's car. Ellie tried not to acknowledge the sinking feeling which the sight of Diana's car had induced in her.

Neither Kate nor Ellie made a move to get out of the car.

Ellie said, 'Quick, before she realizes we're here. Tell me what's going on.'

'The City is putting together a very big deal. Sir Arthur is a key element in it. On Sunday night he returned earlier than expected from a weekend break in the country. Felicity was out. There was a pepperoni pizza in a box in the porch. He thought someone must have left it there by mistake, delivered it to the wrong house. He didn't ring the company who'd delivered it, but said "Finders keepers!" — took it in, cut off a slice and ate it. Thought it tasted odd. Put his fingers down his throat and threw up. While his back was turned, the dog pinched some. Sir Arthur survived. The dog died.'

'Has he any reason to think someone's trying to kill him?'

'He's made more enemies than the Chancellor of the Exchequer. Any one of them could have laced the pizza with poison, but unfortunately, Sir Arthur jumped to the conclusion that an old enemy of his must have been responsible. This morning he arrived at an important board meeting in the City and accused this man of trying to kill him. The meeting broke up in disarray, and the City is not pleased. I'd told Gwyn about you ages ago, about how clever you are with people. He's trying to get both parties back round the table, but Sir Arthur — well, you can see what he's like. If we can find out who really did poison the dog, it would help.'

'Felicity was out at the time?'

'She returned to find her husband lying down, and a large piece of pizza on the kitchen floor with the dog's teeth marks all over it. Rex was hiding in his basket, as any dog would when he's been thieving and expects to be called to account for it. She scolded the dog and said he was to stay in the kitchen all evening as a punishment. She put the remains of the pizza down the waste disposal and threw the carton in the bin. The bin men collected the rubbish the following morning. The dog died in the night, and only then did they suspect poison.'

'Are you sure she didn't poison it herself, to get back at her husband? The way that man treats her . . . !'

'I don't think so, do you?'

Before Ellie could drag any more information out of Kate, Diana erupted from the house.

'Mother! Where have you been? You might at least pick up the phone. You can't pretend you don't know I've been trying to get hold of you.'

Kate flicked a tiny glance of commiseration at Ellie, and got out of the car. 'We were visiting a client, Diana. Your mother has quite a reputation for . . .'

'Oh yes, she's available to everyone except her family!' Diana almost spat in her fury.

Diana was as tall as Kate. Both women were dark-haired and handsome, but there the likeness petered out, for Diana was beginning to wear the haggard expression of the ultrathin woman who only eats lettuce leaves, while Kate — though still slim — had gone up a dress size since she became pregnant.

Ellie smothered a sigh. 'Diana, I was going to ring you this evening, but . . .'

Diana snorted. 'I doubt it!'

Ellie didn't even glance at Kate, but could feel a wave of sympathy coming from her neighbour. Ellie got out her key and let herself and Diana into her house. The light was winking on the answerphone. There'd be a message or two from Diana, of course, but perhaps also one from Aunt Drusilla, whose health was causing everyone concern. She must listen to them later.

'Cup of tea?' She went through into the kitchen, hearing the cat flap click as her cat Midge left the house. Midge disliked Diana as much as Diana disliked him.

'No, I do not want *tea*,' said Diana, much as if Ellie had offered her poison. 'I want . . . I need to talk to you.'

'Talk away, dear.' Ellie put water in the kettle and switched it on, wondering if the downtrodden Felicity really would cook herself a meal this evening. Ellie glanced at the clock. 'Goodness me, is that the time? I promised to go to a meeting at church this evening.'

Actually, she'd been very half-hearted about going, but if Diana were going to hang around, a meeting in the church hall was a better bet than an evening being harangued by Diana.

'You are always so busy!' Diana took hold of her left wrist with her right hand and visibly made herself calm down. 'My blood pressure!'

Ellie was alarmed. 'Have you got high blood pressure, dear?'

'Yes. No.' Irritably. 'I have to watch out for it. Though little you'd care if I did go bankrupt.'

Oh. Ellie made herself a cup of tea, with carefully controlled movements. 'Bankrupt is a strong word, Diana. I thought you were doing so well with that big house you turned into flats. I thought you'd sold nearly all of them.'

'Yes. Well, I did. At least, I sold well over half. But you know what it is. The housing market has slowed down and some people couldn't get their mortgages sorted and there was a long chain with others. The fact is, I have a cash-flow problem. I don't suppose you'd understand it, because you've never had a business head, but . . .'

'Let's go and sit down in the other room, shall we?' Ellie led the way, trying to absorb Diana's news. She set her cup of tea down and went to draw the curtains at both ends of the long sitting room. The central heating had clicked on. Just as well. October nights could be chilly. Also, the flagstones on the patio were wet, so it had begun to rain.

Diana fidgeted with the clasp of a large black handbag. She usually wore black. Skinny jacket, slinky trousers. Fake fur on the lapel of the jacket. The outfit looked expensive but a touch tarty.

Ellie knew that Diana slept around. Diana had slept around even before she'd got rid of her pleasant but somewhat stolid husband. Diana had continued to sleep around since the divorce. She'd made a spectacle of herself some time back with a rather unpleasant estate agent, but had chucked him eventually. Who was her latest? Ellie decided she didn't want to know.

'Well?' Diana had little patience for older women who sat sipping their tea when they should be rushing to help their daughter out of trouble.

Ellie straightened her shoulders. 'Let's get this straight. You bought that big house against my advice. You took out all the period features, even though I warned you that you would be halving the number of potential buyers by doing so. You kept the garden flat — the best flat in the building — for yourself. Now you can't sell the flats as quickly as you expected, you want me to do . . . what?'

'I just need to be tided over until I can sell another flat.'

'You want me to lend you some money at a reasonable rate of interest?'

Diana sprang up, offended. 'Mother, are you out of your mind? You'd charge your own child interest? Naturally, I came to you first, but . . .'

'You've tried your Great-Aunt Drusilla?'

'She's old and doesn't understand.'

Ellie held up her hand. 'Diana, your great-aunt has forgotten more about buying and selling houses than you've had hot meals. She may be old, but . . .'

'She's senile!'

Ellie shook her head. Miss Drusilla Quicke might be getting on in years, she might walk with the aid of a stick, but she had the brightest financial brain on the block.

Ellie looked at the tips of her shoes. They were a trifle tight. She eased them off. She glanced at the clock and calculated how long it would take to get herself something to eat, and get to the church meeting. Annual general meetings were usually boring, but there'd been talk about a developer wanting to rebuild the vicarage. Not before time. Yes, it might be interesting to go to the meeting after all.

Diana began to stride up and down the room, the heels of her boots thumping with every step. Unlike Kate, who almost waltzed around, crooning to her baby.

Diana said, 'I do have other people I can ask, but I'd very much prefer not to.'

'You've tried the bank?'

'They suggest I put my own flat, my lovely garden flat, on the market. They say that's sure to sell quickly. Which of course it would. But then I'd be homeless, and where would I take my darling little boy when I have him at weekends?'

'You could get a job, which would help pay the mortgage.'

'Where would I get a good enough job to pay the mortgage? I tell you, I'm in deep trouble, unless you can help me out.'

Ellie got to her feet, considered putting her shoes back on, decided against it, and padded, shoeless, into the kitchen. 'Let me have a business plan. Set out how much you want and how you'll repay me, and I'll think about it. Meanwhile, I've got to eat before I go out. Do you want to share a shepherd's pie with me? I've got some in the freezer that I made last week.'

Diana shuddered. 'No wonder you've put on so much weight recently.'

Ellie wanted to say that she hadn't, but wasn't sure that would be truthful. Had she put on weight recently? No–o. Her clothes weren't too tight. Not even her beautiful new russet wool suit, which she might wear tonight.

The doorbell rang. Ellie paused with her head in the freezer.

Diana said, 'Salesmen, I suppose! I'll get rid of them,' and stalked to open the front door. Midge's head appeared under the cat flap, enquiring if it were safe to come in. Ellie made a shooing motion with her hand, and Midge's head disappeared.

A confusion of voices. Diana was declaring that Ellie was not in, and two male voices were insisting that she was. *Two* men?

Ellie abandoned her search for food to satisfy her curiosity.

'I know she's in! I saw her draw the curtains just now!' Roy Bartrick, six foot of silver-haired, blue-eyed charm. A cousin of Ellie's dead husband and a respectable architect, he was a good friend who would have liked a closer relationship with Ellie. He was also Aunt Drusilla's long-lost illegitimate son.

None of which endeared him to Diana, who had hoped — without any solid grounds — to inherit Miss Quicke's millions. Diana found it impossible to believe that Roy wasn't as mercenary as she herself was, but in fact he hadn't a mercenary bone in his body, and he and his mother were very fond of one another.

Diana was retreating before Roy's advance. 'I don't know what you think you're—!'

Roy lifted his hand in a salute. 'Ellie, I need to speak to you . . .'

'Let me *in*!' Another man's voice. Roy stepped forward to reveal the plump figure of Archie, church treasurer and another one-time aspirant to Ellie's favours. Archie was looking anxious, as was Roy. Diana looked about to explode with fury.

'Supper, anyone?' said Ellie.

CHAPTER THREE

Sir Arthur was on his mobile, while being driven by Marco towards town.

'Martinez. How did you get on?'

The phone quacked.

'Well, keep at it. We need proof. If he didn't use his car that night, he must have taken a cab. He wouldn't risk asking someone else to dump the pizza on my doorstep. So find it. A lot hangs on this, including your bonus.'

More quacking.

Sir Arthur wrinkled his nose, lifting his upper lip. 'Gwyn's going senile. He sent a middle-aged housewife to see me today. Said she'd find out who's trying to poison me, as if I didn't know! I shot her out quicker than she came in. Ellie Quicke; came in Quicke, went out Quicker.' Sir Arthur snickered.

The phone quacked. 'You've never heard of her? Local busybody. Small-time. Nothing for us to worry about. That Kate creature brought her, the one who's done a lot of work for Gwyn in the past . . . Yeah, I know I thought we might use her, but she's pupped now and off the scene.'

He leaned back against the leather upholstery as they inched their way round the North Circular, which was almost at a standstill. Rain dribbled down the windows. He peered out. 'We're stuck in traffic.

Looks like I might be late. Look. Time's of the essence. You get the proof we need today, or . . . yes, you can switch to plan B.'

He shut off the phone, frowning, fidgeting.

Marco said, 'You want me to do something about Mrs Quicker? Rearrange her garden?'

Sir Arthur snapped at him. 'If I wanted that, I'd tell you, wouldn't I? Where exactly are we? Better drop me off at North Ealing station, I'll take the tube in. You can pick me up later, half ten.'

'I could pay her a visit, that Quicker-Whicker. Give her a warning, like.'

'No need. Or not yet, anyway. I want you to do something else for me tonight . . .'

* * *

Ellie usually had plenty of food in her freezer. Cooking for one can be difficult, so she'd bought herself a big freezer and every now and then she'd spend a morning cooking a large quantity of mince, or a joint or a whole fish, divide the result into individual portions and freeze them. But she hadn't stocked up lately. What had she got? Some frozen shepherd's pies, some stray bags of greens . . . a couple of packages of home-made soups . . . nothing much.

'Mother, we haven't finished our discussion.'

'Yes, we have, dear. Will you join us for supper?'

Diana stormed out of the house, but both Roy and Archie accepted her invitation. Ellie decided against the bother of setting the table in the living room, and suggested they eat in the kitchen.

Neither man was at ease in the kitchen. Roy did his best but he was about as cack-handed as a man could be, and Archie was the sort of man who went out for a meal if he couldn't get some 'little lady' to cook for him.

Ellie wondered how his current bimbo had come to let him out of her sight long enough to visit another woman. Probably she was having her hair or nails done. In any case, bimbo wasn't the type to don an apron and produce food for a man; she was the type who would expect to be taken out for a meal. She'd never believe that the way to a man's heart was through his stomach, although Ellie had proved this to be the case over and over again.

Ellie fed Midge, who'd returned the moment the front door had banged behind Diana. She put some water on to boil to cook the frozen sprouts, told Archie to sit down and not fidget, and asked Roy to pour them each a glass of sherry. Roy could be trusted to do that, at least, and a small glass of sherry might warm the frosty atmosphere which had always existed between the two men.

Ellie whisked individual shepherd's pies in and out of the microwave, while keeping her eye on the sprouts and wondering if the men would want redcurrant jelly or mint sauce with the pies. And what about a pudding? Oh, nonsense. They'd come without an invitation. They could have cheese or fruit or ice cream if they wanted something after the pie. She must keep an eye on the time.

Meanwhile . . . 'Is this about the meeting at church?'

'Yes,' said Roy.

'Certainly not,' said Archie, reddening. Was he lying? 'I was going to ask you, dear lady, to take pity on a lonely bachelor and have supper with me at the Carvery.'

So what had become of his bimbo?

Roy sighed. 'There's going to be trouble tonight. I expect Archie wanted to talk to you about it. I certainly do.'

'Spit it out,' said Ellie.

Archie plumped himself out like a pouter pigeon. He had a gold-glinting smile, which he now turned on Ellie. 'It's purely routine tonight. We don't anticipate any problem.'

Roy cut in. 'Yes, and no. It's—'

'Gentlemen!' Ellie reminded herself that soft words and a smile often produced a better effect than cracking heads together. 'One at a time.' She served up the food, but as she did so, she had a flashback to that poor creature Felicity standing in her superbly fitted-out kitchen, putting the food she'd prepared away . . . and probably not eating herself.

Archie gave every word its weight, as became his position as long-time church treasurer. 'Dear lady, there really is no reason to think there's going to be any trouble. As you know, the diocese has given its consent to the vicarage being pulled down and rebuilt . . .'

Ellie nodded. 'Not before time. I was afraid it might be listed as an example of Victorian Gothic horror, and then where would we be! We really do need something modern, easier to heat and clean. I know we've got to pay for it by giving the end bit of the garden for a developer to build on, but I agree it's the best solution to the problem.'

Archie raised his eyebrows and lifted his hand to rebuke Ellie for speaking before he'd finished. 'Particularly since we're still in debt from the rebuilding of the church hall. We get a new vicarage at no cost to the parish, which will be mightily relieved to hear they aren't expected to shell out another penny.'

Ellie nodded. Yes, the parish was all for it. What with appeals for earthquake victims, children's charities, retirement homes, missions and youth work, there never seemed to be a Sunday when extra money was not being asked for.

'The proposal should go through on the nod,' said Archie, eyeing up his empty sherry glass. Ellie put a jug of water on the table. No way was she getting out a bottle of wine for this meal. 'Allowing the developer to build a block of four flats on part of the vicarage garden will solve—'

Ellie suspended eating. '*Four* flats? I thought there were to be two!'

'Four flats. Outline planning permission was obtained for two flats, but then the developer pointed out that he wouldn't make any profit from two flats, so the diocese agreed that he should build four. This would allow him a reasonable profit, cover the cost of a new vicarage, and pay off our remaining debt. The project solves all our problems at a stroke, and I am one hundred per cent in favour of it.' He shot an aggressive look at Roy, and shovelled food into his mouth to make up for his slow start.

Roy articulated his words with care. 'You're not quite up to date, Archie. The developer doesn't want to build four flats now. He wants six! The garden as we know it will disappear. There will be a small patio for the new vicarage, and the rest will be turned over to parking for the residents of the new luxury flats, which will be sold off on the open market, netting the developer yet another fortune.'

'What?' said Ellie, losing her appetite.

Archie blinked. 'Six? This is the first I've heard of it. Has the diocese agreed to six? Surely not!'

Roy shrugged. 'I've no idea.'

Archie was uneasy. 'No, no. The diocese can't have been consulted. If they had been, surely I'd have been informed. Four flats . . . yes, I can understand that. But six!'

Ellie was bewildered. 'Forgive me for being slow. Why should the garden disappear?'

The best thing about their present vicarage was its large lawn, surrounded by mature trees. Granted, their present vicar was a widower whose children were off his hands, but didn't he need the peace and quiet of a garden just as much as anyone else?

She said, 'What if our next vicar were to be a family man? What's more, the vicarage garden's used by the children's nursery in fine weather, because it's next door to the church hall. Then we have our garden fêtes there in the summer, and all sorts of charity events.'

Archie was thinking hard. 'I suppose the position the diocese would take is that we have plenty of trees in the streets around here. The nearest park isn't far away. As for the nursery, they'd soon get used to it. The fêtes could be held on the church green when it's fine, or inside the church when it's not.'

Ellie could follow the reasoning with her head, but she really didn't like to think of that serene green space disappearing. 'What does the vicar say?'

Archie shrugged. 'If the diocese agrees to the plan, what can he say?'

Roy scraped his plate. 'He can't say anything, for or against. He has to take the view of what's best for the parish.'

Archie pushed back his chair. 'Six flats! I wonder who's been consulted about this. I think I'd better get over to the hall, make sure everyone's been properly briefed.'

Roy stayed put. Ellie followed Archie out into the hall, automatically slipping into hostess mode. 'Are you sure you can't stay for a cup of coffee?'

'No, no. Can I take a rain check?' Somehow he managed to get hold of her hand. 'My dear, I was hoping to have you all to myself for a few minutes . . .'

Ellie tried not to pull her hand away, nor to look at her watch.

'. . . since I regard you as one of my oldest and dearest friends . . .'

Oh dear, thought Ellie. He's not going to propose to me again, is he?

'. . . who always has time to spare for one whom life has treated harshly . . .'

Had his bimbo given him the air?

Roy loomed in the doorway, with a cynical expression on his face. 'Come off it, Archie. In a minute you'll be trying to convince Ellie that your latest girlfriend didn't understand you.'

Archie reddened, and puffed out his chest. 'As a matter of fact . . .'

'The truth is,' said Roy, 'that she understood you all too well. You never had any intention of marrying her, did you?'

'Well! I . . . really!'

'When she worked that out, she hightailed it. I wonder who she's trying to get her claws into now?'

Archie was seriously offended. 'I really don't think you should talk about a nice girl in those terms. Ellie, I'll take my leave, and hope we can get together again soon.'

'Thank you, Archie,' said Ellie, trying not to laugh.

She shut the front door behind him, and turned on Roy. 'That's wasn't very nice of you, was it?'

'I don't feel "nice" tonight. I feel bloody-minded. Now that man's gone, perhaps you can tell me what to do.'

'Coffee?' She'd just about have time. She put the kettle on, throwing the dishes into the sink and running water over them so that they could soak. It was no use expecting Roy to help her do the dishes. He'd probably break as many plates as he dried.

Roy mooched about the kitchen. 'Ellie, I'm in serious trouble. A couple of months ago I was wined and dined by a man I'd met at the golf club. The wine flowed rather too freely, and I accepted a job which, if sober, I'd never have touched.

'I was told the project was very like the one I'd just completed on the Green. An old house was to be pulled down, and modern housing built in its place. I was offered the opportunity to get in on the ground floor, put some of my own money into the project.'

Ellie spooned instant coffee into mugs. They hadn't time to bother with a cafetière tonight. 'How much did you promise to put in?'

Roy lifted his hands and let them fall. 'Too much.'

Ellie didn't like the sound of that. 'But Roy . . .'

'I know, I know. I was told that another architect had started the project, but had had to drop out in tragic circumstances. In short, Anderson had committed suicide. His widow was owed money for the work he'd done, but there were no funds to pay her till the project had been signed off. Outline planning permission had already been obtained, and it was merely a question of updating this and that. However, it all needed to be done in a hurry before the next council planning meeting.

'When I received Anderson's plans, I realized the site concerned was St Thomas' vicarage, and I began to have second thoughts. The earliest plan was for a four-bedroom vicarage and two flats, one above the other, which were to be tucked away to one side of the site. Subsequently the number of flats had been increased to four, taking over much of the existing garden. My instructions were to redraw the plans to accommodate six much larger flats. These new flats were to be aimed at the luxury market, with state of the art wiring, kitchens, wet rooms, floors, balconies. You name it. Anything to put the price up a bracket or two.

'A few of the trees on the boundary wall were to be retained, but most would go. The vicarage itself was to be drastically reduced in size and would be dwarfed by this new, enlarged block of flats. I was to increase the car-parking area and forget the landscaping. Let me sketch it out for you.'

Rapidly, he did so, using Ellie's memo board and washable ink pen. 'The new plans for the flats are going to push the vicarage into a tiny space at the back. It's a totally inappropriate development for the site.'

She blinked. 'We didn't expect anything like this.'

'Once I'd worked out what was required of me, I didn't want anything to do with it. I remembered how much money I'd promised to put up and felt sick. I rang the developer and said I'd changed my mind. He said he knew I could design flats to make buyers' mouths water, and he knew — because I'd told him, fool that I am — that I hadn't any other work on hand. He said I couldn't back out, because he'd taped our conversation at the dinner table, when I'd agreed to everything he'd suggested.'

'Oh, Roy!'

'I know, I know. So I worked twenty-four seven to get the plans done. Though I say it myself, I've made a good job of it, and they go before the planning committee next week. They'll probably get through, unless the parish can mount enough opposition to stall the proceedings, and from what Archie says, they're unlikely to do that.'

Ellie ladled sugar and milk into the mugs and handed Roy his. 'I'm afraid Archie's right. I don't like it, but who's going to fight it? Obviously not Archie. And if the diocese has agreed, I can't see what we can do about it. Anyway, I'm sure you've designed something we can be proud of.'

'You don't understand. He's holding me to my promise to invest in the development, and I don't have that sort of money lying around. My mother invested all the money I made before, because she knows about such things and I don't. I can't — daren't — tell her how stupid I've been. Anyway, I don't trust him. Or like him.

'The man's a bully. You should see the way his staff cringe when he appears. His dog is scared of his own shadow, and I wouldn't be surprised if he didn't beat his wife.'

Ellie exclaimed. 'Not Sir Arthur Kingsley?'

Roy looked surprised. 'You know him?'

'We've met. Roy, this is all very worrying. And what about Mrs Anderson? Newly widowed, short of money. She must be in a terrible state. Where does she live?'

'One of those small streets off the far end of the Avenue, I think.'

Ellie nodded. Her husband had left her very well off, and she'd put most of the money into a trust fund to benefit good causes. Perhaps Mrs Anderson was a good cause? She'd try to visit her. But not this evening. Ellie looked at the clock. Had she time to change before the meeting, and where had she left her good shoes?

'Well, Ellie?' said Roy. 'What do you think?'

Ellie drained her coffee cup. She'd an odd sort of brain, and was at that moment wondering why Mr Anderson had committed suicide. Sir Arthur did seem to have an odd effect on everyone around him. She dumped her mug in the sink.

'If you want my advice . . . no, you don't, really. You know perfectly well what you ought to do.'

He reddened. 'Go to my mother on bended knees? I can't do that, Ellie. She'd think I was just like everyone else, trying to cadge money off her, and I couldn't bear her to think that. I thought you might be able to come up with something.'

Ellie was annoyed. 'What do I know about high finance, Roy? I can't even complete my tax return without help.' A sudden thought. 'You didn't sign anything for Sir Arthur, did you?'

'Of course not!' His colour rose. Was he telling the whole truth? Had he signed something? No, surely he wouldn't have been so stupid.

She said, 'If that's all, then I don't think you've anything to worry about. Tell him to get lost.'

'Ellie, you're so good with people . . .'

'You want me to intercede for you with Sir Arthur? You must be joking!'

He shuffled his feet, his eyes dropping from hers. Yes, that was exactly what he'd hoped she would do. She said, 'Roy, tell your mother. If anyone can sort out Sir Arthur, it's her. Now I've got to change into something warmer, and you need to get across to the hall to make sure the latest plans are on view. We don't want to be late for what promises to be an extremely interesting meeting, do we?'

* * *

She saw him out, glanced at her watch, thought she ought to listen to her phone messages but would have to leave it till later. She didn't really have time to change, either, but she'd better do so. She thought of Kate, who would, even at this moment, be lovingly, smilingly, putting baby Catriona in the bath, and helping her to splash about, and then she thought of that poor creature Felicity, polishing her husband's shoes in that huge, cold house. She wondered if someone really had tried to kill Sir Arthur, and if so . . . who? He seemed to have upset plenty of people, including Roy. Although Roy was not killer material. Was he? No. Definitely not.

Briskly, she went upstairs to change.

* * *

The new church hall was almost full for the annual general meeting. Usually on these occasions about twenty people sat around on uncomfortable chairs, trying to make sense of columns of figures and densely worded motions of no particular importance. They would sit in rigid silence until some vote or other was called for, whereupon hands would be half-raised from laps.

Every now and then someone who liked the sound of his or her own voice would say, 'On a point of order, Mr Chairman,' and everyone else would lapse into a coma until — possibly five or ten minutes later — the speaker would grind to a close, and the chairman would have replied in soothing terms to . . . whatever it was that was upsetting the old dear.

This time the room was crowded because it was rumoured that the bishop had sent his personal envoy, the archdeacon — reputed to be both youngish and dishy — to the meeting. Many people knew that the vicarage was to be rebuilt in exchange for giving up enough ground for two flats. Two, not four or six. Some had come for the excitement of an evening out or to meet their friends and indulge in a biscuit or two with their coffee afterwards.

Some had come because they weren't delirious about the plan to replace the vicarage being imposed upon them from above. These were mostly grumpy, elderly men in greyish clothes; retired, often narrow-minded, but articulate.

The archdeacon was there, early. He asked everyone to call him Paul, and flashed shining teeth. The shrewder members of his audience put this down to his having attended a course on Media Awareness.

The younger members liked Paul's approach and disengaged their minds, sitting back to let him tell them what to think.

Ellie slipped into the hall as the chairman's speech was drawling to a close. Their vicar, Thomas — who shared the same name as their church, St Thomas' — was sitting on the VIP row of chairs facing his parishioners. Thomas, bearded and portly, was known affectionately as Tum-Tum because of his girth. He saw Ellie arrive, and nodded her to the only vacant chair on the far side of the room. She struggled through rows of legs to reach the seat, noting that Roy and Archie had seats in the front row.

As Ellie thankfully sank into the chair, Archie was called upon to review the parish finances. Ellie thought he did it efficiently, showing that though the parish was just about paying its way and meeting the quota set by the diocese, they still had to pay off some thirty thousand pounds for the rebuilding of the hall. And of course, the vicarage was in a dire state of repair, was inconvenient, etc., etc.

Gloom settled on the company. Paul shook his head every now and again, indicating that he was deeply concerned about their poor financial position, but sympathetic. He did it well.

One or two more people arrived and had to stand at the back. Ellie had wondered if Aunt Drusilla might have chosen to attend the meeting; she did attend services at St Thomas' now and again. No, she wasn't there. A pity, because Ellie felt she could have relied on Aunt Drusilla to put a relevant question or two to the chair. She'd be sharp enough to expose the scandal of what was really going on here.

Ellie's view of Paul was almost completely blocked by the massive figure of her old friend Mrs Dawes, leader of the flower-arranging team, an alto in the church choir and veteran gossip. Mrs Dawes' improbably jet-black hair had recently been touched up, and her dangling jet earrings brushed the shoulders of her tartan-lined raincoat. Every now and then, Mrs Dawes' chair creaked in alarming fashion. Ellie hoped it wouldn't collapse. They were still using the rickety chairs from the old hall, because they hadn't got the funds to replace them.

As Archie drew to a close, there came the usual query from the back row about the firm of auditors, replied to with promptitude by Archie. The accounts were accepted with a languid show of hands.

Someone was creating a disturbance on the far side of the hall. Heads turned. A man said, 'Can't you see the sign? No smoking!'

Heads shifted, craning to see who the culprit might be. With a shock, she recognized Marco, the gardener-turned-minder from Sir Arthur's. Was this the meeting Sir Arthur had been intending to go to? No, or he'd be sitting up front with the speakers.

The chairman introduced Paul, and everyone sat up straighter, or angled their chairs to get a better look at him.

Swarthy, well built, well barbered, and incredibly well tailored. His teeth were amazingly white. Did he have them treated?

Paul was one of those people who can manage a PowerPoint presentation without fusing the lights or clicking on to the wrong file. He had the screen at exactly the right angle. His voice was mellifluous. He even managed a small joke, while maintaining the sorrowful air of one attending a funeral.

Which, of course, was what he'd come to do. The poor old vicarage, so much loved, of course! But sadly . . . ah well . . . what was the parish thinking of, to condemn their incumbents to live in such misery? The kitchen . . . the central heating . . . click, click. Peeling paintwork, leaking roof, only one bathroom.

The bishop, said Paul, had been very worried about it for years. But the financial position . . . not improving . . . the enormous efforts that had been made to rebuild the church hall . . . and what an effort that had been! The bishop had been amazed that this remarkable parish had managed to achieve such a high-quality building, though of course much still remained to be done . . . new seating, and so on.

Facts and figures were highlighted. Click, click.

Paul became more and more sorrowful and serious with every click. He'd practically got the front row in tears.

Then the solution! A modern-day miracle!

Hurray! Everyone brightened up as Paul beamed on them. A guardian angel had come into sight. All their problems would be solved at one stroke. The bishop had sent up prayers of thanks. Paul himself had been much relieved, as he'd spent many a long hour worrying about St Thomas'.

Ellie wondered if Paul really expected people to believe he cared about them?

Click. Architect's plans were thrown on to the screen. Ellie found them difficult to understand. She craned to see if these were the plans Roy had drawn up. Roy was sitting with his chin on his chest, but his eyes on the screen. His face showed no emotion. Archie was plumply smiling. Tum-Tum looked wooden.

Paul continued to beam. He didn't expect his audience to understand fully all the details . . . so difficult for us laymen to understand architects' plans . . . but he'd been assured that — click, click — without the parish having to put up one more penny of their own money — their problems had all been solved. Click, click. They were to have a brand-new, purpose-built vicarage in place of the old vicarage.

Click . . . an architect's impression of the new vicarage shot on to the screen.

'Three bedrooms, one en suite with a shower room, and a separate bathroom,' said Paul, displaying radiant charm, like a magician pulling roses out of a top hat to enchant his audience. 'A large living room downstairs which can double up as a committee room whenever necessary, a small study, a kitchen with breakfast bar . . . and off-street parking for a car.' Paul beamed, as if to say, *Look what goodies I'm bestowing on you!*

'What's more, our "angel" proposes, as a gesture to the community, to wipe out the remaining debt on the church hall!'

Ellie screwed up her eyes in an effort to see better. Had he or hadn't he shown the plans for six flats? He'd shot so many slides on to the screen that it had been difficult to see what was going on. How many flats had the plan shown?

She glanced to left and right of her. A murmur of appreciation ran round the hall. The younger people relaxed into smiles. Even the older ones did. Mostly. There was a greyish-looking man three along from Mrs Dawes in the next row, who was frowning, flicking figures with his pen into the margin of his agenda. With an effort, Ellie recalled that he was an occasional church-goer — an estate agent? Not the ghastly creature her daughter Diana had been going out with some time ago, but a reputable man.

The chairman got to his feet, clapping. One or two joined in. The clapping spread slowly to the back of the hall. Only a few people looked half-hearted about it. Even fewer refrained from clapping at all. Ellie didn't clap, for one. Nor did Mrs Dawes, in front of her. Mrs Dawes was no financial brain, but she loved gardens and perhaps she'd realized that this 'miracle' meant they'd lose the vicarage garden. Perhaps Mrs Dawes would start asking pertinent questions about finance etc. Someone ought to.

Not Ellie, of course. She left all that to the men, or to people who were accustomed to speaking in public.

Ellie felt someone tap on her knee. A couple of chairs away sat Jean, who organized the rotas for tea and coffee. Jean was leaning forward, hissing to Ellie. 'I need some help with the coffee. All right?' Jean took it for granted that Ellie would agree. Normally Ellie would agree. But the meeting wasn't over yet, and Ellie wasn't leaving till she was sure everything was out in the open.

CHAPTER FOUR

'If you please, Mr Chairman . . . ?' A voice from the other side of the hall. Ellie relaxed. It had been ridiculous to think the plans would get pushed through without any queries.

'I think we have a lot to be grateful for. For years we've been finding money to keep that white elephant of a vicarage going, propping up the fabric, patching up the central heating . . . not to mention the recurring problem with the kitchen drain . . .'

Some laughter. The saga of the kitchen drain had been going on for twenty years or more.

'. . . and though I personally don't go along with this idea that God dishes out miracles to order . . .'

Ellie craned her neck to see who was speaking. Uh-oh. A self-satisfied member of the PCC, long-retired, member of the golf club.

'. . . yet, in this case, I can't help agreeing with Paul that we have indeed seen a modern miracle . . .'

Some applause. Some sour faces. This sort of oratory didn't go down all that well with the older women. Jean leaned over her neighbour and tugged at Ellie's sleeve. 'We need to get the cups set out now! Come *on*!'

‘Not yet,’ said Ellie, eyes on the man who believed in modern miracles.

‘*What!*’ said Jean, hardly able to believe that Ellie could have refused a direct order. Mrs Dawes stirred in her chair and tried to turn her head round to see who was making all the fuss. Several other people looked round. Ellie blushed and tried to pretend she wasn’t there. How embarrassing! Jean turned to stalk out of the hall, striding over legs and bumping knees as she went, but Ellie stuck to her seat. She wanted to see this through.

The speaker was still in full flight. ‘. . . and therefore, Mr Chairman, I’m wondering if it would be in order to suggest that the new block of flats is named after our benefactor. Naming it “Arthur Court” would be a graceful way of showing our appreciation, don’t you think?’

No! thought Ellie. Around her, people were applauding, some enthusiastically, and others politely. Or looking at their watches. Wondering whether the meeting might by any chance finish early enough for them to get back to see . . . whatever it was on the telly that night.

The chairman was on his feet, relaxed, smiling. ‘An excellent idea. Do I have a proposal from the floor . . . ? And a seconder . . . ? Carried unanimously, then.’

‘No!’ said Ellie, driven to her feet. And there she stuck, not knowing what to say, conscious of many eyes upon her, some looking surprised, others annoyed. And what could she say? That they’d got it all wrong? She wasn’t sure that they had. Perhaps the plans put up this evening were only for two or four flats. Perhaps . . .

She’d never been any good at this public speaking lark anyway.

The chairman was looking at her rather as if she’d grown two heads. She knew him quite well; a church warden, a genial man who believed in running meetings where everything had been cut and dried beforehand.

‘Yes? You have some objection, Mrs Quicke?’

'Yes. I mean . . . are you sure about . . . I've probably got hold of the wrong end of the stick, but . . .' She was furious with herself. Why couldn't she just have let the motion go through without making a spectacle of herself?

'You want us to register an objection to the flats being named after our benefactor?'

'Yes. That is, I'm not sure how much of a benefactor he really is.'

The chairman lost his smile. 'Oh, come now. You've seen the plans, and heard how much good—'

Ellie stiffened her legs, which threatened to give way under her. 'I haven't seen the plans. Well, I heard there were supposed to be only two flats, and that seemed all right. But I haven't seen the latest plans and I haven't seen the figures.'

'Then perhaps you'll let our treasurer — who *is* good at figures — reassure you after the meeting closes.'

A titter ran round the hall. Ellie was the target of unfriendly looks.

She wouldn't give in. Faint but persistent, that was her. 'I realize I may be making a fool of myself, but when it comes down to disposing of something so valuable as our vicarage site . . .'

Paul hadn't lost his smile. He was, perhaps, used to dealing with middle-aged ladies with muddled brains. 'You know, we really have gone into all this very deeply, Mrs . . . er . . . Rich, is it?'

Another titter ran through the room. Ellie went white. How dare he make a mockery of her name. 'Mrs Quicke is my name,' she said, firmly. 'Yes, I'm sure you did your sums perfectly when all this was first thought of. Two flats were to be built on about one third of the existing garden, and that would pay for the rebuilding of the vicarage. I think we all understood the mathematics of that proposal, and agreed with it. Then I understand that the developer felt two flats didn't give him enough of a profit. Is that so?'

'Well, yes. In principle, yes.' Paul didn't like admitting it, but he did so. It was clear that this was news to some if not all of the people in the room. There was a general shifting of chairs, and head-shaking. 'We decided that this would still be a good deal.'

The estate agent gave Ellie a thoughtful look. Clearly, he was one of those who hadn't heard about the number of flats increasing from two to four.

'So,' said Ellie, holding on to her shaking hands, 'when did you hear that there were to be six not four flats? And that they were to be large luxury apartments, and would wipe out the rest of the garden and its trees?'

There was a murmur of incomprehension from the meeting. Everyone looked at everyone else. Did you know about six flats? Lots of head-shaking. No, I didn't. Did you? It's probably not true. No, of course it couldn't be.

The estate agent was doing sums on his copy of the minutes.

Paul did a double take. Didn't he know about the plan to update to six flats? Surely he must have done!

The chairman looked startled. Was it possible he didn't know either? Had she made some horrible, embarrassing mistake?

Archie tapped his teeth with his biro, scowling at Roy. Roy was looking across at Ellie, with a sick look on his face. Did he feel that she'd betrayed him in some way?

The chairman got to his feet, putting on a jolly grin. 'There has been some mention of our allowing six flats, but nothing has been decided. Has it, Paul?'

Perhaps he hoped Paul would rescue him, but Paul wasn't going to play ball. 'I've heard something about the necessity of it being six flats, yes. It still seems to me that you have no option but to agree. The benefits to the parish are obvious.' So he had known.

'Perhaps someone who's good at figures can do the maths for me?' said Ellie. 'These six spacious, luxury flats are going to front on to the Green with plenty of room for car parking, pushing a tiny, much reduced vicarage down an alleyway behind. The flats will have state of the art wiring, kitchens, wet rooms. Four bedrooms, en suite. They will have everything in them to attract people with money to spend. How much would they be expected to sell for?' She looked directly at the estate agent sitting in her row.

He flicked his pen in the air. 'I would value them at upwards of half a million each. That's . . .'

'Three million pounds minimum,' said Ellie. 'How much is it going to cost the developer to put up a very small three-bedroom house to replace the vicarage . . . on land that he doesn't have to pay for, plus six flats, spreading himself over the whole site?'

There was a subdued uproar. Paul looked thunderous. The chairman yelled, 'Order, order!' and was ignored.

Archie sent Ellie a look which should have shot straight through her. Roy leaned back in his chair and looked up at the ceiling. Tum-Tum laughed, his belly shaking, his eyes almost disappearing.

Ellie felt her way back on to her chair and quivered. Her cheeks were aflame, her feet were icy. She was shaking all over. She didn't know how she'd dared!

'Mr Chairman . . .'

They were off. Now they knew what Ellie knew, they were going to worry away at it like a dog at a bone. Everyone could do some simple maths. They realized that the developer had been intending to make the sort of profit you could only dream of . . . and now the Save Our Green Spaces people were going to have their say, too. 'What about the loss of the garden, the trees, the . . .'

'Mr Chair, it seems to me that we can hardly vote on a proposal which has been sprung on us so . . .'

'I second that . . .'

The meeting began to get heated. Mrs Dawes heaved herself to her feet, and started in. 'That new vicarage. You say the living room downstairs is to double up as a committee room. Where's the poor vicar supposed to go when we have our Women's Guild meetings, then?'

Ellie crept out, over legs and in front of knees. People were waving their arms about, trying to catch the chairman's eye. He, poor man, was looking flustered. Archie's blood pressure was going through the roof. Paul was looking down his nose. He was packing up his laptop, unplugging it. Was he really going to turn tail and run away without calming the storm? Yes, he was.

Ellie hovered in the kitchen doorway, watching him having a quiet word with the chairman, who announced that, most unfortunately, Paul had another meeting, would have to dash away, but he was sure they were all very grateful to him for coming to . . .

Ellie closed the kitchen door behind her, trying not to laugh, wondering why she was on the verge of tears.

Jean started in on Ellie straight away. 'What on earth possessed you to interfere in things you know nothing about! You might have realized I'd need—'

Ellie had had enough. 'Put a sock in it, Jean.'

'Well!' Jean's mouth opened and stayed open. Ellie had never, ever, answered her back before like that. Ellie always helped out, whenever she was asked to do so. 'What on earth's got into you?'

Ellie's knees were still trembling. 'I met the developer this afternoon, and I didn't like him.'

'What's that got to do with it? I don't particularly like my milkman, but he's a fact of life, and I don't have to cuddle up to him, do I!'

The thought of frizzy-haired Jean cuddling up to the milkman was too much for Ellie's composure, and she dived for the Ladies so that she could have a good laugh, splash cold water over her face, and blow her nose.

Only then was she calm enough to go back to help serve tea and coffee. And face the music. Luckily for her, the meeting went on for another half an hour, so while Jean fussed about keeping the urn on the boil, Ellie had plenty of time to put out the cups and saucers and tip some packets of biscuits on to large plates. And remember the teaspoons and the sugar.

When the meeting did break up, it was clear that no one was in a happy mood. They'd come expecting to vote through an acceptable proposal to solve all their problems, and now . . .

'We'll have to start all over again,' announced Mrs Dawes. 'Disgraceful, I call it!'

'Next time, *we'll* brief the architect . . . !'

'If we're allowed. The bishop . . . that Paul . . . never could trust . . .'

The chairman was beleaguered, taking refuge in his handkerchief and a timely bout of hayfever. 'We'll have to have another meeting.'

Archie was surrounded by a group determined to 'get to the bottom of this', who were not in the least inclined to listen to his plea that he should at least be allowed to get a cup of coffee.

Roy had disappeared. Wisely, thought Ellie. There was no sign of Marco, who'd been driving Sir Arthur that evening. Was he on his way back to report to his master? What would Sir Arthur do then? Ellie shivered a little at the thought.

Dear Tum-Tum, the vicar, was smiling, consoling, listening to everyone's point of view. 'Nothing to do with me, you know. It's between the parish and the diocese.'

Catching Ellie's eye, he gave her an enormous wink. Which made her feel a lot better.

Nevertheless, she was extremely glad when the last cup and saucer was washed up and put away, the hall swept, and the chairs properly stacked at the sides.

Tum-Tum helped to clear up. Jean stamped off in her car but Tum-Tum fell into step beside Ellie as she crossed the Green on her way home.

'You've no need to see me home,' said Ellie, always nervous that someone would think she was monopolizing Tum-Tum's time. Tongues would wag if anyone saw them, and somebody was bound to see.

'How else can I get a word with you? What an evening! May I ask how you knew about the six flats? I'd heard a rumour which came out of the diocesan office, but when I asked if it were true, I was told that nothing had been officially decided and that I'd be informed if anything came of it.'

Ellie sighed. 'Roy told me. I see now that he set me up. Sir Arthur put pressure on him to redraw the plans, and Roy didn't like what he'd been told to do. He wanted everyone to know what had happened, but he didn't want to be the one who opened his big mouth and put his foot in it.'

'I've heard Sir Arthur makes a bad enemy.'

'Are you warning me?' A shiver went down her spine. 'I've met the man. And yes, I think he'll take this set-back personally. Are you escorting me home to make sure I don't get beaten up on the way?'

She was only half joking. In the dusk, it was hard to penetrate the shadows under the trees.

Tum-Tum said, 'I don't think he'd do anything so obvious, but that man of his — the one who tried to light a cigarette in the meeting — he'll report back.'

They'd reached her gate. Midge was sitting on the gatepost, waiting for her. Tum-Tum tickled Midge around the ears, and Midge yawned mightily, tolerating the vicar's caress. Midge was a good judge of character. Ellie wondered what Midge would make of Sir Arthur.

She said, 'How did you know the man worked for Sir Arthur?'

'I caught him trampling down the flowers in someone's front garden a couple of weeks ago. He told me Sir Arthur owned the house, and that he could do what he liked with the garden, because the tenant was behindhand with the rent. I checked. It was true enough.'

Ellie was silent. She'd had her own garden trampled over once, when she'd offended a neighbour. It had been a shocking experience and at the time she'd been devastated. But she'd survived, and so had the garden.

'Do I know — whoever it was?'

'Possibly not. She doesn't attend our church, and she didn't welcome my talking about it.'

It sounded as though this person might also have had reason to hate Sir Arthur. Ellie was compiling a list. There was the first architect's wife, Mrs Anderson; the person who'd sprayed graffiti on the garage walls; Roy; the man she was supposed to meet tomorrow; and what about the local builders whom he'd displaced in favour of one of his housing developments? The list grew. Kate had hinted that the man had many enemies, and Ellie could well believe it. Perhaps she should add her own name?

But she hadn't poisoned the pizza, and neither had Roy. She was sure of that.

It amused her that Tum-Tum thought he was being so discreet in not naming the woman who'd had her garden trashed. If she was local — and she must be local or Tum-Tum wouldn't have seen it happen — then Ellie thought it would only take her a phone call or two to find out the woman's name and where she lived.

'Goodnight, God bless,' said Tum-Tum, closing the subject.

Ellie went up the pathway, accompanied by Midge, searching for the back door key in her handbag. The house was as she had left it, though the message light was winking on the answerphone.

She could ignore it. Perhaps it wasn't only Diana. Perhaps dear Aunt Drusilla had rung for some reason. Or one of her friends.

Diana's was the first message. Predictable. Threatening. '. . . because if you don't help me out, you'll drive me to do something I really don't want to do, and . . .'

Ellie waited till Diana had run out of steam.

The next message was from an old friend who lived on the other side of London. They'd planned to meet up in town the following week, but something had come up. Could Ellie manage Tuesday instead of Wednesday? Fine by Ellie.

Then a fluttery voice. Dear Rose, the old friend who'd once worked with Ellie in the charity shop in the Avenue, but was now Aunt Drusilla's efficient and loving housekeeper and companion. Rose did go on a bit, but her heart was in the right place.

'. . . because, dear Ellie, I didn't like to say anything to alarm you when it might be nothing at all, and you know what Miss Quicke is like, never making a fuss about anything, and refusing to take painkillers, but she's been using her stick so much more lately, and I've caught her having to rest halfway up the stairs, but she will *not* go to the doctor's, though I've mentioned it at least twice, and I really think she should, you know. It's her hip, I'm sure, but they can replace them nowadays, can't they? Anyway, I thought I'd just mention it, though it might be best if you didn't tell your aunt that I'd been interfering . . .'

Ellie sighed. Yes, she too had noticed that her aunt was in some pain with her hip, and she, too, had had her head bitten off when she'd mentioned it. Now Rose was concerned. Something would have to be done. But what? Miss Quicke had been brought up to present a stoical front to the world, and in her day people did not have parts of their bodies replaced with ironmongery. Perhaps Roy might be able to persuade her to see a doctor?

It was at times like this that Ellie missed her dear husband. It was like a nerve pain. Sometimes she went for days without thinking about him very much, and then . . . ouch!

She told herself she was overtired. Well, she was, of course. But.

While Ellie made herself a cup of instant soup, she sent up a prayer or two. She'd never been any good at praying first thing in the morning. Her time to talk to God was always last thing at night, as she thought over the events of the day.

Ellie didn't think she'd handled things very well that day. What a jumble of impressions she had rolling round her head! That poor Felicity . . . nasty Sir Arthur . . . baby Catriona smiling up at her . . . Diana in a white fury, oh dear!

Aunt Drusilla in pain and Roy getting himself into a financial mess . . . the architect's widow and the woman whose garden had been trashed . . .

Lord protect us, Ellie whispered to herself.

Preceded by Midge, she went up the stairs to bed.

CHAPTER FIVE

Sir Arthur was an early riser. Today he'd got a hangover, so had taken his ill humour out on his wife and would have taken it out on his dog, if the dog had still been around.

Then Marco came in with the bad news about the meeting at the church hall the previous evening, emphasizing Ellie's part in it.

'She did what?'

Marco repeated his words with some relish, thinking that the interfering old bitch had it coming to her. 'She said about the flats going up from two to six. Everything was smelling sweet till then. You hadn't got enough support for six. The man from the bishop, he picked up his skirts and ran. Furious, they was. Then Mrs Quicker went off to make the tea, calm as you please. I told you, din't I? Trouble, she is.'

'What about my architect? He should have stopped the nonsense.'

'Couldn't get a word in edgeways. Nor the chairman, neither. I reckon that scheme's gone down the tubes.'

Sir Arthur slammed his fist down on the arm of his chair.

Marco grinned, anticipating what was to come. 'I'll pay her a visit. Right?'

* * *

It was going to be another blue-sky day. The trees were turning amber, but the leaves had hardly begun to drop to the ground. A good day for gardening. The pink schizostylis which Ellie had planted in clumps in the front garden were coming out nicely, just as the early Michaelmas daisies were beginning to lose their colour. Ellie wondered whether or not to cut some of the lily-like pink flowers to put in a small vase on the mantelpiece in the sitting room — but decided to leave them where they were.

The Japanese anemones were a triumphant mass of white. She could certainly pick some of those.

The phone rang, putting paid to all hopes of getting out into the garden. Kate. Ellie was not particularly surprised to hear that, on such a perfect autumn day, Kate had been persuaded by Armand that she should forgo her trip to the City. Armand said that Ellie was a grown woman and would be perfectly safe going to see her client on her own.

'Do I really have to go?' Ellie would really prefer to work in the garden.

'A car will come for you at nine thirty,' said Kate. 'You'll like Chris Talbot, and he'll like you. I'll be back around three, and look forward to hearing all about it then.'

'Now wait a minute,' said Ellie. 'I'm not going anywhere till you give me a better idea of what's going on. Gwyn is your boss, right? So who is this Talbot? Is he Sir Arthur's enemy, the man he thinks was trying to poison him? And why do you think it wasn't him?'

'Gwyn is the chairman of the merchant bank which employs me. He's been putting together a package to refinance a big corporation that's in trouble, partly through the losses incurred by one of its subsidiaries. There's a lot at stake, not just thousands of jobs, but also national prestige. Chris Talbot came on board at an early stage and it looked as if the City would give its blessing, provided this one loss-making subsidiary would agree to restructure.

'Unfortunately Sir Arthur is a major shareholder in that company, and he's refusing to agree to the plan. He probably thinks that the longer he holds out, the more money he's likely to get as a golden handshake. Then his dog was killed, and Sir Arthur claimed that Chris Talbot — who's an old enemy of his — was responsible. He swore to get even. Gwyn is working behind the scenes to bring Sir Arthur round, but he thinks that if we can only find out who really killed the dog, prove that it isn't Chris Talbot, they'd have a better chance of the deal going through. That's why I asked you to help. You said you would. End of story.'

'But . . .' said Ellie, as Kate disconnected. 'But,' said Ellie to Midge, 'Is my garden going to be safe while I'm away?'

Midge yawned, jumped from the top of the table to the windowsill and proceeded to perform his toilet.

Ellie considered her options. Some people would go on the Internet for the information she required, but she was not one of them. However, she knew a woman who was. Aunt Drusilla did not believe in rising late, and she might well have some useful information about this Mr Talbot — whoever he might be.

* * *

The chauffeur-driven car took Ellie to the very heart of the City, and decanted her in front of the sort of building designed to intimidate those who didn't own houses in Switzerland, Bermuda and Paris, or bank accounts in the Cayman Islands.

The building made Ellie self-conscious. Had her lavender suit, bought in a sale at Selfridges, really been a good buy? Wouldn't everyone be able to tell she was wearing Marks & Spencer underwear?

She had to scold herself into mounting the steps between two modern art statues — what on earth were they meant to represent? Cornucopias, perhaps? Giant fish? Or just twists of steel reaching for the sky?

The foyer was vast. All marble. Or what looked like marble. There were several desks, each manned by the young and the beautiful, who probably — thought Ellie — were expert at judo and would allow her no further into the building. But when she coughed and murmured her name, a man with sharp eyes ushered her round the corner to a lift hidden behind an unobtrusive door. Before she could start worrying whether this was the sort of lift which left your stomach behind, they were on their way, and then of course she began to worry whether they might get stuck between two floors.

Doors whispered apart. A vista of too much sky opened before her and Ellie almost lost her balance, so high up were they. A seagull slid past and Ellie remembered her mother saying that seagulls inland meant storms at sea.

'Mrs Quicke, I presume? My name's Talbot. Delighted to meet you. You don't suffer from heights, do you? Here, take my arm.'

A grey-clad arm took hers and led her away from the expanse of sky to a comfortable chair some distance from the balcony. He spoke to someone behind him. 'Would you close the window, please? And rustle us up some coffee . . .' And to Ellie, 'Or would you prefer tea?'

Ellie made an effort. 'I'm so sorry. Stupid of me. I'm not usually . . . but coffee would be . . . that is, if it's not too much trouble.'

At first sight Mr Talbot appeared to be nothing out of the ordinary. He was a pleasant-looking man of about her own age perhaps, casually but well dressed in grey, but . . . ah, he had the sharpest, bluest eyes she had ever seen. Even bluer than Roy's.

She revised her first impression. There was nothing ordinary about this man. There was a first-class brain behind that pleasant, somewhat bland exterior. Also, she mustn't forget that a man who occupied a penthouse suite in such a building was bound to be a person of importance.

He had a good smile, too. One that crinkled up his eyelids. 'I am delighted to meet you, Mrs Quicke.'

She had an impulse to say — like a nineteenth-century miss — *Charmed to meet you, too*. She refrained from doing so, even while she registered the fact that he *was* charming and had treated her as a gentleman would. And wasn't 'gentleman' an outmoded term? Yet that is what he was. A merchant banker with manners.

He was chatting about the weather, giving her time to recover, saying he hoped his chauffeur had collected her in good enough time. All the time he watched her. Did he guess about the M & S underwear? Possibly. Did he care? No.

Neither did she any longer.

Coffee appeared. Proper ground coffee in a cafetière, of course. Very strong. She took a sip and held back a grimace, reaching for the milk.

'Forgive me,' he said. 'I think you might have preferred hot chocolate?'

'Bad for my figure.'

He smiled. 'Not from where I'm sitting.' He called over his shoulder, 'Can we provide . . . ?'

'Coming up,' said a disembodied voice.

Ellie felt mischievous. 'With a biscuit?'

He capped it. 'Perhaps a Danish pastry?'

She laughed. 'No, that would be overdoing it.'

'Perhaps when this is over, you'll let me give you lunch somewhere we can both be as self-indulgent as we please?'

Her smile vanished. 'I have the feeling you are not often self-indulgent, Mr Talbot.'

'Call me Chris. Perspicacious of you. No, usually I am not.'

A pot of chocolate appeared with a swirl of whipped cream on the side, together with some rich chocolate biscuits. She ignored the cream and the biscuits, but sipped the chocolate with relish. 'You say you are not *usually* self-indulgent. Thereby hangs a tale?'

His eyes wandered away to the window and beyond, to the blue of the sky. Then snapped back to her. 'Mrs Quicke; I was born with a silver spoon in my mouth and I've turned my silver spoon into gold. However, I've a Calvinistic streak, which has perhaps prevented me from making as much money as some of my colleagues. It's also brought me some enemies. One in particular.'

'The man I met yesterday.'

He sighed. 'It all sounds so trivial. Twenty years ago we met on the board of a company which was in trouble. We disagreed about the direction we should take. I swung the rest of the directors over to my point of view without realizing it would prevent Kingsley from making a lot of money on the side. He swore to get even. I think I was a little amused. What did it matter? To him, it seemed to matter a great deal. We've met and clashed every now and again over the years. He seems to take pleasure in opposing everything I do. Usually I win. Occasionally I lose. I've enjoyed the fight, most of the time.'

He leaned forward to pour some more hot chocolate into her cup. His own cup of coffee remained untouched. 'Now he says I'm trying to poison him, and I'm beginning to wonder if he's becoming paranoid. If his allegations reach the press, he could do me a lot of damage. Worse, it would destroy the deal we're trying to put together. I'm beginning to feel my age and this is getting me down. You know the saying about it being fine to ride the tiger, until you want to get off? Well, that's how I feel.'

She revised her first estimate of his age. He was probably nearer sixty than fifty. But still fit. No way was this man too tired to go on fighting. She appreciated the touch about Sir Arthur becoming paranoid, but somehow Chris Talbot's story didn't feel right. With her head she thought, Yes, that all hangs together. With her heart she thought, Bullshit.

She didn't normally express herself in those terms but, to her horror, she heard the word 'Bullshit' leave her mouth.

All the warmth drained out of the air. He was displeased.

Oh well, she'd best be on her way. She reached for her handbag. 'Thank you for the hot chocolate. It was delicious. I've always wanted to meet—' she intended to say *a captain of industry*, but it came out as — 'a gentleman pirate.'

He threw up his head and laughed without sound, wiped his hands down over his face and stood up. He put his hand under her arm and steered her towards the balcony, pushing open the window so that they could feel the breeze cooling this side of the tower.

'Let's get out into the fresh air, shall we?'

Had she just passed some sort of test? Was he now confronting her with another, by leading her out on to the balcony? She felt herself wobble. Well, if she concentrated on something else, such as whether or not to buy some amaryllis bulbs to force for Christmas, she'd be able to manage. After all, she'd managed all right when she'd taken little Frank up on the wheel of the London Eye for his birthday. She'd managed that by being more worried about his wanting to dash from side to side of the capsule, shrieking, than about herself. The trick was to concentrate on something or somebody else.

It wouldn't do to let her mind wander away when a man like Chris Talbot was baring his soul to her. Mind you, she'd believe he really was doing that when full cream milk returned to fashion.

'Perhaps I was less than frank with you earlier. What do you think of the view, by the way? We're not as high as Canary Wharf, but not far off.'

She was pleased to see that the warmth had returned to his manner, but refused to focus on the hundreds of feet between her feet and the ground below. Was it possible that it was not she who was swaying with vertigo, but that the tower itself was gently swinging in the autumn breeze?

'As you probably guessed,' he said, 'all my meetings inside are tape-recorded . . .'

She recalled the word 'bullshit' with horror. Had that really gone on tape? And that gibe about his being a gentleman pirate? Oh.

'But out here there are no mikes and we can talk freely, if the height doesn't bother you too much?'

She nodded, concentrating on his face.

'As you guessed, I'm not usually self-indulgent, but when I was twenty-five I wanted something so badly that I lost my usual sense of balance. For some years I'd had an "understanding" with a childhood friend that we'd marry when she finished her degree at Yale. Our families approved, our temperaments matched. Then I fell in love with a shy, ethereally beautiful girl and her neglected manor house in Oxfordshire.

'Did she love me at all? Perhaps as much as she was able. I promised to restore the house, and she loved me for that. Within weeks of our marriage I discovered that what I'd taken for shyness and modesty was a deep insecurity on her part. She was miserable away from her home, and not clever enough to feel comfortable with my friends. I did what I could to reassure her, but I couldn't at that time pour enough money into her home to transform it overnight, nor could I afford to spend as much time in the country as she wished.'

Ellie nodded. 'You misread one another's characters.'

'I hoped things would improve when the baby came, but caring for our daughter gave Anne the excuse she was looking for. She withdrew to the country for good. My business interests kept me moving around the world. I sent her as much money as I could towards restoring the house, but it was never enough.'

He raised his hands in a helpless gesture. 'She had a no-good cousin who was always there, advising her on restoring the house. He moved in with her and, well, we divorced after two years apart. She married him, and they tried to run the house as a hotel. Neither had any business sense. They failed, of course. He died in a car crash and in the end she had to sell the house to meet their debts.

'She married again. Her new husband drank. She did too. They lived on the money I sent them for my daughter's upkeep. I tried to keep in touch, see my daughter when I could, but Anne was clever about making difficulties and fed the child with the idea that I'd never wanted her in the first place. In consequence my only daughter turned against me and I've seen hardly anything of her.' He held up both his hands in a gesture of defeat.

'I think now that I should have tried harder, but Anne said that my visits upset the child and I–I was always busy.

My fault. Anne thought of nothing but getting enough money together to buy back her home. She blamed me for her having to sell it in the first place. She tried to run a craft shop in Leeds, a café in Sheffield. Those failed, too. Her drinking became an addiction, yet she's still appealing, still beautiful in a fragile way.'

Ellie thought he was probably telling the truth now. 'You married again?'

'Yes.' He relaxed, smiling. 'It took me two years after the divorce to convince Minna that I was in earnest, but I managed it eventually. She's my best friend, my heart and my home. We have two delightful, irritating, amusing, hard-working boys and she understands me perfectly.'

'And your daughter?'

He glanced down at his hand, made a fist, stretched out the fingers. Not to avoid her eye, but because this bit was painful. 'She takes after me in looks. She's almost as anxious and insecure as her mother. She's a home-loving girl who's never really had a home. She devotes herself to looking after her husband and her mother. She married a man who promised to buy back the family house for her and her mother. He's restored it after a fashion, but Anne never got to live there. She's too far gone with the drink, you see. She's in a home now. My daughter pays the bills out of the allowance her husband makes her. I've offered to pay, but she refuses. She won't meet me or even accept birthday presents. She leads an isolated life, has no friends. And her husband does not value her.'

He examined his fingernails, looking anywhere but at Ellie.

Ellie might not be able to read complicated balance sheets, but she could read people, and now she added up this fact and that. And came to a conclusion which surely must be wrong. 'Felicity is your daughter?'

He nodded.

Ellie blinked. If Felicity was Chris Talbot's daughter, had Sir Arthur married her out of spite? Oh, surely not. That would be extremely nasty. Though perhaps not out of character. Ellie shivered.

She said, 'You're worried about your daughter?'

'I don't know who poisoned the dog, but someone certainly did. It gives me the shivers to think that Felicity might well have been the person to take the pizza in and eat it. Kingsley had an autopsy done on the dog, and discovered enough sleeping pills to kill a man, let alone a dog.'

Ellie shook her head. 'Poison would not be your weapon of choice.'

'No.' A brief smile.

'But Sir Arthur thinks you did it. What will he do? Poison you? Sue you for damages? He can't prove anything, if you didn't do it. Or . . . no. He'll try to get back at you in some other way.'

'I can look after myself.'

'What do you think I can do? Surely the police . . . ?'

He shook his head. 'No police.'

Ellie did her sums again. 'You don't want the police because you think that your daughter might have been responsible. You think she tried to kill her husband, but got the dog instead?'

Colour flared in his cheeks. Yes, Felicity was his weak spot. 'I didn't say so.'

'That's what you're afraid of, isn't it?'

He tried to laugh. 'She loved that dog. She was the one who looked after it, groomed it, took it for walks. He regarded the dog as just another disposable asset. He liked to be seen with it because it reflected well on him to own a dog with a good pedigree, especially in the country. The dog was afraid of him, but loved Felicity. And she loved him. She'd never have risked his eating something which might kill him.'

Ellie thought, You're not entirely sure about that, are you?

He said, 'Arthur takes the dog to the country with him at weekends and that's when Felicity goes to see her mother. Arthur came back before Felicity and found the pizza on the doorstep. By the time she returned, it was too late.'

'You know all this because . . . ?'

'There's a woman who goes in to help clean the house. She's on my payroll.'

Ellie nodded. 'I didn't think it would be the gardener-cum-driver.'

'He's hired help, not brains. Have you come across Sir Arthur's PA? A man called Martinez? Looks rather like a snake and thinks like one too.'

She shook her head. 'Suppose I can't find out who sent the pizza? It sounds as if everyone he ever met would have a motive.'

'When Gwyn said he was arranging for Kate to get some woman detective on the case, I was very doubtful that it would do any good. I agreed to meet you because Kate told me you were good with people. Now I've met you . . .'

'And tested me?'

'Yes, and tested you, I see she was right. I don't know whether or not you can discover who sent the poisoned pizza, but it occurs to me that you might help Felicity, befriend her. It would relieve my mind a great deal if I knew she could call on someone like you if ever she needs help. Will you do it?'

Ellie thought of her busy life, of everything she had going on, looking after little Frank, seeing her friends, meeting her friend next week for lunch, worrying about Diana and Aunt Drusilla, and all the problems at church with Roy always wanting more of her company than she had time to give and . . . and . . . and . . . yes, she'd forgotten she'd promised to help serve coffee and tea at the church Autumn Fair on the morrow.

She stood up. 'I don't know whether I can help or not. But I will try.'

* * *

Sir Arthur's mobile rang. He noted that it was Martinez calling, excused himself from the restaurant table and took the call in the foyer. What he heard did not please him. 'That is not what I wanted to hear.

Surely you could have found someone who can connect him with the delivery? Oh, very well. No, you've wasted enough time on it. Move on to plan B. Yes, today. But make sure there's no way they can trace—'

The phone quacked.

Sir Arthur smiled. 'That's good. I like that. Let me know when it's done.'

* * *

Mr Talbot's driver delivered Ellie safely back home. Her garden was untouched and Midge was asleep in the conservatory at the back of the house. There was a flurry of mail on the doormat, but no threatening letters. Perhaps she was too insignificant a person for Sir Arthur to bother with. She changed her good suit — she still wasn't sure that lavender was exactly her colour — for a comfortable warm blue skirt and brushed wool shirt. Then she sat down to consult the phone book.

Ever since Roy had unburdened himself to her last night, Ellie had been worrying about Mrs Anderson, the architect's wife. Ellie knew how difficult it was to cope when your husband died suddenly, and according to Roy, Mr Anderson had killed himself. It didn't sound as if he'd been paid for the work he'd done for Sir Arthur, and Ellie didn't like to think of the poor woman in financial trouble. She found his number, introduced herself as a friend of Roy's and asked if she might pop in for a few minutes on a business matter connected with her husband's work.

She also phoned her aunt, hoping to kill two birds with one stone. Aunt Drusilla was nippier on the Internet than many half her age, and was delighted to be asked to dig up some dirt — if there were any — on Sir Arthur Kingsley and Chris Talbot.

That done, Ellie set out to visit Mrs Anderson. Her house was an ordinary 1930s semi-d, but the small garden in front had been landscaped with unusual plants. Ellie was stooping to inspect a shrub she didn't recognize, when the door opened and Mrs Anderson welcomed her inside.

Ellie had been expecting someone pallid from crying, and neglectful of her appearance, but Mrs Anderson was gorgeous. She was a big, vibrant, thirty-year-old with flashing brown eyes, and a bush of probably dyed blonde hair, dressed in emerald green and black. Possibly there had been some African ancestry a couple of generations back?

'Pretty, isn't it?' said Mrs Anderson. 'It's what I do for a living. Garden design and maintenance. Do come in. Mind the kids' bikes.'

Ellie went in, adjusting her ideas of Mrs Anderson.

'Coffee? I don't, when I'm working, but I've got some herbal tea somewhere. No? It's about the work my husband was doing for Sir Arthur Kingsley? Mind the train set. The children like to play with it as soon as they get home from school, and it's easier to leave it out all the time.'

The interior was slightly shabby but comfortable, with one or two unusual watercolours on the wall — possibly from the hand of a good amateur. A conservatory had been built on to the back of the house, overlooking a garden rich in interest. The conservatory was fitted up as an office, with computers and printers.

Ellie apologized for coming. 'From what Roy told me, I was afraid you might be in trouble after your husband's death, and — I'm doing this very badly — there's a local fund for emergency use . . .'

'Gracious!' The girl threw herself back on to the settee, and ran her fingers back through her mop of hair. On the wall above her was a framed colour photograph of her, two young children, and a man with fair hair and anxious eyes. Her husband? 'I wouldn't mind if you paid last quarter's gas bill for me, but, honest, we can manage.'

'Are you sure? Because when I was widowed, I couldn't even work out which day of the week it was. Also, I heard you'd had trouble with Sir Arthur Kingsley, and were pressing his new architect for some money.'

Mrs Anderson sat upright. She had a decisive manner, and Ellie could well imagine that whatever career she'd chosen, she'd meet with success.

'That wasn't my idea. The new architect sounded nice. Was Sir Arthur putting pressure on him, in order to get money for me? Sweet of him! Not that I'd have seen any of it.' She studied Ellie. 'Look, I did blame Sir Arthur for Pete's death, and yes, he was partly responsible, but the account's been settled. If you've got a minute, I'll tell you about it, and you can decide then if you want to pay the gas bill for me or not.'

Mrs Anderson gestured to the picture on the wall. 'Pete was a fine architect working for a local practice till he was in a car accident. After that his nerves were shot to pieces and he couldn't work. He lost his job. The finances worried him, so we put the house in my name and I took over paying the bills. Towards the end, everything worried him: the children, their noise, me. Don't get me wrong, we were still good friends, and I'd settled for that, but . . . well, it was hard sometimes, remembering what he'd been like when we first met.

'Then came the offer of work from Sir Arthur. I think now that Sir Arthur chose Pete because he could get him cheap. At the time Pete was ecstatic. We thought he'd turned the corner, because he was doing really good work, and sticking at it, too. He planned to take us all on holiday to New Zealand. Then everything went wrong. Sir Arthur wanted changes, but whatever alterations Pete made failed to please. He became depressed. The night Sir Arthur told him he wanted yet more changes, Pete walked over to the park and drowned himself in the river.'

Her face lengthened, her hands clenched. Slowly, in controlled fashion, she spread out her fingers again. 'I miss him terribly. The kids don't miss him so much. They can't remember him as he used to be, only as he has been the last couple of years. In a way, I'm glad about that.'

Ellie said, 'You said you made Sir Arthur pay for it?'

The girl laughed. 'It was a bit naughty of me. I registered a website for him, and emailed details of the website to everyone I thought might be interested, anyone who knew him.'

Ellie began to appreciate the ruse. 'What did you put on the website?'

The girl grinned. 'Caricatures of Sir Arthur's head on animal figures dancing and eating too much, and oh, you know the sort of thing.'

It was Ellie's turn to laugh. 'You made him pay you to close down the site? Wasn't he furious? Didn't he threaten you?'

'I suppose he might have done, if so many people hadn't known about the site and been amused by it. As it was, he paid up like a lamb. So I don't expect any more money from him or his new architect, and I really don't need any help with the gas bill.'

'Worth it,' said Ellie. 'Give it to me, I'll see it gets paid, and I'll tell the architect that he can forget pleasing Sir Arthur to help you.'

'Trying it on someone else now, is he? It almost makes me wish I'd kept the website.'

They parted on excellent terms, and Ellie was still smiling when she arrived at her aunt Drusilla's.

CHAPTER SIX

The large Victorian house which was currently occupied by Miss Drusilla Quicke and Rose actually belonged to Ellie, though few people knew it, and Ellie would never turn the older lady out. Ellie was happy in the three-bedroomed semi-d in which she'd spent nearly all her married life. She was also very fond of her aunt.

Miss Drusilla Quicke was in her late seventies but still ruled an empire of houses and flats to let. She'd never married but had welcomed the reappearance of her long-lost son Roy. She'd been happy to go into partnership with him to develop a site on the Green, while forming no great opinion of his financial ability. As she'd said to Ellie, 'Roy sees the broad picture, but is careless about detail.'

Roy was fond of the 'old dear', as he called her, but, if the truth be known, was also a trifle afraid of her. It was Roy who'd recently drawn the plans to modernize the large Victorian house; providing separate living quarters for Rose, and converting the old coach house into living quarters and an office for himself.

This morning Ellie noticed that Roy's car was absent. Had he confessed 'all' to his mother yet? Or had he shirked it? Ellie liked Roy but was not blind to his faults. He'd probably shirked it.

She let herself into the big house and went through the hall into the high-ceilinged drawing room at the back. You couldn't describe it as a 'lounge', because there was no piece of furniture in it made later than 1910. On this fine day, the French windows stood open on to the conservatory beyond, where Aunt Drusilla was leaning on her stick, looking at a plant which Rose was showing her.

'Ah, there you are at last, Ellie,' said Aunt Drusilla, allowing Ellie to kiss her cheek. 'Just in time, or Rose would have kept me here to admire every single plant in her conservatory.'

Ellie laughed and kissed Rose too. 'A fine example of a *Many-peeplia upside-downia*, isn't it, Rose?'

Rose giggled. '*Many-peep* . . . ? Oh, you are funny, Ellie. Where did you get that from? It's a Jerusalem Cherry, Miss Quicke, and it should give us a nice crop of cheerful red berries all through the winter, if only I can keep the whitefly off it. Home-made soup and a ham salad do you both? I'd bring it out here for you to eat, sitting here in the sun — it's been just like summer — but I think Miss Quicke would rather get back to her chair.'

Ellie knew better than to offer her aunt her arm, but watched anxiously as the elderly lady made her painful way to her high-backed chair by the fireplace. Rose had already laid for lunch on a Queen Anne card table nearby, and now chattered herself away to fetch the soup.

Ellie held back a wince as Aunt Drusilla carefully lowered herself into her chair.

'Don't pull faces,' said Miss Quicke. 'If the wind changes, your face will set like that.'

Ellie stiffened her back. 'Someone's got to say it. If you won't go to the doctor's—'

'Silly old fool. I've known him too long to listen to what *he* says.'

'Then you should see a specialist. Shall I ask my doctor who she'd recommend?'

'Women shouldn't set up as doctors.'

'Come on. There were women practising as doctors before you were born.'

'More fools they. And don't think I don't know you're talking for the sake of talking. What's up with Roy?'

Ellie hesitated. 'I think he ought to tell you himself.'

'He's told you?'

'Yes.' Grimly. 'He wanted me to pull his irons out of the fire for him. Which I did, more fool me. It's something you'd want to know about, but you may have to bully him a bit to get him to open up.'

Rose wafted in bowls of soup. 'Carrot and coriander, with a touch of curry powder. Eat up while it's hot.'

They ate. Rose was an accomplished cook.

Ellie said, 'You're worrying the life out of Rose. She can see you're in pain, and it's upsetting her.'

'I don't pay her to nursemaid me.'

'You invited her to stay as a friend and companion, and she has chosen to cook and housekeep for you. You pay her for that, but she'd still cook and housekeep for you if you didn't pay her a penny.'

'The more fool her.'

Rose brought in slices of home-cooked ham on plates, plus a bowl of mixed salad stuffs. Her home-made salad dressing was a triumph. Ellie said, 'Ah, Rose, I wish you could write down the recipe.'

'It's a bit of this and a touch of that. I'm not really sure what goes into it.'

Rose wafted herself away.

Miss Quicke pushed her plate aside, uneaten. 'What you're trying to say is that I'm a selfish old woman, scared of having an operation on my hip at my age.' She waited for Ellie to deny the charge, but Ellie kept her mouth for eating. Miss Quicke said, 'I'm well over seventy, you know. They don't like operating on people my age.'

'With the heart of a young woman, and the brains of a Nobel Prize winner.'

Miss Quicke snorted. 'Brains don't get you a new hip.'

'Money does. Specialists do. Would you like me to make an appointment for you to see someone good?'

'I'm perfectly capable of lifting the phone if I want to make an appointment.'

'Which you will do?'

'I'm not going to be messed around with at my age.' Miss Quicke speared a piece of ham on her fork, ate it, and took another. She ate slowly, but with relish. Rose had given Miss Quicke half of the amount she'd given Ellie. Both cleared their plates.

'Now,' said Miss Quicke, making as if to struggle to her feet, 'I found some useful information for you on the Internet and ran it off, but I left it on the table in the other room.'

'I'll fetch it,' said Ellie. 'I'd like to know what I've got myself into.'

Miss Quicke rarely used the dining room for eating. Half the long mahogany dining table was her office, and today the very latest of equipment lay on it, ready to spring into life at the touch of a button. A neat pile of paper lay on the laser printer, which Ellie took through to her aunt. 'Is this what you want?'

'Of course. Now, as you can see . . .'

'Aunt Drusilla, you know very well that I can't make head nor tail of balance sheets and company reports.'

'Give them to your friend Kate to interpret for you.'

'Can't you give me the highlights?'

'There's not a pin to choose between Talbot and Kingsley as regards the amount of money they've made. Perhaps Talbot has been slightly more successful at avoiding investigation by the Fraud Squad.'

'Is Chris Talbot really a bad apple? I liked him.'

'I expect he flattered your ego. You don't get to be president of this and that, and consultant to a dozen quangos, without stroking someone's ego along the line.'

'Or crossing their palms with silver?'

Miss Quicke hesitated. 'No, I don't sense corruption. Or not more than the usual "you scratch my back, and I'll scratch yours". He keeps a low profile, but seems to be an able man with a grasp of how the markets move and a sensible habit of withdrawing just before prices peak. I don't say his hands have always been clean — there's some dealings in a steel company in the Far East which look a trifle murky — but on the whole, if I were asked to put money into one of his companies, I'd consider it reasonably safe to do so.'

'What about Sir Arthur?'

Miss Quicke frowned. 'On the surface, a triumphant progress from small developments to large. Many of them. He likes to see his face in the papers, makes a great show of giving to charities, but I don't get the impression that he spends any time working for them. Just puts in the cheques and marks up another photo call. There's more than a whiff of corruption. Perhaps it's the company he keeps? The bimbos who hang on his arm, the Asian businessmen with whom he has many dealings, which to me look like money-laundering?'

'I've heard he's on the board of a company that's going down the tubes, but might be rescued by the parent corporation . . .'

'Common knowledge. To put it in terms you'd understand, he wants a big pay-off for resigning from the board, and it's a key condition of the restructuring of the corporation that he goes. He's managed to cling on, somehow. I'm not sure how. Perhaps he's got something on someone, somewhere? Personally, I wouldn't touch shares in anything he's involved in. Better safe than sorry.'

That made sense, thought Ellie. But . . . bimbos? Felicity wasn't a bimbo. Did she know about them? And if so, did she care?

'There is also,' said Aunt Drusilla, 'the question of Mrs Meadows-Fitch. Rose reminded me of her when I said you'd crossed swords with Sir Arthur.'

Rose had come in and was clearing the table. She nodded at Ellie. 'It's time for Miss Quicke to have her little nap.' Rose shook out a soft rug and laid it over the older woman's knees. Aunt Drusilla closed her eyes, and Ellie followed Rose from the room.

Into the modernized kitchen they went, where Rose already had the kettle on to make coffee. Ellie automatically picked up a tea towel to dry the dishes, expecting Rose to wash up in the sink. Rose took the tea towel off her, pointing to the brand new dishwasher.

'Miss Quicke has taught me how to use this. Isn't it splendid? I didn't think I'd ever be able to master all the twiddles and knobby things, but she sat down and read out the instructions over and over, till I'd got the hang of them. You ought to get one too.'

The combination of what Aunt Drusilla and Rose could do never failed to astonish Ellie. She relinquished the tea towel and sat at the table, watching Rose dispose of the plates and cutlery into the maw of the machine.

In the old days, dear Rose had been the sort of person who couldn't go out in the rain without getting her umbrella turned inside out, and whose buttons were never done up correctly. Her taste in clothes had been governed by what was cheap and brightly coloured in the charity shop. Now Rose was always neatly turned out and could cope with the intricacies of a dishwasher which would have intimidated Catherine the Great.

Ellie imagined Aunt Drusilla making Rose report for kit inspection every morning, saying, 'No, dear! The hem of that skirt is coming down. Why don't you wear the blue we bought last week at John Lewis?'

Rose said, 'Miss Quicke was telling me about that nasty man Kingsley and his pizza. Poison is a woman's weapon, isn't it?'

Ellie was bleak. 'There seem to be quite a few candidates. What about this Mrs Meadows-Fitch?'

'Surely you remember her? She used to come into the charity shop looking for designer wear every Monday morning. Not a very nice woman, dear, though I shouldn't say that really. Tea or coffee? She'd try to haggle the price down, even though she knew very well that we weren't allowed to accept less than what was on the label. Fluffy hair, dyed bright, if you know what I mean. A different colour every couple of months. Usually wore a hat.'

Ellie shook her head. 'Rings a faint bell, but . . .'

'You'd know her if you saw her again. Her husband was Councillor Meadows-Fitch, the little man who used always to be talking about how well the council was doing, even when everyone knew they weren't. Leader of the Council for a long time, remember? Then he was mayor, and after that, chairman of the planning committee. He died, all of a sudden, at a council meeting, if I remember rightly. I expect someone had objected to one of his nasty little plans to take over the world, and he got so upset he had a heart attack, though I shouldn't say that really, dear, should I? But he did have his fingers in a great many pies, or so I'm told.'

'Who told you about him?'

'I think it was that elderly lady who used to come into the charity shop on Mondays, the one who had such trouble with the till, so that in the end they wouldn't let her anywhere near it. Mrs Meadows-Fitch was a friend of "Madam's", who used to run the shop; and I suppose that explains everything.'

'Dreadful woman,' agreed Ellie, who'd suffered from 'Madam's' version of 'leadership' too. 'Madam' had been jealous of Ellie's ability to get on with everyone, and had given her the sack when she was still reeling from the trauma of her husband's death.

Rose nodded. 'Had you heard Madam's been replaced? About time too. I've never met someone who could upset so many people so quickly.'

With an effort — because she really was interested in what had happened to Madam — Ellie stopped Rose taking a diversion. 'Yes, Rose. But what about Mrs Meadows-Fitch?'

'Well, it's only gossip . . .'

'It's not really gossip,' said Ellie. 'It's information we need to understand what's going on with people. Though some of it may not be entirely true, of course.'

'You'll think my tongue's hinged at both ends.'

'I think you understand what makes people tick better than most. You didn't like Mrs Meadows-Fitch because she was mean-minded. What was her link with Sir Arthur Kingsley?'

'Oh, not her, dear. Her husband. The mayor. Easing Sir Arthur's way through the planning committees. At least, that's what they used to say. Wining and dining and dancing in expensive places. Holidays abroad as guests of Sir Arthur. That sort of thing. Of course, they might just have enjoyed one another's company.'

Ellie said, 'I've met Sir Arthur and he's not my idea of a cuddly, reliable friend. At least, not unless he was getting something out of it.'

'No, dear. And that's what upset Mrs Meadows-Fitch. She was talking about it in the queue for the checkout in the supermarket the other day. In a very loud voice. I was always taught not to discuss my private life in public, but she didn't seem to care who heard her. She said promises were made, and now her husband's no longer with us, promises are not being fulfilled. If you see what I mean.'

Ellie finished her coffee. 'Sir Arthur seems to break a lot of promises.'

Rose hovered, fingering a cookery book. 'Shall I bake a Victoria sandwich for tea? Roy usually pops in around tea time to see his mother, and he enjoys a bit of home baking. You wouldn't happen to know what's been wrong with him lately, would you? Bear with a sore head, as my mother used to say.'

Ellie stared into space. 'He got across Sir Arthur. I've advised him to tell his mother, but he's afraid she'll think less of him if he does.'

'Then you'd better do something about it, hadn't you? Can't have him being upset, because that upsets Miss Quicke. I'm worried about Miss Quicke. Why won't she go to the doctor about her hip?'

'I'm not sure. A lot of excuses, none of which hold water by themselves. Perhaps she's just afraid of an operation. She's never had anything serious wrong with her before. I'll ask Roy to talk to her about it. She might listen to him.'

Rose sat down, suddenly tired. 'I think I'll bake the cake a little later on. Miss Quicke says I ought to take a rest when she does, and perhaps she's right. We're none of us getting any younger, are we?'

Rose was quite a bit older than Ellie, though not as old as Miss Quicke. Ellie wondered how soon she'd feel it would be a good idea to have an afternoon nap. When she reached her sixties, perhaps? Well, that was a good way off.

Rose took off her apron. 'Why don't you go round to see Mrs Meadows-Fitch? She lives in one of those big flats on Haven Green, but is having to move to a tiny place on the South Coast. Such a comedown for someone who enjoyed being lady mayoress, don't you think?'

Yes, it was. 'One other thing, Rose. Do you know of someone whose garden's been trashed by vandals around here?'

'Opposite the park, on the other side, you mean?' said Rose, without any hesitation. 'I don't know her name, but someone's made a terrible mess of her herbaceous border. Now, who was it who was telling me about it? It might have been Mrs Dawes . . .' She shook her head. She was tired and needed her afternoon nap. Ellie kissed her and left her to it.

* * *

Sir Arthur's bad temper didn't lift till he took another phone call from Martinez that afternoon.

'Yes? I'm in a meeting.'

A harsh laugh came down the phone. A few more words, and Sir Arthur smiled.

'Good. Excellent. There's no way anyone could trace . . . ? Good. I'll see you this evening.'

Sir Arthur turned his attention back to the man standing before him. Was there anything to be gained by keeping him? No one tried to cheat Sir Arthur and got away with it.

Sir Arthur said, 'It's a good thing you confessed straight away. I will not have any of my staff fiddling expenses. I won't call the police, this time. Provided you sign me an IOU for what you've stolen, plus twenty per cent interest. I'm not a hard man. I'll give you three weeks to raise the money. Now I'm calling security. They'll escort you from the building. No need for you to clear your desk or speak to any of your colleagues.'

He watched the man leave, shoulders sagging. Then smiled, remembering the message from Martinez. 'An eye for an eye, a tooth for a tooth, Mr Talbot. A pity I can't see your face when you hear what's just happened.'

* * *

As Ellie left her aunt's house, she reflected that there seemed to have been quite a few people who had cause to dislike Sir Arthur, but usually the ones who talk about how much they dislike someone aren't the ones who do anything about it. Also, Aunt Drusilla had been dealing in property in this area for years. Had she ever had any dealings with Mr Meadows-Fitch? It might be worth asking her when she woke up from her nap.

At the corner of the street, Ellie hesitated. She did remember Mrs Meadows-Fitch now. An unpleasant woman. She had never been on visiting terms with the lady, and the idea of going in 'cold' did not appeal.

Ellie thought of society as a series of interlocking circles. She knew X number of people, some of whom would know another X number. Circles intersected. There was someone in her circle who might know about the tangled affairs of the ex-lord mayor and Sir Arthur — if he were willing to talk about them, that is — and that was Councillor Patel.

After Diana had divorced her husband Stewart, he'd married Maria, Councillor Patel's only child. Ellie was on excellent terms with Stewart. He and his new wife lived not far away in a three-bedroom semi-detached house which they were renovating. They had managed — with some help from her parents and from Ellie — to put in a loft conversion, renew the central heating and wiring, and were now redecorating.

Stewart worked for Aunt Drusilla, carefully and faithfully managing much of her empire of properties to let. Maria ran an efficient cleaning agency in addition to looking after Stewart and Diana's little boy — with help from an excellent babysitter. Maria had recently produced a pretty poppet of a daughter, with whom her parents were besotted. As — it must be admitted — was Stewart. So far little Frank hadn't exhibited any sibling jealousy.

Councillor Patel would have known the ex-lord mayor and perhaps also have come across Sir Arthur.

This was Friday, and on Friday afternoons Councillor and Mrs Patel were often to be found at Maria and Stewart's house, playing with little Frank, and taking turns to hold the baby. Ellie mentally reviewed what she ought to be doing that afternoon and evening — shopping for the weekend, calling on an elderly neighbour, doing some gardening — and decided that checking on Maria and Stewart would be much more interesting. Besides, baby Yasmin was a charmer, and Ellie hadn't seen her for a fortnight, which was far too long.

The fine weather had held. Stewart was at work, of course. Little Frank was pleased to see his 'ganny', as he called Ellie, and Mrs Patel was hovering over Yazzy's cradle, hoping she'd wake up soon. Maria was always quietly pleased to see Ellie, however unexpectedly she might call, and Councillor Patel was delighted to have an excuse to get up off the floor, where he'd been helping little Frank to run a train. Ellie smiled to herself, remembering much the same layout at Mrs Anderson's.

As usual, Ellie admired the rose-pink shalwar kameez — tunic and trousers — which Mrs Patel was wearing, and as usual laughingly declined to accept the offer to go shopping with Mrs Patel for something similar for herself to wear.

'Not till I've lost another stone in weight.'

'Nonsense,' said Mrs Patel, who was of statuesque proportions and comfortable with it.

Ellie caught Councillor Patel's eye. 'Might I pick your brains? A small problem but I'd value your opinion.'

Frank launched himself at Mr Patel. 'Make it go! Make it go fast!'

Councillor Patel laughed, and obligingly pushed the train along the track, under the bridge and past the toy station.

Maria smiled, but said, 'Five minutes, now. It's all got to be cleared away by the time Daddy gets home.'

Frank went red and screamed with fury. His tantrums were famous, and dreaded by everyone. 'Now then, little man!' said Councillor Patel.

'I hate you!' screamed Frank, attacking him.

'That's enough!' Maria picked him up, and bore him into the hall and sat him on the bottom step, still screaming. They heard her say, 'You stay on the naughty step till you behave.'

Frank went on screaming as Maria returned to the room. The other adults held their breath, expecting Frank to follow her. He didn't. The screams subsided.

Maria pushed the dark hair back from her forehead and sighed. She too was wearing the shalwar kameez today, although she normally favoured Western clothing. 'The poor little man got overtired this morning at nursery school, but I can't let him get away with it.'

The adults shook their heads in agreement. They all knew that when Diana had Frank at weekends, she indulged him all the time, and never checked his tantrums.

Baby Yazz opened her eyes and smiled at everyone. Everyone smiled back. What a contrast to the awkward little boy who was even now inching his way around the door. Maria extended her hand to him. 'You want to say sorry now?'

Little Frank nodded. He buried his head in Maria's lap, and huffed and puffed a bit. But finally got it out. 'Sorry.' Maria wiped his nose and eyes, and said he could help Grandpa put the train set back in its plastic box. Which — amazingly — he did. The adults let out the breaths which they hadn't realized they'd been holding.

Everyone — apart from Diana — thought that Maria was doing a magnificent job in bringing up little Frank.

Councillor Patel praised Frank for helping him put away his train set. Everyone praised Frank. Maria gave him a kiss and a cuddle and a fruit juice in his child-sized wooden chair. Mrs Patel picked Yazz up, and cooed at her. Peace descended.

Councillor Patel raised an eyebrow at Ellie, and wondered if she'd like to inspect the dahlias in the garden with him.

Ellie agreed. Once outside, she told him how she'd been dragged into Sir Arthur's orbit. She did not tell him that Sir Arthur had married his old enemy's daughter, but she did say she was worried how Sir Arthur might react to her interference in his plans for developing the vicarage site. 'Tell me I'm foolish to worry if I've offended him.'

'Not foolish, no. I'd be wary of offending him myself.'

'What do you know about his relations with Councillor Meadows-Fitch?'

'Very little. I'm not on the planning committee. Never have been. Leisure is my concern. The committees are ranked in order of importance, according to how large their budgets may be. Education and housing, they're the top. Planning? A tricky one. A political hot potato. There are undoubtedly opportunities to make money there, if you have that type of mind.'

'Tainted money, for pushing through dicey plans?'

Councillor Patel was silent. Then he shrugged. 'I am not of the ex-mayor's political persuasion, and have no insight into how he uses his influence. Yes, there has been some gossip, but such things are difficult to prove. It's true that some of us were perturbed when a big superstore was given permission to double its size at the expense of its car park. Also when a certain school's playing fields were sold off for development purposes. And . . . yes, when a certain factory complex was given permission for a change of use which wiped out nearly a hundred jobs but built a lot of housing for the private market.'

'Did you vote against these things?'

He grimaced. 'I am not a member of the cabinet.'

Ellie nodded her understanding. The volume of work which passed through the council every day was far beyond what could reasonably be dealt with by the councillors, who attended meetings in their free time. Therefore they had changed to a cabinet system, which meant that an inner select group approved any matters which had previously been decided upon by the various committees. It sounded all right. Most people thought it was . . . or didn't think about it at all, which was more likely.

'Councillor Meadows-Fitch was a member of the cabinet? Right. But you will have heard people commenting on his behaviour from time to time. Have you heard it said that he had his holidays paid for, or was given other favours by developers from time to time?'

He nodded. 'I have heard that said, yes. I speak as I find. I have had no first-hand information about these matters. Now the man is dead.'

'And Sir Arthur?'

'I have had no dealings with him.'

'And will not?'

Another shrug. 'Sometimes we have to deal with people when we'd rather not. I have been fortunate so far.'

'What about Mrs Meadows-Fitch?'

He was reluctant. 'I have heard . . . but it is only gossip, you understand . . . that Sir Arthur persuaded her husband to remortgage his nice big flat at Haven Green, in order to invest in one of Sir Arthur's schemes, and that he lost the lot. I have heard that Mrs Meadows-Fitch was talking of suing Sir Arthur but had to drop the case, and that she now has to sell her flat and move to a small place. There is a general feeling that if you wish to dine with Sir Arthur, you should equip yourself with a long spoon . . . have I got that idiom right?'

'You have indeed,' said Ellie, remembering the old saying that he who sups with the devil should have a long spoon. So, Mr Patel — discreet as he might be — thought Sir Arthur was the devil?

CHAPTER SEVEN

She wondered about taking a cab home. Or should she walk, because she could do with the exercise? After all, there was no one waiting for her at home to ask how her day had been, and what was for supper.

She recollected with a start of dismay that it was desperately important to find out who had poisoned the dog. How on earth was she going to fulfill her promise to Chris Talbot to befriend his daughter? She used her mobile to phone for a cab. Waiting for it to come, she wondered what her dear husband would have advised her to do when faced with the problem of the dog's death.

She sighed. When her dear husband Frank was alive, she hadn't had the time or the energy to get caught up in other people's problems like this. Nor, let's face it, would he have been amused if she had. He'd wanted her to stick to the role of little wifey. He'd made all the decisions, and she'd gone along with them. It would have been out of the question for her to go visiting gentlemen pirates or indeed visiting gentlemen of any kind, while he'd been alive.

Still, she did wonder what he'd have made of Sir Arthur, Felicity, and Chris Talbot. Would he have been as intimidated by Sir Arthur as she had been? Would he have talked to Chris Talbot on equal terms?

The cab came and she asked him to cruise round the far end of the park. Perhaps she'd be able to spot the ravaged garden.

Dear Frank, she realized, would have recognized Sir Arthur's nastiness and had as little to do with him as he could. Ellie concurred.

How would Chris Talbot have struck Frank? Ellie's imagination refused to cope with this question. She could no more picture Frank being whisked up to the penthouse suite in the City to be given details of Chris Talbot's private life, than . . . pigs might fly. Her dear husband had had many excellent qualities, but sympathy . . . empathy . . . putting himself out for others . . . no, that had not been his forte.

Which brought Ellie to the point where she wondered what would happen if Frank were suddenly resurrected and standing in front of her. He wouldn't want her 'wasting time poking her nose into other people's business'. He'd be asking why his supper wasn't in the oven at this very minute, and had she taken his suit to the dry-cleaner's as he'd asked her to do, and why was she allowing his aunt to be looked after by a stranger instead of doing it herself?

Yet — sigh — he'd been a faithful and loving husband and the centre of her life for all those years.

The cab driver wasn't paying much attention to what Ellie had asked him to do, but halfway along a road lined with nice-looking houses overlooking the park, she cried out to him to stop. He drew up twenty feet along from where a For Sale sign had been set up outside a dingy, rather neglected-looking house. Quite a contrast to the other houses in the road. The front garden looked as if someone had run a chainsaw through it. Yes, this was it. Now what should she do? Ring the estate agent and ask for details to view the house?

A man with a clipboard came out of the house, smiling, ushering a depressed-looking middle-aged couple along the drive to the pavement. They stood there, talking for a bit, then the couple got into their car, the agent got into his, and all three of them drove off.

A mousy little woman, sixty-ish, stood in the doorway, watching them go. She was not smiling.

Ellie dismissed the cab, walked along to the house and rang the doorbell. The mousy woman had put the door on the chain, and saw no reason to open up for a stranger.

'I'm so sorry,' said Ellie. 'Am I too late? I thought I could catch up with the estate agent here, but I was delayed in traffic.'

A beady eye inspected Ellie from head to foot. 'Come in if you like. But he's gone.' The woman was dressed in grey and beige, clothes which had once been good but were now limp from many years of laundering. Had she come down in the world? Her grey hair was thin, her skin was pasty, her eyes slightly protruding, giving her a tortoise look. A greater contrast to Mrs Anderson you couldn't find.

The chain was undone, and the door opened just enough to let Ellie slip into the hall, which was of a good size but gloomy, cluttered with china in old-fashioned cabinets and on picture rails.

'I was looking for a house for my mother,' said Ellie, whose mother had actually died many years ago. 'Something near me, but not too near. This has three bedrooms, hasn't it?'

'Only one bathroom. This is the sitting room.' The woman showed Ellie into a room which was so closely curtained and warmly heated that it made her gasp. It was actually not a bad shape and size, but looked smaller because it was so crowded with cabinets and mismatched chairs and small tables. Everything here was brown too. Yet more china occupied cabinets and shelving. Nothing looked quite clean, or maybe that was an effect produced by the drawn curtains and low-wattage light bulb.

'Ellie Quicke,' said Ellie, holding out her hand.

'Mrs Alexis,' the woman responded, her hand brittle and dry-skinned. 'My husband was Greek.'

Ellie was shown into a large, bare dining room. Was it ever used? Probably not. 'This is a good-sized room. Have you lived here a long time?'

'Twenty years.'

'What a nice long garden you have at the back,' said Ellie, trying to find something to praise in the chill of a small kitchen which ought to have been in a museum. 'You must be sad to lose it. Are you going far?'

Silence. Mrs Alexis mounted the stairs ahead of Ellie. A carpet runner, ill-secured with old-fashioned brass rails. Dust in the corners. Woodchip on the walls. The woman threw open the door of the bedroom at the front of the house, but stood so that Ellie could not enter, though she could see what was within. Another large room. A mismatched thirties bedroom suite, candlewick bedspread.

'What a pleasant room,' said Ellie, trying to keep cheerful. 'Is there much traffic noise at night?'

The woman didn't answer. She threw open the door to a small bedroom, furnished with a single bed and some cardboard boxes. Then a bathroom with a cracked basin which could have done with a good clean, and finally a second bedroom, with two single beds in it and more cardboard boxes. Everything was brown, if it wasn't grey. No wonder the people who'd just looked round had come out looking depressed.

Ellie followed the woman down the stairs, wondering how to prise more information out of her. Ellie's brain was empty of ideas. The house, the woman, were so depressing that Ellie herself was becoming downhearted.

Mrs Alexis said, 'The garage is full of my husband's things, but if you want to see it, I suppose I can find the key to the padlock. If you like the house — which I don't suppose you do, because I haven't done any decorating for years — then you'll have to take it as seen. I can't afford a new kitchen, or another bathroom, or a loft extension or anything. I'm only the tenant. The landlord can do as he likes once I'm gone.'

'It must be hard for you to have to go, after living here for so long,' said Ellie, trying to feel sorry for the woman, while thinking she could at least have cleaned the place up to make it look better. 'Can't you get him to extend your lease?'

'There's plenty worse off than me. So, do you like the house?'

Ellie shook her head. 'I don't think my mother, at her age, could take on a house which needs so much doing to it.'

The woman shrugged, and held the front door open for Ellie to pass through. Ellie did so, thinking that she could draw Mrs Alexis into conversation about the ruined front garden, but the door closed on her heels and Ellie could hear the chain being replaced.

Ellie shivered. Had it turned colder? Or was it just the depressing effect that Mrs Alexis had on people? She would stride out, walk home. Shake off the nasty feeling she'd experienced in that house. So lifeless. Introverted. A suspicion of things lurking in corners.

No, it really hadn't been that dirty. She was imagining things. Was Mrs Alexis the poisoner? Probably not. Too ground down to take any action to help herself, poor thing.

When she reached the Green around the church, Ellie paused to cast a critical eye over the terrace of town houses which Roy and his mother had developed. All sold, of course. Ellie had been responsible for the planting of the landscaping along the side of the development, and liked to check on it now and then. She bent down to stir the mulch she'd laid on the surface, to feel the soil beneath. Yes, it was still damp. The recent rain had refreshed the leaves nicely.

She shook her head. Frank wouldn't have approved of her getting involved in that either. She sighed, wondering how he'd have dealt with Diana's latest demands for help. He'd reached the end of his patience with her schemes before he died, so perhaps she knew the answer to that one.

She tried to draw up a balance sheet; when Frank had been alive, she'd been nothing but a timorous wee mousie. Now she had to strike out for herself, and did. Sometimes her courage failed her, especially when she thought about Sir Arthur — the man exuded menace — but on the whole life was a lot more interesting than it had been in the past. She'd even stood up to Jean over preparing coffee the other night, and she'd never have been able to do that in the old days.

She turned into the alley which ran along the bottom of her garden, and caught her breath.

There was a lot of activity in her garden. People. Men in uniform. Police? Armand up a ladder resting against the poplar tree which was on the boundary between her garden and a neighbour's and . . .

. . . some of the great panes of glass which protected the tender plants in her beloved conservatory were in fragments.

She put her hand to her heart, which she could feel thudding in her breast.

Who . . . ? Sir Arthur, of course. In retaliation for blowing the whistle last night.

Kate spotted her. Kate was carrying baby Catriona in a sling across her body. 'Oh, Ellie! We were just too late to stop him! I've been phoning you, but . . .'

Ellie never remembered to keep her mobile phone on. Hadn't checked for messages that day.

She opened the gate into the bottom of her garden, and felt her pulse quicken. The glass . . . her plants . . . if there were a frost tonight they'd all be killed.

What was Armand doing up the tree? She looked up and up, but the sun was in her eyes, and she couldn't see.

A policeman was asking her questions. Did she know him? She knew some of the local police, but they did tend to get moved around a bit, and . . . no. She didn't think she knew this one. She answered more or less at random. Yes, she was Mrs Quicke, and yes, she'd been out, away from the house since . . . she couldn't remember . . . oh, that morning, quite early. No, wait a minute. She'd come back about . . . noon? Yes. To change her clothes before she went to see some people. Everything had been all right then.

Kate was talking. 'We came back a bit later than we'd intended, because it was such a lovely day and Catriona fell asleep in the back of the car after her last feed, and just as we opened the back door of our house, I heard the most almighty crash, and I thought at first it might be a chimney coming down.'

Armand was up the tree still, saying, 'Midge! Here, Midge!'

Ellie gasped. 'Midge?'

Kate was wringing her hands. Kate had lost her cool completely, which was most unlike her. 'This man — whoever it was — had a hood over his head and he had what looked like a metal bar and was bashing at your conservatory, and Midge must have been sleeping there, you know how he does, and just as I was yelling at Armand to come, because I thought he was a burglar, the man started cursing, and he must have caught Midge a whack, because the next thing it sounded like a major cat-fight . . . and, oh, I shouldn't laugh, but Midge must have bitten him or scratched him because he was yowling, and just as Armand came out to see what all the fuss was about, the man shook Midge off and ran away down the garden, but he must have scared the cat, because he streaked for that tree and went up it, and I don't think he can get down!'

'Calm down, dear,' said Ellie, who was shaking, herself. 'Think of Catriona.' She took a deep breath. A burglar? No way. 'Was it that man Marco?'

'Marco.' Kate brought her voice down from the stratosphere. 'Why him? Well, yes!'

The policeman had his notebook out. 'You think you know who did this?'

'Yes,' said Ellie. 'At least, I suppose I can't prove it, but . . .'

'Yes, it might very well have been him,' said Kate. 'Only, I didn't see his face.'

Armand was getting red in the face. A second policeman was holding the bottom of the ladder while Armand tried reaching higher and higher . . . to where Midge, fluffed out to twice his normal size, was clinging to the main trunk. Far above Armand. 'Midge, come on down!'

Catriona woke up and began to wail.

Ellie said, 'My knees are shaking. Let's go inside and have a cup of tea.'

Kate struck the side of her head. 'After I phoned the police, I got in touch with the builder, asked him to come straight round to assess the damage. He should be here in a minute.'

The policeman persevered. 'You think you know who did this, Mrs Quicke?'

'Yes, it's possible, but . . . thank you, Kate,' said Ellie, trying to sort out her priorities. 'Armand, you'll fall and then we'll have to take you to hospital and that won't do any good.'

'I'm not leaving Midge up here. Shall I get the fire brigade?'

Ellie 'washed' her face with both hands, thinking over what she knew about cats. 'Midge will come down when he considers it safe.'

'Mrs Quicke!' said the policeman.

Kate said, 'Ellie!'

Catriona stepped up the volume.

Ellie's faithful builder appeared at the bottom of the garden. 'Hallo, hallo? What's all this about, then?'

'Time for tea,' said Ellie and led the way up the garden path, noting that the intruder had managed somehow to topple her stone sundial in his flight. She hoped he'd stubbed his toe on it. He'd also managed to decapitate one of her favourite delphiniums. She hoped Midge had scratched or bitten him really badly. She crunched over broken glass as she stepped into the conservatory. This was going to take some clearing up.

At the back of her mind, her dear husband Frank shook his finger at her. 'This is what comes of interfering in other people's business.'

Yes, it did indeed. But if there was one thing she'd learned since Frank died, it was that she was a survivor.

CHAPTER EIGHT

Friday evening. The nights were drawing in. Ellie told herself to make an effort. She blew her nose, got up off the chair into which she'd sunk an hour ago, and drew the curtains at the window looking up to the road. Then she went through the French windows into her conservatory. Most of the glass had been cleared away. Some of the tender pelargoniums had been chopped to pieces, but others could be tied up and might survive.

The tiled floor showed glints of light here and there where tiny shards of glass still lay. The broken glass had luckily not reached the goldfish, swimming sedately in their lead tank against the inner wall. It took a lot to frighten a goldfish.

Marco — if it was he, and she must be careful not to make allegations which might turn out to be false — had only managed to smash two large panes. The builder had boarded these spaces over for the time being, and would bring replacement glass tomorrow. Ellie had rung Maria Patel, and asked if she could get someone from her cleaning agency along tomorrow with a vacuum cleaner to suck up any remaining fragments of glass. Maria — shocked — had agreed to arrange it.

The insurance would cover the damage, of course.

Except that a rather pretty creeper, tropaeolum something, which was a relation of the common nasturtium but much daintier, would never be quite the same again. Also, Midge was still up the tree, though not, thank heaven, clinging to the trunk any more. Rather, perched over a branch and surveying the neighbourhood for foes.

Ellie opened the door on to the garden, and called Midge once again.

Midge took not the slightest bit of notice. Midge was offended. He'd been attacked without warning and without provocation, and his minder — Ellie — hadn't been there to defend him. It was not, Midge seemed to be thinking, what any self-respecting cat should have to put up with.

In the dusk Ellie stood and looked down the length of her pretty garden. The builder had righted the sundial but left it slightly out of position. Typical.

Her next-door neighbour — a nice woman, the one in whose garden the tree was — had also come out to see what she could do to coax the cat down. Midge ignored her. Midge was ignoring everyone. His attitude was that he was safe where he was, and he was staying put until he decided otherwise.

Armand had left his ladder against the poplar, saying it might be easier for Midge to come down the ladder than the trunk of the tree. Armand had the softest heart and the hottest temper you could imagine. Ellie was grateful to him. He and Kate were now safely indoors with all the curtains drawn and the doors locked, but had made Ellie promise to leave her mobile on and to carry it with her at all times, in case there was another visitation.

The police had gone. She'd told them she suspected Sir Arthur's driver might have wished her harm, and why, and seen only scepticism in their eyes.

'So you think someone would bother to bash in your windows, just because you objected to a planning application? Isn't it more likely to have been someone high on drugs, looking for a way to break into your house? We get plenty of that.'

Perhaps it had been. Perhaps she'd been on the wrong track all the time. Then she remembered that Chris Talbot hadn't wanted her to involve the police. Oh dear.

She felt limp, but her brain was informing her that she had to tell Mr Talbot about this — as soon as she'd coaxed Midge down from the tree. Only how did you get a cat down from a tree which must be sixty feet high if it was an inch?

Knowing it was useless, she said, 'Oh, Midge! Do come down!'

Armand unlocked his back door and came out into his garden. Seeing Ellie standing there looking helpless, he asked if he should have yet another try at getting Midge down. She clutched at her common sense and said, No. Midge would come down when he was ready.

Armand declared that he was not wasting any more time on that cat. Which was a lie. Even as he went back inside, Ellie thought she'd bet on it that he'd be back out again in a few minutes.

Chris Talbot had exchanged telephone numbers with Ellie. He'd even written his home number on the back of his business card. She got out her mobile phone and rang him at home. No reply. An answerphone clicked in.

She tried to keep her message succinct. 'Mr Talbot, a man broke some windows at my house this afternoon. I think it might have been Marco, Sir Arthur's driver, in retaliation for my spoiling a local planning application last night. The thing is, I know you didn't want the police involved, but my neighbour rang them before I got back and I told them about Marco. I don't think they took it seriously, and I'll keep your name out of it if I can. I'm all right, just shaken. I'll try to contact Felicity this weekend.'

There was a crackling sound from the poplar tree. Midge was making his move. He dropped a couple of feet, and clung to a lower branch, digging his claws in. Ellie ran down the garden, looking up, praying the cat would be safe. Midge inspected the next few feet, and decided it didn't look too good. But he hadn't eaten since breakfast time. One or two birds were skittering around above him in the tree, ready to roost for the night. Too high for him to reach.

He decided to take a chance and half slid and half jumped down a few more feet. Now he was within reach of the topmost rung of the ladder.

Ellie held her breath.

Exactly as if he were walking down a staircase in the house, Midge descended the ladder.

'Well done, Midge!' said Ellie.

Promptly on cue, Armand appeared in his garden, and punched the air, cheering. His pretended indifference to Midge forgotten, Armand called Kate out to see. Their neighbour on the other side came out, and congratulated Ellie. Armand removed the ladder, while Kate beamed on everyone from her garden.

Once on the ground, Midge turned his back on Ellie and marched up the garden path towards the kitchen and food. He allowed Ellie to provide him with some of his favourite tuna, and a bowl of milk and water, plus a frosting of crunchies.

Ellie knew better than to touch him while he ate. She sat at the kitchen table, waiting for him to acknowledge her existence.

He didn't jump on her lap after he'd eaten. He hadn't forgiven her yet. He jumped up on to the boiler, and proceeded to his toilet. Ellie was only too grateful that he *could* still jump up on to the boiler. At least he hadn't suffered any injuries from the tussle with the intruder. Or had he?

'Hold on a minute, Midge,' said Ellie. 'What's that on your chin? Is it blood?' She dampened a tissue and rubbed at the cat's chin and jaw. The tissue came away red. Blood? Ellie wondered if she could still get hold of a vet to attend to Midge if he'd been cut . . . but no. No cut. The blood must have come from Marco. Midge objected to her attentions, but not too strongly. He was full and wanted to sleep it off.

There was more dark red on and between his claws. Midge allowed Ellie to swab away at one paw, and then withdrew, offended. He knew how to clean himself up far better than Ellie.

Could they extract some DNA from the blood left on the cat? It might be worth a try.

Ellie bagged the tissues up and sealed the top with Sellotape.

She realized she was extremely hungry. She'd made cups of tea and even drunk one earlier. She'd fed Midge. Now it was time to feed herself, or she'd be tossing and turning all night.

She made herself an all-in-one omelette, with bits of leftovers from the fridge. Taking it through to the sitting room to eat in front of the telly, she listened to the news — more tragedies. Why did she bother? It only upset her to hear about more tragedies just before she went to bed.

Only then did she remember the answerphone, and listened to her messages.

One: Diana. Oh dear. The usual threats. Ellie wondered if she were being a cold-hearted mother, refusing to help her only child out of difficulty. Except that there'd been too many crises over the years, too many cries for help. Ellie resolved that tomorrow she'd try again to talk to Diana, see what she could do.

Two: Roy. He'd wanted to take her out to supper at the Carvery that evening. Tough. The evening had come and gone. He also wanted to talk to her, urgently. He didn't say about what, but she could guess. Would Sir Arthur blame him for the fiasco last night? Had he spoken to his mother about the mess he'd got himself into? *Had he lied to Ellie about his involvement with Sir Arthur?*

Three: Mrs Dawes, Ellie's flower-arranging friend with the improbably jet-black hair. She wanted to remind Ellie that the Autumn Fair was to be held in the church hall the following morning, and could Ellie help out on the bric-a-brac stall, as they were short. Tough; Ellie had already promised to help Jean with the teas and coffees.

Four: someone who did a bit of heavy breathing and hung up. It might be a salesman. It might not. It might be Marco wanting to gloat.

Ellie didn't want to think about that.

Midge decided he'd had enough of this long and tiring day and was going up to bed, without her if necessary. It wasn't yet ten o'clock, but Ellie had also had enough. She locked up the house, and took her mobile to bed with her, praying that they'd be safe that night. In God's hands. Guardian angels round us keep. Etcetera. Please.

Her mobile phone trilled. She shot upright in bed, checked the digital bedside clock — just after eleven — managed to switch on the bedside light, found her mobile and pressed the right button.

Chris Talbot, sounding tired. 'Mrs Quicke, I've just picked up my messages. Are you all right? I'm phoning from the hospital. My younger son, Julian, was knocked down on his way home from school this afternoon . . .'

Midge got up from where he'd been nestling at Ellie's back, and gave her a look which meant, *How dare you disturb my sleep?*

'Is he all right?'

'His right leg's broken and he's badly bruised. They've set and pinned the bone and he's going to be just fine, but they're keeping him in overnight to check he doesn't have any ill effects from a knock on his head.'

This was shocking news. The attack on her conservatory was nothing by comparison. Ellie murmured, 'Sir Arthur?'

'Julian didn't see what hit him. He heard a car with what he says was a "ropey engine" coming up fast behind him, he was on the pavement, was thrown forward and hit his head against the wall. He's not sure if he blacked out or not. He thinks the car had a leaky exhaust because he could smell fumes as it roared off. No one got out of the car to check on him or to rob him. It's a quiet road with little traffic in it. There wasn't anyone else to be seen. Julian knew his mother was out and his elder brother not due home yet, so he fished out his mobile to dial nine-nine-nine, and then rang my office. I got through to my wife and told her not to go home but to collect our other son from school and go to a hotel for the night.'

'Sir Arthur's car is a Mercedes, isn't it? Runs as smooth as silk. It couldn't have been him. What time was it? About four? I don't think it can have been Marco either, because he was over here bashing in my conservatory about that time of day. The car that hit your son sounds like an old banger, picked out for the job. Possibly stolen?'

'I'm trying not to be paranoid about this. It may have been two lads joyriding, who lost control of the car, panicked and drove off without bothering to check on their victim.'

'You don't think it was, do you? Would Sir Arthur use hired hit men?' said Ellie, thinking that all this was unreal. Talking about hit men? In this quiet London suburb?

Chris Talbot hesitated. 'I haven't heard of him using those tactics before, but that doesn't mean he hasn't done so. I got to the hospital to find Julian being interviewed by a couple of local police. He told them he hadn't seen anything, and doesn't know why anyone would want to kill him. They incline to the joyrider theory.'

Ellie frowned. 'You didn't enlighten them?'

'It never occurred to me before today that Kingsley would take it out on my family. If Julian hadn't been attacked I'd have kept quiet, but this alters things. I can't have my family put at risk. So yes, I told them I suspected Sir Arthur. They said they thought it unlikely that a respectable businessman would resort to such measures.'

Ellie remembered the devastation in her conservatory. 'He's not a respectable businessman. He's a thug.'

Grimly. 'He's not been caught before and it's unlikely we can prove anything now.'

Ellie said, 'There might be some proof. Oh, not for the attack on Julian, but for the assault on my conservatory. If we can get Marco for that, it might help. The local police came round to view the damage because my neighbour reported it in my absence. They thought it was a burglar trying to obtain entry and there didn't seem to be any proof that it was anything but that. Only after they'd gone, I found that my cat had dug his claws into the man who broke my windows, and had also bitten him. There was blood on Midge's fur, although he's no cut that I can see. I've swabbed off as much blood as I could and kept the swabs. Would that help?'

Chris Talbot became crisp and efficient. 'I'll send someone to pick them up from you in the morning. Put the samples into a sealed plastic bag. I'll send it off for analysis, and tell the local police what I've done. They won't have linked the two cases. Two different local forces. If I can get hold of Marco's DNA somehow, possibly from a mug he's drunk from — yes, I can do that through my contacts — then the police would have two cases to work on. Yes, it might help.'

'You'll take extra care from now on?'

'Of course. Are you going to see Felicity tomorrow? Kingsley usually goes down to the country at weekends.'

'I'll try. Hopefully he'll take Marco with him.'

'He'll take his shadow, Martinez, too. I expect it was Martinez who organized the attack on Julian. I'll have to investigate that. I'm sorry, I never asked how you were. I feel responsible.'

'I was attacked because I upset his plans for a local housing development. Nothing to do with you. And I have no proof that Marco was the assailant, unless my cat can provide it.'

'We'll see what we can do. Are you covered by insurance, because if not . . . ?'

'I am. Thank you.'

'I'll be in touch.' He rang off. Ellie imagined him sitting back in his car, being driven through the night to the City, planning this and that. She thought that Sir Arthur had made a mistake in attacking Julian. Chris Talbot probably wouldn't retaliate in kind . . . no. His revenge would be more subtle, probably financial. But if Sir Arthur were up to attacking a teenage boy, what else might he not think of doing? Throwing acid at Mrs Talbot's face? Kidnapping her?

It was a nightmare scenario, but in the dark hours of the night, Ellie couldn't rule any of it out. Sir Arthur was not your common or garden white-collar criminal. He was Taurus, the bull. Uncontrollable.

Was the gentlemanly Chris Talbot up to Sir Arthur's weight? Probably. Remembering that he wasn't just a gentleman, but a 'gentleman pirate'.

She turned off the bedside light and lay back, listening to the usual night-time sounds. Traffic: distant. A police-car siren: distant. The far-off rumble of a late-night tube train. Sound travelled for miles at night time.

An owl. The squeak of a bat.

A couple walking down the road, talking a little too loudly. A television, muted. The cry of a fretful baby next door. Was Catriona teething?

Dear Lord, I'm way out of my depth here. Help, please. Keep me safe.

She thought she saw Frank sitting on the side of the bed, putting on his shoes . . .

. . . and woke to hear the telephone ringing downstairs.

It was midnight, and Midge had moved to the bottom of the bed.

Ellie tried to shake herself awake, reaching for the bedside light, running over the list of people who might be in such trouble that they'd ring her at this time of night. Someone had had an accident, of course. They were ringing from the hospital. Diana? Oh dear. Had she really carried out her threat to do something dreadful that would make her mother sorry about not helping her? Or was it Maria, saying one of the children was dead, or . . . ?

The answerphone was switched on. By the time she reached the landing, the phone had stopped ringing. She listened for whatever the dread message might be.

No message. Just heavy breathing again. She could hear it even from where she stood at the head of the stairs.

Marco?

She went back to bed, feeling anxious. It took her a while to get to sleep again, but finally she did . . . only to be woken again at one o'clock. This time she made it to the phone before the answerphone kicked in. More heavy breathing. And then the phone was disconnected.

Fear for her family turned to anger. She turned the bell on the phone down to silent. There! That would let her have a few hours' sleep.

Anger carried her back upstairs and into bed, where reaction set in, and she began to fret about what she ought to say to the police in the morning. If she let Mr Talbot have the bloodstained swabs, she couldn't give them to the police, and the police wouldn't like that, would they? She turned over in bed and banged the pillow into a different shape.

Perhaps she hadn't rescued enough blood from Midge to prove it was Marco who had attacked her conservatory. It was probably too diluted to help. She ought to have taken Midge straight away to the vet's. But he hated that so much! He'd probably have scratched and bitten everyone in sight, and then how could they have rescued any DNA?

Oh, her poor plants! What would Frank have said if he'd still been alive? And what could she do about that unfortunate creature Felicity? And how on earth was she to manage to get through everything she had to do tomorrow . . . Felicity . . . Mrs Dawes and the Autumn Fair at church . . . Jean and the coffee cups . . .

Please Lord . . . and she fell asleep.

* * *

At some point in the night she'd had an idea about how to combine two of the calls on her time, but over an early breakfast she realized her idea simply wasn't feasible. Surely Felicity wouldn't want to help out at the church, and in any case, Ellie couldn't leave the house with builders wanting to replace the glass in the conservatory, and Maria's people coming to hoover up the broken glass. Then there was Diana.

Yes, she'd phone Diana first. Was it too early? Not in view of the emergency, no.

There was no reply at Diana's flat. Ellie thought to try Diana's mobile number, which she could never remember offhand, but which she'd written down somewhere . . . if she could find the piece of paper . . . Had she left it in the study? No, here it was, tucked into an electricity bill that she must pay today, or she'd be getting a reminder.

Diana's mobile was never switched off. Ever. She seemed to have a new mobile every other month, keeping abreast of the latest technology. It probably cost her more than she spent on having her hair done, and that was an arm and a leg.

'Yes?' Diana. Terse to the point of rudeness. Was she still in bed?

'It's me,' said Ellie, ungrammatically. 'Sorry it's so early, but I only got your message late last night, and couldn't ring back because . . .'

'You needn't have bothered. I'm not counting on you for anything any more. And by the way, I'm not able to have little Frank this weekend, so you might check with Maria and Stewart that it's all right for him to stay on with them.'

'What? But . . . Diana, you have warned them you can't have Frank, haven't you? Otherwise he'll be looking out of the window, waiting for you to—'

'Do you think I enjoy disappointing him? But you've given me no option. Give him a kiss from me. I expect you'll think of something to make it up to him. You enjoy spoiling him, don't you?'

'But . . .'

'Must go. Speak to you later.'

The phone went dead. So much for thinking she could have a quiet, reasonable talk with Diana about her finances.

Kate rapped on the back door and Ellie went to let her in.

Kate said, 'We were worried about you — and Midge. And I completely forgot — how did you get on with Chris Talbot?'

'I'm all right, and I liked Mr Talbot very much; it certainly wasn't him who sent the pizza. He was, I think, afraid that his daughter might have done it, but I don't buy that either.'

Kate nodded. 'I agree. I thought it was unlikely that Chris had done it, but we had to exclude him. I'll tell Gwyn. They'll be buzzing around all this weekend, trying to mend fences. So what's your next move?'

'I've got to be at church all day. Autumn Fair for church funds. Would you or Armand look out for the builders when they come to replace the glass? And there's someone coming to hoover up all the bits of broken glass, too. Oh, and is there anything on the Internet which would help about poison and poisoners? I just don't understand what would make someone do that.'

'Ellie, you can access the Internet yourself.'

'You know I'm hopeless at getting on to the Internet. It all takes so long to find anything, and I'm afraid of getting viruses and . . . no, don't tell me there's a way round that. I can't cope at the moment.'

Kate gave in. 'All right, I'll see what I can do. Have you time for a cup of coffee?'

Ellie glanced at the clock. 'Just about. But first I've got to phone Maria and Stewart . . .'

* * *

Maria sounded distracted. 'Was there something, Ellie? We're about to go out for the day, leaving as soon as Diana collects little Frank. He's got a drawing of a train he's done this morning, that he's dying to show her.'

'I've just been on the phone to her. She's not able to have him this weekend.'

Silence.

'I know,' said Ellie. 'It's not right. Frank's going to be upset, and you've made other arrangements and Diana didn't even tell me why she can't have him this weekend.'

Maria was a remarkably fair-minded woman, and although anyone else would have shouted at Ellie, Maria didn't. She sighed instead. 'That's the second weekend in a row. It's bad for Frank to be messed around like this. Now how are we going to manage? We've arranged to go with my parents to a family wedding in Southall. It wouldn't be appropriate to take Frank with us.'

Ellie grimaced. No, it wouldn't. If he threw one of his tantrums in front of a room full of nicely brought-up Patels . . . No, it didn't bear thinking about. Ellie anticipated Maria's next question.

'You want me to have him for the day? I don't think I can. Not this morning, anyway. Suppose you take him with you for the morning, and then if he gets fractious, perhaps Stewart can bring him over to me, and I'll look after him this afternoon?' She wondered how she'd cope with serving coffee, builders, police, Felicity and possibly another visit from Marco.

'We'll do that,' said Maria. 'Now I've got to go and break the bad news to Frank.' She tried to laugh. 'You'll probably hear his howls of protest where you are.'

Ellie put the phone down. Kate had been listening, of course.

Ellie said, 'Diana!' As if that explained everything, which it did.

Kate nodded. 'Are you OK? I thought I heard you moving around in the night and wondered if you'd disturbed another burglar.' She grinned. 'I tried to nudge Armand awake enough to come round to see if you were all right, but he was out to the world.'

'I'm OK. Just. There's something else you need to know; someone ran down one of Chris Talbot's sons yesterday. Broke his leg. Not Sir Arthur. Not Marco, if we assume it was him over here.'

'Oh.' Kate fished out her mobile phone, and keyed in a number.

Ellie's doorbell rang. It was Chris Talbot's chauffeur. Ellie recognized him, and was happy enough to hand over the bag of bloodied swabs, enquiring whether Mr Talbot were all right this morning.

'Sure he is.' Irish? Second generation? Large and reliable-looking.

Kate was walking about, listening to her mobile when Ellie got back. She nodded several times, said she'd get on to it, and switched off. 'Ellie, I've just spoken to Mr Talbot and he said you should fill me in on your talk yesterday. Armand's looking after Catriona while he marks some papers, so we've got a minute.'

Kate was a good listener. When she'd finished, Ellie sat back watching Kate test all the links in the chain in her head. 'Basically, you've been caught up between a couple of feuding heavyweights.'

'I know, and I've promised to try to befriend Felicity. I dread to think what Sir Arthur will make of that. What do I do to protect myself, Kate?'

CHAPTER NINE

Kate said, 'Let me think.' She couldn't sit still, but moved around the kitchen, picking things up and putting them down again.

'The restructuring of the corporation is only one aspect of the ongoing feud between the two men. If Sir Arthur is forced out, he loses face and a fortune and that's why he's fighting it. But the City wants the restructuring to go through, and the City knows how to bring pressure to bear here, and offer an "incentive" there. Sir Arthur will come out of it well enough, provided he sees reason and doesn't insist on carrying the feud to its logical conclusion.'

'Doesn't his resorting to force mean that he's lost his sense of balance?'

Kate went all broody.

Ellie persisted. 'This feud has been going on for years, and presumably everyone thought this restructuring — whether it meant Sir Arthur came out of it with a golden handshake or not — would be conducted in the boardroom as usual. But Sir Arthur left the boardroom behind when he attacked Julian Talbot. Isn't that going to upset the City? Are they really going to encourage Sir Arthur to look for a handout, if he's gone over the edge?'

Kate's brows twitched, and her hand strayed to her mobile. 'I don't know. I'll have to check. I'll speak to Gwyn. He needs to know what's happening.'

Ellie shoved her breakfast things into the sink and poured water on them. 'Of course, Sir Arthur will disclaim all knowledge of the attack on young Julian, and even if we can link Marco with the assault on my conservatory, Sir Arthur can deny he was involved. But he's been involved in all sorts of other shady deals recently, such as the plan to redevelop the vicarage site. Oughtn't you to tell your boss about them too?'

Kate was dubious. 'Look, I know I don't go to church much, but I do value it and it has a place in my life. I saw there was a meeting about it, and I would have gone but . . . what with the baby and all. Tell me.'

Ellie filled Kate in, while rapidly washing the dishes and leaving them to dry on the rack. '. . . so now I'm worried about what Sir Arthur might do to Roy. Can he really force Roy to come up with all that money?'

'Not if there's nothing in writing.'

'I agree. I advised him to consult his mother, but he didn't want to because it might make her think badly of him.' And he might have been stupid enough to sign something, even though he said he didn't.

Kate brushed this aside. 'Sir Arthur is not a nice man, but everyone knows that already. It's not worth bothering Gwyn with.'

Ellie said, 'What about Sir Arthur's promise to give the widow of his first architect some money if Roy produced the right sort of plans for him?'

Kate frowned. 'A generous gesture, which was then withdrawn. Hardly illegal.'

Ellie grinned, thinking of what the resourceful Mrs Anderson had done to make Sir Arthur pay up. 'Roy does feel threatened, though. Look, I'll phone him now, and you can listen in, judge for yourself.' She tried his home number.

No reply. Left a message. Hunted down his mobile number, and tried that. He answered on the third ring.

'Roy!' She was surprised at how relieved she felt to hear him sounding normal. 'Sorry I couldn't make supper last night. I didn't get your message till too late. How are you? Have you heard from Sir Arthur?'

'Several times. He's being polite but with an undercurrent of menace, assuming I'll fall in with his plans. He's commanded me to go down to his country house this weekend, but I said I'd a previous engagement that I couldn't break. He was not amused. Actually, I'm running the tombola at the Autumn Fair today, though I didn't tell him that.'

'Roy, your mother has ears like a bat. If you don't tell her, someone else will.'

'You won't tell her, will you?'

'No, I won't. But yesterday afternoon, someone — possibly the man Marco who works for Sir Arthur . . .'

She told him what had happened to her conservatory, but didn't mention Mr Talbot.

Roy groaned. 'It's got all the hallmarks, hasn't it? If he threatens my mother . . .'

'She's a feisty old lady but she's not made of cast iron. Roy, you've got to warn her.'

Heavy breathing. A muttered, 'I suppose so. I did go in to see her but just couldn't admit what an idiot I've been. Strangely enough, some more work has just come in through a chap I know at the golf club.'

'He's not a friend of Sir Arthur's, by any chance?'

'No, no. His company's bought a very basic sixties office block on the Uxbridge Road, and they want to put up some classy flats instead. Given the need for housing, and the drop in usefulness of old office blocks, the planning permission should be a doddle. Never fear, I'll be looking at all the small print this time. I suppose I'll see you at church this morning? Perhaps we can have that meal together this evening?'

He rang off.

Kate had been making them both a cup of coffee, and now shoved some in Ellie's direction. 'Roy's an optimist, if he thinks he can brush Sir Arthur off like that.'

'My sentiments precisely,' said Ellie, ladling in some sugar. She glanced at the clock. She ought to be on her way to church now. Jean would be cross if Ellie were late . . . again. 'One more phone call. This time I'm really going to poke Sir Arthur in the eye.'

Luckily, Sir Arthur was in the phone book.

'Hello, is that Felicity? This is Ellie Quicke. We met briefly the other evening, you remember? I haven't been able to get the thought of your poor dog out of my mind. I only have a cat, but if anything were to happen to him . . . oh, please don't cry . . . it's only natural for you to be upset . . . but I was just wondering, if your husband is away this weekend and you haven't anything on today, I've got to help out at a fair in the church hall, and there's going to be a Royal Society for the Protection of Birds stand, and the Cats Protection League will also be there, and we're desperate for help and I was just thinking that it might take your mind off things, even though it's birds and cats and not dogs . . . you wouldn't mind? Nothing else to do? Oh, that's just great. It's St Thomas', you know it? At the end of the Avenue. I'll be going over there in a minute. I'm on teas and coffees, but I'm sure we can find time to sit down and have a chat.'

Ellie put the phone down, pulling a face at Kate, who was killing herself with laughter. 'Oh, I know I sounded like a gibbering monkey on a stick. A caricature of a Little Woman whose mind never rises above gossip and the price of cauliflowers. But it worked. She's going to meet me there in an hour.'

'Sir Arthur will kill you.'

'Will she tell him? Especially if I bring up the subject of the bimbos he's supposed to have.'

'Be careful, Ellie. That's all. And now, I'd better find out if Armand can look after Catriona for a bit longer while I get on to Gwyn and . . .' She looked stricken. 'For a moment there I'd forgotten Catriona. How could I?'

Ellie patted her hand. 'My dear. I know. But needs must. Or words to that effect. And as you said it to me, I'll say it to you . . . be careful!'

* * *

On her way out, Ellie checked the contents of her fridge. There wasn't much there for the weekend. There wasn't even much in the freezer. She really did need to stock up again. But if Roy took her out this evening, and she ran over to the new mini-supermarket in the Avenue first thing in the morning, she could manage. She didn't really approve of Sunday shopping, but sometimes it came in useful.

She collected her shopping basket from under the stairs, pushed in an apron and some clean tea towels. The hall was let out all the week and however many tea towels were left in the kitchen, there were never enough clean ones by the weekend. Rubber gloves, yes. Purse, keys, mobile phone. Was it going to rain? Jacket, umbrella.

Lock and bolt the front door. Go out the back way down the garden path. Kate and Armand had a key to the back door.

There was a shuffle of dried leaves in the alleyway, floating down from the trees around the church. Ellie tried to relax. Tried to forget all about Sir Arthur, and feuding magnates and nasty people who made silent phone calls in the dark. Think of Marco as if he were a cockroach, to be dealt with and disposed of.

Sir Arthur, of course, was more like a hyena. Or a charging rhinoceros.

She'd take a bet on it that he'd married Felicity partly to get himself an unpaid housekeeper and cook, but mostly to spite his old enemy. He didn't treat her well. He'd broken her spirit; that is, if she'd had any in the first place. She had to pay for her mother's stay in a home out of her own allowance, and it didn't look as though this left anything over for hairdressers and good clothes. It seemed he didn't take her out into society, didn't need her at weekends in the country . . . did he have a bimbo there? Aunt Drusilla had referred to bimbos in the plural. If she were right, then perhaps he had a country bimbo and a town bimbo.

Either way, he'd taught Felicity her place, which was, presumably, in the kitchen. No children, and now no dog to love. He encouraged Marco to treat her as if she were a skivvy.

Felicity must be feeling desperate, but what could she do about it? Where would she go? She'd been taught to distrust her father, and her mother was in a home. She'd no money, no skills apart from homemaking, and apparently no friends.

It had been clever of Chris Talbot to suggest Ellie befriended his daughter. In his own way, he was just as manipulative as Sir Arthur. Did Chris Talbot really care for Felicity, or was he just using her as a pawn, as her husband did? Ellie had a fanciful thought that Sir Arthur had tried to murder his rival, by marrying his daughter. Oh well . . .

There was a queue forming outside the church hall already, though the doors wouldn't be officially opened for another five minutes. Ellie pushed her way in, and nodded to Archie, who was on the door, ready to take entrance fees. Fifty pence for adults, children free.

The Autumn Fair was a mix of church-operated stalls and a table sale for crafts, plus a few charitable organizations who could pick up money and membership at such times. The main hall was crowded with stalls, and the small room off the kitchen was also in use.

The weather was not brilliant, but the side door into the vicarage garden was open and there were a few stalls and some children's play equipment set up outside. If it didn't rain, that play area would be a godsend. If she had to look after little Frank this afternoon, then he could play outside. If she were able to take time out to look after him.

The organist was setting up a barbecue in the garden with his wife, who was dear Rose's only daughter, and a difficult girl to get along with. Though efficient.

The majestic Mrs Dawes was presiding over a table full of flower arrangements, and waved to Ellie. 'Good timing, dear. I've got an old friend to help out on the bric-a-brac stall, but if you could manage an hour here . . . ?'

'I'll see what I can do, but Jean wants me in the kitchen.'

Mrs Dawes shook her head in sympathy, making her long earrings jangle. Everyone knew what a slave-driver Jean could be.

Ellie hurried into the kitchen, where Jean was already scolding away. Maggie, a large, comfortable-looking woman who'd recently joined the choir, was taking not a blind bit of notice of Jean. Nice woman, Maggie. Ellie and she exchanged nods and smiles, while Jean switched her tirade to Ellie for being late. Which she was not. Or almost not.

'. . . and we're short-handed as it is. I was relying on your friend Rose to help us, but she's cried off. Says she's too tied up with looking after that old skinflint she works for, begging your pardon, Ellie; I know she's your aunt—'

'Husband's aunt,' said Ellie, automatically.

'—but everyone knows she could buy and sell this place a dozen times over, and what she needs Rose for as well, I really don't know.'

'The doors are open and they're off!' cried Tum-Tum, appearing to snatch a slice of cake. 'Jean, I'm on the video and DVD stall till lunchtime. Needing sustenance every hour. One large cuppa, one even larger slice of cake. Can do?'

'For you, vicar. Anything!' The sharp lines of Jean's face relaxed into what she imagined was a smile. It made Ellie shudder, but Tum-Tum — brave man — never blenched.

Maggie and Ellie flicked glances at one another, and got down to spreading tablecloths on the half dozen tables in the side room where people could sit and eat. It was going to be a busy day for all concerned, and hopefully make a few hundred for the church funds. Especially if the plan to develop the vicarage site had fallen through.

* * *

Sir Arthur had been almost too busy to take the phone call from his wife. He didn't usually allow himself to dwell on thoughts of her when he was in the country, but this was different. The girl had her uses, after all.

He listened, and even encouraged her.

'Yes, you do that. Find out what you can and keep me informed. Yes, I know I said I'd be in a meeting all day, but this is important. Well done, Felicity.'

* * *

The first of the hungry and thirsty customers had begun to trickle through, demanding coffee, tea, soft drinks, cakes, crisps . . . something on a stick for little Danny, and haven't you got any straws, because my daughter's just lost her front teeth . . . ?

To give credit where it was due, Jean worked as hard as Maggie and Ellie, but they never seemed quite able to catch up with the queue of people wanting to be fed and watered. The new kitchen was wonderful, of course, but the urn was temperamental, and before long Jean was saying they'd have to dig out the old one, even if it did leak and had to be stood on a tray to catch the drips.

'Well, look who's here!' Roy, reaching the head of the queue with a fair-haired girl in tow. 'Ellie, she's been looking for you everywhere, but I said you were likely to be in the thick of it. Two coffees, one black, one white, and a couple of doughnuts.' Turning to the girl, 'You'd like a doughnut, wouldn't you? You look as if you could do with feeding up.'

'Oh, Mrs Quicke,' said the girl. 'What a crush! I was just on the point of going home when Roy rescued me.'

'Felicity, my dear,' said Ellie, pouring out coffees and slipping doughnuts on to two plates. 'As you can see, I'm—'

Jean broke in, 'Those tables need clearing, Ellie.'

'—a bit pushed at the moment.'

Roy pushed a couple of pound coins into Maggie's hands. 'Keep the change. Come on, Felicity, I'm on my break now, so I'll grab a couple of chairs, and we can take ten minutes to get reacquainted. This way.'

He wafted her away. Ellie told her jaw to resume its normal position. Felicity was still dressed all in black, yes; but she'd taken the trouble to wash her hair, which was blonde rather than mousy. She was wearing a bra today — not that she'd much to worry about in that direction, being so slim. Far from being a downcast little bunny, she was actually smiling up at Roy, and even as Ellie watched, Felicity reached up to pull her fair hair free of the elastic band which had tied it back.

'That one knows a good thing when she sees it,' said Maggie, swabbing down the surfaces. 'Where did he dig her out from?'

'She's a client's wife,' said Ellie, wondering if she'd completely misread Felicity. The girl didn't look particularly pale or uninteresting today. She had a fine creamy skin and her hair wasn't a bad colour, though it could perhaps do with some highlights and a more fashionable cut.

Roy certainly seemed to admire her. It might be because her husband was away for the weekend and she knew she wouldn't be shouted at and belittled, but there was even a little colour in her cheeks.

Well, bully for Roy.

Jean was sour. 'You'd best take care, Ellie, or your fine beau will be looking elsewhere.'

Ellie blushed, and was furious with herself for doing so. 'He's not my beau. He's my husband's cousin, we're good friends, and poor Felicity could do with a few hours away from a difficult husband.'

'Hah!' said Jean, meaning that she didn't believe a word of it. 'And those tables still need clearing.'

Ellie went to clear the tables, trying to convince herself that Chris Talbot would be pleased with the way things had turned out. Roy was handsome and charming. Roy was delightfully devoted to his mother. Roy was a good architect, who was perfectly capable of supporting a wife and child, if he could find the right person to marry.

True, Roy had many times asked Ellie to marry him; but Ellie had never taken him seriously, and had always told him so. Perhaps that had been a mistake?

Nonsense. She'd long ago decided that she didn't want to marry Roy and nothing she'd seen of him had inclined her to change her mind. He was self-centred and lacking in empathy. He'd been married to a pretty flibbertigibbet years ago, and didn't want to go down that line again. He did yearn for domestic bliss, but didn't realize it might entail putting his own wishes second to someone else's.

He wasn't good with the small print of contracts and needed a sharp eye overseeing his finances, he was perhaps spending too much time with his cronies at the golf club. And yet, by and large, taking everything into consideration, he might well make a good husband and father to the right woman.

But to tangle with Felicity? His bête noire's despised wife? It was asking for trouble.

Rose popped her head around the door. 'Are you worked off your feet, Ellie? Oh, I see you are. I've brought dear Miss Quicke over for a look-see. She wanted to inspect the new hall in action, so to speak. She's catching up with Roy at the moment.'

Jean opened her mouth. 'Well, if you're at a loose end, we could certainly do with some help in here.'

Rose winked at Ellie and faded from the scene.

Ellie closed her eyes for a moment, imagining the confrontation that might even now be taking place over Roy's body. One elderly lady, who'd never been married, could never have been described as a beauty and who had a bad hip, versus youth and some beauty. Ouch. But, come to think of it, Ellie's money would be on the older lady.

Mrs Dawes came surging in. 'Isn't anyone coming round to take orders from the stallholders for lunch? And who's that blonde that Roy's squiring round? Anyone we know?'

'It's Lady Kingsley,' said Ellie. 'He knows her through his work. Her dog has just died, and she was at a loose end. Perhaps we can get her on the bric-a-brac stall this afternoon?'

'Chance would be a fine thing,' said Jean, giving a twist to the — metaphorical — blade she'd dug into Ellie's back. 'That one's got her claws firmly in, take my word for it.'

'Really!' snapped Mrs Dawes, who detested Jean. 'Well, if you've quite finished gossiping, perhaps you'd take my order for lunch. A ploughman's would do, with home-made soup. I assume you do have some home-made soup, and not that gruel made from a packet?'

Patches of red showed up on Jean's cheeks. 'A ploughman's, and some tomato soup. Right. Ellie will bring it out to you *when* she's finished those dishes.'

And, thought Ellie, Roy's a good twenty years older than her. Which makes me about twenty years older than her too. Ouch. Oh dear, I am being so stupid. What does it matter if he's interested in someone else? I should be cheering him on.

'*Whose mobile phone is that?*' Jean screeched so hard that Ellie almost dropped the tray she was carrying. Was it hers? Yes, it was.

Another problem. Balancing the tray on one hand, she fished out her mobile and answered it.

It was Kate. 'Ellie, listen: I don't know what the police want with you, but they've been round here — the builders have turned up, by the way, arguing with the cleaners about who's got priority in the conservatory — anyway, Armand told the police you weren't here and they're coming over to the church hall to—'

'Mrs Quicke? Is she here?' A youngish, bulky man who had 'police' written all over him. One she hadn't seen before. Accompanied by a young policewoman almost as bulky as her partner.

'Now what?' said Jean, arms akimbo.

The policeman addressed Jean. 'Mrs Quicke? May we have a moment?'

'What?'

There were about twenty people crammed into the small room, having early lunches or coffees or whatever, and they all turned round to see what was happening. Maggie looked at Ellie and signalled with her eyebrows towards the back door. Maggie evidently thought Ellie would like to make her escape that way.

'Er, no,' said Ellie. 'I'm Mrs Quicke. But as you can see . . .'

'We are rather busy, in case you hadn't noticed!' said Jean. Jean wasn't a large woman, but as she advanced on the policeman, he quailed. Ellie was amused and alarmed by turn. What had gone wrong? Diana! No, perhaps little Frank had met with an accident, or . . .

She took off her apron. 'May I see your identification, please?'

The policeman disconnected from Jean's basilisk gaze, and held up a shield.

'DS Robertson.' His mate produced another badge. 'DC Smith. Is there somewhere we can talk?'

Tum-Tum appeared, reducing everything to normal. 'A problem, is there? Ellie, you've not been caught drunk in the street again, have you?' As Ellie hardly touched liquor — except for the odd glass of sherry — this sally was greeted with relieved laughter by everyone except Ellie and the police.

Ellie was still anxious. 'Nobody's dead or anything, are they?'

'No, no. Just a quiet word, if we may.'

Tum-Tum opened the back door which led from the kitchens on to the garden and waved them towards the vicarage. 'Use my study. Just don't disturb anything on my desk, right? Ellie, do you need anything?'

Did he mean she ought to be asking for her solicitor?

She shook her head. 'It's probably about the burglar — if that is what he was — and I suppose I ought to have reported the silent calls he made in the night. If it was him. It probably wasn't. I'm sorry about that.' She looked up at the policeman, who had pale grey eyes that signalled intelligence.

He was a ferrety-faced man, a little like Armand in that he had the same type of golden red hair, matched to skin reddened and not browned by the sun. Robertson sounded

Scots. His companion looked stolid. She had acne, poor thing.

Ellie threaded her way through the back quarters of the vicarage to the room which Tum-Tum used as his study, overlooking the drive. Like all the other rooms here, it had a ceiling almost higher than the room was wide. Faded brown curtains matched faded carpet — brought from some larger room, to judge by the way the pattern was cut short at the edges. The furniture consisted of a few large, shabby pieces and a host of books. Surprisingly pretty watercolours of birds and flowers livened the walls.

Ellie didn't take the vicar's chair, and neither did the police. They sat rather awkwardly side by side on an ancient horsehair settee, while Ellie took a single chair from its place by the wall.

It appeared that DS Robertson was going to do the questioning. 'Now, Mrs Quicke, can you account for your movements yesterday?'

That was a surprise. 'Well, I suppose so. I was up in town in the morning, then . . . What is all this? You haven't called about my break-in, have you? You're not local. So . . .'

'Your local nick has been investigating a break-in at your place? What time was this?'

'Yesterday afternoon, about half past four. A man tried to—'

'You weren't there at the time?'

'Well, no. I was on my way back from—'

'You know a Mr Talbot?'

Ellie nodded. 'Yes, but—'

'What went wrong?'

'Nothing. I don't understand what—'

'How did you come to know him? Were you employed by him in one of his companies, perhaps?'

Ellie gaped. 'What on earth are you talking about?'

'You knew where he lived, of course.'

'No, I'm afraid I—'

'You knew his son, Julian, though.'

'No, though I heard that—'

'Mrs Quicke, we *know* what happened. You were seen. The number of your car was noted down by a passer-by. We have information that you knocked that boy down and drove off without bothering to get out of the car, or to check how badly he was hurt!'

CHAPTER TEN

Ellie opened and closed her mouth.

Blinked.

'I could pinch myself to see if I was awake, but I think on the whole I'd prefer to pinch you. I have never heard such nonsense in my life! I am so angry I could . . . I would like to . . . ! If I weren't so . . . ! Heavens above! Where did you get that story from? No. Don't say anything. And don't you dare interrupt me again, do you hear?'

She wanted to smash something. Someone.

This is what came of trying to help someone in distress.

Ah.

A thought. A nasty little thought that grew and grew in her mind.

She said, 'What a very clever little man it is, then! This story — this fantasy of yours — it came straight from the rhinoceros's mouth, didn't it? No, wait a bit. He wouldn't risk bringing his own name into it. It would have been either an anonymous letter, or better still, he'd have got someone to ring up and accuse me of attempted murder. Am I right?'

DS Robertson looked wooden. 'Let's hear your story, then.'

Ellie fluffed out her hair, thinking hard. 'Well! I hope you've got the message properly recorded, because I'd like to hear it. I wonder, would he use Marco for this?'

'Marco who?'

'I said, don't interrupt! No, I don't think he'd have used Marco. But he's got this other man working for him. Now, what's his name? Chris Talbot did tell me.'

'Talbot. You admit you know him?'

'Yes, of course. Martine something. Martins? No, Martinez. I'm told he "looks like a snake and thinks like one, too". It would be him, probably. And no, I've never met him and I don't know what his voice sounds like. Very clever of you, Sir Arthur.'

'Sir Arthur who?' The man sounded genuinely puzzled.

Ellie felt sorry for him. A little. 'Look, I know most people can drive, but I can't. I can't even wobble about on a bicycle. Ask our vicar. Ask anyone. Now, I think what we had better do is have a bite to eat — I can get someone to bring something over from the kitchen — and I'll tell you everything I know. Then you can fill me in on what's been happening your end. All right?'

'I don't think that—'

'No, I realize you don't think, but that's only because you haven't enough data to go on yet. I'm not sure that I fully understand all the ins and outs of this affair, but at least I'm further on than you. Now, would a ploughman's lunch do you? Would you like some soup? I'm afraid it's out of a packet.'

The policewoman stirred for the first time. Ellie had begun to wonder if she were deaf, or thinking about something more important. 'Shall I check?' DS Robertson nodded. The policewoman got out a mobile and left the room, speaking softly into it.

There was a knock on the door, and Tum-Tum put his head round. 'You all right, Ellie? Jean's foaming at the mouth.'

'I'm fine. That is, I will be when you tell the police what type of car I drive.'

He grinned. 'Your vehicle of choice is a minicab.'

DS Robertson looked resigned. 'She doesn't drive?'

'Perish the thought.'

'Never owned a blue saloon, registration TOP something? Got a dicky exhaust?'

'She's taken driving lessons now and again, but it's really not her scene. She has an account with a local minicab firm. What's she supposed to have done?'

'What I have done,' said Ellie, 'is made an enemy of Sir Arthur Kingsley, as you very well know.'

Tum-Tum's eyebrows peaked. 'Ah. Was he responsible for smashing up your conservatory? Everyone's talking about it. What can I do to help?'

'Help me to flee the country, without leaving a forwarding address. What I need at the moment,' said Ellie forcefully, 'is a good long holiday abroad.'

'At Her Majesty's Pleasure?' said the policeman, showing an unexpected streak of humour. 'Now, can we have it from the top, please?'

Ellie sighed. 'Where to begin? And if you say, "at the beginning", I'll . . . I'll . . .'

The door burst open, and in strode Roy, with pink-cheeked Felicity glued to his heels. Felicity had not only spread her hair over her shoulders, but had also picked up a gauzy pink overblouse to wear . . . from one of the stalls? She was unrecognizable from the dispirited figure she'd cut the other evening. Ellie revised her opinion of Felicity. Away from her husband, it seemed she was capable of holding her own in the world.

Roy was half amused, and half annoyed. 'Ellie, you're needed in six different places. Jean's sending people out to look for you, and what's more, Stewart's arrived and is asking for you.'

DC Smith slid back into the room, looking as bored with life as ever. She nodded to her partner, and muttered,

'They traced the call to this telephone number.' She held out her notebook so that he could see it.

A small child was wailing outside, and the wails were getting louder.

'Is she in there?' Stewart hove into sight, carrying his son at arm's length. Everyone in the room recoiled. 'He was sick in the car, all over everything, and worse!' The 'worse' was evident to everyone whose sense of smell was functioning.

Frank was covered with vomit and snot, and still howling, helplessly, furiously.

Stewart didn't look too dapper himself. 'He's been appalling. He scratched Yazz hard enough to break the skin. Then he bit Maria, gorged himself on some food he'd been told not to touch, screamed when he was stopped, hit his granny Patel and threw up. When I removed him from the scene, he swore and kicked at me, so I put him in the car to bring him back, where he threw up again, and . . . I've got to clean myself up, clean the car, and get back.'

'I hate you!' screamed Frank, trying to hit his father, who was still holding him at arm's length. 'I want my Mummy!'

Felicity got behind Roy, while still clinging to his arm. 'Whose is that brat? Don't let him come near me.'

Roy was distracted, half wanting to shield Felicity, and half anxious for little Frank. 'It's all right, Felicity. He's my nephew, sort of. Come along, Frank. Come to Uncle Roy.' He tried to disengage himself from Felicity, who shrieked a ladylike little shriek and clung on.

Frank gulped, red-faced, and heaved as if to vomit again.

Ellie wished she'd kept her apron on, but made a heroic gesture. 'Come to Granny, then.'

Tum-Tum was quicker. He picked Frank up and held him at arm's length. 'Let's get him cleaned up, shall we?'

'It's my job,' said Ellie. 'Only, Jean will kill me if I don't get back to the kitchen.'

The police looked amused — even the blank-faced policewoman's wooden expression momentarily relaxed — but everyone else took this seriously.

Roy said, 'That's true.' He looked at Felicity. 'You wouldn't sacrifice an hour of your time to help out in the kitchen, would you?'

'Me?' Felicity was undecided. Clearly she didn't want to spend the next hour washing up dishes, but she did want to impress Roy.

Jean appeared in the doorway, her blood pressure clearly mounting to danger levels. 'Ellie, I don't know what you think you're playing at but . . .' She recoiled as Tum-Tum advanced on her holding Frank before him.

'That's it, Jean,' said Tum-Tum. 'Hold the door open for me.'

Jean stood aside to let him through, but caught Ellie by the arm when she would have followed. 'You're not going anywhere, Ellie Quicke, until—'

Ellie brushed her aside. 'Try Felicity.'

She heard DS Robertson saying, 'Hold on, there!' as she followed Tum-Tum up the imposing staircase to the high-ceilinged, echoing, dingy first floor. Tum-Tum elbowed open a door and dumped the little boy, still wailing and retching, in a large, claw-footed enamel bath, and turned on the shower.

'Stand clear!' he sang out, and turned the spray on to Frank.

'His shoes,' said Ellie. 'Shall I take them off first?'

'Ruined already,' said Tum-Tum. 'Here we go! Rub-a-dub-dub. Three men in a tub. Do you sing in the bath, Frank?'

Frank hiccupped and tried to climb out of the bath. Tum-Tum gently but firmly pushed him back in. Frank began to howl again, but Tum-Tum sang louder and louder. 'Rub-a-dub-dub . . . Three men in a tub . . . Rub-a-dub-dub . . . Here we go, little man. Soon be nice and clean again . . . Ellie, hold the spray for me, will you, while I strip him off.'

Frank stopped howling, needing the air in his lungs for breathing purposes.

Ellie held the shower head while Tum-Tum stripped off the little boy's clothes and lathered him, still protesting, with shampoo. 'Rub-a-dub-dub . . . I used to do this with my old dog, and he never liked it either. But what has to be . . . has to be. Ellie, can you find me a large, clean towel from the linen cupboard over there? That's the ticket.'

Frank was weeping now, but quietly.

Ellie found a towel and held it ready while Tum-Tum inspected little Frank from head to toe, and pronounced him clean. Once wrapped in the towel, Tum-Tum lifted the boy out of the bath and stood him on a nearby stool. 'Rub-a-dub-dub. That's the way to dry you, all over, between toes and fingers and into all the nooks and crannies. That's the ticket!'

'R-r-r-r-!' Frank was shivering. Ellie took over from Tum-Tum, towelling the little boy till his skin was pink.

Something large loomed in the doorway. DS Robertson was not giving up easily.

'Is the wee one feeling better now? My sister gives her girls sugared water to drink, if they're sick. Or flat Coca Cola.'

'Good idea,' said Tum-Tum, using the spray to clean round the bath. 'Can you get some for him? The kitchen's at the bottom of the stairs, through the passage to the back and turn left.'

The policeman nodded. 'Don't you go away, Mrs Quicke. Right?'

Roy added to the blockage in the doorway. 'Have you got any clothes at home for him, Ellie? Yes? Felicity's gone to help in the kitchens, and I had a word with Rose, who agreed to lend a hand there as well. Rose didn't want to leave my mother, but seeing as she's deep in gossip with some crony of hers, I said I'd see her safely home in a little while.'

'Ellie, find another clean towel to wrap him in till the clothes situation has been sorted out. I'll have to get back, show my face around,' said Tum-Tum, efficiently stowing Frank's dirty clothing in a large plastic bag.

Ellie found another large towel, and wrapped a now docile Frank up in it.

Tum-Tum handed her the bag of dirty clothes. 'You take this, and let me carry the boy downstairs for you. Use my study for as long as you like, but remember that I'll need a full explanation later as to why the police are chasing you.'

'I'll get some food organized, shall I?' said Roy. 'Soup and a sandwich do you, Ellie?'

Following Tum-Tum down the stairs, Ellie reflected on how easy it was for men to say they'd only do a couple of hours on a stall, and then be free to go ahead with their own lives, while women felt obliged to work on till the bitter end, and then clear up the mess. Rose would tire herself out . . . how did Jean keep going? Mrs Dawes' bad leg would play up tomorrow. How was Maggie coping on her first exposure to the sweatshop atmosphere in the kitchens?

Tum-Tum dropped little Frank on to Ellie's lap when she got herself settled in the big leather armchair with its worn arms. Frank was still shivering, but not much. His eyes were closing on him. Worn out with fighting the world.

The policewoman was on her mobile again, taking more notes.

Ellie fished out her own mobile and tried Diana. For once, Diana's mobile was turned off. Ellie left a message. 'Diana, little Frank is in a bit of a state, missing you. If you could ring him, have a chat? It might help. He'll probably be staying overnight with me, as Stewart and Maria are not available.'

She leaned back, closing her eyes for a moment. *Dear Lord, help. I'm so tired of all this. I don't know what to say to little Frank. Maria's so much better at this than I am, but if Frank has attacked little Yasmin, I'm not sure Maria'll be able to cope in future.*

DS Robertson came back with a mug. 'Sugared water from the kitchen. Amazing place, this. Like something out of a museum. Get it down him or he'll be dehydrated.'

The policewoman turned her back on them, still on the phone, still taking notes.

Ellie managed to get Frank to drink most of the water, while the DS watched her with what looked like sympathy. She gave him a wan smile. 'His mother's off somewhere this weekend, chasing business, and he's one very angry little boy. Now, what is it you want to know?'

The door banged open and in hobbled Miss Drusilla Quicke, leaning heavily on her stick. 'There's nowhere to sit down out there, and the vicar kindly said I could rest in his study till Roy can take me home. It's a fine thing if I have to learn what's going on from complete strangers. Where is Roy, anyway? Why didn't you stop him making a fool of himself, Ellie? And what's all this about you getting all your windows smashed in?

'And,' to the policeman, 'who are you? Hold your badge up so that I can see it. Higher. That's better. And your partner? Too busy to turn round? Well, I suppose I have to assume that she's a genuine policewoman. I'm Miss Quicke, by the way, and it looks as if my son and my niece have been mixing in bad company. No, no,' as he offered her a low, cushioned chair, 'I can't possibly sit on that. I'd never get up again.'

Roy thrust open the door as it was about to close again, propelling himself and a tray full of goodies into the room. 'Ellie, this is all I could . . . Mother, what are you doing here?'

'Waiting for you, Roy. Is that food for me? Good.' She subsided into the chair behind Tum-Tum's desk and settled the tray on top of his papers. 'Now, sit down, all of you, and tell me exactly what's been going on.'

'Well . . .' said Roy, looking embarrassed.

DS Robertson showed a modicum of intelligence. 'I'm DS Robertson, investigating a complaint placed against Mrs Quicke here.'

Miss Quicke said, 'Really? You surprise me.' Without further ado, she started on the bowl of soup Roy had brought in for Ellie.

Roy looked anguished. 'I'll go and get some more food, shall I?'

His mother pointed with her soup spoon to the low chair. 'Sit down, Roy, and explain to me how you came to be embroiled in this affair.' Roy sat.

DS Robertson flicked a glance at Ellie in which — she was almost sure — there was a gleam of humour. 'We need a word with Mrs Quicke — in private.'

'I'm not going anywhere,' said Ellie. 'But everyone here knows what's been happening, so why don't you just get on with it?' She settled little Frank more comfortably on her lap, hoping he'd drop off to sleep for a while.

'I suppose it all started with me,' said Roy. Even his ears had gone red. 'But it all seemed so straightforward at first. Just another job. I'm an architect, you see, and I met this man — Sir Arthur Kingsley — at the golf club, and . . .'

'You haven't the sense you were born with,' said Miss Quicke. 'Roy, this soup lacks seasoning.' But she finished every drop.

Roy fidgeted. 'I know I ought to have consulted you, but I thought I knew what I was doing. He wined and dined me, and somehow, I don't know exactly how . . .'

He told the sorry story up to the meeting in the church hall. '. . . and then it all came out — thanks to Ellie, who stood up in front of everybody and asked the right questions — and I was naive enough to think that would be the end of it, but of course Sir Arthur still wants his pound of flesh.'

'And,' said his mother, looking around her, 'the vicarage still needs rebuilding. It's a disgrace. How far have they got with planning permission? You may bring round your plans to show me later on, Roy. Perhaps you and I together can come up with an acceptable solution to the problem.'

Roy's relief was tangible. 'Mother, you're an angel, but you don't want to tangle with Sir Arthur.'

'I'm no angel, but I can see there's money to be made on a sympathetic development on this site. Sir Arthur doesn't frighten me. Now, Ellie. Where do you come in?'

While Roy had been talking, Ellie had wondered how much or how little she should mention about her dealings with Chris Talbot, but came to the conclusion that if she kept it short and sweet, all she need say was that Sir Arthur and Mr Talbot had been enemies for ever, and leave the tangled relationship with Felicity out of it.

The policewoman switched off her mobile and paid attention.

Ellie said, 'I'll have to go back a bit. A couple of days ago I called with my neighbour to visit Sir Arthur and his wife. It was a sympathy call, because their dog had been poisoned. Nasty. I met Marco — Sir Arthur's handyman — and thought him extremely rude. He didn't like me much either. Sir Arthur sent Marco to the meeting in the church hall. He heard me rubbish their plans, and he must have taken the bad news back to his master.

'I think the poisoning of his dog must have pushed Sir Arthur over the edge, because he accused Mr Talbot — a longtime rival of his — of trying to kill him and of poisoning the dog instead. He did this before witnesses in a board meeting! Mr Talbot hadn't had anything to do with the poisoning, of course.'

Ellie had been concentrating on saying enough to satisfy the police, but not too much, and hadn't noticed that Felicity had returned to the room. But there she was now, sitting on the arm of Roy's chair.

She looked flushed and almost pretty. 'You're talking about my husband? He wouldn't get mixed up with anything underhand!'

'Wouldn't he?' Ellie felt sorry for Felicity, but continued, 'When I got back yesterday afternoon, I found that my conservatory windows had been smashed in. My neighbours had called in the police. I'm sorry if it distresses you, Felicity, but I think it was Marco, getting back at me. My neighbour caught sight of the man who did it, and she thinks it was him too. We told the local police what we thought, but I'm not sure they took it seriously. I'm not sure that I would have taken it seriously either, if I hadn't heard other stories about Sir Arthur's business methods, and met the man myself.'

The policeman looked at Felicity, who said, 'Absolute nonsense!' and pushed her hands up the sleeves of her sweater.

Ellie concluded, 'Later yesterday evening I phoned Mr Talbot to tell him what had happened at my place. That's when he told me his son had been attacked on his way home from school. He was distressed, of course. He suspected it might be Sir Arthur striking back at him, but of course there was no proof. I believe he took his family to a hotel for the night for safety's sake.'

Felicity turned her head to look directly at Ellie. *Yes, this is your father and your half-brother we're talking about.*

'My builder boarded over the broken windows and I went to bed. I had a couple of silent phone calls in the night, but I turned the volume down on the bell, so I could get some sleep. I think that's about it.'

'You mean,' said the policeman, 'that this lady's husband—?'

Felicity attempted a laugh. 'As if he would! She's making it all up.'

The policewoman consulted her partner in an undertone, and showed him various entries she'd made in her notebook. He read off a telephone number. 'Mrs Kingsley—'

'Lady Kingsley,' Roy corrected him.

'—is that your home telephone number?'

Felicity went pale. She nodded. 'Yes, but . . .'

'Where can I find your husband now?'

For the first time Felicity looked nervous. 'He went down to the manor yesterday evening as usual. But he couldn't possibly be linked to—'

'What time?'

'I'm not sure. Six? Half past? He has a housekeeper down there who gives him supper on Friday nights.'

'You don't go with him?'

Felicity reddened. 'He has other company down there.'

'Did this man Marco go with him?'

'No, Marco had the weekend off.'

'So, at eight in the evening, your husband couldn't have been using the phone at home? What about this Marco, or his PA?'

Felicity was paler than ever. 'I don't know. Marco was home last night, yes. He has a flat over the garage.'

'Could he have used your phone?'

She shrugged. 'He comes and goes as he pleases.'

'You didn't use the phone yourself, by any chance?'

Felicity's skin looked transparent. 'I went out after my husband left. I got back in time to watch the sitcom at half past eight.'

'Seeing someone?' There was almost a leer in the policeman's voice.

Felicity frowned. 'My mother. In a home on the Common.'

'What about the PA, Martinez?'

'I didn't see him last night, but that's not unusual. He doesn't live in our house. He's got a flat overlooking the park.'

Ellie remembered something. 'I ought to have said before, but the man who broke my windows upset my cat, who bit and scratched him. I wiped what looked like blood off my cat and kept the tissues.'

'What have you done with them?' The policeman looked interested.

'I bagged them up and gave them to Mr Talbot's driver, to see if he could find some DNA on them.' She faltered. 'It was probably the wrong thing to do. I suppose I ought to have given them to the police, but they'd gone by then and . . . well, Mr Talbot offered. So he has them now.'

The policeman was not amused. 'You do realize you've compromised the evidence by giving it to Mr Talbot, if indeed there was any?'

Miss Quicke had finished up everything on the tray. 'Lady Kingsley, did Marco look as if he'd been scratched or bitten when you saw him last night?'

Felicity nodded. She looked as if she were going to cry. 'I had to clean him up. He said he'd disturbed a feral cat.'

Miss Quicke dabbed her lips with a paper serviette, and summed up for the police. 'Well, Detective Sergeant Robertson, you'd better be on your way, find this Marco, check if he's had a tetanus injection, ask him why he broke my niece's windows and then accused her of dangerous driving. Someone senior to you had better tie the two cases together and then you can find this man Kingsley and tell him to stop it. If you need a statement from Ellie . . . ?'

'We'd like her to accompany us down to—'

'As she couldn't possibly have committed the crime, taking a statement from her can be deferred to a more suitable time, don't you think? As you can see, she's got her hands full at the moment. In the meantime, Roy, you may take me home. It's time for my afternoon nap. And rescue Rose from the kitchens. I don't want her being worn out. I think that's all. Someone hand me my stick and I'll be off.'

* * *

Sir Arthur was showing off the view from his terrace. 'As far as you can see,' he said, gesturing widely. 'Been in the family for generations. What do you think?'

Diana smiled. 'I've always been attracted to powerful men. Men who know what they want.' He wanted her, she knew that.

He was enjoying himself too. His enemy had been taught a much-needed lesson, the interfering Quicker woman punished, Martinez was working on a plan to bring the architect to heel, and his wife was actually pulling her weight for once. It was a pleasant change to play the game with a stylish career woman instead of pretty girls with nothing between their ears.

She said, 'I haven't seen your dog around. I thought you always brought him down to the manor at weekends?'

His mood darkened. 'He died. I'm getting another.'

'I like men who own dogs. It gives them an air of respectability.'

That made him laugh. 'You don't think I'm respectable?'

'That's what I like about you. Also, you never say your wife doesn't understand you.'

His mood was genial again. 'I have a wife, yes. But she knows her place.'

Diana looked back at the house. An anorexic fortyish blonde was hovering in the doorway, watching them. 'Your housekeeper tells me she's been with you for years. Lucky you.'

'She knows her place, too.'

'Really?' Diana wasn't so sure about that. The woman had intimated a very close relationship with Sir Arthur.

'Now and again I have to remind her.'

Diana suppressed a delighted shiver. The man could be frightening. She liked that about him too.

He caught her arm. 'You said you had a proposition for me.'

She dropped her eyelids, looked demure. 'I'd do anything for my son. You know that.'

'I know you'd do anything for money.'

'Only if it pleases me as much as it pleases you.'

He laughed. Tucked her arm within his. 'Let's discuss this proposition of yours, shall we?'

CHAPTER ELEVEN

The Autumn Fair was winding down. Girl Guides and Brownies were beginning to pick up litter and stack furniture. It hadn't rained, which was a blessing. Tum-Tum said the takings on the door appeared to have been satisfactory, and Mrs Dawes was triumphant because she'd sold nearly all her flower arrangements.

Felicity had tied back her hair and disappeared — on a bicycle, if you please! Didn't her husband allow her the use of a car?

Miss Quicke had been chauffeured back home by Roy, with Rose holding a clutch of things she'd bought at various stalls. Miss Quicke had said she hadn't seen anything worth spending her hard-earned money on, but had given Tum-Tum a cheque to swell his funds.

DS Robertson carried the sleeping Frank back to Ellie's place for her. As Ellie let them into her house, she was relieved to see that her conservatory was once more glazed, even if the panes now needed cleaning; the floor, too. There didn't seem to be any more glass shards twinkling from corners. Good. Presumably the insurance would pay. She must remember to report it to them.

The policeman deposited Frank on the settee in the living room. 'Cuppa?' said Ellie. He shook his head. 'I'd best get back.'

She saw him off, double-locked the front door, and sat down with a deep sigh, easing off her shoes . . .

. . . and the next thing she knew, someone was ringing the doorbell.

She struggled awake, glanced at the clock — it had stopped, drat it. Her watch said it was after six o'clock. Little Frank was beginning to stir. She must find him some clothes to wear and oh, heavens! She'd no decent food in the house. What could she give him for supper?

The doorbell was insistent. As she made her way into the hall, she noticed the light was flashing on her answerphone. It could wait.

Surprise! It was Felicity on the doorstep, still wearing her black clothes, but without the pink overblouse. Hair tied back, no make-up. She was retreating up the path to the road with her bicycle even as Ellie opened the door.

Ellie had the odd fancy that whatever she did or said in the next few minutes was going to affect the reconstruction of a national corporation and the jobs of countless men and women across the UK. Which was, of course, ridiculous.

'Come on in,' said Ellie, opening her door wide. A cold wind, spattering with rain, blew in on her. There was a wail from Frank in the living room. Well, he could wait.

Felicity dithered. 'No, I wouldn't want to . . . I was just . . . I expect you're busy.'

'Bring your bike through to the conservatory, or it'll get pinched.'

Felicity obeyed. 'Yes, I . . . my car's in the garage, and anyway, it saves petrol to use the bike.' Her colour was coming and going. She looked like a white rabbit, nose twitching, not sure whether to advance into the big wide world, or to scamper back to its warren. But there was some determination there. The girl had a chin. She also had the remains of a bruise on the side of her face which Ellie hadn't noticed in the general gloom of the vicarage study.

Frank was fretful. Ellie beckoned Felicity into the living room. 'There, there, Frank. Granny's here. Look, we have a visitor. Isn't that nice? Now we'll just find some clothes for you to wear and—'

'I'm hungry!'

Ellie had ceased to be surprised at the capacity of the young to throw up one minute and eat a hearty meal the next, but it did pose a problem.

'Oh, I'm sorry,' said Felicity, hovering. 'I didn't realize . . .'

'Come on in. I don't suppose you've eaten much today, have you? There are some menus by the phone in the hall. Takeaways. Chinese, Indian, pizza. Perhaps we can choose.'

'McDonald's,' said Frank, firmly. 'I want a Big Mac and chips and Coca Cola and everything. Now!'

Ellie blenched. Junk food had never appealed to her. Felicity, however, looked interested. 'I haven't been to McDonald's for ever.'

'Then we'll go,' said Ellie, recognizing a majority decision. 'I'll get Frank dressed and call a cab.'

* * *

McDonald's was, in fact, just the sort of place to go on a dreary October evening. It was bright, cheerful, family-friendly, and clean. There was plenty there to amuse children, and the adults didn't have to eat the same food as the young ones. Felicity, in fact, ate as much — if not more — than Frank.

'I ought to apologize for bursting in on you,' said Felicity.

Frank remarked, 'Mummy brings me here on Saturdays. Where is she?'

'Not at all,' Ellie said to Felicity. 'I've been thinking about you.' And to Frank, 'I rang your mummy and left her a message. She'll ring you as soon as she can.'

Frank pulled a face. 'When she's able to get out of bed.' Was this a direct quote from something Diana had said? Felicity and Ellie exchanged startled glances.

'Little pitchers,' said Ellie to Felicity. Felicity looked puzzled, but Frank treated them to a bright, intelligent look. He said to Felicity, 'She means I've got big ears. But I haven't. I've got nice ears.'

'Of course you have, darling,' said Ellie. Seeing his attention turned to watching a party of children nearby, she said, 'You've lost your pretty pink blouse, Felicity? What a shame. I thought it looked nice on you.'

Felicity was refusing to make eye contact. 'I gave it to Mummy. She looks lovely in pink.' She took a gulp of Coca Cola. 'You must think me very odd, dumping myself on you like this, but you see, when I got back home — that was after I'd been to see Mummy, as I always do when Arthur's out, especially in the afternoons at weekends — anyway, there was a police car in the driveway. I expect they were looking for Marco, but I just felt I couldn't face any more hassle, so I turned my bike round and . . . I suppose I lost my nerve. If they were going to take him away for questioning, I didn't want to see it. I couldn't think where to go at first. Then I thought you'd all been so kind to me that afternoon . . .'

Ellie guessed, 'You went looking for Roy?'

Felicity reddened. 'Well, I did think he might . . . but he'd gone . . . and that big bossy woman who'd been on the flower stall directed me to your place. I'm so sorry.'

That would have been Mrs Dawes, an avid gossip, who liked to stir things up, and who would want to hear all about it after church tomorrow.

'I'm sorry I'm not Roy.'

Felicity had a very pale, transparent skin and when she blushed, she did it properly. As the blood receded, the bruise on her cheek showed more clearly.

Ellie said, 'Your husband hits you, of course. He used to hit the dog too, didn't he?'

Felicity excused him. 'He only does it when we're stupid. Poor Rex got so nervous that he used to widdle everywhere, and naturally Arthur had to teach him to mind his manners.'

Ellie shuddered. 'What do you do to make him angry?'

'I'm really not very clever, and I do make silly mistakes.'

'So does everyone. So what?'

Felicity wriggled. 'Well, I'm not exactly what he thought he was getting when he married me. Not a social asset, I mean.'

'Children?'

'I had a miscarriage at four months, soon after we married, and since then it seems I can't. I've been to doctor after doctor, but they can't find what's wrong.'

'And Arthur?'

'Oh, he says it's not him. It's definitely me.'

'Why don't you leave him?' Yet Ellie thought she knew the answer.

'Oh, I couldn't possibly. He loves me really, you know. Besides, I promised Mummy I'd never, ever, put her into a horrid National Health home, though really they're quite nice, because I did some voluntary work in one till Arthur said it wasn't a suitable thing for his wife to do. It's very expensive where Mummy is, but she's happy there, and I couldn't afford it if Arthur stopped my allowance.'

Frank produced a burp loud enough to attract attention from everyone within earshot, and leaned back in his chair.

Felicity fiddled with her last few chips, without eating any more. 'All that stuff about my father. Did you really go to see him? Where was it? At his home? I don't understand. He doesn't give a stuff about me. Arthur has never liked him either, but it's stupid to think my husband would arrange a car accident for anyone.'

'I've heard stories about your husband taking it out on people who've crossed him.'

Felicity managed a smile. 'When you're as successful as Arthur, people will always make up stories, try to pull you down. It's just envy.'

Ellie changed the subject. 'Have you ever met your half-brothers?'

Felicity shook her head. 'I promised Mummy I'd never have anything to do with them, and I won't.'

Ellie tried to clean Frank up. 'Your father still cares for you. Worries about you.'

'Don't make me laugh.' Yes, the girl was bitter. 'He never wanted children, and as soon as I was born, he was off. He only remembers he has a daughter twice a year, for birthdays and Christmas. He promised Mummy enough money to restore the manor, but he never gave her enough. She worked so hard to keep the place going but she's never had a head for business, and no matter how much I tried to help . . .'

'I need to go to the toilet,' Frank announced, in a loud voice.

'In a minute, dear,' said Ellie, not wanting to interrupt Felicity.

'I need to!' said Frank.

'Oh, dear. Well, come along, then. Felicity . . . ?'

Felicity blew her nose on a paper serviette. 'I'm not going anywhere.'

Ellie wasn't that sure that Felicity would wait, but in fact she did. Frank didn't linger too long in the loo, and she made him wash his hands and face before returning to the restaurant, where he informed them he wanted to go and play in the children's area.

'Good,' said Ellie, making sure she could see him from their table.

Felicity had ordered some coffee, but said, 'I've just realized I've come out without any money. I'm so ashamed, cadging off you like this.'

'Think nothing of it. Tell me how you came to marry Sir Arthur. How long ago was it?'

'Nearly ten years now. Mummy was feeling very down after she lost the shop up north, and thought she'd try her luck in London, so we moved down here. I got a job working on the information desk at the town hall, and found this little flat to rent, though of course it wasn't at all what she'd been used to. Poor Mummy. She did try so hard to find work, but she hadn't been trained for anything. I gave her as much as I could from my wages and she had lots of friends who invited her out, because she was so pretty, you've no idea how pretty she was, especially when she was all dressed up with her hair done nicely. One evening she met Sir Arthur at a do in town and discovered they'd lots in common . . .'

'Such as a relationship with your father?'

'I suppose so. He took one look at me and . . . I don't know why, because I wasn't prettily dressed or made-up or anything . . . but he asked me out. I didn't want to go at first, because I couldn't think what he'd see in me. Mummy insisted, saying he could do so much for us if I were nice to him, and of course I wanted to be nice to him. Arthur was wonderful. He made me feel so . . . special. He took me to all sorts of places I'd never have dreamed of going to, and promised to get the manor back for Mummy. She was so happy!'

'And you?'

Felicity smiled. 'Of course. We were married and he bought the manor, but I'm afraid I disappointed him dreadfully. He expected me to be a social asset, like Mummy. The more I tried, the more I failed him. Then I had the miscarriage, which was all my fault because I would exercise his dogs — he had two darling little spaniels at the time, and they needed a lot of walks, but it was dark and raining, and I slipped. Then Mummy had this awful accident. She'd been to a party and perhaps she'd had too much to drink. She doesn't know exactly how it happened herself, but she fell and cut herself terribly . . . the blood was everywhere . . . so she never got to move back to the manor. Arthur was forced to put her in a home because she couldn't be trusted to live on her own any more. Really, she's like a child now.'

'I think,' said Ellie gently, 'that you've been more of a mother to her than she has to you.'

Felicity shook her head violently, and dabbed her eyes with a paper serviette. 'Tell me why you went to see my father. Was it at his home? Are you keeping in touch with him now?'

Ellie craned her neck to follow young Frank as he disported himself. Would he make himself sick again, if he persisted in turning himself upside-down?

'It's a complicated story and I'm not sure I understand all of it, but this is how I came into it . . .' She told how Kate had asked her to visit 'a man about a dog', and that Kate really thought Sir Arthur's life was at risk.

Felicity's eyes grew round. The idea that her husband was in danger seemed to excite her. Poor thing, if her husband really was treating her so badly, then his death might well seem a release.

'. . . and then the next day I was sent for to the City to meet your father, and he told me of his long-standing feud with Sir Arthur and how — forgive me — he feared you might have been used as a pawn in the game the two of them are playing.'

'No! Ridiculous!' Colour stained Felicity's cheeks.

'Well, that's what your father was afraid of. He's very concerned about you, you know. You should hear his side of the story some time.'

Felicity pushed back her chair. 'He's a monster!'

'He's worried sick that you might have poisoned your husband.'

'What?' An angry laugh.

'And now his younger boy has been attacked. He might have been killed. He's got a broken leg and they fear concussion. Your father has — I think wisely — taken the rest of his family to a hotel for safety's sake.'

'Well, at least he's showing some concern for his second family!'

Ellie sighed. She thought she'd said enough. Probably more than enough. She looked around for Frank. How had it happened that she'd taken her eyes off him, when she knew his propensity for getting into trouble? She couldn't see him in the play area.

So where had he gone? The people on the next table were collecting their children together, talking loudly, joking.

A small girl hurtled through the tables, yelling and pointing to the play area at the back. Ellie guessed Frank was at the bottom of whatever it was. She made her way there as fast as she could. Frank was crowding a small child under a low table, laden with Lego. He was pinching her. She was weeping, crying for her mummy. Another child kept saying, 'I told him not to!'

Ellie plucked Frank from his victim, stood him upright. 'Oh, Frank! How could you! Don't you realize how much you were hurting that little girl? You must say you're sorry, at once!'

Frank kicked Ellie. It hurt. He said, 'She hit me first.'

'I never!' cried the little girl, whose parents were now swooping upon her with cries of alarm.

'I'm so sorry,' Ellie apologized to the parents. 'I'm afraid he's missing his mummy today. I oughtn't to have let him out of my sight.'

'That's all very well,' blustered the father, 'but if your child has—'

'Oh, leave it. Let's just get out of here.' The mother gathered up her weeping toddler and bore her away. The father followed.

'Frank, I could smack you!' said Ellie.

'No, you can't,' said Frank, looking a lot older than his years. ''Cause a policeman will kill you if you do.'

There was no answer to that. Ellie dragged Frank back to their table. Felicity had disappeared. Of course.

Ellie pushed and pulled Frank into his jacket, and towed him outside, so that she could phone for a minicab to get them home.

Felicity was waiting outside. 'This is so embarrassing. I haven't enough money to call a cab, and I've left my bike at your place. My car's in the garage for repairs, you see.'

Ellie was getting a strange feeling about Felicity. Why had the girl sought her out, and then clung to Ellie's side? Was it just because she didn't want to face the police, or . . . what else might it be? Ellie decided to test out her suspicions.

‘Would it be a good idea for you to stay over at my house tonight?’

‘You’re very kind,’ said Felicity, smiling in approved Nice Girl fashion.

‘Not at all,’ said Ellie, thinking that she’d misread Felicity once, and might still have to adjust her opinion. ‘I could do with the company. Apart from Frank, that is. And what I’m going to do with him, I don’t know.’

‘I want to sit in the front of the cab!’ said Frank.

‘No, you can’t,’ said Ellie, envisaging Frank grabbing at the wheel and causing an accident.

‘Mummy lets me. If you don’t let me, I’ll make myself sick!’

Felicity recoiled and Ellie eyed him with horror. She knew it was no idle threat. She put away her mobile. ‘If you feel like that, then we’d better walk home. It won’t take us more than half an hour.’

She caught Felicity’s eye and, towing Frank, started along the pavement. Frank screamed and twisted, trying to release himself from her grasp. Ellie hung on, ignoring him. Felicity kept pace with them.

‘I’ll be sick, I will!’ shouted Frank.

‘All right. If you want to be sick, just do it in the gutter. The walk home will make you feel better.’

Frank began to weep. ‘I want my mummy.’

‘I expect there’ll be a message from her on the answer-phone by the time we get back. So don’t drag your feet. One, two. One, two. Best foot forward. Do you know any good marching songs, Felicity?’

‘Er . . . no. I mean, what about “The Grand Old Duke of York”?’

Ellie carolled,

‘Oh, the Grand Old Duke of York,
He had ten thousand men,
He marched them up to the top of the hill
And he marched them down again.’

Felicity joined in.

'And when he was up, he was up,
And when he was down, he was down,
And when he was only half way up,
He was neither up nor down.'

Frank was furious. 'Stop singing! I hate it.'

'You hate a lot of things,' said Ellie. 'Which is a pity, because the world's not a bad sort of place if you approach it with a smile instead of a scowl.'

'I hate you!' He hit at her with his free hand. Since she was wearing a thick jacket, the blow didn't hurt. Except in her spirit. Her spirit quailed. However was she to deal with this angry, violent child?

'Don't do that, Frank. Behave nicely, or else . . .'

He jeered at her. 'Or else? You can't do nothing to me, or my mummy'll do something dreadful to you.'

Ellie exchanged glances with Felicity. 'Any ideas?' asked Ellie.

'He's a brat. I'm just thinking how Arthur would deal with him.'

Ellie smiled. Reprehensible though the thought might be, it gave her some pleasure to imagine Arthur giving young Frank a good spanking. She sighed. 'Unfortunately, we can't. Sanctions are limited nowadays.'

'I'm tired.' Frank was dragging his feet, making them carry him along.

'What a pity,' said Ellie. 'We've hardly gone any distance. Of course, if you aren't going to be sick, we could get a taxi home.'

'Probbly I might not be sick now.'

'Good,' said Ellie, being cheerful. She got out her mobile and asked for a minicab to pick them up.

Felicity said, quietly, 'Well done.'

Equally quietly, Ellie said, 'I may have won a battle, but I haven't won the war.'

CHAPTER TWELVE

It was getting towards Frank's bedtime but since he'd had a good sleep that afternoon, it was hopeless trying to put him to bed early.

Ellie turned on all the lights, drew the curtains, and sat Frank in front of the television, selecting a cartoon video for him to watch. She didn't approve of the violence in the cartoons, but Frank did. Ellie was too grateful for his absorption in the video to quibble about the content.

Felicity asked if she could help to make up beds for herself and Frank, but Ellie had got into the habit of having the spare-room bed always made up ready for unexpected guests, and the little bedroom was known as Frank's room anyway.

'Not to worry,' said Ellie. 'I'll find you a disposable toothbrush, and I've got a clean cotton nightie that might do you.'

'Oh, I don't need anything like that. Just a towel and a toothbrush.'

Ellie nodded, went upstairs to put out clean towels and check that the back bedroom was in good order. Which it was.

Midge appeared, was fed and watered, and made himself comfortable on the warm window ledge above the central heating radiator in the hall. He seemed to be moving into his winter quarters early, but she couldn't blame him for that. She didn't particularly want to sit in the conservatory herself at the moment.

Ellie listened to her answerphone messages while Felicity slumped into a big chair, half watching the cartoons with Frank. The girl looked as tired and dispirited as on the first occasion Ellie had met her.

The first message was from Jean, much annoyed that Ellie had 'skived off' early and left her and Maggie to do all the clearing up. Jean wanted to remind Ellie that she was down to do the tea and coffee after church the following morning. If it wasn't going to be too much trouble, heavily ironic!

Ellie grimaced. If she still had little Frank in tow, what price his creating mayhem at church while she sang in the choir? He'd need policing during and after the service.

Ellie tried to imagine what he'd grow up like, if he continued on his present course. She shuddered. A delinquent at ten, an Anti-Social Behaviour Order at twelve? A string of appearances in court, followed eventually by some kind of confinement at Her Majesty's Pleasure?

The problem was how to break the cycle. Was Diana aware of what was happening? Did she care, or was she so self-absorbed that she couldn't see it?

Could Stewart cope? Probably not. Far too soft-hearted.

Maria? Ah, but if Frank had started to attack little Yasmin, then how much would Maria put up with?

The second message was from Stewart, enquiring anxiously how Frank was. Stewart was a straightforward sort of chap and would no more have dreamed of making himself ill to get his own way than of walloping his only son. Although a walloping might have helped, if only it weren't against the law.

What was a harried parent to do, in such cases? What sanctions did one have against a potential juvenile delinquent? The Naughty Step had worked for Maria. But then Frank had attacked Yasmin. Would Maria be able to cope in future?

Ellie realized she was thinking in circles.

The third message was another silent one. It might be a salesperson trying and failing to get through, or it might be Marco. Again. Ellie had checked her conservatory when she came in. All was in order. Well, it would be when she'd got the glass cleaned, and the broken plants replaced. She must remember to phone the insurance people.

The next message was from Kate next door. Anxious. 'Are you all right, Ellie? Was it OK to send the police round to the church? The builders seemed to know what they were doing but there was a row with the cleaners, who wanted to stay on to clean the newly fitted panes of glass, but the builders said the panes mustn't be touched for weeks, to let the putty dry. So I'm afraid the place doesn't look quite right yet.

'Oh yes. And I've been in touch with Gwyn and Talbot about You Know What. Most interesting. There's an emergency meeting up in the City about it this afternoon and they want me to go. I'll tell you all about it when I get back.'

The last message was from Chris Talbot himself. 'Mrs Quicke, have you seen Felicity? How is she? Julian's doing all right, but I'm packing the family off to stay with friends in the country for a few days, out of harm's way. Please ring me on the following number . . .'

Nothing from Diana, drat it.

Ellie poked her head into the living room. 'Fancy another cuppa?'

Felicity shook her head. 'I'd forgotten cartoons could be such fun.'

Ellie dumped Frank's filthy clothing in the washing machine, adding lots of washing powder. There was no point in trying to rescue the shoes; Tum-Tum had been right about them. They went in the bin.

Frank appeared, still watching his cartoon through the open door to the living room. 'I want some hot chocolate.'

Hot chocolate on top of Coca Cola on top of Big Macs? Ellie said he could have orange juice and like it. He opened his mouth to howl, so she said he'd better be quiet, because she was just going to try to phone his mummy. Thankfully, he shut his mouth again. Diana's mobile was still switched off.

Ellie left another message. 'Diana, please ring me. Frank's missing you very much. Can I tell him you'll pick him up tomorrow morning before church?'

'Before breakfast!' Frank insisted.

'Perhaps,' said Ellie, cravenly, 'she'll even be here when you wake up in the morning. Now, off to bed with you.'

Frank had just started to howl when the doorbell rang, as did the telephone. Ellie scooped up the phone, told it to wait, and opened the door. It was raining hard.

Stewart stood on the doorstep, looking anxious, and down the path from the road came Tum-Tum, also looking worried, under an enormous, colourful umbrella.

Ellie waved them both in. 'The more the merrier! Frank, stop that noise. Can't you see your father's here?' And to the phone, 'Yes?'

It was Roy. 'Heavens, Ellie; what's going on there? I wondered if you'd like a bite to eat at the Carvery tonight. Or perhaps we could go over to the golf club for a drink?'

'You've forgotten; I've got Frank here.' Ought she to mention Felicity, or not?

Perhaps not. Especially if her suspicions of the girl proved correct.

Roy had forgotten. Remembering the boy's behaviour that day, Roy wasn't going to offer to take him out too. 'Oh. Well, perhaps another time?'

'Go and see your mother instead.'

Roy groaned. 'You won't believe the trouble I'm in there. Sir Arthur's PA was waiting for me when I got back, with a letter from his solicitor. Can I bring it round to show you?'

'Take it to your mother. If we're talking solicitors, she's got a heavyweight one in tow, remember?'

Roy sighed. 'Well, I don't know. But if you're not free . . .'

'No, I'm not. See you tomorrow at church, right?'

Roy sighed again. Disconnected.

While she'd been talking on the phone, Frank had been excitedly telling his father all about his day. '. . . and Tum-Tum dumped me in the bath with all my clothes on, and he says my shoes are ruined, and then the policeman gave me some horrid water and *she* made me drink it and I went to sleep all afternoon and then we went to McDonald's and there was this stupid girl who screamed like a mouse, like this . . . eeeh! So I pushed her a bit and then *she* spoiled everything and made me walk home, all the way . . . till we took a minicab, but she wouldn't let me sit up front and Mummy's not answering the phone but she'll be here tomorrow before breakfast . . .'

Ellie shooed the menfolk into her sitting room. 'It's time Frank was in bed. Are you going to take him back with you now, Stewart?'

'No!' said Frank. ''Cos Mummy's coming here tomorrow before breakfast.'

Ellie took the coward's way out. 'I'll ring her back and tell her where you're going to be. Perhaps it would be best if you went back with your father.'

'No!' Frank went bright red, squinched his eyes shut and prepared to have a tantrum.

'Oh, come on, Frank,' said his father. 'You know Maria puts you on the Naughty Step if you lose your temper.' He didn't say that *he* did it himself, and it was obvious from Frank's reaction that Stewart didn't.

Frank opened his mouth to yell. Stewart dithered, but Tum-Tum picked the little boy up, took him out to the hall and dumped him on the bottom step. Frank was so surprised, he forgot to scream.

Tum-Tum said, in a firm but kindly voice, 'Stay there till you're prepared to say thank you to your granny for having taken care of you today, and then you can go home to your own bed with your father, right?'

Frank's eyes were round. He looked at Tum-Tum with awe. Everyone looked at Tum-Tum with awe.

'Splendid,' said Stewart, in a gobsmacked voice. 'How's about we get going then, Frank?'

Frank got off the step and went to stand beside his father — on the side away from Tum-Tum. 'I'm going to sit in the front.'

'No, you're not,' said Ellie, relief that he was going and common sense fighting for ascendancy. 'Your special seat is in the back of the car, and we don't want to lose you if there's an accident, do we?'

He ignored her. Pretended he hadn't even heard her. Didn't thank her for looking after him.

Tum-Tum said, still in that kind but firm tone, 'Haven't you forgotten something, Frank?'

As if under a spell, Frank turned to Ellie and said, 'Thank you for having me.'

Tum-Tum said, 'There's a good boy.'

Stewart ushered Frank out to the car. The boy's voice floated back to them. 'Tum-Tum's cool, isn't he?'

Silence. Blessed relief as the front door shut behind the pair.

'Phew!' said Felicity, who'd been observing the tussle from a safe distance.

'Thomas,' Ellie gave him his proper name for once, 'I'm deeply moved and very grateful. How do you do it? He's been a little monster all day. I know he's missing his mother. This is the second weekend on the trot that she's failed to take him out. I feel as if I've been fighting a tornado with poor results, then you walk in and tame him with a look.'

'It's not the look that counts,' said Tum-Tum, sitting in the big armchair. 'It's being consistent. Give him lots of praise when he's done something good. I suppose he's been playing you off against Maria, and Maria off against Diana. The usual.'

Ellie rescued the biscuit tin from a high shelf, which so far Frank hadn't managed to reach, opened it and put it on the arm of Tum-Tum's chair. 'Help yourself. Cuppa? No?

Frank's miserable. Diana's not consistent, though I think she does love him in her own way.'

'It doesn't matter where he gets his love from, so long as he gets it from someone.' He took a couple of biscuits and turned his not inconsiderable bulk towards Felicity. 'How are you coping, my dear? Roy was telling me, when we were clearing up after the fair this evening, how he came to meet you. I very much appreciated your helping us out today. I hope the police presence didn't put you off us for good.'

Felicity blushed. She certainly blossomed in the presence of a man. 'You were all very kind. I was feeling so down this morning. Ellie was so kind about our dog being poisoned. It just seemed meant, you know?'

'Mm,' said Tum-Tum, whose eyes saw further than most. 'So, shall I give you a lift back home in a minute? You won't want to walk in this weather. It's raining quite hard.'

Ellie waited for Felicity's reply with interest. What did the girl really want? A refuge from a violent husband, for whom she still carried a torch? Or something else?

Felicity gave a little wriggle. 'Ellie has been so kind as to ask me to stay here overnight, which is wonderful, because it can be a bit lonely at home when my husband's away.'

Which sounded fine if it had come from a sixteen-year-old who'd known Ellie all her life, but didn't quite ring true from a thirty-something woman who'd only just met her that week.

'Ah,' said Tum-Tum, nodding. Probably not believing a word of it. 'Well, Ellie, I really dropped in to give you a bit of bad news. Mrs Dawes managed to fall and twist her bad knee during the clearing-up. It's swollen to twice the size. Archie took her off to hospital to get it checked out, and brought her home afterwards. Nothing's broken, but she's going to have to keep off that leg for some days. Archie said she was worrying herself silly about not being able to do this and that, so I dropped in to see her just now, and promised to tell you what's happened. Perhaps you can give her a ring? She's got the telephone by her bedside and I fixed her up with a snack and a thermos for later.'

Ellie exclaimed, 'Oh, poor dear. Yes, of course I'll ring her. Does she need any food?'

'She's well stocked for food, but in a right fantod about making it to the church hall for her flower-arranging class on Thursday, and whether she can get to meet up with her old friends for their weekly get-together, and I don't know what else. Oh yes, and she wanted to remind you that you're on the coffee rota for tomorrow morning.'

'Jean's already been on to me about it.'

'There was something else bothering her, but she wouldn't tell me what it was. She said you'd know, and she was sorry if it had inconvenienced you.'

'Thank you,' said Ellie, nailing this one down with ease. It sounded as if — when Felicity returned to the church enquiring after Roy — Mrs Dawes had told a porky. She'd told Felicity he'd already left and directed her to Ellie's house. But he hadn't gone home. Or rather, he'd taken his mother away, and then come back. Because he'd been helping Tum-Tum clear up later on.

Had Mrs Dawes thought that she was helping Ellie by misleading Felicity as to Roy's whereabouts? Had Mrs Dawes thought Ellie would be hurt if Felicity annexed Roy? Oh dear. Probably.

Ellie looked at Felicity, but the girl was gazing blandly out into the conservatory. Possibly she hadn't understood the ramifications of the message which Tum-Tum had delivered to Ellie. Or maybe she had, and was choosing not to hear.

Tum-Tum shook the empty biscuit tin, and replaced the lid. Laying his capable-looking hands on the arms of the chair, he heaved himself upright. 'Well, must be off. See you in the morning, Ellie. And you . . . my dear?'

Felicity managed to blush again. She did it very prettily. 'Oh, perhaps.'

Ellie accompanied Tum-Tum to the front door. She said, 'Thank you, Thomas. For everything.'

'Not at all.' He opened the front door, unfurled his giant umbrella and sailed forth into the wind and rain. There was something of the jolly sailor about Tum-Tum.

Ellie returned to the living room to find Felicity yawning. 'Is that the time? I don't know why I'm so tired.'

'Not too tired, I hope, to tell me why you're here? Not too tired to get fresh instructions from your husband? You were asking me where your father is going to be tonight? Don't you want me to find out for you? Or did you take down his telephone number from the messages he left on my answer machine?'

Ellie had heard of people who could cry to order, but had been sceptical. But Felicity, apparently, could do just that. Tears began to well over her eyelids, and run down her cheeks. 'Oh, how could you?'

Ellie sat down beside Felicity, and patted her knee. 'Come on, you can tell me.'

'You're all being so horrible about Arthur!'

'Who abuses you.'

'No, no! He doesn't!'

'What about that bruise on your face?'

'A cupboard door swung out on me. Arthur didn't do that. Honest!'

It was possible she was speaking the truth. Yet, earlier on she'd admitted that Arthur had disciplined her. And the dog.

'He used to beat his dog. You told me so yourself. And he bullies you, doesn't he?'

Felicity tried to laugh. 'Arthur, a bully? You've got him all wrong!'

'He's a bully and a sadist. He employs Marco, who is also a bully and a sadist.'

Felicity drew in a sharp breath. Her eyes switched from side to side. 'Marco's a bit rough, yes, but he doesn't mean any harm. I'm sure it wasn't him who damaged your conservatory, even though he did get himself badly scratched. Anyway, I can't see any damage now. You probably made it all up, to get back at Arthur.'

'Why would I want to get back at him?'

'Because he's rich and important and . . .' She hesitated.

'I'm not?' Ellie shook her head. 'Felicity, I understand that you want to be loyal to your husband, in spite of the evidence, but . . .'

She was interrupted by someone tapping on the door from the conservatory into the garden. It was Kate, letting herself into the house. Ellie and Kate kept keys for one another as a matter of course. Kate wore her work clothes — a trouser suit of impeccable cut, in dove grey — but was holding baby Catriona over her shoulder.

'Ellie, are you there? Armand's been a poppet all day, looking after the baby, but of course he hasn't done a stroke of work, playing with her. She had a nap at the wrong time and now, of course, she's wide awake.' Kate brought Catriona into the living room, but stopped short when she saw Felicity. 'Sorry, I didn't realize you had company. Ellie, if I can have a quick word?'

'Sit down, Kate,' said Ellie. 'Felicity is staying the night, because her husband wants her to discover where Mr Talbot might be hiding out.'

Kate was startled. 'But . . . !'

Felicity turned her tearful gaze on Kate. 'I know you've all got a down on Arthur, but honestly, he'd never in this world put Julian in hospital just to get back at my father, even though they don't see eye to eye about things.'

Kate sat with care not to disturb Catriona, who was munching on her fist and looking around her with bright, wide-open eyes.

Kate and Ellie regarded Felicity with identically sceptical gazes. Felicity managed to sniffle, while fumbling in her shoulder bag for a tissue. Not finding one straight away, she dumped the bag on the settee beside her. In doing so, some of its contents fell to the floor. She dived for her purse, but Ellie beat her to it.

'Five ten pound notes, and plenty of coins. Felicity, you said you hadn't any money.'

Felicity sniffled again. 'You just don't understand. Anyway, it's all your fault. You invited me to the church in the first place—'

'I was sorry for you, more fool I.'

'—and my father was paying you to rubbish Arthur to me.'

'Not a penny.'

Felicity was wide-eyed, no longer crying. 'Then why . . . ?'

'Because,' said Kate, 'your dog died, and that's upset the delicate balance of City business. Your husband thought your father had done it, and started World War Three. He was wrong, as it happens.'

Felicity reddened. 'You're trying to make out that Arthur's gone round the twist.'

'So you think so too? Your father was afraid that you yourself might have poisoned the dog, in an attempt to rid yourself of your husband.'

Felicity's mouth opened wide, and her eyes shut. Was she going to scream? No, she was going to laugh. In a horrible, retching way.

Ellie got to her feet. 'If you're going to have hysterics, I'll slap you. Do you hear?'

Felicity gulped once or twice, but her colour remained high. 'You don't understand. I love my husband and I'd never want to kill him. And if he did die, I wouldn't be able to pay the bills for my mother's care.'

'Nonsense,' said Kate, the brisk businesswoman uppermost in her, even while she rubbed baby Catriona's back. 'As his widow, you'd be entitled to claim the house and a reasonable sum to support you.'

Felicity was unconvinced. 'He's got ways of tying his money up. He explained it to me when we got married. It's to prevent anyone trying to grab his assets if one of his businesses goes pear-shaped.'

Kate said, 'Which they have. Felicity, your husband has got across one too many powerful people. He's in deep trouble, but doesn't seem to realize it. In conducting this vendetta against your father, he's lost sight of the real issue.'

'I don't know anything about it.' Sullenly.

'Of course you don't,' said Kate, all brisk and business-like. 'Neither does Ellie. But I do. Powerful interests in the City want the restructuring of a particular company to go through and your husband is blocking it, partly because he's holding out for a giant pay-off, and partly because your father is on the side of the restructuring.'

Felicity shrugged. 'Nothing to do with me.'

'I know that.' Kate was patience itself. 'What you do need to know is that the City wants that restructuring to go through, and they don't think it would be good public relations to encourage your husband to get away with a golden handshake. There have been meetings going on yesterday and today which your husband doesn't know about. He's been boasting that his board of directors are behind him in refusing to restructure. He's wrong. On Monday he's going to discover he's lost all his support.'

'You mean the others have been bought off?' said Felicity, trying hard to follow.

'Not bought off,' said Kate, with a grimace. 'Made to see reason. If the restructuring doesn't go through, the company goes to the wall — and bang goes their money tree.'

Silence. Felicity tried to think this through. 'You mean my husband will lose a lot of money too?'

Kate nodded.

'I don't understand what you want me to do,' said Felicity.

Kate held back a sigh. 'Warn him, obviously. If he can only forget his feud with Chris Talbot and concentrate on the real issue, he can still come out of this smelling sweet enough, if not smelling of roses. True, he'll have lost control of his company, but he'll have a nice block of shares in the new corporation to make up for it. The merger will go through and he'll live to fight another day.'

Felicity fingered her mobile. 'He'll be so angry. He wants me to find out where my father's going to be this weekend.'

'Why? To have another attempt at murder?'

'No!' Explosively. 'To talk to him, of course. To make him see reason.'

'It's not Chris Talbot he has to talk to now, but Gwyn. Tell him Gwyn wants to speak to him urgently.'

Felicity did her helpless, dithery act. 'I just don't think I can make him understand.'

Ellie said, 'For heavens' sake, girl! Get through to him, and then pass the phone over to Kate!'

CHAPTER THIRTEEN

Ellie rather expected Felicity to whine that she didn't need to shout at her, but she didn't. She pressed buttons and listened. They could all hear the phone ringing at the other end. The answerphone kicked in.

'He's got it switched off,' said Felicity. She glanced at the clock — it had stopped — and at her watch. 'He never switches it off . . . unless . . . I suppose it's about the time of day that he . . . well, he may be with someone.'

Ellie said, 'Try the landline. Maybe he'll hear that.'

'The thing is,' Felicity hesitated, and then rushed on. 'He might be with Anita, the housekeeper. Together, if you know what I mean.'

Ellie and Kate flicked glances at one another. Like that, was it?

Catriona burped. Smiling, Kate laid the baby down on the settee beside her.

Ellie said, 'What about that man Martinez? He's been round to see Roy this evening . . .'

Felicity perked up at the mention of Roy.

'. . . on a blackmail mission for his master . . .'

'I wish you wouldn't say such things,' said Felicity, resorting to tears once more.

'So I assume he's in London at the moment. Suppose you try his mobile number, get him to understand that it's in Sir Arthur's best interests to call off his vendetta? If he can't get through on the phone either, perhaps he could actually go down to the manor and speak to your husband in person? Unless, of course, he's already been arrested by the police for arranging your half-brother's little accident.'

Felicity applied a tissue to her eyes. 'I can't believe this is really happening.'

Kate rolled her eyes.

Ellie had had enough. 'Felicity Kingsley, stop that this instant! You're not a child any more, and if you don't snap out of it, I'll tell the police that you've been obstructing their enquiries into your half-brother's "accident", and you can spend the night at the station, being interviewed. I can just about believe you didn't know everything your husband's been getting up to. Tearing up people's gardens. Corrupting councillors to get planning permission through. Breaking promises to pay people when it no longer suits him to do so. Getting poor Roy drunk and taping promises he'd never have made in his right mind. Destroying my conservatory. Arranging an accident for Julian . . .'

Felicity had both hands over her ears. 'Stop! It's not true!'

'So I'll give you the benefit of the doubt and say that you chose not to know what was going on, rather than actively participated.'

'Da-da-di-da-da! I won't listen!'

'You can't deny you more or less invited yourself into my house, in order to find out where your father was?'

Felicity avoided eye contact. 'All right, I did listen in to his phone message, but the number he left is no use, because it's obviously a mobile. He could be anywhere. Arthur told me to find out where he is and ring him back, but I really don't want to get involved. Anyway, I can't get through to him now, can I?'

Kate rolled her eyes again. Kate didn't suffer fools at all, never mind suffer them gladly. She was gently rubbing

Catriona's tummy. The baby laughed up at her, pumping arms and legs. Kate smiled down at her child. Kate was opting out of the conversation.

Ellie said, 'I'll give you one last chance, Felicity. Get hold of Martinez and tell him to stop bothering Roy.'

'He takes orders from Arthur, not me. He won't listen to anything I say.'

Ellie ground her teeth. 'All right. Try Marco's mobile. If he's still at liberty.'

With a bad grace, Felicity punched in numbers. The phone rang. She listened. It was just going to cut off, when Marco answered. Ellie and Kate could both hear him, because he was bellowing down the phone. There was a lot of background noise.

'Yes?'

'It's me, Felicity. Have the police been round?'

'I just missed them. What's going on?'

'They know about your breaking Mrs Quicke's windows.'

Marco laughed. 'So what? She won't dare complain.'

'You're wrong there,' said Felicity, showing fight. 'She has. She told the police she thought it was you, so . . .'

'She weren't there, so she can't have seen me.'

'They know her cat scratched you. When they see your hands, they'll know it was you.'

Kate lifted her eyes from adoration of her baby. 'Tell him I saw him. And told the police I thought it was him.'

Marco heard that. 'What? Who's that? Hello? What's going on? Where are you? Down at the manor? No, can't be. He's got someone else there this weekend. Does His Majesty know Mrs Quicker's put the police on to me? I'll half murder her.'

'No, don't do that,' said Felicity, dealing with this inadequately. 'Are you at the house, or—'

'In the pub, of course. Saturday night, innit? Dunno where Martinez is. Tell you what, I'll pay the old girl another visit, warn her to keep her mouth shut, that'll do it.'

'No, you mustn't!'

He rang off.

Ellie leaned back in her chair. 'Did I mention that I'd like an extended holiday somewhere warm? The South of France, perhaps?'

Felicity burbled, 'Oh, I'm so sorry. He doesn't mean it, of course he doesn't. I'll have a word with him in the morning. Or get Arthur to do so. I'm afraid that if I say anything, Marco might take it into his head to do the opposite. Anyway, if I ring him back while he's at the pub, he might be angry, you know? Drinking time, and all that?'

Kate and Ellie regarded Felicity with the weariness of adults faced with a toddler who's forgotten her nappy training. Again.

Ellie said, 'Why not try your husband just once more?'

Cowed, Felicity tried. No answer. 'It doesn't usually take him this long to . . . he's probably forgotten to switch it on again . . . after . . . you know?'

'She must be good,' said Kate, lifting Catriona back on to her shoulder. 'Well, this little one's ready for bed.'

'So am I,' said Felicity, giving an appealing look at Ellie. 'You won't turn me out, will you? I really don't have my car this weekend, and I don't want to go home till Arthur gets back. Because Marco, when he gets back late tonight, well, he might get aggressive and then I'll have to lock my door and . . . it's not very nice when that happens.'

'I'd walk away from the whole sorry mess, if I were you,' said Kate, getting ready to depart.

'Can't,' said Felicity, and her chin came out to reinforce this statement.

Kate blew a kiss at Ellie. 'See you in the morning, maybe?'

Ellie nodded. 'Church. Then I've got to visit Mrs Dawes. Or maybe the other way round.' She saw Kate safely down the path, locking and bolting the door from the conservatory after her. Would Marco really pay her another visit? And if so, when? After he'd had enough to drink in the pub?

Ellie offered Felicity a hot drink to take to bed. Would the girl really go up without reminding Ellie to get back to her father?

'No, thanks. Nothing for me. You've been so kind.'

Ellie put a mug of water into the microwave to heat up for herself, waiting for Felicity to make her move.

The girl got as far as the bottom of the stairs. 'Oh, I've just remembered. You still have some telephone calls to make tonight, don't you?'

Ellie sipped her hot water. It was as good an aid to digestion as she knew, and she needed it after supper at McDonald's. 'Ah. A good thing you reminded me. Poor Mrs Dawes. Yes, of course I must ring her. It's not too late, is it?'

Felicity pinched in her lips. 'I was thinking that my father must be waiting to hear from you.'

'I've nothing to report. But you have, haven't you? Do you want to try your husband again?'

'Why, I suppose I could, but . . .'

'But you don't want me to hear what you say. I noticed you didn't leave a message for him, either time you rang.'

Felicity went up the stairs without another word.

Ellie called after her. 'Your bedroom is at the back of the house, straight ahead at the top of the stairs. Bathroom to your left. Use that first. I've got to ring Mrs Dawes before I come up.'

Felicity closed the bedroom door with extreme care. Ellie smiled to herself. The girl would be on the phone to her husband within minutes, of course. Ellie rather hoped he would have turned his mobile on again. Anita must have been proving rather more fascinating than usual.

Ellie took her hot water and the notebook from the hall into the study, where there was an extension phone. Firmly shutting the door behind her, she rang Chris Talbot's number. Unlike Sir Arthur, Chris Talbot had left his phone switched on.

'It's good to hear from you, Mrs Quicke. I'd been imagining all sorts, and feeling guilty that I'd dragged you into this mess.'

And charm will get you anywhere, thought Ellie. 'I'm fine. I have Felicity staying the night.'

'What?'

'She hasn't left her husband. She insists he's white as driven snow. He encouraged her to spend time with me, in order to learn your whereabouts, which I sincerely hope you're not going to tell me.'

He was amused. 'Mrs Quicke, you are an amazing woman.'

It was getting late, and Ellie was tired. 'Don't patronize me, please.'

'I'm sorry.'

'As to what I've found out; Kate tells me there've been meetings today to persuade Sir Arthur's supporters that he's on the losing side—'

'Yes, I was there.'

'—but I'm afraid Sir Arthur is still using Martinez to pressurize someone into putting money into another of his schemes. I may be able to stop that. I hope so. But I haven't found out who sent the poisoned pizza yet, because too much else has been going on. Not least an attempt to implicate me as the driver who ran your son down.'

'Really?' His voice cooled with suspicion, then warmed again. 'That makes no sense.'

'As it happens, I don't drive. But the police did question me about it.'

'Clever,' he said, slowly. 'But not clever enough.'

'I imagine it was Martinez's idea. It wasn't Sir Arthur who made the phone call, anyway. It might have been Marco. The police went round to pick him up, but missed him. He's in a pub drinking at the moment, and threatening to pay me another visit to shut me up.'

He drew in his breath. 'I'm truly sorry, Mrs Quicke. I'd no idea Sir Arthur'd resort to such tactics.'

'I think the death of his dog has tipped him over the edge, and there I can't help you. Yet.'

'It wasn't Felicity?'

'No. She married him because he made a dead set at her, and promised to restore the manor. He gives her enough money to cover her mother's incarceration in a home, but not enough for her to appear well-groomed. Felicity visits her mother whenever his back is turned at weekends. Sir Arthur doesn't want her at the manor, where he seems to have installed a mistress-cum-housekeeper.'

'I could pay for her mother to—'

'She promised her mother not to have anything to do with you. She has poor self-worth. Her devotion to her mother overrules everything, except her terror of her husband. She won't meet you, or talk to you, yet. She's in denial about her husband's ruthless activities. Her need to provide for her mother will probably keep her tied to Sir Arthur for the foreseeable future.'

Silence.

'I'm sorry if that all sounds rather depressing,' said Ellie, 'but it's the truth as I see it.'

'I repeat, you are amazing, Mrs Quicke. Thank you.' This time he didn't sound patronizing. 'You can reach me any time on this number. Take care.'

He rang off. Another soft 'click' sounded on the phone. Ellie replaced her own receiver, and glanced back at the door. That soft 'click' was a giveaway. Felicity must have crept down the stairs and lifted the handset of the phone in the hall, to listen in on Ellie's report to her father.

Ellie had always been told that 'listeners never hear any good of themselves'. She didn't suppose Felicity had enjoyed what she'd heard, but it might have made her think; *if* she was capable of thinking for herself, of course, which was quite a different matter.

Ellie made herself relax. She'd been horribly tense throughout the phone call. She glanced at the clock. Would Mrs Dawes have taken some painkillers and gone to sleep? She'd risk it.

Mrs Dawes answered the phone at the first ring, sounding as loud and confident as if she'd been in the same room. 'Ellie dear, I've been so worried. You've heard, have you? So stupid. I was trying to collapse one of those metal tables, you know how awkward they can be. I overbalanced and fell. It would be my bad knee, of course.'

'I'm so sorry to hear it. I wish I could have stayed to help clear up, but little Frank . . .'

'The young rascal!' Indulgently. 'Jean was in such a temper, hearing you'd taken him home, but as I said to her, what else were you to do? Anyway, Archie took me to the hospital and they didn't keep me waiting above half an hour, fancy that! And this Indian doctor, I wondered if he could even speak English, but of course he did, and he had the gentlest hands, and was so kind. Nothing broken, but a strained muscle, so I have to keep my leg up for a few days, and then I'll be out and about with the help of my stick.'

'You won't like being stuck indoors for days.'

'No more I will. But Tum-Tum — Thomas — told me you were trying to find out who else might have suffered from Sir Arthur Kingsley recently. Dreadful man! Who does he think he is, planning to build all those flats in our vicarage garden? Dear Tum-Tum — Thomas — dropped in to see me after Archie brought me back, and I was asking him about your conservatory — has the stephanotis survived, dear? — and he seemed to think it was Sir Arthur who arranged it.'

'Well, yes, but—'

'Thomas — I really can't go on calling him by that ridiculous nickname, even if it does suit him — thought I might dig up some information on Sir Arthur for you, since I'm not going to be so active for a few days. You heard about the woman who had her garden trampled down, did you?'

'Yes, I went to see her. I don't think it's her. Too downtrodden, poor thing.'

'Oh. Well, there's the odd-job man who Sir Arthur cheated . . . now what was his name? It'll come to me in a minute. Or I could ask around. One or two of my old friends have promised to drop in, keep me company. One of them is sure to know.'

'Mrs Dawes, you are incredible. May I bring you in some food or flowers — or perhaps a bottle of sherry tomorrow, to cheer you up?'

'Not that very sweet sherry, dear. I don't think it agrees with me. Oh, and Jean wanted to make sure you were going to do coffee after church, and I said you'd never forget! So don't, will you? Forget, I mean.'

Laughing, Ellie put the phone down. How clever of Tum-Tum — Thomas — to provide Mrs Dawes with something to keep her mind occupied during her enforced period of leisure. Mrs Dawes loved poking into other people's business.

Mrs Dawes was right about not calling him Tum-Tum in future, as well. That nickname had been applied to him on his very first day in the parish, but it really wasn't suitable. Of course he did look like a Tum-Tum, with that solid corporation of his. But he was a wise and experienced minister and he deserved to be called by his proper name. Thomas. Yes.

Ellie called Midge in from the garden, and gave him a late-night snack. She made sure the telephone bell was turned right down, and put her mobile phone in her pocket. Turning off the lights, checking that the bolt and chain was on the front door, she went up to bed. Felicity's light was on in the spare room.

She undressed with one eye on her bed, which appeared particularly soft and inviting tonight, especially with Midge spread out upon it. Would she get a good night's sleep, or would Marco pay her a visit?

Dear Lord, what a tangle. I don't know whether to feel sorry for Felicity; or to shake her. Uh-oh. When I don't know what to ask for, I should just say, Please, Lord. You know what's best for her.

And poor Roy. He really isn't fit to be let out alone. Though, to give him his credit, he is a good architect. I do hope he's taken the whole sorry mess to his mother.

I wonder if she will do something about the vicarage. Poor Aunt Drusilla, her hip. How can I get her to see a specialist? Rose is so worried about her, and so am I, dear Lord. Please, Lord, remember Aunt Drusilla tonight, perhaps unable to get to sleep, uncomfortable even in her big bed.

And Mrs Dawes. That leg of hers . . .

Ellie had a quick shower and, after checking that Felicity's light was out, got into bed and turned out her own light. Midge snuggled into her back, purring. He seemed to have recovered from the fright Marco had given him. How on earth had he managed to get so far up that tree so quickly?

Dear Lord, take care of me now I lie down to sleep . . . something about guardian angels round me keep . . . these childhood rhymes . . . the Grand Old Duke of York . . . little Frank . . . must do some tidying up in the garden . . . baby Catriona, so sweet . . . I am so fortune in my friends, Lord . . . thank you, thank you . . .

* * *

'What! What did you say?' Sir Arthur was not taking the news well, especially as this unexpected visitor was interrupting his late-night supper with Diana.

His P.A, Martinez, hooded his eyes. He was a long streak of a man with a narrow head. His skin was pale, as if he rarely exposed himself to sunlight. He didn't bother to repeat his words. He knew his employer well. Sir Arthur might bluster and shout, but there was a shrewd brain behind all that unnecessary noise.

Diana had enough sense to keep quiet, knowing enough about business men to realize there was no point complaining when a crisis blew up. And this was evidently a crisis, since Martinez had taken the trouble to come out from London to give his boss the bad news.

Sir Arthur blundered off into his study, letting the door bang to behind him. Martinez gave Diana a sleek, poisonous glance, and followed.

Anita, the faded blonde housekeeper, watched from the shadows. She didn't seem displeased that Sir Arthur's time with Diana had been interrupted.

Anita topped up Diana's cup of coffee. 'He won't be requiring you again tonight. Do you want to be on your way back to London now? You'd be in before midnight.'

Sir Arthur was speaking on the phone next door. No. Shouting into it.

Diana shrugged. You win some, you lose some. And she was on the winning side this time. 'I don't like driving this late at night. I'll be off first thing in the morning.'

Anita began to pile the dirty plates from supper on to a tray. 'Likely he'll work all night, now. I just hope he doesn't forget to collect his new dog tomorrow.'

Diana leaned back in her chair. She'd no intention of letting the housekeeper hustle her away. Not after all that had happened that day. She smiled.

All things come to those who wait . . . and are prepared to give fate a gentle push now and then. Great-Aunt Drusilla would have to eat crow. And so would her mother. She was looking forward to seeing her mother's face when she told her.

CHAPTER FOURTEEN

A good night's sleep is a blessing. Ellie woke at her usual time, stretched, opened one eye to check on the time. Just before the seven o'clock news. Good. She switched on the wireless, remembering to keep the sound low in case it wakened her guest.

Midge had been sitting on the windowsill, between the curtains and the glass. He stirred when she did, elongating himself to double his usual length, yawning with gaping pink jaws.

Sunday. That meant church and — of course! — doing the coffee. Nothing must stand in the way of her doing the coffee, or Jean would go bananas. Ellie must also visit Mrs Dawes. Before or after church? Probably it would be best after church, because she hadn't any sherry in the house to take to her old friend. Or much food, either.

How long was Felicity going to stay?

Ellie shrugged. Did it matter?

Yes, it did. Kate — always so clear-thinking — had said all along that the key to this whole mess was the killing of the dog. That was why she'd called Ellie in. Chris Talbot had had other ideas, of course He'd wanted Ellie to befriend Felicity and possibly to wean her away from her husband.

Everyone had their own agenda.

Roy wanted Sir Arthur off his back.

Sir Arthur wanted Roy to divvy up some money. Sir Arthur wanted to prove Chris Talbot had poisoned his dog. Sir Arthur wanted his own way in all things and wasn't too worried how he got results. Sir Arthur was a thoroughly nasty piece of work and no one would have shed a tear if he *had* fallen victim to the poisoned pizza. Ellie was normally the most charitable of persons, but in this case she felt — sincerely — that it would have saved everyone a lot of trouble if he had.

Not, of course, that one was supposed to think that way. Though one did.

Ellie sighed, half listened to the news, properly listened to the weather forecast — more wind, more showers — some of which might be heavy — and got washed and dressed. Nothing too fancy, because she'd be doing the coffee at church. One of her ivory blouses with a pretty neckline, over a dark blue skirt. With a navy blue gilet on top, in case the weather did turn nasty.

There was no sign of Felicity as Ellie made her way down the stairs, accompanied by Midge, who knew when breakfast was due. She fed Midge, checked the fridge and freezer. Oh dear. She'd hardly anything suitable to give a guest for breakfast. A stale heel of a loaf, only one egg, a dried-up bit of bacon that ought to have been thrown away a few days ago. No fresh orange juice, or ground coffee.

She glanced at the clock. If she hurried, she could whiz over to the supermarket, stock up on basics and be back before Felicity got out of bed.

She left her guest a note on the kitchen table, snatched up her purse and jacket, and let herself quietly out of the house.

The sky looked unpromising. She hadn't brought an umbrella. She must hurry, or she'd be caught in the rain. Luckily it wasn't far to the shopping parade. The supermarket was at the far end, of course. Nearly opposite Bill Weatherspoon's office. Bill was a solicitor and a family friend, who liked to invite Ellie out now and then. If Roy didn't take his mother into his confidence, Ellie would have to see that he consulted Bill. Soon.

There were plenty of people in the supermarket, which was always a surprise this early in the morning, and on a Sunday too. Eggs, milk, bread, bacon, orange juice, ground coffee . . . some chops for lunch . . . the broccoli didn't look too fresh, but there were some decent French beans. Potatoes? No, she'd enough at home. Mushrooms. Fruit. Newspaper. What else?

She dithered at the checkout and then remembered. Sherry for Mrs Dawes. Apologizing to the customer in the queue after her, she went back for some sherry, and nearly bumped into someone she thought she recognized, but couldn't for the life of her remember the name. Only when she was back at the checkout and paying for her purchases did she remember who it was. She turned round to apologize to Mrs Alexis for not having greeted her, but there was no sign of the woman. Oh. Just one of those missed opportunities.

A thought to make her giggle: was Mrs Alexis buying frozen pizza? It had rather looked like it. To poison someone with? No, no. Ellie slapped her wrist mentally. Ridiculous!

Laden with two shopping bags plus her basket, she considered calling a minicab to get her back home. She could walk it, but the bags were heavy, and she'd wear herself out. She'd call a minicab. No mobile. Where had she left it? Upstairs in her bedroom?

Bother. She used the phone box at the supermarket, and soon was being driven home again, worrying about where she'd left her mobile. She thought she'd taken it out of her pocket when she undressed last night, but if so, where had she put it?

Home again. Everything looked nice and peaceful . . . except for a sleek car parked on the opposite side of the road. Diana's.

Diana would have let herself into the house, of course. Would she have encountered Felicity, and if so, what would have happened? Had they ever met? Possibly not.

Ellie let herself into her house. 'Yoohoo! I'm back. Breakfast in ten minutes.'

Diana appeared in the doorway to the living room.

'What a lovely surprise!' said Ellie. Though it wasn't. Something told Ellie that this visit of Diana's was not going to be all sweetness and light. Diana was looking too smug for that.

'Who's your lady friend?' asked Diana, not moving to help her mother heave the shopping on to the kitchen table. 'I saw someone scuttle into the bathroom, but when I called out, she yelped and slammed the door on me. Anyone I know?'

'Probably not, dear. Lady Kingsley. Felicity. Her husband's away in the country, she was lonely and somehow she ended up in the spare room.'

Something had changed in the atmosphere of the room, though Ellie couldn't quite put her finger on it. Had Diana reacted to Felicity's name? Yes? But her face was deadpan.

'Ah. Ground coffee. I'll make it, shall I?' Diana could make excellent coffee, when she felt inclined. 'I dropped by to pick up Frank. Since you sent me an SOS about him, I assumed he must be here, but his room's empty.'

'Frank was very upset when you didn't collect him yesterday. He behaved so badly that Stewart and Maria asked me to look after him for the rest of the day. Which I did. Then Stewart collected him again in the evening. This chopping and changing is bad for him, and he acts out.'

'Poor little mite. I'll make it up to him next weekend. Take him to Disney in Paris, or something.'

'It isn't treats that he wants, it's consistent parenting.'

'Are you criticizing me, mother? You, of all people!'

Ellie felt herself go pink. 'I did my best. You know very well that I had to work to help with the mortgage. I worked short hours so that I could always be at the school gates to collect you.' Ellie drew in her breath. Diana had been a demanding and difficult child, but she could hardly say that. Or could she? No, probably not.

She said, 'This sort of slanging match gets us nowhere. It's little Frank we're talking about now, not you.'

Diana spooned coffee into the cafetière, while Ellie laid the table for three. Fresh orange juice. Get the frying pan out. Eggs, bacon and mushrooms ready for an omelette or a fry-up, whichever was required. Bread sliced for toast. No cereal. She'd forgotten to get any. Well, tough.

'It's because of Frank that I've been working so hard,' said Diana. 'You of all people should understand that I sometimes have to sacrifice the amount of time I spend with him, to make sure he gets a decent standard of living.'

Ellie eyed her daughter with apprehension. The girl was positively glowing with inner amusement. What had she been up to now?

Diana poured on boiling water from the kettle, and settled the lid on the cafetière. Smiling. Not nicely. 'I'm a very lucky girl. I found someone who wants something I possess, and he's prepared to pay me handsomely for it.'

Ellie thought, Your body? No, you give that away. You don't sell it, judging by recent history.

Diana depressed the plunger. 'Under my father's will, you get to live in this house for life. After your death, the house becomes mine.'

'Not quite,' said Ellie, unsure where this was leading. 'The house was in joint ownership; mine and your father's, so he couldn't dispose of my half. I have the house for life, and on my death, you get the half which he owned outright. I can leave my half to whoever I like. I might leave it to the Cats Protection League. Or Children in Need. Or Oxfam.'

'Nonsense,' said Diana. 'You'll leave your half to me, which means that after your death, I'll own the whole house. I've just sold my interest in it to a developer, which will give me enough cash to live on till I've got rid of the rest of the flats I've been renovating.'

Ellie sat down with a bump. She stared at the boiler, not seeing it. Diana had sold the house over her mother's head? Well, not precisely over her head, but looking forward to the day when her mother would be dead? And taking not a blind bit of notice of the fact that she might not inherit all of it? It was . . . gruesome. Hurtful.

It tipped up the balance of what Ellie had always considered to be stable in her life.

Of course she oughtn't to be worried about what might happen to her house after she died. She knew in her head that other people would live there afterwards. They probably wouldn't like the way she'd decorated the house. They might neglect the garden, her lovely garden.

She closed her eyes. Clenched her fists.

She told herself she was being unreasonable, but it hurt to think of her house and garden being torn apart by someone who didn't give a damn about what a happy home it had been for so many years.

Something else was worrying her. 'A developer, you said?'

'Yes, he's long wanted to get hold of a couple of houses in this road, tear them down, build flats. The outlook on to the church should be worth a few bob.'

'Two houses? You mean, he's after Kate and Armand's as well? But they won't want to move.'

Diana shrugged. 'He's a pretty determined customer. I expect he'll make them a fair offer at first, and if they don't play ball, then . . . well, as I said, he's a determined customer.'

Ellie gazed at the opposite wall. Frank had put up those wall units. He hadn't done it very well, and they'd always meant to have the kitchen refitted, some time. The kitchen wasn't very up to date. Anybody buying this house would want the kitchen replaced.

But it wasn't going to be replaced. It was going to be torn down. The garden wiped out. Her pretty conservatory . . . gone. Her goldfish in their lead tank. Midge!

Midge had gone out through the cat flap as soon as he heard Diana come in. Midge and Diana had never got on. Midge might live to be twenty. Might even outlive her.

Ellie grabbed at something, some hint, in Diana's announcement which could do with elucidation. 'This man. This developer. Who . . . ?'

Diana poured herself out a cup of coffee, black. 'Sir Arthur Kingsley, of course.'

Felicity appeared in the doorway, looking wan. 'You're talking about my husband?'

'Are you Felicity? I've heard a lot about you.' Diana looked Felicity up and down and laughed.

Ellie was shocked. Felicity recoiled. Both women understood in that moment that Diana was the latest woman in Sir Arthur's life. Diana and Sir Arthur? That would be a powerful combination, indeed.

Ellie couldn't think of anything to say which would be helpful. She'd been schooled to ignore her own problems and to look after guests, so now she did her best to appear normal. 'Felicity, this is my daughter, Diana, who's dropped in unexpectedly. What would you like for breakfast?'

'Just tea, thank you.' In a whisper.

Really, thought Ellie, the girl might make an effort. Ellie could understand how Felicity's whipped-dog attitude might encourage a bully to put the boot in. She herself wouldn't mind shaking the girl, who looked washed-out and drab in her unbecoming black garb, as compared to Diana, who was all sleek grooming and expensive clothes.

'Well, I'm having the lot,' said Ellie, determinedly breaking eggs into her pan. 'An omelette, toast, everything.'

'Don't overdo it, mother,' said Diana, draining her cup. 'That skirt of yours is tight enough as it is.'

Ellie considered hurling the contents of the pan at Diana's face but resisted, though her breath came fast, and her wrists shook with the effort she made not to raise the pan from the stove. 'Get out of here, Diana, before I lose my temper. I want a sight of whatever agreement you've made with that man. I wouldn't put it past you to falsify your expectations, and if he found out that you'd double-crossed him, well . . .'

Diana laughed again, but this time there was a note of unease in her laughter. 'You wouldn't do that, mother dear. I know you. You'd never be so unkind to your darling daughter. Well, I must be on my way. Arthur's got some emergency meetings up in the City first, and when he's dealt with them, he's collecting me from the flat. Nice meeting you, Felicity. He told me what you were like, and I didn't believe him. Silly me.'

Felicity reddened. She was not up to fighting back. Perhaps wisely.

Diana picked up her expensive black leather handbag, checked that her lipstick was not smudged, and twitched a red and grey scarf into place around her neck. 'See you later, mother. Kiss, kiss.'

She left the house, leaving Ellie staring at the wall and not seeing it. Leaving Felicity staring at the table, and not seeing that either.

'Gracious me,' said Ellie, rescuing her overcooked eggs. 'I need some solid sustenance for the day ahead. How about you, Felicity? Did you say you wanted tea?'

Felicity burst into tears. Ellie told herself she didn't give a toss, and tipped her omelette out on to her plate. She put the plate on the table, poured herself out a coffee, added milk and sugar, and then abandoned both to put an arm around the weeping girl.

'There, there. It's nothing new, is it? I mean, he's had women before, hasn't he? I don't suppose Diana will be the last.'

'You don't understand. He was so pleased with me for warning him about the meetings that were going on behind his back that he was going to bring me back some flowers tonight, and he's picking up a new dog tomorrow. He knew that would please me. I went to bed feeling so happy for a change.'

Ellie forked some omelette into her mouth, dropped her fork to pour herself some coffee. She patted Felicity on her back. Wondered where her box of tissues had gone.

'I got used to his playing around with Anita down at the manor, but she's quite old, and he said he'd never divorce me for her. There were other "pretty little chicks" — that's what he used to call them — but they were all terribly young with not much in the way of brains, and quite useless about the house, so he always went back to Anita because she kept the manor looking so nice. But Diana . . . !'

Yes, Ellie could see that Diana was different. Diana didn't give a toss about keeping a house clean. She was an ambitious career woman, handsome rather than beautiful, but fashionably dressed and accustomed to move in society of a certain type. Her morals were dodgy, she had an iron will, and hardly any conscience.

Plus she seemed to be good in bed. Or so she said. Ellie had no reason to doubt it.

Yes, Diana would be a suitable consort for a powerful man like Sir Arthur. Ellie could well imagine he'd discard Felicity for Diana. Diana would enjoy being Lady Kingsley. Oh yes. Wouldn't she just!

'No, no.' Ellie shook her head. 'He wouldn't marry her. She's not got enough to offer.' Except this house, and a way of getting at Kate and Armand's house, too. If he knocked down this house, say . . . and did it carelessly, so that the party wall was breached . . . or somehow dumped building material in their garden, by mistake . . . or worse still, threatened baby Catriona.

It didn't bear thinking about. There were building regulations against his damaging someone else's property, of course, and planning permissions would be needed. But he'd got round such things before, hadn't he?

Well, that was one thing Ellie could do — if she lived through this. She could go to her MP and lobby councillors, dear Mr Patel for a start, and contact the local press and make sure that Sir Arthur didn't have it all his own way in local affairs in future.

She squeezed Felicity's shoulder. 'Come on. You've got to keep your strength up. Do you fancy a boiled egg, perhaps?'

Felicity put her head down on the table and wailed.

Ellie stifled impatience. She forked up another mouthful of omelette and took a gulp of coffee.

She tried to reassure Felicity. 'Your husband would never discard you. You know that. You're necessary to him.

You keep his home immaculate, and while married to you, he has the perfect weapon to hold your father in check.'

Felicity wailed again. 'Oh, how could you!'

Ellie spotted the box of tissues, which was on the floor. Midge must have dislodged it from the top of the boiler, where it was usually kept. She dived for the box and dumped it in front of Felicity. Then paused in the act of lowering herself back on to her chair.

Shock.

No, it couldn't be.

Or, could it?

Felicity struggled to lift her head from the table, and reached for the tissues.

Ellie said, more to herself than to the girl, 'Diana's just signed my death warrant.'

'What?' Felicity went on weeping.

Ellie repeated the words, more loudly. 'Diana's signed over her interest in this house to your husband for redevelopment. She inherits half on my death.'

Felicity snorted into her tissue. Took another. Stopped crying. 'So . . . ?'

Ellie looked around her. The old, familiar, slightly shabby kitchen. 'I haven't made a will, so Diana — as my nearest relative — gets this house on my death. How long do you think I've got?'

'Well . . . I suppose you're not that old really,' said Felicity, reaching for another tissue and blowing her nose thoroughly. 'Some people live till they're seventy. Or even older. Mummy's just fifty, though you wouldn't think it. Some days she can still look thirty. As young as me.'

Ellie nodded. 'How many years would you give a woman who stood in the way of your husband making a fortune?'

Felicity froze. Shook her head. 'You don't mean what I think you mean. He wouldn't ever . . . I mean, no!'

'A week?' said Ellie. 'What if he arranges for me to be run over — as he did your half-brother? A couple of days?'

How soon could she arrange with Bill to make a will? How soon could she get a copy to Sir Arthur? Today was Sunday. How could she ensure her safety till she could get to see Bill?

Silence. Felicity sniffed. 'You're being ridiculous.' Faintly.

'Am I?' said Ellie, draining her coffee cup. 'Let's look on the bright side. Maybe he'll be a bit more careful now the police are investigating Julian's "accident". He'll wait till things have settled down again. I assume Martinez has provided himself with a good alibi. Marco too.'

Felicity was silent.

Ellie stacked dishes in the sink. 'I have to go off to church in a minute. I suppose I'll be safer there than staying here. Felicity, will you do me a favour? Ring your husband on your mobile. Tell him that you've seen Diana, and heard all about her plan to sell him my house. Tell him that Diana has misled him because she only gets half the house at my death.'

'Half the house . . .' The girl was trying to understand, but not succeeding too well.

Ellie considered going through it in words of one syllable, but decided life was too short. 'Get through to him, then hand the phone over to me. I'll tell him myself.'

Felicity produced her mobile. Sniffed twice. Punched a number. Waited.

Ellie switched on the kettle to make Felicity a cup of tea. She was thinking. She had Bill's home number. She could ring him before she went off to church. Perhaps he could inform Sir Arthur that Diana had misled him about the house.

Felicity put on a bright, false tone. 'Arthur, is that you?'

Of course it was, thought Ellie. Silly girl.

'Arthur, I'm sorry to ring you when I know you must be terribly busy . . .'

'Yes, I am.' Sir Arthur's forceful personality entered the room with his voice. He was not pleased at being interrupted. 'What is it?'

'Something you ought to know. Diana's played a nasty trick on you . . . Are you there?' So far, so good. The girl was holding together better than Ellie had expected.

Silence at the other end. Voices were heard, arguing, in the background.

Ellie reached for the phone, but Felicity eluded her. 'Diana's cheated you!'

'Nonsense! I know why you're doing this, Felicity, and it won't do you any good, do you hear? Don't expect me back tonight, either. I have other plans.'

The phone clicked off.

Felicity was trembling, ashen-faced.

Ellie poured hot water on a tea-bag in a mug, and put it on the table in front of Felicity. Subduing an impulse to tell the girl she'd have done better to have handed the phone over to her, Ellie patted her on her shoulder. 'Well, you tried.'

Felicity whispered, 'He always comes back to me on Sunday nights, no matter who he takes down to the manor. Always. I get back from visiting Mummy and he gets back from the manor and that's our special time together. He thinks I'm jealous of Diana, and of course I am, but . . . I've just realized, if I'm no longer important to him, then . . . I'm at risk too. He insured my life for a million.'

CHAPTER FIFTEEN

Ellie looked at Felicity with horror. A million to insure her life? Felicity explained. 'We made wills in each other's favour and took out insurance as soon as we got married. Arthur said he was often travelling and if there was an accident, I'd have something to fall back on. He said I was worth a million pounds to him. He was being nice to me then.'

Ellie closed her eyes for a second. Was the girl really so naive? Well, yes; she was.

'What am I going to do?' said Felicity, looking to Ellie for help.

Ellie didn't feel like helping. She felt like throwing Felicity out of the house, banging the door shut behind her, and phoning Bill Weatherspoon for help. *Come quickly, Bill! My life is in danger. Please tell the nasty man to run away and play.*

She braced herself. Tears wouldn't help. Yelling and screaming at Felicity wouldn't help, either. She glanced at the clock.

'First things first. I have to be at church to sing in the choir in twenty minutes. I'll be safe there. You'd better come with me, unless you know of a better place to go?'

Felicity was calming down. She was still pale, but the threat of personal danger seemed to have steadied her. 'I used my mobile to ring him, but he'll probably think I'm at home. I don't want to go back there, especially now, especially if . . . he might try to . . . oh, this is just a nasty dream, isn't it? He wouldn't really . . . would he? But I must admit, I don't want to go back there by myself. Also, if Marco's recovering from an all-night drinking session, he can be very rude to me.

'I'd feel safer if I came with you. Mummy always used to take me to the little village church beside the manor. I used to like that. Mummy used to say she preferred "bells and smells" in church, but I like it plain.'

Everything for Felicity and her mother went back to nostalgia for the manor. Ellie was inclined to be impatient until she remembered what a shock it had been for her to realize her own home might soon be demolished. Not that she'd know anything about it, if she were dead.

Though possibly — if her present attempts to help other people were to count against her sins — she might end up on a fluffy cloud, playing a harp, and looking down with a smile on future occupants of the flats which were to replace her home. That is, if you thought of heaven that way, which on the whole Ellie didn't. She'd never been that musical, even if she had been dragooned into singing in the choir.

'I think that's sensible,' she said. 'I see it's started to rain. Drink your tea, wash your face, brush your hair and I'll see if I can find something warm for you to wear. The weather's turning nasty and they've only just turned the heating on in church. Meanwhile I've a couple of phone calls to make.'

Ellie tried Diana's landline and her mobile. She wasn't answering either. On both lines Ellie left a message to the effect that she'd warned Sir Arthur that Diana had misled him about inheriting the whole house. Maybe that would prevent his acting straight away. Maybe not.

She rang Bill Weatherspoon at home. He was out too. Bother. She left a message asking him to ring her, urgently.

What else could she do to protect herself?

She glanced at her watch. She could hear Felicity splashing about in the bathroom. She must leave the house within the next five minutes, or she'd be late. Sometimes, if she were late, Mrs Dawes would get Ellie's music ready for her. But Mrs Dawes was laid up with her bad knee, and Jean would be checking her watch every few seconds, waiting for Ellie to appear.

She rang Chris Talbot's number. He answered, cool and precise as ever.

'Mrs Quicke?'

'Yes. Problems. Sir Arthur's gone into the City to try to stop—'

'I know. He won't succeed.'

'There's another player entered the game. My daughter, Diana. She's threatening Felicity's position vis à vis Sir Arthur. Diana's also sold her half-interest in my house to Sir Arthur, who wants it for redevelopment. He insured Felicity's life for a million. We're both more than slightly worried.'

Silence. 'I see. Where are you?'

'At home. Felicity is with me. We're both due at church in a minute.'

'And after?'

'I don't know. I have to visit an old friend, and possibly my aunt, also. I'll have to think.'

'Ring me when you leave church.'

* * *

As Ellie and Felicity left the house, they heard someone call after them.

'Yoohoo!' It was Kate from next door, with baby Catriona asleep in her pram. 'I gather there's ructions going on up in the City, but my money's on Gwyn. Are you off to church? I thought I'd come too. Armand needs space to do his marking.'

'Fine,' said Ellie. 'Can you take Felicity in for me and look after her?'

Somewhat breathlessly, Ellie dashed round the church to enter the vestry just as Tum-Tum — Thomas — was beginning to marshal his troops.

'Sorry, sorry,' said Ellie, struggling into her robes, and looking wildly around for the music she needed. No Mrs Dawes, of course.

Nice Maggie — who'd been working in the kitchens with her yesterday — helped her. 'Thanks,' whispered Ellie, as they fell into line and Thomas led the way out into the church. The organist was playing something rousing. For a moment Ellie couldn't think what it was. Then she got it, and had to stifle a laugh.

'Onward, Christian soldiers' was a bit dated, perhaps, but it struck a chord in Ellie today. She certainly felt like a soldier under fire.

The first hymn . . . the confession . . . the children's talk . . . the second hymn. Where was Felicity? Ellie had found her a jacket in a soft coral to wear and it should be possible to pick that out. Yes, over by the pillar. No one could get at her there, wedged in by Kate, who'd kept the pram by her side. Catriona seemed to be fast asleep. Good. It could be awkward, having a baby wake up in the service. Some people objected strongly to hearing babies cry for attention, though Tum-Tum — Thomas — never seemed to mind.

Whatever were they going to do after the service? Felicity had used her mobile, so Sir Arthur wouldn't know where she might be, but he knew where Ellie lived all right.

Ellie's eye, roaming over the congregation, located Roy sitting at the back of the church. Gossip had it that he'd soon be asked to consider becoming a sidesman. He'd do the meeting and greeting bit well. Beside him — wonder of wonders — was Aunt Drusilla, with Rose. Well, Rose did often come, of course. But Aunt Drusilla? Not in living memory. Well, not in Ellie's memory, anyway.

Why was Aunt Drusilla there? She had her own morality, but was she a Christian? She'd been brought up to consider the state of her soul a private matter. She'd suffered minor ailments all her life: teeth, feet. But nothing really serious until her hip had started to play up. Ellie wasn't sure how long her aunt's hip had been giving her trouble. She'd carried a stick about with her for years, but recently she'd actually been leaning on it. And in considerable pain. Perhaps this hip trouble had reminded her that earthly bodies do wear out, and that she ought to think about making her peace with God. Perhaps.

Thomas didn't preach long sermons from the pulpit. He wasn't that sort. He stood at the top of the steps down into the chancel, and treated the congregation to something multilayered. His sermons were light on top with a joke somewhere inside. The middle had something thoughtful in it. And the bottom layer was good, solid comment.

So what would he have to say today?

'Friends . . . a good result yesterday, don't you think? For Brentford Football Club, I mean. Not the Autumn Fair.'

Everyone relaxed, most laughed or smiled. Brentford Football Club indeed! Most people had never even heard of it, even though it had many enthusiastic supporters in the borough.

'A local Derby, of course,' said Thomas. 'I was amazed that so many of you turned up to do your bit for the church, instead of enjoying yourselves on the terraces, shouting till you got laryngitis, sitting outside in a cold wind, missing your tea . . . well, perhaps not missing your teas. I gather the fish-and-chip shop in the Avenue did well last night—'

More low laughter. The fish and chip shop in the Avenue was always under siege at weekends.

'—whereas we poor souls had nothing much to shout about. Or perhaps we did, come to think of it. Instead of bellowing for Brentford, we turned out to work for the good of others. We sorted and priced books and bric-a-brac. We toasted and turned the food on the barbecue. We pulled the handle on the urn — instead of pulling pints. We served food all day, we cleaned up after mucky eaters, and washed and dried cups on a production line. We sold tickets for games, and supervised the children in the play area. We worked our socks off — for our own home team. Not Brentford, but the church.

‘It was hard work, wasn’t it? Backs ached, feet swelled up, tempers frayed all over the place. It didn’t actually rain yesterday, though the clouds may have kept some people away. Somehow, the work got done. Even the clearing-up got done, eventually.

‘There were casualties, of course. The most important was that Mrs Dawes fell over and hurt her bad knee, trying to collapse one of our awkward metal tables. I worry a bit that this elderly lady felt she ought to tackle a job which should have been done by someone younger and fitter.’

Ellie was amused. If Mrs Dawes heard that Thomas had called her ‘elderly’ in front of the whole congregation, she’d be livid!

‘Also,’ said Thomas, with a change of pace, ‘they tell me that there were five cups broken, two plates have gone missing, and the urn is leaking again! Talk about stress! No—’ he held up his hand to quell amusement — ‘I am not joking now. These occasions can be very stressful, and stress takes its toll just as much as laryngitis or a chill on the kidneys. The result of all that effort was an unexpectedly high sum to add to our rebuilding fund. It’s not going to be enough to rebuild the vicarage, of course. For that, we need to take someone else into partnership.

‘But we must choose our partner wisely. I think all of us here know how important that is. We have had an offer of partnership recently which proved to be from a man who thought less of the glory of God and the good of this parish, than of his bank balance. I didn’t think that we should accept such a partner. Your reaction to the offer showed that you don’t either. The fact that you turned out in such numbers yesterday, to work without pay or even commendation, shows that you all know what’s important in your lives.’

He held up both hands in the surrender position. ‘And before anyone starts taking pot shots at me, I know Brentford is important in our lives, too.’

Everyone smiled. Everyone was intent on his words.

‘You might say it was peer pressure that brought you all out to help. If one of your friends had offered to help with the candyfloss, then you didn't want to be left out, so you offered to do a stint face-painting. Perhaps you came to make some money; you'd made some colourful scarves, and you didn't mind paying to rent a table in the hall, if you could cover your costs and make a bit on the side. There's all sorts of reasons why people come to help, but the one I like best is the one that flourishes in this particular church — and that is what I call the servant syndrome. Jesus called himself the Servant, didn't he? If He'd been around yesterday, would he have been sitting around in an armchair, smiling benignly at everyone working their socks off for him?

'I don't think so. I think he'd have taken an apron and helped out washing floors and feet, and humped chairs and tables when it was all over.

'There are a lot of you servants about. Would you be justified in calling yourselves minor saints? Perhaps you would. You work without pay, or thought for your own comfort. Sometimes you overestimate your strength and it knocks you up. You never expect praise or thanks. It's . . . remarkable.'

Everyone was very quiet. One or two people glanced sideways at their neighbours. Some people looked uncomfortable, and shifted in their seats. Perhaps they hadn't pulled their weight? One or two looked wooden-faced, pretending they didn't know what Thomas was driving at. Possibly they hadn't helped at all, but now wished they had.

'People make choices all the time. Some people yesterday could have gone to watch the match at Brentford. They could have gone to the cinema, taken the car out into the country for the day, mucked around doing nothing much, watched a video, partied with friends. But they didn't. They chose to come here to work for the good of the parish, for the good of St Thomas' Church. And I, for one, am very grateful that they did.

'Now don't get me wrong. All was not sweetness and light. Sometimes we make choices which are not always appreciated by others. For instance, if the person who'd agreed to take the money on the door had skived off to see the Brentford match at the last minute, he'd have been decidedly unpopular hereabouts, wouldn't he? But suppose he'd had a phone call at the last minute asking him to replace the referee for the match, who'd been injured in a car crash? And he'd tried to get a substitute? Wouldn't that be a reasonable excuse for going missing? We can't judge till we know everything . . . and let's face it, we're not omnipotent.'

Ellie thought, Is he talking about me, ducking out from helping in the kitchen? Where's Jean? Does she realize what he's saying?

Thomas said, 'Jesus said the greatest commandment was that we should Love One Another. Many of you proved that you did yesterday. You came, you worked, you achieved. Some of you went home in a glow of satisfaction, and that glow of satisfaction, that knowledge that you had worked for the good of the parish, was part of your reward.

'Some of you had difficult choices to make as the day went on, and not all those choices will have been clearly understood by others. I don't know why the end of the book stall fell off its trestle table and precipitated a hundred books on to the grass.

'I've heard that someone placed the trestle — without noticing it — so that it dropped off the path into a patch of soft earth. Perhaps they were overtaxing their strength, in putting the table up, and therefore we must not cry "Shame!" on them, but cry "Shame!" on those who should have helped but didn't. If Jesus had been here, we could have called on his carpentry skills to make sure the table didn't collapse. He wasn't here in person, but two young people rushed forward to sort out the mess. Wasn't Jesus using their hands?

'Yes, he often uses our hands, our feet, our tongues. I don't know how long it will be before he sends us another partner for our rebuilding programme, but I do know that we have to be very sure what we are doing when he does. We need a partner who understands our problems and helps us discover the best possible solution to them — from our point of view as well as from his.

'Remember, we don't only need a partnership for the rebuilding. We need a partner — a role model — someone to guide us through life. Who will you choose? A man whose sights are set on money? Or one who will help you make the right choices in life, one who has your best interests at heart, someone who will bring out the best in you?

'Who will you, personally, choose to guide you in the days, weeks, and years to come?'

There was a long silence. Thomas held it for a count of ten, then announced the next hymn.

* * *

At the end of the service, Ellie threw off her robe and ran round the outside of the church to the hall. It was bad enough that she hadn't got to church before the service, in order to lay out cups and saucers and fill the urn with water, but to be dawdling after the service as well . . . ! Jean would skin her alive!

Dragging on an apron, Ellie avoided Jean's wrathful eye, and concentrated on serving tea and coffee. Also biscuits; someone had very kindly donated a box of biscuits. A real treat. There was a certain satisfaction to be had in mindless occupations such as doling out drinks and, even, in washing up. Being busy occupied the front of your mind and held back panic.

Don't think about what you're going to do when you finish here. Concentrate on giving Mrs Thing her weak tea with one drop — only one drop, please — of milk in it.

Baby Catriona had woken up, and was now being dandled on someone's knee while Kate talked to Aunt Drusilla. Felicity had cornered Roy, and was talking at him, hankie in hand, dabbing at her eyes, no doubt pouring out the whole sorry story about Diana. Hoping, no doubt, that he'd throw out his chest and say, Leave it all to me!

Roy looked harried. Having a nice-looking female hang on his sleeve was one thing, but being presented with an Orphan of the Storm was quite another. He could barely cope with looking after his own interests, never mind taking on someone else's.

Jean nudged Ellie back to attending to her work. 'Will you collect the dirty cups, or do I have to do everything?'

'I'll do it.' Ellie seized a tray and started to work through the room. Several people enquired after Mrs Dawes and Ellie said she'd be seeing her that afternoon.

Though whether it would be wise to walk there on her own, she didn't know.

Kate waved goodbye, Catriona safely tucked back into her pram.

Thomas appeared at her elbow. 'Everything all right, Ellie?'

'Not really, no.' Thomas had broad shoulders and wasn't going to faint if she asked him for help. Unlike Roy, who was looking around for help. Or her.

Thomas said, 'Police trouble?'

'Diana trouble. Sir Arthur trouble. I need to make a will. Fast. This morning. Do you know how to do it?'

'Sure. Every now and then I get asked to help a parishioner make a will, and I have a form somewhere. Come to my study when you've cleared up here. Now, what are you doing about Felicity? I was glad to see her in church, but . . .'

'She came because I came. She's frightened her husband might want to dispose of her.'

Thomas's eyebrows peaked. 'Dispose of her? As in divorce?'

'I don't think divorce would be his chosen method of disposal. Too expensive, if she could claim half his wealth.'

'Ah. Does she want to make a will too?'

Ellie hesitated. 'I'll ask her. She may not have anything to leave, but . . . let me think about that.'

'Bring her too.'

'Ellie!' Jean was not having her helpers avoid their duties. Especially if they were monopolizing the vicar.

'Coming!' said Ellie. She made a beeline for Aunt Drusilla. Most people had already left, or were leaving for their Sunday lunch. Aunt Drusilla sat on, hooded eyes on Roy, whom Felicity had managed to pin into a corner. Aunt Drusilla was weighing up the chances of Roy's getting tangled with Felicity. Ellie could almost hear her aunt's thoughts: *Good hips for child-bearing and would scrub up nicely, but a silly, weakly sort of creature. Not a good match for my son.*

Rose was standing beside Aunt Drusilla, holding her stick. Rose was also looking at Roy and Felicity. Rose would be thinking in terms of her beloved gardening, *Men quickly tire of clinging women. She looks as if the first frost would kill her. Definitely not a hardy perennial.*

'Aunt Drusilla,' said Ellie. 'I've got to make a will, quickly. Thomas will help me. If I can get it written out within the next quarter of an hour, will you and Rose witness it?'

'So long as we're not beneficiaries.'

'Bother,' said Ellie. 'I'd like to leave something to Rose. I'll ask Roy, then, shall I?'

Rose went pink. 'Ellie, dear! I wouldn't wish to . . . I don't expect . . .'

'Why the haste?' enquired Aunt Drusilla, cutting to the chase as usual. 'You're not ill, so far as I know. If you can wait till tomorrow, I'll get my own solicitor to—'

'No, it has to be today. I'll explain in a minute. Thomas has said we can use his study for a few minutes, but I've got to finish clearing up first.'

'Ellie!' Jean was looking thunderous.

'Coming,' said Ellie. 'Aunt Drusilla, could you ask Roy if he'd stay to be a witness? Oh, and I suppose Felicity too? She won't have anywhere else to go.'

Aunt Drusilla directed her eyes towards the pair, and nodded. Ellie darted back to her duties, confident that the required witnesses would be on hand when she had finished putting everything away and swept the floor. She wasn't terribly surprised when Rose came to help her, even though she was wearing her best suit and a really good pair of shoes. Rose loved good shoes.

'Thank you, dear Rose,' said Ellie.

Rose — the meekest of people — replied that she was surprised at Ellie allowing Jean to push her around.

'I've done enough pushing around this week,' said Ellie, thinking of how this had all gone back to her getting cross with Marco. 'It's got me into a lot of trouble.'

* * *

Ellie had imagined that she could just scribble her will down in a few lines on a piece of paper and be done with it, but it didn't work out like that. For one thing, she had an audience of Thomas, Aunt Drusilla and Rose, plus Roy and Felicity.

Felicity was still talking non-stop. '. . . and then I realized that if he's going to take that woman into his bed, he won't want me hanging around any longer and . . .'

By this time Roy was trying to disengage himself from her. Aunt Drusilla took pity on him.

'Felicity, come and sit here by me. Now, what's all this about your husband wanting to kill you for the insurance?'

CHAPTER SIXTEEN

Thomas had unearthed a will form from his desk. 'Ellie, I suggest you draft it out first on some scrap paper, and then write it up on the actual form.'

'I repeat,' said Aunt Drusilla, 'why the haste?'

Ellie seated herself at Thomas's desk and reached for some scrap paper. 'Diana has sold her interest in my house to Sir Arthur, who apparently wants to tear it down — and next door, too — and build a block of flats. Backing on to the Green, the site would be worth a mint.'

Miss Quicke nodded. 'Why do you think that puts you in danger?'

Ellie tried to do two things at once, to explain why, and to draft her will. She didn't think she did either very well, but with Felicity filling in some details, Miss Quicke seemed satisfied. 'Very well. You'll leave your half of the house to . . . ?'

'Kate,' said Ellie. 'Because she's been better than a daughter to me, and I'm extremely fond of her. If I leave her my share of the house, she'll be in a better position to see Sir Arthur off. I'm not leaving anything to Diana, or little Frank.'

'Sensible,' nodded Miss Quicke. 'What about the house I live in, including Roy's converted garage? They belong to you, remember.'

Ellie stared at her. 'I hadn't thought. There's all the money my husband left me, as well, and the trust fund which I set up to benefit good causes.'

Miss Quicke nodded. 'The trust fund is safe; the trustees will simply need to appoint someone else in your place when you die. The rest of your money you'd better leave to the trust itself to carry on the good works.'

'With some for Rose, of course. And your big house . . . to you, dear Aunt.'

'Not to me?' Roy, trying to smile.

His mother tapped his arm. 'No, dear boy. Not after you've allowed Sir Arthur to tie you into knots. I haven't got to the bottom of that affair yet, but I will. And don't interrupt; people like him eat people like you for breakfast. I myself will make a new will tomorrow. I'll put everything in trust for you, Roy — apart from one or two legacies, one to Rose in particular.'

'Mother,' protested Roy. But subsided. Rose went pink, but said nothing.

Felicity put up her hand to speak, just like a small child in class. 'Do you think I should make a will too? I've got one or two pieces of jewellery that my grandmother left me, and the car, of course. Not much else, I'm afraid.'

'Of course,' said Roy, chewing his thumbnail. 'Everyone should make a will, really. I suppose I ought to as well. If I ever get free of Sir Arthur.'

Thomas put his hand over the will form, so that Ellie couldn't write. 'May I make a suggestion? If you name Kate as your heir, won't it put her in danger too? And your aunt? Especially if Diana thinks she's going to inherit something from her.'

'She isn't,' said Miss Quicke. 'But you've got a point.' She applied her mind to the problem. 'I suggest Ellie leaves her whole estate to the trust fund. Even Sir Arthur can't arrange fatal accidents for an entire board of trustees. When the man's been neutralized, Ellie can make another will.'

Everyone nodded.

Ellie began to copy out what they'd decided. Her hand wanted to tremble, but she wouldn't allow it to do so. She'd get cramp, holding the pen so tightly. 'I need to get a copy to Sir Arthur this afternoon. And Diana.'

'Be my guest,' said Thomas, taking the cover off a photocopier in the corner. 'Fax machine here, too. Where is he likely to be this afternoon? In the country? At home in London? At his office? We could fax him to all those places. Where can we find the numbers?'

Felicity put up her hand again. 'I'm good at remembering numbers. I never need to keep an address book. I can operate a fax machine. I used to do it all the time when I was working.'

'Amazing,' said Miss Quicke, speaking for all of them.

Ellie read over what she'd written. 'Roy, will you and Thomas witness my signature?' She signed, and they witnessed her signature.

Ellie handed the will form over to Felicity. 'The sooner he accepts he's been misled by Diana, the better. Then, perhaps, we'll all have some peace.'

'Unless,' said Felicity, going pink, 'he's already sent someone out to kill us. Before he found out that Diana's cheated him, I mean.'

Silence.

Thomas gave a great sigh. 'I'm afraid she's right. Until we can get him to acknowledge he's been sold a pup, we ought to take some elementary precautions. 'I'd better chaperone Ellie around this afternoon.'

Felicity was wringing her hands. 'Oh dear, and me, too? I just dread what he's going to say! I mean, he relies on me to look after the house, so what will he say when he finds out that I didn't go home last night? And I have to pop in to see Mummy this afternoon, or she'll get into a state. She gets in a terrible fret when I miss a day, and sometimes when I go she says I haven't been for ages, though I was there only the day before.'

The girl's muddled thinking seemed to bemuse Roy. 'I'll take you round to see her. You'll be safe with me.' Though he didn't sound too convinced of that. Neither did anyone else.

'It would be best if we stuck together,' said Thomas. 'Felicity can come with us to see Mrs Dawes, and then we'll all go to visit your mother. After that, we'll see.'

Felicity was handling the photocopier as to the manner born, which surprised Ellie, who'd written the girl off as inefficiency itself. Perhaps, if Felicity ever got clear of Sir Arthur, she might one day be able to hold down an office job somewhere.

Meanwhile, Ellie looked for Chris Talbot's card, on which he'd written his mobile number. She hadn't found her own mobile yet, so she asked Thomas if she could use his landline. As Felicity was using the fax machine, he handed her his mobile instead. Ellie punched in the numbers.

'Yes, Mrs Quicke?' He sounded strained, not quite at ease.

'You asked me to keep in touch. I'm faxing a copy of a new will I've made to Sir Arthur, and once he's read it, I imagine I'll be safe. Do you know how negotiations in the City are going?'

'As well as can be expected.'

'Is anything the matter?' Cautiously.

'My son, Julian. He's taken a turn for the worse. It's more than just concussion. They're operating now.'

Ellie was shocked. 'I'll pray for him.'

'Thank you. And Felicity? Have you managed to see her?'

'Here with me. We're going to see her mother later on. We'll be well protected.'

'Ah. Thank you. I must go. Tell Felicity . . . no, I can't do this now. I'll speak to you again later.'

Ellie handed Thomas back his phone, and repeated what Chris Talbot had said to the others. Everyone looked thoughtful, and Roy said it didn't sound too good, did it? Especially needing to operate on a Sunday.

Thomas said, 'Ellie offered to pray for him. I suggest that we all take a minute to think about him, in silence. And his family. And ask God to look after him.'

The fax machine bleeped and everyone jumped. But then they all did as Thomas had suggested. Even — Ellie peeked with one eye — Miss Quicke seemed to be following Thomas's lead.

'Right,' said Thomas, when they all began to stir. 'Let's see how we can organize this. I have to be back at six, ready for evensong. Suppose Roy takes his mother and Rose back to their house, while I chauffeur Ellie and Felicity around.'

Rose put up her hand. Felicity's influence was beginning to spread. 'Suppose I make supper for everyone at about half past seven at our place?'

'Bless you, my dear,' said Thomas. 'But there are rather too many of us. No, we couldn't possibly impose.'

Miss Quicke cut him short. She was the only person Ellie knew who could cut Thomas short, but she did it. 'Nonsense. Rose is one of those people you were talking about this morning. She's only happy when she's looking after other people. She's a freezer full of food, far more than I can ever manage to eat, and it pleases her deeply to see clean plates. Roy will take us back and we'll put our heads together over the plans for rebuilding the vicarage, while Rose enjoys herself in the kitchen.'

Felicity said, 'Oh, do you like cooking too? I like cooking, but I'm hopeless at sorting out what wines go with what. Arthur does all that . . .' Her voice trailed away and she looked miserable.

Roy patted her on her shoulder, but made no move to keep her at his side while Thomas efficiently chivvied him and the two older ladies out of the house.

'Food first,' said Thomas, when the others had disappeared into Roy's car. 'I'll make sandwiches for us three, and then we'll be on the road ourselves.' He led the way to his antiquated kitchen, and with his usual efficiency built substantial sandwiches while directing Ellie to make them a big pot of tea. He was, of course, right to think they needed sustenance. Ellie felt much better when she'd eaten. Even Felicity managed to eat a reasonable amount. Thomas cleaned up the crumbs and led them out to the garage, which housed a surprisingly stylish new car.

Ellie remembered that Thomas had in the past written books and held down an important job in a college somewhere. The car was certainly pricier than those usually run by parish vicars. Good for Thomas.

Thomas steered Ellie into the front seat, making sure that Felicity sat in the back. It pleased Ellie that she was given the front seat — the seat of honour — while Felicity had to sit in the back. While her husband had been alive, Diana had always been given the front seat, and Ellie had had to sit at the back. She hadn't thought it had mattered at the time, but she saw now that it had mattered, quite a lot. It had rankled, definitely.

'Are you all right there in the back — front?' asked Thomas, while the engine obediently roared into life.

'Oh, I usually sit in the back,' said Felicity. 'Arthur likes to have his dog on the front seat, though I've wondered sometimes if it's entirely safe.'

There wasn't any suitable answer to that. Thomas turned into the road that wound up the hill to Mrs Dawes'. 'Onwards and upwards,' he said. Ellie kept a sharp lookout but no cars seemed to be following them as they wound round corners to the steepish road in which Mrs Dawes resided. It wasn't far from Ellie; you could almost sling a shot from Mrs Dawes' front garden into Ellie's down the hill, but it took a while when you followed the roads.

'Pretty,' commented Felicity, getting out of the car and gazing at the neat front garden, full of heathers, miniature cyclamens and white Japanese anemones. 'What are those pink things called?'

Ellie didn't want to get cross with Felicity, but really the girl was intensely irritating. She curbed her annoyance; not everyone knew the names of garden flowers. 'The tiny ones are called cyclamens.'

'Oh, I know that. No, those lily-like ones under the viburnum. You've got some in your garden, too, but yours are a paler pink.'

Ellie could have kicked herself. Why did she keep assuming that Felicity knew nothing about anything? 'Schizostylis. A bulb. Pretty, aren't they?'

'Mm. I'd like some in my garden, but . . . oh well. Arthur bought a whole lot of cyclamens for indoors last winter, but they didn't last.'

'It was too hot for them inside, I expect,' said Ellie. 'Indoor cyclamens like to be kept cool, or their leaves turn yellow and they die.'

'That's exactly what I said, but he didn't take any notice. Perhaps he'll listen to me next time.' Her smile faded as she remembered there might not be a next time.

Thomas rang the bell and peered through the front window, tapping on the pane.

Someone thump-thumped their way to the door and let them in.

'Mrs Dawes, you shouldn't be on your feet,' said Thomas, ushering the others inside.

'How exactly do you expect me to manage if I don't get up to let people in? My friend Mrs Mays was with me all morning, and she was up and down answering the door to people, bringing me flowers and fruit and I don't know what else, till her poor legs gave out on her, and now she's nodded off in her chair, poor soul. Her grandson brought her down to spend the day with me. Now she's dozed off and I'm making use of her Zimmerframe, dratted thing.'

Mrs Dawes slowly led the way into her small sitting room, which was crowded with too much furniture, including a large, high-backed chair in which dozed a tiny sparrow of a woman. Mrs Dawes was in a plum velvet housecoat with her bad knee heavily bandaged, but her colour was good, and she'd managed to dress her jet-black hair as usual. There were the remains of a sandwich lunch beside both ladies' chairs.

'You're marvellous, Mrs Dawes,' said Ellie, kissing her cheek, and depositing the bottle of sherry on her hostess's coffee table.

'Don't leave it there, dear, or Mrs Mays will be wanting some too. Put it in the bag on the side of my chair. It's all very well people bringing me things, but they don't realize that what a person really needs is another pair of legs. Good ones, this time round.'

'Can I do anything to help, Mrs Dawes?' enquired Felicity, doing her polite-little-girl act. 'I could cook something for you for tonight.'

'There's enough food in the kitchen to last me a week.'

'Did you mention people had brought you flowers?' Felicity looked around, but there were no flowers in the room. 'Shall I arrange them for you? I'm quite good at that.'

Ellie held her breath. Felicity couldn't know, of course, that Mrs Dawes was the head of the flower-arranging team at church, that she was renowned throughout West London for judging at flower shows. She attended conferences on flower-arranging. She was invited to steward at the Chelsea Flower Show. Felicity's offer was rather like a toddler offering to help David Hockney paint a portrait.

Mrs Dawes let the girl down lightly. 'Just find a bucket — there's one outside the back door — and put them all in water. That would be helpful.' As Felicity darted off, Mrs Dawes signalled with her eyebrows to Ellie. 'Why's she still around?'

'It's a long story,' said Ellie, settling cushions behind her old friend, and making sure a stool was close enough so that Mrs Dawes could put her foot up. 'She's got it into her head that her husband might want to kill her, which may or may not be true.'

'Probably is,' said Thomas, neatly stowing himself into a chair in the opposite corner.

'Ah. Sir Arthur. Now, did you say you'd heard about the woman whose garden he destroyed? That was a dreadful thing to do.'

'Yes, I've been to see her,' said Ellie.

'Oh,' said Mrs Dawes, deflated. 'Well, did you hear what he did to the odd-job man? Sir Arthur refused to pay his bill, would you believe! Only, I can't remember his name.'

'It'll come to you in the middle of the night, I expect,' said Ellie.

'That's just what I said, dear. I said, "What's his name?" And Mrs Mays — she's a little bit deaf, you know, and I had to shout — she said she didn't think she'd ever heard it, but he did some work for her niece over the other side of the Avenue, and she'd recommend him to anyone.'

'Do you have her niece's name and address?' asked Ellie.

'It's Trisha, that I do know. But have I ever heard her married name? I don't think I have, and I'm not waking my friend up to ask her now. It's the house with the strange pagoda-like structure over the front gate, you can't miss it. She'd had this man in to take up and relay her front path. They're all old tiles on the front paths around here, and they crack and shift about till they're quite dangerous to walk on and have to be taken up and relaid on a new foundation.

'She said this chap told her he'd been doing some work for Sir Arthur, edging paths in the back garden. Sir Arthur insisted on having original Edwardian tiles around the flower beds, the ones that look like rope edging. You can get repro, of course, any amount, but the originals are hard to come by. This chap couldn't get quite enough of one type so he got a few repro which look exactly the same, almost. He said it would take a sharp eye to notice the difference, but Sir Arthur saw and refused to pay his bill, and wouldn't let him take the tiles away either.'

Ellie said, 'I wonder, did he try to get his own back on Sir Arthur?'

Mrs Dawes shifted in her chair. 'I don't know what you mean, dear. What could he do?'

Ellie grinned. Mrs Dawes knew very well what the man had done. 'He sprayed some graffiti on the door of Sir Arthur's garage, didn't he?'

'What was that?' asked Felicity, entering the room with a charming arrangement of chrysanthemums in a vase. 'Were you talking about poor Paddy? I told Arthur I couldn't see the difference between the two lots of tiles, but he was livid.

I tried to clean the paint off, but I don't think I made a very good job of it. Where shall I put these?'

Mrs Dawes expressed approval, in a grudging sort of way. 'Not bad for a beginner. You should come to my flower-arranging classes on Thursday morning, Felicity. Put them on the mantelpiece for the time being, and I'll just give them a tweak here and there later.'

Thomas looked at his watch. 'We ought to be going. I'll pop in again tomorrow, Mrs Dawes, if you'll let me know what I can bring you?'

'Nothing, vicar. But Ellie . . .' Mrs Dawes beckoned Ellie to come closer, and whispered in her ear.

Ellie nodded. 'Of course. I'll bring some in tomorrow.'

'What?' asked Felicity, but Ellie just shook her head and said they must indeed be moving.

There were only a few friends to whom you could mention the delicate matter of your bowels, and Ellie was not going to give Mrs Dawes' whispered request airtime.

Ellie said, 'Don't get up. We'll see ourselves out.' She saw Thomas slide a box of chocolates into the capacious bag that hung from the arm of Mrs Dawes' chair, but pretended not to notice.

Felicity got into the back of the car, and directed them down the hill and towards the park. 'The home that Mummy's in faces on to the park. It's not an old building, not really, but they're talking about pulling it down because not every bedroom has a bathroom en suite, and that's what's needed in future. I don't know how I'll manage if Mummy has to move out till it's rebuilt. I've tried to talk to her about it, but she refuses to believe it will ever happen. It's too worrying for her to take in. I mean, she's happy at the home now, or as much as she can be, given the circumstances. She does get a sherry before meals, and she has a nice room on the ground floor overlooking the park, but of course the company's not what she's used to.'

'I suppose anything would be a comedown after the manor,' said Ellie, trying to be polite. Trying not to think about cars whizzing round corners and crashing into them . . . or snipers taking potshots at them from the horse chestnut tree on the corner.

It was all nonsense, of course. Sir Arthur hadn't the faintest idea where they might be at the moment.

'Here we are,' said Thomas, parking neatly in the forecourt of a rambling, sixties-built place. 'I do drop in here from time to time to see someone, though I don't think I've had the pleasure of your mother's acquaintance, Felicity. Would you like us to come in with you to see your mother, or shall I spend some time with my old friend?'

'Oh, do come and meet her,' said Felicity, exhibiting signs of nerves. 'Mummy will love to have someone new to visit her. She doesn't get many visitors and has to keep herself to herself here because . . . well, the other people are not quite . . . you know?'

'Compos mentis?' said Thomas. 'The one I visit can beat me at chess any day.'

'That's not quite what I meant,' said Felicity, with a tinge of colour in her cheeks.

Ellie wondered if the girl was a snob? Or was it the mother?

Felicity's mother Anne was ensconced in an armchair by one of the windows of the large sitting room, with a moustached elderly man bending over her.

'Oh dear,' said Felicity, hanging back. 'She's got the commodore in tow. It's lovely for her to have an admirer, of course, but he does bring her gin when he shouldn't, and he takes her on outings which sometimes . . . oh well, I must be pleased for anything which makes her happy.'

The commodore was wearing a blazer and grey slacks. His hair was thick and plentiful, but his eyes were reddened and watery. Anne seemed to be flirting with him — until she caught sight of her daughter, when she pressed his hand and told him to run away and play. To Ellie's amusement, the commodore kissed Anne's hand before leaving the room.

Ellie saw what Felicity meant when she said her mother could pass for thirty — with the light behind her. From a distance she gave the impression of being quite a young woman; fragile and lovely.

She was beautifully dressed in what Ellie recognized as designer clothes, topped off by a Hermes scarf draped around her neck. A cashmere rug had been tucked in over her legs. Her hair was died blonde and perfectly arranged. She wore a fine string of pearls, plus several diamond and emerald rings on her fingers. Her hands and neck gave away her age and — when Ellie got closer — she could see a fine network of lines about her mouth and eyes.

Ellie disliked the woman on sight. How much did it cost Felicity to keep her mother dressed and coiffured like that? How could Anne let her daughter beggar herself that way?

Felicity stooped to kiss her mother's cheek. 'Mummy dear, may I introduce some friends? This is Thomas, who—'

'I know you,' said Felicity's mother, smiling up at Thomas. 'You come to see that disgusting old man in the corner there. You'd far better spend time with me.'

'Madam,' said Thomas, bending over her hand in a manner suggesting that he'd like to kiss it too. 'A vicar doesn't choose his parishioners.'

'But he can choose to visit a lonely widow now and then?' She was a coquette. She was signalling she'd be very happy to flirt with Thomas, and Felicity was looking pleased, like a cat who's brought its kitten something amusing to play with.

Anne looked beyond Thomas to Ellie, and her mouth took on a downward curve. 'Who's this?'

'Ellie Quicke, another widow,' said Ellie, grimly contrasting her own workaday attire with that of the exquisite Anne. 'I'll just go and talk to that disgusting old man in the corner there. That is, if you'll introduce me, Thomas?'

Thomas obliged. The 'disgusting old man in the corner' was a particularly clean old man who had once been tall and well built. An old soldier? There was something in the way he held himself which made her think that. Now he'd shrunk to a skeleton, but his eyes still gleamed bright under shaggy eyebrows, and he still had all his marbles.

Thomas said, 'Perce, good to see you up and about again. I'll pop in to see you as usual in the week, but can you look after this lady for me for a while? I have to visit with someone else this afternoon.'

Perce — short for Percy? — patted the chair beside him, on which Ellie duly sat. He said, 'Found someone else to pay court to her, has she, our Lady Muck?'

'You're not her favourite either, I gather.'

'She never lets a day go by without telling us how she's had to lower herself to live here. If her daughter weren't beggaring herself to pay her bills in this place, she'd be down the council home, and serve her bloody well right.'

'And you, Perce? Old soldier, aren't you? Why don't you put your medals on, to show her what's what?'

He crowed with laughter, shook a bony finger at her. 'Got me weighed up, have you? Well, we have to take our fun where we can. I admit she rubs me up the wrong way. One of these days, when I'm carried out of here by the back door, they can tell her about my chest full of medals and I shan't half have a laugh. Catch me passing the time of day with her before then . . . ? She's had three husbands so far, did you know that? Looking around for a fourth. The commodore's too old and short of cash, so he's no good to her that way, though she doesn't mind his spending money to take her on outings and keep her supplied with gin. I hope Tommy knows what he's doing, getting so close to her.'

'Tommy's a wily old bird,' said Ellie, enjoying herself very much.

'So are you, my dear.' The sharpness faded from his eyes and, with a trembling hand, he extracted a large clean handkerchief from his pocket, and wiped a tear from his cheek.

'Tea, Perce? Choccy bikkie?' said a middle-aged woman in an overall. She handed him a mug, which he accepted with both hands. She put a plate with a biscuit on the arm of his chair. 'And you, dear?'

Ellie accepted a cup of strong tea, but declined the biscuit. Perce managed not to slop his tea, but it was obviously an effort. Parkinson's disease? Advanced. Across the room, Thomas and Anne were animated, in flirting mode, while Felicity looked on, proud of her mother and, for once, smiling contentedly.

When Perce had finished his biscuit, he said, 'Why did you come to see her?'

'Her husband — her first husband — has been trying to build fences with his daughter, but she's fiercely loyal to Anne and won't have anything to do with him.'

'Why should you care?'

She gave an answer which she thought would appeal to him, and which also happened to be true. 'I don't like to see dumb animals suffer.'

'From her mother . . . or from her husband?'

'What do you know about Sir Arthur?'

'Anne talks about "my daughter, Lady Kingsley" all the time. Duchesses or dustmen, all the same to me. I can tell you this, though, Anne's afraid of Sir Arthur.'

'Do you know why?'

'Because he put her in here? Because it's his wife who pays the bills?' He shrugged.

'Isn't she a bit young to be here?'

'She can hardly walk. Both legs were broken in an accident and the tendons damaged. She was drunk, of course. She'd be drunk all the time now, if she could get it. She always asks her visitors to bring her in some gin.'

'What sort of accident?'

'She tripped and fell down a flight of stairs and through some glass doors. They say. Or was pushed.'

Ellie was startled. 'What do you mean by that?'

CHAPTER SEVENTEEN

Perce played dumb. 'What? What's that? An old man's ramblings don't mean anything.'

He hadn't been rambling. Ellie tried to work out a new scenario, involving Anne. 'You think her son-in-law caused her accident? Why would he want to do that?' She answered her own question. 'Oh. Because she expected to be reinstated at the manor when he married Felicity, and he wouldn't have liked that? But . . . she's stuck in here, so how could she doctor a pizza and deliver it to Sir Arthur's house?'

'Is that what someone did?' He laughed till he got hiccups, and then let his hands relax so that she had to rescue his mug before it fell to the floor. He slumped in his chair, closing his eyes, and letting his jaw drop. He was closing the conversation by going to sleep on her.

He'd made Ellie extremely uneasy. She looked around for Thomas and Felicity, who were now bending over Anne, taking their farewells, promising to come again on the morrow; Yes, of course dear Mummy, don't you worry about anything.

Anne was saying, in a carrying voice, 'Couldn't you just take a little more care with your appearance, Felicity? For my sake, if not for your own.'

A grim-faced woman was watching them from the doorway, and as they left, she drew Felicity to one side. Thomas and Ellie tried not to look as if they could hear what was going on, but of course they could. 'Your mother's been out again! She bamboozled the commodore into giving her a lift into the West End to have her hair done. Of course, she hadn't enough money to pay the bill, and they've been on to us, wanting to know who to send the bill to, and you know it's absolutely out of the question for us to . . .'

'Of course,' said Felicity, blushing. 'I'll see to it, of course I will. How much is it? I'll bring the money in tomorrow, or perhaps the next day.'

If she were going to leave her husband, what were the chances of getting the bill paid?

Thomas looked at his watch as they got back into his car. 'Where to now, ladies?'

Felicity was frowning, biting her lip. Undecided.

'Felicity, dear.' The endearment came easily, because Ellie was indeed very sorry for the girl. 'What do you want to do? Are you ready to leave your husband? It's a big step to take, and you must be sure of what you're doing. If you do decide you've had enough, then you're very welcome to stay with me for a while.'

'Do you think Arthur would care?' Felicity was biting her lip. 'Or even notice, if he's got your daughter to keep his bed warm?'

Ellie blinked. That hurt. 'I can't answer for Diana, and I don't know the answer to your question. Do you want to leave him? You've grounds enough.'

'I can't. You know why. Mummy. I could go on as we are for a bit. Only, your daughter's different, isn't she? I know I irritate him sometimes, though I do try, I really do. But he wouldn't really go so far as to get rid of me, would he? I mean, divorce. Not . . . not anything else.'

They'd been over this ground before.

Felicity sniffed. 'He'll never find anyone who can keep his house looking so nice as I do, or look after his dogs and take them for walks and groom them, and be there when he wants me, and not there when he doesn't. I mean, Diana couldn't do all that, could she?'

'No, she couldn't.' But Diana could do other things, which he might be finding more attractive at the moment.

'I must admit that it's a teensy bit lonely sometimes. And Marco is getting really nasty! Ordering me about just as if he were the master, and I was a cleaner. A couple of times lately he's tried my door at night when Arthur's away. I said I'd tell Arthur if he tried that again, but he just laughed. He said Arthur wouldn't believe me, and I suppose he's right. And that Martinez gives me the creeps!'

'Yes.'

Felicity fidgeted. 'Suppose I were to get away somewhere, just for a few days? I could leave him a note saying that when he'd decided what he wanted, he should let me know and I could come back? Give him time to think. If only it weren't for Mummy . . .'

Thomas said, with care, 'If you divorced your husband, you'd be entitled to a comfortable income, and could easily pay for your mother's care out of that.'

Felicity was silent. Head down. Plucking at her black T-shirt. 'Or he could have me killed. To avoid a divorce.'

Silence.

Felicity made up her mind. 'If I can stay with you for a bit, Ellie, that would be good. I need to collect one or two things from the house first. He's out with Diana this evening, so it should be quite safe. If you'd come in with me, just in case Marco's there, I could pack a bag and get away before he realizes.'

'Fine,' said Thomas, starting the car. 'But we'll have to do it pretty quickly. Evensong in twenty minutes.'

Ellie said, 'Drop us at Felicity's. I'll call a cab to take us both back home. May I borrow your mobile again?'

'Don't you have a mobile?' asked Felicity, surprise and a little contempt colouring her tone.

Ellie felt the sting. 'Yes, I do, but I don't know what I've done with it. It's not in my handbag, that's for sure.'

'You can borrow mine,' said Felicity, producing hers. 'I always keep it by me.'

Ellie blushed for shame. From the start, she'd written Felicity off as a dimwit, but the girl was constantly proving her wrong. It was Ellie who was the dimwit, mislaying papers and forgetting where she'd put things. It was humiliating. 'Thank you, Felicity, I appreciate it.'

The girl let her down lightly. 'You don't drive, either, do you? I don't know what I'd do without my car, though it's terribly old and often in the garage. I must ring them tomorrow and see what the latest bill is . . . unless . . .' She left the sentence unfinished. If she left her husband she wouldn't have the money to pay the garage bill. Was she going to dissolve into helplessness again?

No, she wasn't, but her voice trembled as she said, 'I'll have to get a job, and move Mummy into a cheaper place.'

'Good for you,' said Ellie. 'And of course you're welcome to stay with me till you're on your feet again.'

'Bravo, Felicity,' said Thomas. He drove them down the hill and parked in the drive of her home. The windows looked blank and dull, giving the house an unoccupied air. There was a drift of fallen leaves on the gravel of the drive and in the porch. There was also fresh graffiti on the garage doors.

'Will you be all right?' asked Thomas, looking at his watch. 'I could wait, but . . .'

'We'll be fine,' said Ellie, knowing he was due back at the church. 'Thanks for the lift.'

Felicity got out of the car, looking at the graffiti. 'Oh, I did hope Paddy would have forgotten about it by now. Arthur'll be furious! I wish Marco had made an effort to clean it off, but he doesn't appear to be here. Arthur won't like that, either.' She looked up at the blank, uncurtained windows above the garage. The evenings were getting darker, and the whole house seemed to be in shadow.

Ellie had the odd fancy that if the sun struck the building, it would disappear like a soap bubble. Perhaps it was all that dark red paint against red brick. A dispiriting combination.

Felicity let them into the great house. The air struck Ellie as being slightly damp. Felicity exclaimed, and turned up the thermostat so that the central heating clicked on. She didn't bother to turn on any lights, but led the way up the imposing staircase to the first floor and down a corridor, sorting out a key from her bunch.

'Arthur sleeps in the big bedroom at the front, but when he's away I like to sleep in a small bedroom at the back, because it overlooks the garden. I keep my clothes there, so that Arthur's got plenty of room for his wardrobe. I always keep my door locked when I'm out, because of Marco and . . . oh!'

It wasn't going to be necessary to use the key in the door. It was ajar. A tyre lever lay on the floor — was that the instrument that had been used to break Ellie's windows? — and the splintered edge of the door showed where someone had jimmied it from the frame.

Felicity gave the door a push and it swung open, revealing a pink bedroom which looked out on to the garden. The curtains had been roughly drawn across the window and a bedside light left on. A dishevelled, unshaven figure lay flat on his back on the single bed. There were half-healed scratches on his hands showing where Midge had defended himself.

Marco had been sick at some point. Carpet and bedding — not to mention his clothes — bore evidence of this. Five empty beer cans lay around, with one spilling half its contents on to the carpet. Ellie disturbed another with her foot, and it rolled away from her.

Marco must have come back from the pub drunk. He'd known the police wanted to question him about Ellie's windows. Perhaps that's why he'd not returned to his own quarters? Or perhaps he'd simply been drunk enough to hunt for Felicity? Either way, he'd forced his way into her room sometime during the night. It must still have been dark, to judge by the evidence of the half-drawn curtains and the bedside light. He'd stayed there, drinking, till he'd passed out.

Women's clothes had been pulled from the wardrobe, and emptied out of a chest of drawers. Not many clothes, and none of them could have cost much.

Felicity picked up a pretty blue scarf. 'Mummy gave me this for Christmas!'

It was stained too.

Ellie saw that Marco was beginning to stir out of his drunken slumber. 'Come away. I'll take you shopping in the morning.'

'But . . .' Felicity picked up a sweater, some underwear, a pair of black jeans. 'I can't just . . . these are all I've . . .'

Ellie put her arm round the girl's shoulders. 'The only things worth keeping are items of sentimental value. Did you say your granny left you some jewellery? Are there any family photos you'd like to keep? Where would they be?'

Felicity made a sound as if she were in pain, but stood on a chair to rescue a worn leather jewellery case from the top of the wardrobe. From under her bed she pulled out a plastic bag containing a couple of old-fashioned photograph albums.

Marco was definitely stirring. He would have a terrible headache. Hopefully.

Ellie tugged on Felicity's arm. 'Let me take those for you. Now, is there anything else you need?' The girl scooped up an armful of clothes, and looked around, chewing her lip, undecided, on the verge of tears.

Ellie prompted her. 'What about recipe books? Gardening books? That sort of thing?'

'My own trowel, that my papa — that's my second papa — gave me when I was little. It's stainless steel. And my winter boots and coat . . . oh, I can't think.'

'Can you find a suitcase to put your things in?'

Felicity was going to cry again. 'The matching cases are all Arthur's.'

'Then we'll find a couple of large plastic bags for these things, shall we?'

They got as far as the corridor, then Felicity stopped to pluck a watercolour of some bluebells off the wall. 'That's mine, that Mummy gave me when I was tiny, and I've always had it.'

Ellie added the picture to the jewellery box and albums. Felicity's arms were full of clothing, some of which she dropped as she led the way to the head of the stairs. Ellie stooped to pick up one of Felicity's boots.

The front door swung open, letting in a blast of cold air. In strode the master of the house, bringing with him an air of good wine, cigars and aftershave. And menace.

Arthur was feeling pleased with himself. Which didn't last long. He threw a laptop and his mobile on to the hall table. 'Felicity!' He switched on the light in the hall. 'Why hasn't the heating been turned on? You know I don't like coming into a cold house.'

He hadn't yet caught sight of Ellie, deep in the shadow of the landing.

'Arthur!' Felicity cringed, clutching her possessions. 'I thought . . . didn't you say that . . . ? I've been out all day!'

'Why are you wandering around in the dark? And what are you doing with all that washing on a Sunday night? You know it gives me a headache when you run the washing machine.' He turned to usher a companion into the hall. 'Come on in, my dear. Welcome to the ancestral home.'

Oh, no! Ellie's mind leaped at the truth before the woman came into sight. But no! He wouldn't bring Diana here, before he'd rid himself of Felicity, would he? But that's exactly what he had done.

Diana moved into the light, wearing a sleek black dress which looked new and had certainly not come from Marks & Spencer. A light, glittery wrap was around her shoulders, picking up the pinpoints of diamond studs in her ears. Where had those jewels come from? Guess! Diana had been shopping with her credit cards, setting lures to catch the eye of a wealthy man.

Diana, whose eyes were everywhere, was trying to look bored, but taking everything in. Yes, this was what Diana wanted. A house and a lifestyle to die for!

Felicity could read the signs as well as Ellie.

Arthur heaved off his overcoat, and threw it over a chair. He helped unwind Diana from her gauzy wrap. 'We'll soon have the house warm enough, my dear.' And to Felicity, 'Well, don't just stand there! It's been quite a day, and I don't want any lip from you. I've had enough of that from . . .' He scowled. 'Well, never mind, that little rebellion's been quelled, and I won't be having any more trouble from that direction.'

Ellie flinched. So Arthur had overcome the 'little rebellion', had he? Then Mr Talbot and Gwyn had lost!

'We could do with a drink. In my den. Straight away.'

Felicity gasped, and more clothing slipped from her arms. She looked as if she were about to faint.

'Goodness gracious me.' Diana was amused. 'Is it always like this?'

Arthur's mood switched to outrage. 'Snap out of it, girl! Drinks! Now! Chop-chop!'

At this point Marco came blundering out into the corridor, holding his head, and moaning.

Arthur heard him. 'What's that! A burglar?'

Felicity quavered. 'It's Marco. He broke into my room and has been sick.'

Arthur was astonished. 'What did he do that for?'

'He wanted . . . he wanted me.'

Diana smiled, all disbelief. 'Oh, really!'

Arthur shouted with laughter. 'Don't be silly, old girl. What would he want with you, eh?'

Felicity reddened, and was mute.

Marco hadn't realized his boss was back. He could see Felicity at the top of the stairs, and that was enough for him. He bounced off the wall and reached for her, leering. 'Oi! You! Come back here and let's have a tumble!'

Felicity attempted a scream, but managed no more than a squeak. As Marco lunged for her, she tried to recoil, and lost her footing. She tumbled down a couple of steps, dropping everything she was carrying, before catching hold of a baluster to halt her descent.

Ellie jettisoned her own load and rushed down after Felicity, cradling her. Felicity held her breath.

'Mother! What are you doing here?' Diana was aghast, as well she should be.

Arthur saw Ellie for the first time too. 'What . . . ? You . . . ?' He strode up the stairs, pausing momentarily when he reached Felicity, but making no move to touch her. He loomed over Ellie. 'Didn't I tell you to get out and stay out? Get the hell away from my wife, do you hear?'

He looked up at Marco. 'What the hell do you think you're playing at? Did you really dare go into my wife's bedroom? Out of my way!' He took the last few steps at a run and blundered along the corridor, switching on lights as he went. They all heard his roar of anger when he saw the bedroom door jimmied open and the mess within.

Marco's knees gave way. 'I can explain . . . !'

Wheeling back down the corridor, Arthur swung at Marco, who tried to duck but couldn't get out from under in time. Marco half fell and half stumbled down the stairs past Felicity and Ellie, with Arthur lumbering after him.

At the bottom Arthur picked up Marco, squealing, and kicked him across the hall.

Diana laughed. Felicity let go of the breath she'd been holding, and turned her face into Ellie's shoulder.

Arthur opened the front door, and swung Marco out into the night. 'You're sacked! Get your things, and leave! Now!'

Marco sprawled on the gravel. He shook his head to clear it. He hadn't expected Sir Arthur back, and he hadn't expected an audience when he went after Felicity. Marco chose, perhaps unwisely, to fight. He staggered to his feet. 'You won't sack me. You daren't!'

Arthur stood in the doorway, towering over him. 'You tell me what I can do and can't do? I could stamp you into the mud and not even notice it.'

Marco took a step back, but wasn't finished yet. 'There's things I could tell, if I had a mind!'

'Try it! Would anyone take the word of a worm like you, against me? I know nothing of what you may have been doing behind my back. Understand?'

Marco retreated a few steps, then returned to the fight. 'I know stuff! Stuff you wouldn't like told.'

Arthur was contemptuous. 'If I hear you've been making trouble for me, I'll ask Martinez to pay you a visit. Understand?'

The threat sobered Marco. He swayed on his feet, muttering. Then said, in a calmer voice, 'You can't turn me out just like that. I'll go in the morning. And you owe me a month's wages, right?'

'A month's wages won't pay the damage you've done to my property. Now, get out. Remember, if I hear that you've been gossiping . . .'

Marco had had enough. 'You'll be sorry for this, you will!' The sound of his footsteps retreated.

Arthur shut and bolted the front door. He looked for approbation not to his wife, but to Diana.

Diana ran her hand down his sleeve. 'Fisticuffs! Adorable!'

He laughed, good humour restored.

Then scowled up at his wife. 'Get up, girl! Drinks. Now. Then a little supper in half an hour, say. As for you, Mrs Quickie, or whatever your name is . . . out!'

Ellie said, 'I don't think your wife's broken any bones in her fall, but it has shaken her up.' No, nothing appeared broken — except for the girl's spirit. She was like a rag doll. No backbone. Ellie coaxed the girl to stand. It would be easy to take over, to tell Arthur that Felicity was leaving him, and to sweep her out of the house.

No. That wouldn't be right. This was a decision that Felicity must make and communicate to her husband herself. Or not. The girl was trembling, clinging to Ellie.

Arthur's lip was lifting. 'Pull yourself together, girl. Our guest will think poorly of your hospitality.'

Felicity pushed back her hair, which had come loose. 'Arthur, you said you wouldn't be coming back tonight, and then I found Marco in my room. But that's not it. What it is . .

.' she faltered, then went on in a stronger voice. 'What it is, I've had enough. You've been good to me in lots of ways, I know that, and I'm grateful. But it's not enough and I'm leaving you.'

Arthur's eyes narrowed to slits. 'Has your father been getting at you? You know he's lost his latest battle with me?'

Felicity shook her head. 'I haven't been in contact with him. I know that leaving you means Mummy may suffer terribly, but I can't go on like this . . .' Her voice broke, and she brushed her forearm across her face. 'So I'm going. I'll get a job, somewhere. My car's in the garage still. You can pick it up tomorrow. I'll just take one or two things now, and come back for the rest tomorrow.'

Arthur's eyes went from side to side. Ellie could read him easily enough. This was a surprise, yes; but it wasn't unwelcome news. His eyes went to Diana, who was ironing out a smile, but otherwise seemed content to let events take their course. If Felicity went, it would ease his path with Diana. Perhaps he'd get another housekeeper, and then move Diana in?

Ellie thought that they deserved one another.

He didn't reply to Felicity. Just stood there, frowning slightly. He said, 'I need a drink.' He set off down the corridor which led to his den, leaving the three women alone.

Felicity began to gather her things together again. Ellie helped her.

Diana perched herself on a hall chair. 'Can I be of any assistance?'

'No, thank you,' said Felicity, dumping her clothing on the hall table. 'I'll get some plastic bags from the kitchen to put these in, and then I'll go.'

Ellie added the jewellery case and photo albums to the heap, but didn't follow Felicity out to the kitchen.

Instead, she faced Diana across the hall. She said, 'Diana, don't do this.'

'Why ever not? Their marriage is well and truly broken. Nothing to do with me.'

'Arthur is not a nice man.'

Diana smiled. 'I don't have any choice. I have to make my own way in the world — since you refused to help me.'

'You can't put this on me. I've helped you many times in the past, but there has to be a limit.'

'If you loved me . . .'

Ellie sighed. 'I love you, but I don't think I like you very much.'

'I do what I have to do to survive.'

'Does that include signing my death warrant?'

'What?'

'You know Arthur's reputation. He's ruthless and not above using questionable tactics to get his own way. When you sold your interest in my house, didn't it occur to you to wonder how soon I'd meet with a fatal accident, so that he could develop the site?'

Diana gaped.

Ellie clasped her hands together. 'Use your head, Diana! He's no philanthropist. Why should he pay you all that money, if he didn't think he could cash in pretty soon?'

A tiny sound made both women look up. Felicity had come through from the kitchen, with another armful of belongings and some large plastic bags, which she dumped with the rest of her things on the table.

Ellie turned back to Diana, but it was too late, for her daughter's face was set against her. Ellie sighed. 'You'd better tell Arthur straight away — if he hasn't already found out by looking at his faxes — I made a new will this afternoon leaving everything to the trust. You don't get anything from me.'

'Diana, what does this mean?' said Arthur, reappearing with a large glass of whisky in one hand and a fax in the other. 'You showed me a copy of your father's will, which left you half the house at your mother's death, and you said you'd get the other half when she died. Here's a copy of a will she's just made, and it doesn't leave you anything. If you've tried to cheat me . . .'

Felicity repeated what Ellie had said. 'Ellie made a will this afternoon, leaving everything to a trust fund. You can't touch her now.'

Diana looked into space. Then — and Ellie had to admire her for this — she stood to face Arthur. 'I'd no idea my mother hated me so much. I'll tear your cheque up, now.'

She delved into the pretty bag that hung over one shoulder, and produced a cheque, which she tore into small pieces and let fall to the floor.

She took a step towards him. She didn't cringe or plead as Felicity might have done. She challenged him instead. 'On the other hand, you said you'd made a killing this morning . . . and half a loaf's better than none, isn't it? And perhaps I have other — qualities — which might compensate . . .'

She raised her arms and put them around his neck. His breathing quickened. He dropped his glass on to the table, and crushed the fax in his fist as she closed her eyes and kissed him. His arms went around her, and he kissed her back.

Felicity said, in a tiny voice, 'I think I've seen enough.' She'd already filled two plastic bags with her belongings, and now she shook out another, to fill that.

Arthur broke away from Diana, but retained her hand in his. He said to Felicity, 'I want to see what you're removing from my house.'

'Be my guest,' said Felicity. She held things up so that he could see them as she stuffed them into the bags. 'My recipe books, my gardening books, my trowel and small fork, my gardening gloves, my favourite saucepan, which I bought with my own money . . .'

'All right, all right. Why don't you take a suitcase?'

'They're all marked with your initials,' said Felicity. 'This is my library book, the picture my mother gave me, my winter boots and coat, my black ski pants — not that you ever took me skiing . . .'

'Enough! Leave your keys on the table. Keep the car, if you can pay the garage bill. I'll need your address. You'll hear from my solicitor about a divorce, but don't expect alimony. If you choose to leave me, then that's desertion, and you don't get a penny.'

Felicity stuffed her remaining belongings into the last plastic bag, and got out her mobile. 'I'll get in touch with a solicitor as soon as I can, and we'll work something out that's fair to everybody. Ellie, what's the number of your minicab firm?'

Ellie wasn't good at remembering numbers, but she could remember that one. She gave it to Felicity, who asked for a cab straight away.

Felicity started to carry her bags out to the porch, and Ellie helped her. Diana stayed close to Arthur, smiling at him, and not taking any notice of her mother at all.

Oh, Diana, thought Ellie. *How could you?*

Arthur watched them go. Ellie wondered how soon he'd regret having lost his wife. He must have appreciated her once. Surely he hadn't married her solely out of spite?

One last trip. Felicity draped her winter coat over her shoulders and looked around the hall. Saying goodbye? Would she miss the big house, and the status her marriage had given her? Possibly she'd miss the dog most.

Arthur shed Diana's hand. Perhaps he still had some feelings for Felicity. He said, 'You can tell your father . . .'

Felicity shook her head. 'I haven't seen or talked to my father since I was a child, and I've no intention of seeing him again. Or you. But I think you should know that my half-brother Julian has taken a turn for the worse, and it's touch and go whether he lives or dies. I hope the police get you for that.'

Arthur stared at her, and made as if to speak. Diana touched him on the shoulder, but he ignored her.

Felicity joined Ellie in the porch, slamming the door behind her. She looked around her. 'I'll miss not having a dog. He was going to get a bigger dog this time. A Labrador. I would have liked that. But . . . I'll survive.'

CHAPTER EIGHTEEN

The minicab came, and in no time at all they drew up outside Ellie's house. 'I'll pay,' said Felicity. 'I've enough money for that.'

'No need. I've an account with the firm.'

The cab driver knew Ellie, of course, and was happy to help them struggle down the pathway and dump the luggage into the hall.

Ellie picked up a couple of bags. 'I think there's enough room in the wardrobe and chest of drawers in your bedroom.'

Felicity stopped her. 'Hold on a minute. I just want to make sure the cab's gone.'

She looked out of the door. It had. She shut the door, and set her back to it. 'You'll think me paranoid, but Arthur heard you give the telephone number of the cab firm, and knowing him, he'll ring them soon, to check that you've actually brought me here.'

Ellie nodded. 'So . . . ?'

'There's rather more in one of those bags than my belongings. I put Arthur's laptop and mobile in, before he started checking on me. They were on the table with all my stuff, you see.' The girl could act innocent when she wanted to.

'Ah,' said Ellie. 'So what do you want to do with them?'

Felicity's chin came out. 'I thought Miss Quicke might help us, if we took the laptop over there. Or your friend . . . Kate, is it? Someone who'd be able to use the information on the laptop and mobile to upset Arthur's nasty little plans. As for the mobile, don't you think the police would be interested in hearing what he's been up to, if my half-brother dies?'

'Felicity, you're amazing!' Ellie looked at the phone. The answerphone light was flashing. As usual. She never seemed able to leave the house without someone ringing her, wanting something from her.

Ellie tried to think quickly. 'Not Kate. It wouldn't be fair to involve her. She's too vulnerable, because of the baby. It would be best to take the stuff straight away to Aunt Drusilla's. They're expecting us for supper, and she's got the sharpest brain on the block. We can ring the police from there. I'll get hold of a black taxi cab; they've got a rank outside the station. Then if Arthur checks with the minicab firm, he won't be able to trace us.'

Felicity dragged some of her bags upstairs, while Ellie phoned. She ignored the flashing light on the answerphone, and found a shopping basket to put the laptop and mobile in. She looked in a couple of obvious places, but still couldn't find her own mobile.

Unlike Arthur's mansion, Miss Quicke's house looked very much alive. It was well cared for, nowadays, and no one had sprayed graffiti on its doors. Welcoming lights were on in the porch, Roy was just coming across from his quarters in the converted garage at the side, and into the drive behind them drove Thomas, tooting merrily.

Rose opened the door, wiping her hands on her apron, and crying out a welcome.

Felicity gave a little sob. 'You're so lucky to have all this, Ellie!'

'I know I am,' said Ellie. 'But each of these people has had to overcome — oh, not what you've been through — but still, a lot.'

Felicity followed Ellie into the hall, where Miss Quicke leaned on her stick, lifting her face to be kissed by one and all.

'Supper's ready,' cried Rose.

Ellie stopped her. 'Could it wait? Maybe half an hour? We've got something that needs doing first. Urgently.'

Miss Quicke nodded and led the way to the drawing room, while Rose squawked and dived off to the kitchen to turn the oven off.

In the drawing room, long velvet curtains had been closely drawn against the dank evening outside, and there was a simulated-log gas fire burning in the hearth, adding to the overall warmth of the central heating.

'Pour us all a sherry, will you, Roy?' said Miss Quicke, ensconcing herself in her high-backed chair.

'Not for me,' said Felicity, nervous now that she had to explain herself. 'Ellie, will you tell them?'

So Ellie did. They all knew some of it, but not everything. Enough that they could follow and understand the importance of what Felicity had done.

Felicity drew out the mobile and laptop. 'So, what do I do now? I took them on impulse, and immediately regretted it because if he'd caught me . . .' She drew in her breath. 'If I could have taken them out of the bag again, I would have done so, but he'd have seen me and realized what I'd done. He'll miss them quite soon, unless Diana gives him something else to think about for a while. When he does miss them, he'll know what's happened to them, and he'll come after me. I don't know exactly what incriminating information he may have here, but . . .'

'Enough.' Miss Quicke set her sherry glass down with a snap. 'We must copy the hard drive, of course. I have my computer set up next door. Felicity, you will help me.'

Ellie eyed her aunt with admiration. 'I wouldn't know how to begin.'

'There are such things as manuals, aren't there? Also, I have an excellent relationship with the little man who supplies me with all my equipment, and if I run into trouble, I can always ring him up and ask his advice.'

'On a Sunday night?' asked Roy.

'At any time,' said Miss Quicke. 'I make it worth his while.'

Thomas stroked his beard. 'It's theft, of course.'

'Thomas,' said Miss Quicke, 'if you feel that helping us would compromise your position, then you must leave immediately. Only, I do trust that you won't give us away to Sir Arthur.'

'No, I won't do that.'

'Good. Now, Thomas, you forget about the laptop and concentrate on getting the information on the mobile to the police. It's my belief they can find out what calls he's been making without having the mobile actually in their hands, but they might find it useful to check on any recorded messages and copy them.'

She held out her hand to Felicity, who helped her to stand. Miss Quicke's face quivered with pain, but she was not about to give in.

Felicity said, 'I suppose I'd better turn off my own mobile, because he'll ring me as soon as . . .'

Her mobile trilled at that point. She turned paper-white and swayed, but Miss Quicke's grasp on her arm tightened. 'Turn it off, girl. Now!'

Felicity fumbled for her mobile and turned it off. She looked at it. 'It was him.'

'Right. So now we know what we're up against. He's discovered his loss and is looking for you. He may go to Ellie's but he won't know where else to look if you're not there. Roy! Tell Rose that supper will have to wait.'

As they went out, Thomas picked up the phone. 'I'll try to get hold of the policeman we saw yesterday.' He hung on for ages till someone finally answered. No, DS Robertson was not available. Neither was DC Smith. Someone would take a message, if it was important.

'Can I speak to someone dealing with the attempted murder of the Talbot boy?'

A long wait. Thomas beat tattoos on the table. Ellie sank into a chair and gazed into the fireplace. How long before Arthur tracked them down?

Eventually Thomas put the phone down with what was, for him, a rare moment of anger. 'They've taken a note that we have some important information for them, and will pass the information on soonest. Which is not going to help us if Sir Arthur tracks us down. What to do now?'

Ellie said, 'I could speak to Chris Talbot. I used your mobile to ring him earlier, so you should be able to raise him. Maybe he'll have some ideas.'

Chris Talbot replied on the third ring.

'Mr Talbot. Ellie Quicke here, with some good and some bad news. But first, how is Julian?'

The calm voice was as controlled as ever, but a slight tremor showed fear had entered his life. 'He's a fighter. We hope, we pray.'

'Same here. The bad news first. Arthur thinks he sorted everything out this morning with his friends. You might like to check that your alliance is still in place. Now for the good news: Felicity has left Arthur and managed to bring away his laptop and mobile with her . . . what did you say? Are you still there?'

'Yes. Continue.'

'He may have missed them already. We're going to try to copy the hard drive, get as much information as we can, and return both to him quickly. Hopefully without him suspecting anything. Only, although my aunt knows a lot about computers, we don't necessarily have the right equipment. We thought it might be good to copy the recorded messages on the mobile, but again, we're not sure how. We've tried the police, but there's no one there who knows anything about the case at the moment.'

'Let me think.' He sounded stronger now. 'Can you bring them up to my office in town? I can get someone to meet us there, someone who knows how to copy hard drives. I can't send my car for you, since I'll need it to get there myself. Take a cab. I'll pay. Bring the mobile too.'

Thomas frowned, but Roy called out, 'I'll bring them. Tell me where and when.'

Chris Talbot heard that. He said, 'Mrs Quicke, you know where. I'll have someone meet you in the foyer. Um, will Felicity . . . ?'

'I don't know. I'll ask her,' said Ellie.

He rang off, and Ellie went through into the dining room next door, which Miss Quicke used as her office. Miss Quicke had the laptop open, and was talking on her phone. 'So you see, it's really urgent. You say all you need is your laptop and a connection to make them speak to one another? You can do it straight away? Good. We'll give you supper, of course, and make it worth your while. Now, what about the mobile . . . ? No, I understand.'

She switched off. 'He'll be here in half an hour with his laptop. He says it'll take about an hour to copy the hard drive on to his computer, and then we can access the information at our leisure. Unfortunately he doesn't know how to transfer messages from a mobile phone. I suggest we listen to what messages there may be on the mobile and Ellie can take them down in shorthand and type them out for us. No need to involve Mr Talbot.'

'He's very keen to do something,' said Ellie. 'His son's fighting for his life.'

'I realize that,' said Miss Quicke, 'but he's too deeply involved in this to be an impartial witness. If we get Jock to do it, he's an independent expert and the police can use whatever he can get for us. Mr Talbot is an interested party and the police could say that he might have tampered with the evidence.'

Ellie said, 'You're right, as usual. I'll ring him back and tell him what we've arranged. Save him a trip into London.'

Rose was twittering in the doorway. 'Is it all right to take the food in now? I've already dished up and it's been keeping warm, but I don't want it to spoil.'

Miss Quicke struggled to her feet, her face calm but her hands trembling. 'Yes, take it in, Rose. We might as well eat while we're waiting for Jock. Remember to put some aside for him. That boy doesn't eat enough to keep a cat alive.'

Everyone processed back to the drawing room, where Rose had put up the side leaves of a pretty Pembroke table, and laid it for four: Thomas and Roy, Ellie and Felicity. Miss Quicke had hers on a tray on her lap beside the fire.

As Ellie got through to Mr Talbot, Rose brought in plates of roast beef, Yorkshire pudding, roast potatoes, parsnips and Brussels sprouts. Thomas's eye brightened. 'Rose, if ever you get tired of working for Miss Quicke, you can come and be my housekeeper and cook!'

Rose went pink. 'Oh, but I'd never get tired of . . . Ellie knows . . . and Miss Quicke, too! It's a pleasure to . . .'

Miss Quicke patted her arm, smiling. 'My dear Rose, take it as a compliment.'

Ellie went out into the hall to hear Mr Talbot better on Thomas's mobile. 'Mr Talbot? Panic over. My aunt's got some expert to come in and copy the hard drive. It'll only take about an hour. So there's no need for you to traipse all the way into town. Save you a journey.'

'I'd prefer to supervise this myself. I don't trust anonymous "experts".'

'I daresay,' said Ellie, who was hungry and noticed that the others had started to eat. 'But the police might not trust your people either. I can assure you this is an independent expert, who'd stand up to scrutiny by the police. Best leave it at that.'

Was he grinding his teeth? Was he already in his car on the way back to town? It sounded rather like it. He said, 'Do you know if Arthur's missed his laptop yet?'

'We think he may have done. He's tried to ring Felicity, but she turned her mobile off, and I'm not at home. He may look there, of course, but the house will be in darkness. He doesn't know anything about my aunt, so we're safe enough here for the moment.'

'How do you propose to return his laptop and mobile without his bringing a charge of theft against you?'

'I'm not sure. We'll probably say Felicity was so flustered when she left, that she didn't realize that she'd packed them with her things. We'll get them back to him this evening.'

'You're at your aunt's, you say. Where is that?'

Ellie thought it over. 'I think I'd prefer not to tell you. Better safe than sorry. I do hope your son pulls through. Goodbye.' She shut off the phone and took her place at the table. The others were halfway through their platefuls, and eyeing hers, so she tucked in.

Aunt Drusilla was pecking at something bland. She was not resting easily in her chair either. Her hip must be causing her a lot of pain.

A ring at the door, and Rose called out, 'Yoohoo! Jock's here. I'll take him straight in, shall I?'

Aunt Drusilla tried to rise, and fell back in her chair with a suppressed exclamation of pain. 'Ellie, you explain what we need done.'

Ellie abandoned her half-empty plate, hoping the rest of her food would still be there when she returned, and went into the dining room, where a young black man, sporting gold rings at ears, nose and eyebrow, was setting up a laptop on the table. Miss Quicke had referred to Jock as a 'boy', and to her he must seem youthful, though he must have been in his late twenties. He was dressed all in black, with every item of clothing sporting a name. Nike, mostly.

'I'm Miss Quicke's niece,' said Ellie. 'What she wants is to—'

'Have a look at what this other fella's been up to, right?' He had the typical West Londoner's glottal stop, missing off the end of words. He didn't seem bothered about the ethics of what he was about to do.

'Yes. You see, the police—'

'Sure.' He opened his own laptop, produced a wire, and connected it to Sir Arthur's. His fingers danced over keys. He sniffed. Coughed. He seemed to have a cold.

Rose came through with a tray for him. A full-size plate of roast beef with all the trimmings, plus a can of beer. 'How's your wife, Jock? And the little one?'

'Fine, Rose. The little one's teething. No need for you ladies to hang around. I'll be all right now. Let you know when I'm done.'

Dismissed, Rose and Ellie retreated to the hall. Ellie lowered her voice to say to Rose, 'My aunt's in a lot of pain, Has she got something to help her sleep?'

Rose replied, also low down. 'I'm not supposed to tell you, but after you'd all had a go at her the other day, she did make an appointment to see the specialist next week.' She raised her voice again. 'I'll bring in the coffee in just a minute.'

The two women nodded at one another, well pleased by this exchange of information, and Ellie returned to the drawing room to find the others starting on apple pie with cream. Nine o'clock. How long would it be before Sir Arthur tracked them down? How long was Jock going to take to copy the hard disc?

When Ellie had cleared her plate of apple pie, Miss Quicke announced that they really must get on and deal with the mobile.

Her phone rang. Everyone froze, looking at it. Then relaxed, for it couldn't be Sir Arthur, could it? Miss Quicke picked it up, and handed it over to Ellie.

'Ellie, thank God you're there. What's going on? It's Kate. Sorry. Should have said. The thing is, I wasn't sure where you'd be. Took a chance.' It wasn't like Kate to panic.

'What is it, Kate?' Ellie saw the others were all listening.

'Sir Arthur came to the door here about a quarter of an hour ago. Diana was with him. Very angry. Wanted to know where you were. I said I hadn't the slightest idea, which was the truth, of course. He didn't believe me. He pushed past me, knocked Armand down, and searched the house, waking the baby, can you believe? He shoved me against the wall and said I'd better tell him where you were. So I asked him whatever was the matter, had there been an accident, because I hadn't seen you all day. Armand agreed. Armand was furious — you know how he can be — and said he was calling the police. He got as far as dialing nine-nine-nine before Sir Arthur pulled the phone away from the wall and stormed out.'

Ellie sank on to the nearest chair, trying to think. Arthur was looking for her already!

Kate continued, 'Armand phoned the police on his mobile, but while he did so, Sir Arthur got into his car and stormed off. There are lights on in every room in your house. The curtains haven't been drawn, though, and I can see Diana is there . . .'

'Diana has her own key. She must have let them in.'

'Yes, and made a mess. They've been looking for something, to judge by the way things have been thrown around. I rang the bell and Diana came to the door. Said you'd stolen something of Sir Arthur's and he wanted it back. She seemed to think you might have gone up to see Mrs Dawes . . .'

'No. Tomorrow.'

'Well, apparently there was a message on the answerphone from Mrs Dawes and they thought you might be there, and that's where he's gone.'

Ellie put her hand over her eyes. 'Kate, that's terrible! Mrs Dawes has got nothing to do with this, and at the moment she can hardly walk because she's hurt her bad knee. She'll have difficulty getting to the door to answer it, and if he were to push her over . . .'

'I'll get Armand to tell the police that, get them to go round there. Do I need to ask what this is all about?'

'The less you know, the better. Except, you might tell Gwyn that Sir Arthur thinks he's shored up his defences today. I'll be back later. Catch up with you tomorrow, with any luck.'

'Oh, before you go,' said Kate, 'you wanted some information on poisoners. I ran off some stuff from the Internet, and dropped it through your letter box, all right?'

Ellie thanked Kate, put the phone down and relayed what she'd learned to the others. 'I can trust Armand to get the police to go round to Mrs Dawes', I think. She may even have gone to bed by now, and if Sir Arthur finds the house in darkness, presumably he won't try to get in.'

Thomas grunted, 'I wouldn't put it past him. Tell you what, I know a retired soldier lives in that road. How's about I give him a ring, ask him to keep an eye out for any ructions? I'll tell him not to get involved, but if there's any trouble, he can ring the police too. That should do it.'

Felicity asked, 'If Arthur's not at home, would it be a good idea if I rang there and left a message, saying I was having supper with friends but I'd found his laptop among my things, and would drop it back there later this evening?'

Thomas considered that. 'He may not believe you, but it's as good an excuse as any.'

The others agreed, so Felicity got out her mobile, and made the call.

'You won't go back there by yourself,' said Roy, coming over all noble and protective.

'Of course not,' said Felicity, giving him a baby stare. 'With a bit of luck, he'll still be out searching for us when I take the stuff back. I'll get a minicab to take me there. The cab driver can watch while I drop it in the porch and then I'll make a quick getaway. Arthur won't do anything in front of a minicab driver — especially if I haven't paid him.'

Felicity had, in effect, refused Roy's offer of assistance, so presumably she'd discounted him as a future boyfriend? Good. Roy wasn't making too good a showing at the moment. He seemed to be forthcoming and withdrawn by fits and starts. He definitely had something on his mind. She caught Miss Quicke's eye, and they exchanged a moment of concern about Roy. Well, one or other of them would get it — whatever 'it' was — out of him sooner rather than later.

Thomas was fiddling with Sir Arthur's mobile. Time to listen to the messages.

CHAPTER NINETEEN

Thomas said, 'There seem to be two messages. What do you make of this, Ellie? The first message was recorded at seven p.m. on Saturday evening. He's speaking quite loudly. Can you all hear it?'

He pressed the button, and they heard a man's voice speaking above traffic noise. 'Mutt and Jeff are OK, no problem. I've seen Leonardo, and he's wriggling, but he'll come through in the end. I'll be at home if you need me.'

Ellie seized a piece of paper and looked for a pen in her bag. 'Mutt and Jeff . . .'

Felicity said, 'Can you really do shorthand? I thought all that went out with the Ark.'

'It did,' said Ellie, refusing to take umbrage. 'But it's useful. Now, have I got this right? "Mutt and Jeff are OK." Did he say, "Leonardo"? As in "da Vinci"?'

'That's what I heard. Who's Leonardo?' said Thomas.

'Leonardo di Caprio,' said Felicity, looking smug. 'The film star, of course.'

Once again Ellie met her aunt's eye, and this time both looked away. They'd guessed who "Leonardo" was. "Leonardo da Vinci" had been rather clever with a pen and pencil, and so was Roy. But they were not going to say anything before the others, unless Roy admitted to it, and it appeared he wasn't going to. No way.

'"Mutt and Jeff?"' Roy was frowning at the ceiling. 'Pseudonyms, I assume. Hit men?'

'The men who ran young Julian down?' This was Thomas. 'Anyone recognize the man's voice?'

'I think it's Martinez,' said Felicity. 'Arthur's PA. He's slimy.' She shuddered. 'But clever. If the accident with Julian was arranged, then he'd have been the one to do it. You can be pretty sure that "Mutt and Jeff" won't talk. Even if we could find them.'

'We leave all that to the police,' said Miss Quicke. 'What about the other message?'

It was Martinez again. This time there was no sound of traffic in the background, and the voice was clearer. 'I'm taking a few days off. Family trouble back home. I'll be in touch.'

Thomas said, 'Recorded this afternoon, Sunday, two p.m. Do you think he'd just heard that the boy whose "accident" he'd arranged was fighting for his life? So he's making himself scarce? Felicity, do you know where his home is?'

Felicity shrugged. 'Spain? Morocco?'

Ellie finished writing it down, and read it out. Everyone nodded. She'd transcribed it perfectly.

Miss Quicke said, 'You can type it out and we'll all sign it as being a correct record of what we've heard. Is there anything else we can learn from the phone before we give it back?'

'Address book,' suggested Ellie. 'Read out all the numbers, Thomas. The police may find them useful.'

Rose had cleared the table, so Ellie and Thomas got into a huddle, taking down the numbers. Felicity twirled a lock of hair round her finger. Roy fidgeted until his mother told him not to. Then he suggested a game of whist to pass the time.

Everyone looked at him in amazement, and he reddened, apologized, said he didn't know what he was thinking of. Ellie met Miss Quicke's eye, and they both sighed gently.

'Roy,' said Miss Quicke. 'Go and see if Jock wants any more food, there's a dear. Ask him how long he's going to be.

It's past my bedtime, but I can't leave things up in the air like this. Felicity, my dear, would you like to stay here tonight?'

Felicity shook her head. 'I've got to get the laptop and mobile back to Arthur, and all my things are at Ellie's.'

Diana was also at Ellie's. How long would she stay? Would Arthur meet her back there? Ellie had quite often regretted letting her daughter have a key, but she'd never gone so far as to demand it back, or have the locks changed. Perhaps she'd do just that, now.

Jock appeared in the doorway, cheerful but coughing. 'All done. Who wants the disc?'

Miss Quicke held up her hand, and beckoned him over to her. She pulled him down so that she could speak in his ear. He nodded once or twice, said 'Can do!' and reached for a tissue to blow his nose. Miss Quicke said, 'Jock, you aren't going down with another cold, are you?'

'No, no. The wife says I ought to take time off, but you know how it is.'

'I do.' Miss Quicke said. 'Let me have a bill, as usual. Treble time on Sundays, remember. My regards to your wife.'

Rose appeared, holding the tray she'd taken in to Jock. 'He's only eaten half his food, Miss Quicke.'

'You're too good to me, and I'd eaten already,' said Jock, and removed himself. Ellie listened for the front door closing, but it didn't. Had Jock gone back into the dining room to collect his things? Oh, probably.

Everyone looked at the clock. Nearly ten. 'Past my bedtime,' said Miss Quicke.

Ellie said, 'Give me a few minutes on your computer, Aunt Drusilla, and I'll run this stuff off for you. If someone can dictate the numbers to me, that would make it even quicker.'

Felicity didn't volunteer, but Thomas did. He followed her into the dining room, where Miss Quicke's computer was all set up and running. Also set up and running was a strange laptop. Jock's? Thomas didn't notice anything out of the ordinary, because he hadn't been in this room before, but Ellie did.

As she settled herself at her aunt's computer, she began to wonder about the last-minute whispered instructions Miss Quicke had given to Jock. He'd had the hard drive in his hand when he came into the room. And when he went out again. So what had he done with it?

Thomas cleared his throat. 'Do you want to open a new document?'

Flustered, Ellie concentrated on opening a document and started to type in her transcription of the messages on the mobile, and also the address-book details. Thomas's diction was good. She was getting a little tired, but by dint of concentrating hard, they had soon run off a couple of copies of all the information they'd gleaned from the mobile phone.

All the while, Ellie wondered why Jock had left his own laptop all set up and running, for Miss Quicke to use. Had he replaced his own hard drive with the copy of Sir Arthur's? So that Miss Quicke could access the information straight away? Probably. Should she say anything about it? Well, probably not. No.

'Oof,' said Ellie, easing her back. 'Aunt's computer's at the wrong height for me. Now to get everyone to sign them as a true record, etcetera.'

Time to restore Arthur's belongings to him. Hopefully when he wasn't there.

Felicity signed the sheets and passed them to Miss Quicke. 'I've no keys to get back in with, so I'll have to leave his things in the porch and then ring him, tell him what I've done.'

Ellie crossed her fingers. Like Felicity, she sincerely hoped Arthur would be out when they dumped the stuff on his doorstep. Only, if he were out . . . where would he be?

'I'll phone for a cab,' said Ellie, stooping to kiss her aunt's cheek.

'I'll take you,' said Thomas, getting out his keys.

'No, let me,' said Roy, a fraction too late.

'Thank you, Thomas,' said Ellie. 'I'd appreciate it. Thank you, Roy, but you don't need to get your car out again tonight.'

She collected Arthur's mobile from the dining room, and put it in her basket with his laptop. 'Ready, Felicity?'

Felicity shuddered, but nodded.

'Courage, girl,' said Miss Quicke, and uncharacteristically added, 'You may kiss me goodnight, if you wish.'

This from a woman who had despised all gestures of affection till recently.

Felicity was dabbing at her eyes as Thomas inserted her into the back seat of the car, and helped Ellie to belt up in the front. It was a dark night, threatening rain again.

Thomas's car was reassuringly large and felt protective as they crossed the Avenue and turned into the road where Arthur lived. His house was in darkness except for a light in one downstairs room and the hall, but as they turned into the drive, security lights flashed on. There was also a light on in the flat above the garage. No one had yet cleaned the graffiti off the garage doors.

Felicity said, 'It looks as if Marco's still there. Those lights inside the main house are on time switches. If Arthur were in, there'd be a light on in his den — it's at the back, but you can see a reflection in the sky if it's on. If Arthur's in his bedroom, then the bedroom light would be on, and it isn't. None of the curtains have been drawn. He's still out.' She got out of the car, taking the laptop and mobile with her, put them tidily in a large wooden mailbox in the porch, and returned to the car. 'I'd better ring his landline, tell him what I've done.'

She got out her phone. They could all hear the phone in the hall ringing, ringing. The answerphone clicked in. Felicity said, no sign of nerves in her voice, 'Sorry about taking your stuff. I didn't realize I'd got it till too late. It's in the box in the porch.'

Thomas set the car in motion again.

'Home, please,' said Ellie, wondering if Diana were still there. Or Arthur. Wondering if the light was still on up in Felicity's old bedroom, or if it would stay on till the cleaner came on the morrow.

Thomas was obviously thinking along the same lines. 'I'll come in with you, of course.'

'Thank you, Thomas.'

It wasn't far to her house. She wished it were further. Diana's car was outside her house. So was another big car, which she assumed must be Arthur's.

There were lights on upstairs at Kate and Armand's, but none on downstairs.

Her own house showed lights in every window. No curtains had been drawn. As she walked down the path to the front door, she could see into her front room. The television was on, and Diana sat there, watching it. With Arthur.

Ellie took a deep breath. 'Yes, Thomas. Please do come in with us.'

She got out her key, and let them into the house. On the floor in the hall there was a re-used envelope addressed to her in Kate's writing. That would contain information about poisoners. Some of Felicity's clothes had been strewn all the way up the staircase. Her grandmother's jewel box lay open at the foot of the stairs, a couple of old-fashioned necklaces and three pearl drop earrings exposed to view.

Someone switched off the television. Bracing herself, Ellie opened the door to the living room. There were no great signs of a search here, though cupboard doors had been pulled open and left that way. Also, the coffee table was out of alignment with the settee.

'About time, too,' said Diana. 'Where have you been?' An empty bottle of wine and a couple of glasses lay on the coffee table between her and Arthur. He was very much at his ease, lying back on the settee next to Diana. He looked somewhat dishevelled. Diana looked immaculate, but then she always did. Perhaps she'd been 'entertaining' him, and it had blunted the edge of his usual ferocity? He didn't even bother to rise when they came in. Perhaps he'd even been dozing?

'Hello, Diana. Sir Arthur? This is a surprise. We've been out to supper,' said Ellie, playing the part of the innocent little woman. 'Do you know Thomas, our vicar, by the way? Sir Arthur, have you come for the things Felicity took by mistake? She *was* upset when she realized what she'd done, but there . . . it's not every day you catch your husband kissing his mistress in front of you, is it? You've had a wasted journey, I'm afraid. We've just dropped the things back at your house.'

'I did phone you, Arthur,' said Felicity, in a trembling voice. 'As soon as I found out. But you weren't there. We were invited out for supper, but as soon as I could get away, I dropped the things back at the house for you.'

He struggled to his feet, glowering, suspicious but not entirely sure of his ground. If they'd been alone, he'd probably have hit Felicity, but he couldn't do that with so many witnesses, especially with thickset Thomas standing at Felicity's side. 'That's all very well, but you sent me on a wild goose chase, up hill and down dale, knocking up neighbours, being shouted at by some stupid old guy who flourished an air rifle at me, if you please.'

Thomas's face never moved a muscle, but Ellie felt like cracking up. It was all too funny, too dreadful. Altogether too much.

'Well, if that's all,' she said, brightly, 'it's off to beddy-byes for us. It's been a long day and . . .'

The doorbell rang. Insistently. Everyone froze. Ellie didn't know that ring. People rang the doorbell in different ways; some were tentative, some took two goes at it. Some held on to it for an extended count. This wasn't anyone she knew, but she guessed straight away who it might be.

Chris Talbot. She let him in, not knowing how to refuse him entry. He wiped his shoes on the mat and stepped inside. 'Forgive the late hour.'

He had every intention of coming in, of course, despite his apology.

Arthur's face turned purple with fury. 'What the . . . !'

Chris Talbot didn't extend his hand, but looked around with interest. Ellie was struck for the first time by how small and shabby her house was, compared with his grand penthouse suite, or with Arthur's imposing mansion.

Felicity gasped. She was quivering. 'Go away. I haven't anything to say to you.'

Ellie said, 'Anyone like a coffee? Mr Talbot, this is Thomas, our vicar. And the girl on the settee is my daughter, Diana.'

Chris nodded pleasantly to Thomas, and turned his bright blue gaze on Arthur. 'I didn't expect to find you here, Arthur. I believe the police are looking for your man Martinez, as well as for Marco. A little matter of murder. I hope they find them soon.'

'Murder!'

Who'd said that? The room was still. Nobody seemed to breathe, even.

'Murder?' Arthur stood with his legs apart on the hearthrug. 'I haven't murdered anyone.' But a flush rose into his face.

'Really?' Chris Talbot proceeded to unbutton and take off a superb cashmere and wool coat. He was wearing a casual but beautifully cut cashmere sweater over grey trousers underneath. 'Well, that's for a jury to decide, isn't it?'

'I've no need to commit murder,' said Arthur, with a hint of uncertainty in his voice. Did he know exactly what 'Mutt and Jeff' had done?

'Haven't you?' Chris Talbot smiled, and laid his coat down over the back of a chair. Ellie had an impulse to take it out and hang it up in the hall — on a hanger, of course. Not by a loop. That coat demanded reverential treatment.

She said, 'As it happens, Arthur's just leaving. My daughter, too. By the way, Diana; I'm having the locks changed, so will you let me have your front door key before you go?'

Thomas held the door open, and somehow this action released the others from their frozen state. Diana picked up her handbag and walked out, closely followed by Arthur until he swung round in the doorway to face Felicity.

'If you've tampered with my laptop . . . !'

'I never even opened it,' said Felicity, which was, of course, the literal truth. If misleading.

Arthur stared at her but when Diana called to him from the hall, he followed her out. The door banged to behind them.

'It's beginning to rain quite hard,' said Chris Talbot, seating himself unasked. 'Did you manage to copy his hard drive, and who's got the copy now?'

'It was successfully copied,' said Ellie, 'and it's being dropped into the police station together with a transcript of the messages on his phone. Both phone and laptop are now back at Sir Arthur's house, awaiting collection. Kate will warn Gwyn that Arthur thinks he's reinforced his alliances today. I'm afraid you've had a wasted journey.'

'Not at all. I've been wanting to meet my daughter again for a very long time.'

Felicity dropped on to a chair, looking away from him. 'Nothing to say.'

'I know your mother felt I'd let you both down, but I did try to keep in touch with you.'

'That's not what Mummy said.'

'Sometimes she hears only what she wants to hear. I did want to keep in touch, Felicity. I still do. More. I want to help, if you'll let me.'

Thomas had taken a seat by the door, and was blending into the background. Ellie tried to do the same.

Felicity twirled a lock of hair between her fingers, her eyes on the carpet. 'I've left Arthur.'

'I'm glad about that. I wasn't sure that he treated you well.'

'He didn't, but that's not it. I can stand on my own two feet. I've done it in the past, and I can do it again. I can get a job, find myself somewhere to live. Start again. But Mummy can't.'

'Will you allow me to take care of her bills at the home? I won't even make it a condition that you have supper with me every now and again.'

She threw him a frown. Ducked her eyes down again. 'You're trying to make conditions already, just by saying that.'

'I withdraw any hint of a condition. Unconditionally, I undertake to cover your mother's care.' He was clever enough not to say that he hoped for more.

Felicity thought that through. She had found some backbone from somewhere. Perhaps there was more of her father in her than was apparent at first sight? She nodded. 'I'll tell them at the home to send the bills to you in future.'

'You'll let me have your address?'

'I'm staying here with Ellie for a few days, until I can find something for myself.'

Ellie intervened. 'I'll make an appointment for her with my solicitor in the morning, to get started on divorce proceedings.'

Chris Talbot said, 'Why don't you let me . . . ?' He stopped, nodded. 'Right. I respect you for that too. The only thing I'd say is, if Arthur gives you any more grief, will you remember that I really do want to help?'

Felicity nodded, but didn't meet his eyes.

He picked up his beautiful coat, smoothed down the nap, and held out his hand to Ellie. 'Thank you for everything you've done. I hope the police will be able to act quickly on the information you've given them. I'm most grateful. By the way, I may have exaggerated a trifle back there. Julian is still alive. Just.'

He hesitated, looking towards Felicity, but she kept her eyes averted. He nodded to Thomas, smiled at Ellie, and made his exit, pulling the front door quietly shut behind him.

Thomas let out a long sigh of relief. 'You need oxygen tanks to move in these rarefied circles. Your father's got better manners than Arthur, Felicity, but I wouldn't care to cross either of them.'

The phone rang. From high tragedy to low comedy. It was Kate, wanting to know if they'd survived the visitations. 'Yes, we're all right,' said Ellie. 'I hear there was trouble at Mrs Dawes' but a neighbour stepped in to defuse the situation.'

'Armand rang the police. He went round there as well. I didn't want him to, but you know what he's like. Has to dash in and play the hero. He got there just as Sir Arthur was being prodded into his car by an elderly man with a fixed bayonet! Can you believe? Mrs Dawes must have taken a sleeping pill, for there were no lights on. The police arrived just as Armand and the old soldier parted company.'

'Bravo. I'll be going up to see Mrs Dawes tomorrow.'

'I've just thought,' said Kate. 'Who's got the hard drive? The police?'

'No,' said Ellie, beginning to smile. 'My aunt's got it, and I suspect she's making use of it right this minute. You can deal in shares round the clock nowadays, can't you?'

Kate laughed. 'Let's hope Gwyn gets his own way, then.'

She put the phone down. Ellie pressed the play button on her answerphone, but it was no good. 'You have no messages.' There had been at least one message on the phone before she went out, which meant that Diana had listened in, and deleted whatever voicemail was on the phone. Bother Diana! One would have been from Mrs Dawes, presumably? Otherwise Arthur wouldn't have gone haring up there. Ellie decided it was too late to ring her now.

Ellie drew the curtains, feeling tension seep away. 'I suppose it's all over now bar the shouting. We'll get the disc and the messages to the police tomorrow, and they can take it from there. So much sound and fury, and all because a dog died. We never did find out who'd done it, did we? I wonder if Mrs Dawes has any more news for us on that front, or should we just let it drop?'

'I think I'd like to know who killed Rex,' said Felicity. 'Poor Rex.'

Ellie tried to be positive. 'Shall we have a hot cuppa before we call it a day?'

They sat round the kitchen table and drank herbal tea, hoping it'd have a soothing effect.

Thomas was thoughtful.

Ellie was contrite. 'Thomas, I should never have got you involved in all this. All the lies we've told today! From your point of view, it must have been difficult to take.'

'White lies, fibs and misdirection. It's been an education. Felicity—' and here he put his large hand over hers — 'told white lies in order to survive. My dear, be brave; that part of your life is over now.'

Ellie pushed the box of tissues towards Felicity, who sniffled but didn't break down.

Ellie said, 'I lied too. I told Chris Talbot the hard drive was on its way to the police. I'm not a hundred per cent sure why. He's on our side, isn't he?'

Thomas shook his head. 'He's on his own side. We're caught between tycoons.'

'The only person to benefit from that lie is my aunt, who is probably accessing the information on the disc at this very moment, with a view to making yet another fortune on the Stock Exchange.'

'Three tycoons,' said Thomas, smiling. 'When is Miss Quicke going to do something about her hip?'

'Next week, Rose says.'

'*Deo gratias*,' said Thomas. 'The Lord be praised. I admire Miss Quicke enormously, and that has nothing to do with the fact that she may help us rebuild the vicarage.'

Felicity mopped her eyes. 'I wasn't always a good wife to Arthur. Sometimes — just occasionally, you know — I almost hated him. He can't help having high standards. I should have tried harder to live up to them.'

Ellie eyed her with irritation, but Thomas knew how to soothe her. 'My dear, everyone has regrets in such circumstances. May I ask whether you were married in church or not?'

'Registry office. It was all done in a hurry, and we couldn't have a big "do" because Mummy was in hospital after her accident.'

Thomas nodded. He'd find it easier to come to terms with a civil marriage which had broken up — especially one entered into under such circumstances — than one celebrated in church.

'I feel awful,' Felicity confessed, 'because I think I'll miss not having a dog more than I'll miss Arthur. I was often a bit . . . well, anxious . . . about what mood he'd be in when he came home. But the dogs were always loving. I think they loved me more than they loved him, though of course they were his dogs really. I wonder who he'll get to look after his new dog.'

'Cheer up,' said Ellie. 'We'll make an appointment to see a good solicitor in the morning.' Come to think of it, another message on the answerphone might have been from Bill Weatherspoon, whom she'd asked to ring back, urgently. 'And perhaps you'd better check your bank account. Have you a joint account?'

Felicity shook her head. 'A household account in my name. There's nothing much in it. Not even enough for me to put down a deposit on a flat. That's another thing I'll miss: not having a garden. Oh dear, I'm going to cry again.'

'Bedtime,' said Ellie, who was also feeling rather tired. 'Things will look better in the morning. It will be the first day of the rest of your life, remember. We'll sort things out. Meanwhile, you can stay here.'

Thomas got to his feet and stretched. 'Keep in touch, right?'

'Dear Thomas. Thank you for everything.'

Felicity was preoccupied. 'I'll still go to visit Mummy, of course, but perhaps not as much as before.'

'That's right, dear,' said Ellie, seeing Thomas to the front door, and shooting the bolts behind him. 'Felicity, would you like a hot-water bottle to take to bed with you?'

Felicity was slowly going up the stairs to bed, gathering up her belongings on the way. 'Mummy's going to be furious about me accepting help from my father.'

'Does she need to know?' said Ellie, collecting the envelope of data which Kate had left for her. She'd try to look at it before she fell asleep. 'Now, what sort of mess has Arthur made up here?'

It wasn't too bad. Felicity folded and placed her clothes into the chest of drawers, and replaced the duvet, which had been shucked on to the floor. She sat on the bed to open one of her photograph albums. 'Would you like to see a picture of the manor?'

'Not tonight, dear,' said Ellie, drawing the curtains and making sure the bedside light — which had been tossed to the floor — still worked. Which it did. 'I must go to find Midge. My cat, you know? I'd forgotten all about him, but he doesn't like Diana, so he may still be outside.'

Felicity started to turn over the pages of the album. Ellie left her to it.

Midge met her on the landing and together they inspected Ellie's bedroom — where doors had been left open, and drawers pulled out, but nothing much else disturbed. Midge jumped on to the bed and made himself comfortable. Ellie opened the envelope Kate had left for her. Sheets and sheets of information. She started reading, but was too tired to make sense of it.

Famous poisoners . . . some pictures, mostly women . . . they all looked as if butter wouldn't melt . . . poison seemed to be the weapon used by people who had no other means of inflicting harm . . .

There was something knocking at the back of her mind . . . someone's knocking at my window . . . someone's knocking at my door . . . it was too late to think straight. She yawned.

The end of a trying day, Lord. Much to be thankful for. Not least, Thomas, who was quite wonderful . . . so glad Aunt Drusilla's doing something about her hip . . . thank you, Lord . . . and please look after young Julian, who I do hope will survive . . . strange to think Felicity's never even met her half-brothers . . . please look after Felicity . . . and all of us . . .

CHAPTER TWENTY

A wet Monday morning. Yuk. Dark and gloomy, and not all that warm either.

Ellie felt the let-down after all the excitement of the night before. Now, it was just a matter of clearing up. Wasn't it? Then why did she feel so tense? She tidied up and put away the papers that Kate had sent her on poisoners. Then took them out and looked at them again. The trouble was that she knew so little about people who'd commit murder at long distance. It wasn't something a normal housewife came across often.

She decided to discuss the subject with Kate some time. But not now.

Felicity must be feeling downhearted, too. Ellie decided to ignore her own forebodings and be positive about everything.

When did the hour go back? Next week? Better try to get the garden tidied up before then, and replace those broken plants in the conservatory. Perhaps think about having some decorating done? The house hadn't been touched since before dear Frank died, and it could do with a facelift. Something really ought to be done about the kitchen.

There was no sound from Felicity's room as Ellie showered, dressed, went down to give Midge his breakfast, and then get her own. The newspaper had come, but the paperboy had left it on the floor of the porch so that the rain had wet it. Bother. That box in Arthur's porch must be a good thing in wet weather, keeping all the post out of the rain. Perhaps she could have something like that in her own porch?

The rain looked as if it were setting in for the day. Ellie made a shopping list. Felicity came down, looking washed out but consenting to eat some tea and toast.

'The first day of the rest of my life,' said Felicity, looking out of the window at the rain. 'I couldn't sleep, thinking of all the things I ought to have taken from the house and didn't. There's some family papers and my birth and marriage certificates for a start. My christening cup that my godmother gave me. My building society book, though it hasn't got much in it. How could I have left them?'

'You weren't thinking straight, and no wonder. We'll collect them today.'

'I haven't got keys to the house now, but Arthur will be up in the City, so I thought if we waited till Maureen gets there about ten — Maureen's the cleaner and a really nice person — then she could let us in, and I could take the most important things, and perhaps pack up some of the other stuff to be collected later.'

Ellie noted the 'we'. Obviously she'd have to jettison whatever she'd planned for that day — except for visiting Mrs Dawes. 'I'll look out a couple of suitcases for you.'

She noticed that one of the replacement glass panes in the conservatory was letting in water. Not enough putty? Bother. 'Let's make lists, shall we?' There was no point both of them feeling dreary. 'At nine o'clock we'll ring Bill for an appointment. Then you can ring the garage and find out how much your car's going to cost.'

'Too much. I'll have to leave it there.'

'Felicity, I have a trust fund which disburses money for deserving causes. Kate is one of the trustees, and I'm another. I'm going to suggest we make you a grant of a couple of thousand pounds to tide you over.'

Felicity gaped. 'Why would you do that?'

'Because I was once as downtrodden and apologetic a little wifey as you. I couldn't say boo to a goose, and that's partly why Diana is like she is. When my husband died, I had good friends to help me sort myself out, and now I'd like to help you in the same way. No strings. A proper loan, to be repaid when you get your maintenance sorted out.'

'Arthur won't want to pay me anything.' She shivered. 'Honest, it would be better not to ask.'

'*You* won't ask. Your solicitor will. Right? So ring the garage, discover the total, and get your car back.'

The phone rang, and Felicity jumped. 'Sorry. I keep thinking he's going to come round and . . . stupid of me!'

It was Mrs Dawes on the phone, booming away. 'Ellie, dear. Did you get my message last night?'

Ellie explained that no, she hadn't, unfortunately. It turned out that Mrs Dawes had forgotten to ask Ellie to fetch some powder for her athlete's foot from the chemist, so would she . . . ? Of course Ellie would. And added it to her list. 'Did you sleep all right, then?'

'Like a top. The knee's a lot better today, too. Oh, and my friend who lives by the park is coming round this morning. She says Mrs Meadows-Fitch is moving out of London very soon, so you'd better get round there if you want to catch her.'

'Mrs Meadows-Fitch?' Ellie couldn't for the moment place her. Then she remembered Rose and Aunt Drusilla talking about the ex-mayor's wife, who'd been accustomed to the high life when her husband was alive and allegedly had helped Sir Arthur to push some highly questionable planning permissions through. It wasn't worth going to see her now, though. Was it?

As she put the phone down, it rang again. Aunt Drusilla, at her most imperious.

'Ellie, do you know when the police are coming round to collect this hard drive? I really don't care to have such sensitive material lying around.'

'I'm not sure. Thomas asked . . .'

'I wasn't particularly impressed with either of the junior police we saw yesterday. Don't we know someone a little higher up the chain?'

'I suppose that . . .'

'Ah yes, I remember now. There's a detective inspector I met some time ago. A difficult woman, but then, it's a difficult job, isn't it? I'll get on to her straight away.' The phone clicked off.

Trust Aunt Drusilla to get things done.

'Come on, Felicity. Ring the garage.'

Felicity took the receiver as if it would bite her, but did ring the garage. When told the cost, she bit her lip, but said she'd be round in half an hour to pay the bill and collect the car. 'Then I can drive us over to the house.'

'First we find out if Bill can see you today.' He could, that afternoon. 'Bill's nice,' said Ellie. 'You'll like him.'

'Who's Mrs Meadows-Fitch? Did she kill Rex?'

'I really don't know. She's someone else your husband's done down, and who's feeling annoyed about it.'

Felicity brightened up. 'I think I met her at some reception at the town hall. I used to go with Arthur sometimes. Awfully hot and crowded, but he knew so many people, and liked to keep in touch. She's funny.'

'Funny as in making you laugh?'

Felicity screwed up her face. 'Funny as in how many Botox injections can you have before your face falls apart? She ought to wear a wig because her hair's got awfully thin. Also, she doesn't like dogs. What makes you think it wasn't her? I'd really like it to be her.'

'I don't really think we can go crashing in on people just because they don't like dogs.'

'I do.' Felicity's chin came out. 'If I could find out who killed Rex, I'd . . . I don't know what I'd do, but I'd make them pay for it. If you won't go and see her, then I will.'

'Before or after you get yourself a job and somewhere to live?'

The girl flushed. 'I'm sorry. I'm all over the place, aren't I? One minute I feel fine and strong, and the next — you'll laugh — I want to crawl to Arthur, beg him to take me back, tell him that I don't mind what he does with Diana so long as I don't have to see it.'

Ellie patted her arm. 'But you won't. Now your bike's still here, but it's not safe for you to ride it in this rain. Let's get a minicab to the garage and collect your car. Then do a bit of shopping in the Avenue and take it up to Mrs Dawes. After that, we'll swing by your house and collect what you want, have a spot of lunch back here and then I'll take you up to see Bill this afternoon. Isn't that enough for one day?'

'We could drop in on the ex-lady mayoress before we do the shopping.'

Ellie shrugged. Well, why not? She went to ring Kate to make sure all was well with her — it was. Armand had gone back to school now the half term was over, Catriona was teething, oh dear, and Gwyn had reported overnight dealings in the corporation's stock which were — rather surprising.

'Aunt Drusilla?' guessed Ellie. 'I think she had Jock set up the hard drive for her on his laptop last night, so that she could access Sir Arthur's secrets without us knowing.'

'I wouldn't put it past her,' said Kate, who admired Miss Quicke.

Ellie said, 'She's handing the hard drive over to the police this morning.'

'I wouldn't have minded a sight of it.'

'Neither would Chris Talbot, but he didn't get it. Any news of young Julian?'

'Nothing new. Did you get the information I left for you? If you want more, I can always get it for you.'

'Yes,' said Ellie, frowning. 'I found it surprising, and it made me worry a bit about someone I've met recently. But then, what do I know about it?'

'You know people. Who do you suspect? Will you drop by later? Of course I'm not bored. How could I be, with Catriona to look after? She's quite adorable. But I'm screaming inside, Ellie. I should be up in the City, working out how to foil Sir Arthur's little plots, but I can't leave Catriona. I don't want to leave her.'

'No, of course you don't,' said Ellie, wondering if she ought to offer to babysit, but deciding that babysitting Felicity was enough for one day. The girl had washed up the breakfast things and was fidgeting, ready to go.

'Hold on a mo,' said Ellie. 'There's a couple of umbrellas in the hall which we'll need today, and I'll get out a couple of suitcases while you ring the minicab people. The number's by the phone in the hall. Then if you can find Mrs Meadows-Fitch's number in the book, perhaps you'd give her a call, ask if we can drop in for a few minutes . . . that is, if you still want to.'

'Yes, I do,' said Felicity, her chin coming out. Ellie shrugged. If the girl wanted to chase shadows, then why not?

The garage first. It was the sort of place that was a proper workshop and didn't try to sell cars on its forecourt. 'Arthur put some money into it, I think,' said Felicity. 'They always service our cars.'

They stood in the rain while Ellie paid off the minicab driver, settled the garage bill, and transferred her old suitcases to Felicity's car, which was not new but was dent-free. Felicity was a competent driver, Ellie noted.

As Ellie belted up, she said, 'Are you sure you want to go chasing up Mrs Meadows-Fitch?'

'Positive,' said Felicity. 'I hate loose ends. She said she'd be in, but couldn't give us long, because she's moving at the end of the week.'

Mrs Meadows-Fitch lived in a second-floor flat in an expensive block overlooking Haven Green. Felicity shook out her umbrella as she led the way to the lift. Ellie rang the bell, and they were let into a big, airy flat which was currently being dismantled. Brighter patches on the wallpaper showed where large pieces of furniture had once stood. Cardboard boxes were everywhere.

Mrs Meadows-Fitch advanced to meet them. Felicity's description of her had been cruelly accurate. The woman was wearing a brightly coloured scarf over her curls. The scarf was tied in a coquettish knot but didn't disguise the fact that the hair beneath was too thin, and too peroxided.

She looked disappointed at seeing Ellie and Felicity. 'I thought you said your husband wanted to see me?'

'Just me,' said Felicity. 'I heard you were having to move and I wanted to say how sorry I was to hear it.'

The woman's face settled back into lines of disappointment. Judging by the downward slant of her mouth, this was her usual expression. 'Well, I did think, after all we've done for him . . . but there's no expecting thanks or gratitude nowadays, is there? If there was any justice in this world, I wouldn't be moving into a poky little granny flat at the back of my son's place on the south coast, where I won't know anyone and there are no decent shops! It'll take me hours to get back up to Harrods, and the salt in the air will ruin the car. I'll have to leave it on the street in all weathers, which, as you can imagine, would make my poor husband turn in his grave if he were to see it.' She applied a tissue to the inner corner of each eye.

'So sad,' murmured Ellie. Their hostess had not invited them to take a seat, but Ellie did so, and gestured to Felicity to do the same. 'Everyone thought your husband was so close to Sir Arthur too.'

'Yes, he was.' The woman sniffed. 'I can't offer you coffee, I'm afraid. The good cups have all been packed up, though goodness knows when I shall have opportunity to use them, in my exile.'

'I thought the south coast very nice,' said Felicity, and was stopped by Ellie pressing on her foot.

Ellie gave Felicity a warning look, and continued, 'But no doubt your solicitor will be able to—'

'Huh! Him! My dear husband was conned into using Arthur's own solicitor, and it seems I haven't anything in writing to prove what we were promised, only four months ago! The life insurance! The portfolio of gilt-edged! Everything gone! I blame my husband, I do, even though I shouldn't, I know that. It's wrong to speak ill of the dead, but when I think . . . !' Here the tissue was applied again. Her mascara was beginning to smudge.

'Dear me,' said Ellie, all sympathy. 'Surely Sir Arthur didn't intend this?'

The woman sniffed. 'I've never been so completely taken in, in all my life. I thought him a perfect gentleman. He's all sorrowful now, of course. Says he's lost a packet, too, or otherwise he'd have done his best to see me right, which I don't believe! I've spiked his guns, I can tell you! I wasn't Lady Mayoress for nothing. I know a lot of important people. I heard he was keen to be elected to the Inner Wheel, so I've blackballed him!' She nodded in triumph.

'You didn't!' said Ellie, wondering if the woman had lost all her marbles. No word of censure from her was going to mar Sir Arthur's election to any club, however exclusive.

'I did! And the chairman told me himself that he was going to pass the word around. That'll larn him!'

'It will, indeed,' said Ellie, getting to her feet, and signalling to Felicity to do the same. 'I'm sure he'll really feel it. I do wish you all the very best in your new home.'

'Are you going already?' Mrs Meadows-Fitch had been glad of a sympathetic ear, and was not that keen to let them depart, but Ellie and Felicity managed to escape with only a few more polite words.

It was still raining when they got out again.

'Phew!' said Ellie as they got back into the car. 'Poor creature. I feel sorry for her. Well, it definitely wasn't her who sent the poisoned pizza.'

'How do you make that out? I'd really like it to be her.'

'Because . . .' Ellie thought about it. 'Because she took her revenge another way.'

'She's still a horrid thing,' said Felicity, turning on the ignition and setting the windscreen wipers twitching. 'Shopping next?'

Ellie was trying to remember everything Kate had dug up for her about poisoners. She really must go through it with Kate sometime. Meanwhile . . .

'Do you ever get time to yourself?' asked Felicity, as they drove down the hill. 'I mean, you're always running around after other people. Don't you get tired of it?'

'Sometimes. I like people.'

'You mean as in, "Love One Another"?'

Ellie blushed. 'I wouldn't say I'm that . . . I just do things. You know? Or try to.'

The shopping was soon done. As they got back into the car, Ellie noticed that Felicity had become very silent. She was probably dreading the return to the Kingsley residence. 'Mrs Dawes next, to drop off her things.'

Felicity nodded. 'You won't mind if I don't come in with you, will you? I've got a lot to think about.'

'Not at all. I'll be in and out in a trice, and then we can get the things from your house.' Ellie was as good as her word, flitting in and out under her umbrella, glad to hear that Mrs Dawes' knee was improving and that she had another old friend with her. It was still raining when Ellie got back into the car.

They parked in Sir Arthur's drive, both looking at a well-known car by the front door. Diana's. Felicity was very pale, but she got out of the car, ignoring the umbrella which Ellie offered her, and rang the doorbell. Ellie extricated the suitcases and followed her into the porch.

A stout, middle-aged woman came to the door, breathing heavily. When she saw who it was, she held the door wide open, while rolling her eyes to one side to indicate that all was not well within.

'Thank you, Maureen,' said Felicity. 'I'm glad you're here, so that I can explain what—'

'I think I explained everything to her, quite perfectly,' said Diana, who was standing in the hall with a clipboard in her hands. 'You're the ex-wife, and I'm the new Lady Kingsley. So what are you doing here?'

Felicity crimsoned. 'You're not Lady Kingsley yet. I keep the title, unless I marry again, of course.'

Ellie silently applauded, then turned to lug the suitcases inside.

'Mother, you here? You've hitched your wagon to a fading star this time, haven't you?'

'I don't think so, dear. Now, if you'll let me have the key to my house? I asked you for it yesterday, remember? I'll just help Felicity pack one or two things, and we'll be on our way.'

Diana twisted a key from her key ring and threw it on to the table. Ellie retrieved it.

Diana turned back to her clipboard. 'Now, if you don't mind, I have some measuring-up to do. This house needs redecorating from top to bottom.' She wandered up the stairs and out of sight.

Maureen watched her go. 'I'm not going to work for her, that's for sure. Not unless she doubles my wages. Where will you be, Lady Kingsley? In case there's some post for you?'

'I'm staying with my friend Mrs Quicke for a while. I've only come back to collect one or two things.'

'You fetch what you need,' said Ellie. 'Bring them down here, and I'll pack.'

It didn't take them long, because there wasn't all that much Felicity wanted to take, when it came down to it.

Felicity kissed Maureen and promised to keep in touch, they piled everything into the car and left. Was Diana watching from an upstairs window? Possibly.

Ellie fingered Diana's key, and put it in a side pocket of her purse. It occurred to her that Diana might well have thought to have a duplicate made, after Ellie had asked for it. It was — regrettably — the sort of thing Diana might do. Best get the locks changed.

Ellie and Felicity both tried to be cheerful over a scratch lunch. Felicity said how much she liked Ellie's conservatory, and could they eat out there? Which they did.

The rain thudded down on the glass roof. Ellie considered saying how cosy it was to be inside in the rain, but refrained.

Felicity said, 'I feel so odd. As if I'm waiting for something. Is there thunder in the air? I feel like that. I mean, we're quite safe now, aren't we?'

'Of course we are.' They were safe, weren't they? But yes, Ellie felt the tension too.

The phone rang and they both jumped. It was Roy, asking if Ellie might be free for a meal that evening. Ellie said no, because she had a guest staying. She didn't say it was Felicity, and Roy didn't ask. He sounded miserable.

As she returned to the kitchen, where Felicity was washing up, Ellie said, in a flat voice, 'That was Roy.'

Felicity nodded. 'Another casualty of my husband's.'

Ellie put into words what had been worrying her about Roy. 'Did he sign anything, promising to give your husband all that money?'

'They all do. I have to provide a savoury meal, which makes them drink a lot. I don't *think* Arthur puts anything in the wine, but they do all get drunk quickly, while Arthur never seems to be affected. Then Arthur holds out a plan for a golden future to them, and they swallow it whole. He always tells them there's a risk, but they never believe him. He said everyone wants something for nothing and that "when stupidity is allied to cupidity, he's on to a winner".'

'I thought you liked Roy.'

'I did at first, but he's let Arthur walk all over him, and I don't like that.'

Ellie made a note to get Roy to talk to his mother, soonest! Only she could sort this out.

The phone rang again, and again they both jumped. It was Thomas this time, ringing to see how they were coping. Felicity went into the study to speak to him privately. Ellie dusted and hoovered and paid the outstanding bills. She made another list of things to do. She knew some people found solace in making lists, but she wasn't normally one of them. Only, somehow it helped when you were trying to organize someone else's life as well as your own. Or when you were trying to get through a tiresome patch.

Kate didn't ring. Ellie sewed a button on a blouse, fretting. How were they getting on in the City? Had Sir Arthur been defeated, or had he triumphed yet again? How was Julian Talbot doing? Would the rain never stop?

Three o'clock found them in Bill Weatherspoon's office, explaining as best they could what had happened. Bill was an old family friend of Ellie's. He had a wise, monkey-like face on top of a tall — not to say gangling — body. Older than her and supposedly thinking about retiring, he was her first port of call whenever she got into trouble. He heard them out, blinked once or twice, and asked for some parts of the narrative to be repeated.

Then he leaned back in his chair, and laced his fingers together. 'Do I understand that you had information which was relevant to several crimes, including attempted murder . . . and you left it with Miss Quicke, instead of handing it over to the police?'

'Oh,' said Ellie. 'I see what you mean. But we did try to tell the police, honest.'

Bill washed his face with both hands. 'Lady Kingsley walked out of her house, leaving her husband in possession, instead of asking him to leave?'

'Yes,' said Felicity in a small voice. 'He frightens me.'

Bill exhaled. 'You do realize you've both placed yourselves in the wrong? Yes?'

They nodded, forlornly.

'Well, we'll just have to see what we can do about it. Ellie, would you care to use the phone in the outer office to see if your aunt has turned the evidence over to the police yet? Meanwhile, I need to take some details from Lady Kingsley.'

Dismissed, Ellie did as she was told. She rang her aunt's and Rose answered the phone, to say that Miss Quicke had gone out somewhere quite early, and Roy had been fussing, coming in and out asking where she was, and getting in the way something terrible. No, the police hadn't been round, but Rose thought Miss Quicke was going to see them, because she'd told Rose not to worry if she was some time, which of course made her worry all the more. Rose left the phone for a moment, telling Ellie to hold on, which she did.

Had Sir Arthur somehow found out that Miss Quicke had the copy of his hard drive, and moved on her? No. How could he? Well, he could guess, perhaps, that Ellie would take money troubles to her aunt. Or Roy would. Then he could have phoned her, offered to meet to discuss the matter.

Or, she might have offered to meet him, to try to extract Roy from his predicament. And then . . . it didn't bear thinking about.

The phone quacked in Ellie's ear. 'It's me, Rose, again. Your aunt's just come back and . . . what's that? Ellie, I'll hand you over to her.'

Aunt Drusilla. 'Ellie? Where are you? No, don't bother to tell me. I'm soaking wet because the cab driver wouldn't park right up by the porch. Yes, of course I've taken the hard drive and the messages in to the police. They tried to fob me off with some sergeant or other, but I did manage to speak to someone senior in the end. Then I went on to see the specialist about my hip. Luckily I've got private health insurance and he says he can do it quickly . . .' A man's voice in the distance. 'Here's Roy come in. I want a word with you, Roy! Ellie, I'll just hand you back to Rose.'

Rose was all excited and happy. 'Oh, Ellie, isn't that just like her, to go off and see the specialist without telling us? Poor Roy — he does look hangdog — but she'll sort him out, never fear.'

Ellie put the phone down, smiling. Good. Extra good. Now let's hope Chris Talbot has some good news, too. She found the number with some difficulty — where was her mobile? She really must look for it properly — and got through to him straight away.

'Ellie Quicke here. How is your son?'

'A little better. We're hopeful. And you? And my daughter?'

'Your daughter is in with a solicitor, discussing a divorce. I went with her this morning to collect some more of her things. Diana seems to have moved in.'

'Felicity should have kicked him out, and not left him in possession.'

'She's frightened of him.'

'Yes, he can be very frightening. You haven't asked how things went this morning. Kingsley expected to win. He thought he'd promised a couple of the directors enough money to keep them loyal to him. He was mistaken. They faded away, and he lost. The board asked for his resignation, and though he refused, he won't be able to maintain that position. The restructuring will take place as planned. The announcement will be in the press tomorrow.'

He ended the conversation, as Felicity came out of Bill's room. She'd been crying. Bill always kept a big box of tissues on his desk for clients.

'Tell you what,' said Ellie. 'What do you say to going out to supper somewhere cheerful? Just the two of us. No men, no hassle. My invitation.'

Felicity did her best to smile. 'I have to pop in to see Mummy first, and tell the people at the home to send all the bills to my father in future. After that, yes; that would be nice.'

CHAPTER TWENTY-ONE

What woke her?

Was that the crash of more glass being broken in the conservatory? No, she didn't think that was what had wakened her. The digital clock on her bedside table said half past twelve. It appeared to be a quiet night. No cars in the street; not that there were usually many on this quiet side road. An owl hooting?

No, a man shouting in the distance.

Midge wasn't where he'd started the night, tucked up at her back. She turned on the bedside light. The cat was standing at the foot of the bed, ears pricked, looking at the door.

Ellie's mind went into overdrive. Was Sir Arthur trying to break in to punish her for her interference? Or his wife, for daring to leave him? He'd had hours to work himself up into a murderous state.

It was very dark out. Suppose he did try to get at her, how would he do it?

He'd drive his big car to her road, leave it there and . . . try to batter the front door down? She'd put the chain on, hadn't she? She was pretty sure she had. And shot the bolts on the door. Or, if Diana had cut another key, he could borrow that to get in.

The shouting had seemed to come from the back of the house. Would he know about the back alley, which gave on to her garden? No, surely not. He wouldn't even be able to find his way up the garden path, would he?

Except that there was a street light in the alley at the bottom of her garden, and it did allow you to see where the path ran up the slope. People came and went that way all the time.

The shouting was . . . where? Not at the front of the house, which was where she slept. Had he got into the garden? Perhaps he thought that Ellie slept in the back bedroom, which was now occupied by Felicity?

Ellie groped for her mobile phone before she remembered that she'd lost it. Where had she left it? Out of bed, into slippers. The night was warm enough. She pawed through the clothes she'd left on a chair. No mobile. Her dressing gown, hanging on the back of the door. Yes! The mobile was in there. She hesitated. She didn't want to ring the police if it were just some ordinary drunk yelling at the moon.

She opened her bedroom door. Midge poked his head out, and shot through the gap. She whispered, 'Come back, Midge!' He took no notice.

Felicity's light wasn't on, so she hadn't heard anything.

Ellie shivered. Not such a warm night, after all. Seeing the house all in darkness, Sir Arthur — if it was he — would no doubt think better of any idea of getting even with her. He sounded drunken. He might be so drunk that he'd stumble around for a bit, mistake the gate into her garden, fall and lie there in a stupor till he'd slept it off.

She really did not need to stand there on the landing, holding her mobile, shivering. The nights were noticeably colder this last week. She wasn't even wearing a winter-weight nightie yet. Just a cotton one. Quite a pretty one, with a motif of tiny blue flowers on a white ground, and lacey inserts around the top. No sleeves.

She'd over-reacted. There was no danger. She'd be jumping at shadows next.

Except, she'd turned off all the lights before she came up to bed, and now there was a light on downstairs.

She could persuade herself that she'd forgotten to turn it off, and go back to bed. Or . . . she could go downstairs in the dark and see who had turned on the light in the kitchen.

Cra-sh! A horrible, grinding crash.

Followed by the unmistakable sound of breaking glass.

Was he forcing his way into the conservatory? Ellie spared a thought, a hope, that Kate and Armand next door would be woken by the noise and call the police . . . which would be a good idea . . . except that Armand was the sort of person who always Had a Go when faced with lawbreaking and Ellie really didn't want Armand facing up to a drunken madman armed with . . . who knew what?

And then . . . the sound of someone swearing in whispers.

Then a waiting silence.

Ellie could hear herself breathe.

Her phone rang down below. Kate, wondering what was wrong? There was no way Ellie was going out there to answer it. Her mobile rang. Ellie ducked back into her bedroom, closed the door, and answered it.

It was Kate. 'Ellie, what's happening? Are you all right? Where are you? Is it your conservatory windows again? Look, Armand's coming round, I told him not to, but you know what he's like . . . oh, Catriona's woken up, and I'll have to . . .'

'I'm all right,' said Ellie. 'There does seem to be someone downstairs. I'll wait for Armand to get here before I go down.'

'Oh, my baby!' The phone was cut off as Kate fled to rescue Catriona, who was indeed wailing.

Still no sound from below. Ellie told herself that he wasn't waiting outside her bedroom door. She'd have heard him if he'd climbed the stairs. Wouldn't she? Maybe he was searching for something downstairs, making sure there was no one else in the house before coming up to find them.

A voice downstairs. Two voices. Someone laughed. Armand, laughing? Whatever was going on? She opened her door a crack.

'Hello, there! Ellie?' It was Armand's voice in the hall.

Ellie shot out on to the landing. 'Are you all right, Armand?' All the lights were on downstairs and standing there, holding a reddening tea towel to her hand was Felicity, dressed in jeans and a sweater, and Armand, brandishing a stout walking stick.

'No burglars,' said Armand. 'Felicity fell over her bicycle and dropped a glass on to the tiled floor.'

'I'm so sorry!' Felicity was in tears, again. 'I didn't mean to wake you. I couldn't sleep and came down for a glass of water. I was going to sit in the conservatory for a bit, and I only put on the little light over the sink so as not to disturb you, only I forgot my bike was there, and fell over it and then I dropped my glass and it broke and when I went to pick up the pieces, I cut myself.'

Ellie began to laugh, until she realized that Felicity was dripping blood on to the hall floor. 'Let's have a look at what you've done to yourself.'

Midge jumped up on to the boiler, to indicate he'd like some food. Normality returned.

* * *

The rain was bouncing off the road and that wasn't the only reason Sir Arthur was in a foul mood. Who'd have thought so much could go wrong so quickly!

He'd gone from one colleague to another, cajoling, threatening; but for once he'd failed to get his own way. They'd been bought off, of course. One of them even suggested it would be best if Arthur did resign . . . save his face . . . cut his losses . . .

Cowards! Stupid fools!

He'd have their guts for garters. He never forgot a bad turn, and this was one of the worst he'd ever had. He'd get Martinez to . . .

He hit the steering wheel of the car in frustration, peering through the whirring windscreen wipers at the dark road ahead. Damn Martinez! Why did he have to go missing now?

Martinez hadn't been careless, had he? Could the police really trace the 'accident' back to him? If so, then that was just one more thing he'd have to see to.

The dog whined and pawed at the back of his seat. She wasn't used to travelling in cars. He couldn't trust her in the front with him, so had tied her up in the back where she kept up a continuous whining that was getting on his nerves.

He took the car round the bend at speed, spraying water from potholes in the lane. The car skidded. He corrected the skid. His mobile rang. Not his hands-free car mobile, but his personal one. He fumbled in his pocket for it.

Diana. 'Are you all right, Arthur? I've been waiting for you for ages. Do you know what time it is?'

Curses. Was it that late? He could do without Diana demanding attention at the moment. 'On my way back. Had to pick up my new dog on the way. Half an hour?'

'I'll be waiting!' Oh, but she could put such an intonation in her voice. When he got back, he'd throw her on the floor and . . . a pity that Felicity had decided to go. He'd miss her in some ways, but Diana . . .

Dropping the mobile on the seat beside him, he jerked as the dog threw all her weight against the back of his seat, making it shudder . . . a bend was coming up . . . the bright lights of an oncoming car, too high to . . .

He fought to keep the car to the left, but the oncoming car was too far into the centre of the road, and the rain . . . the skid took the car crashing through spindly trees that lined the road . . . down a steep embankment . . . he was going to make it . . . a larger tree loomed up ahead, and he tried to turn the wheel, but it was too late . . .

He put both arms above his head as the airbags inflated . . . the wheel was wrenched round and struck something unseen, and the car tipped over . . . and over . . . down the slope . . .

The last thing he heard was the dog howling with fear.

The dog survived and was found a new owner. Sir Arthur died.

* * *

The police arrived at Sir Arthur's house next morning at the same time as Maureen trudged up the drive, wondering how much extra she could demand for her services in future.

Maureen directed them to Ellie's house, where she and Felicity were having a late breakfast, both listless from lack of sleep and anxiety.

Felicity answered the front door to a strange policeman, accompanied by a policewoman. The policewoman said, 'Are you Lady Kingsley? May we come in? I'm afraid there's some bad news.'

Felicity said, 'Arthur?' and slid to the floor in a faint. She was only out for a second or two, but that was long enough for Ellie to wonder if the girl were anaemic, and could she get the doctor out to visit.

Ellie accompanied Felicity to identify her husband in the morgue.

* * *

Later, Felicity sat with both hands around a mug of coffee in the kitchen, while Ellie peeled potatoes for their lunch. Felicity had been very quiet since the police left. She'd refused to see the doctor, or to take a tranquilliser. When Ellie had spoken to her, Felicity hadn't seemed to hear. So Ellie had left her alone.

Now Ellie saw that Felicity was crying, soundlessly, hopelessly.

Ellie drew up a chair, and put her arm around Felicity. 'Cry it all out.' She remembered how she'd cried for days and days after her husband died. He'd been the centre of her life for thirty years. He'd always dealt with business affairs for both of them. When he died, she'd felt helpless, couldn't think how she'd manage. Felicity must be going through the same thing.

Felicity brushed tears away. 'I'm not crying for him. Or am I? He was kind to me, in his own peculiar way. We did have some good times together. I loved having the garden, and a dog, and someone to look after. I wouldn't have been able to look after Mummy if it hadn't been for him.'

'I know. It comes back and hits you when you least expect it, and you find yourself crying all over again, even when you think you've got over it.'

'How did you manage?'

'Good friends. Good advice. Prayer.'

'Prayer?' Felicity tested the word and found it alien. 'Thomas prayed with me over the phone yesterday, but he used ordinary words. I didn't think prayer could be like that. Just everyday words.'

'Why not? Didn't you feel better afterwards?'

'I suppose I did. Can you catch the habit of praying from other people? I've hardly ever been to church since I grew up, but last night I did try to pray. I was so afraid that Arthur would come after me. And now, he's dead.'

Did Felicity think her husband died because she'd prayed? No, surely not. Ellie said, 'It was an accident, remember.'

'Mm. I know. You were saying that after your husband died you had friends to help you. Arthur and I had no friends, only business acquaintances. They all think I'm clueless. Now . . .' She shuddered. 'I suppose I inherit the house, and the manor and the life insurance and all his business interests, and trouble with the police, and I don't know where to start.'

'Your solicitor will help you, surely.'

'Arthur's solicitor's like Martinez. He looks at me and is polite, sort of, but makes it clear he thinks I'm a birdbrain. He did all Arthur's dirty work. He'll run rings around me, and I won't know how to stop him. I don't want to do business like Arthur, but all his business associates will want me to give them my backing, or sell to them, and the police say the newspapers will be featuring his death and will want me to comment, and I don't know what to say or do. Tell me what to do, Ellie.'

'Take time to think and make up your own mind. There's lots of people will want to advise you, Felicity. I suppose the trick is to work out whose advice you should take.'

'*Not* Arthur's solicitor. I don't trust him. *Not* his business associates. *Not* Mummy, who's got no business sense at all and who'll want me to install her back at the manor and wait on her hand and foot. You must think me very hard, but I don't think I could bear that. She sort of mops me up, if you know what I mean. I'd like to have her out of the home to stay with me for the odd weekend, but not for good, because I can't cope with her when she gets drunk and . . . I don't like to say this about my own mother, but she's horrid when she's drunk, and if I give her any money she buys gin with it, and she can't climb stairs any more and . . . oh, I oughtn't to be so ungrateful, but I don't think I could do it.'

Ellie stroked Felicity's hand, but didn't comment. She didn't think she could have done it either.

Felicity mopped her eyes. 'You put everything in a trust fund, didn't you, Ellie? Suppose I sell everything and do the same?'

'If you do that, then you must choose your trustees wisely, people who can deal with City sharks and come away with a whole skin. They do say that widows shouldn't make any decisions about moving house, or selling up, for at least a year. What about your father? He'd help.'

Felicity sniffed. 'Can I trust him?'

Ellie was silent for a while, thinking. 'He does care for you. He volunteered to take care of your mother's bills out of concern for you and not because he'd be getting anything out of it. If I were you, I'd listen to what he has to say very carefully, but not make any decisions about the future, or Arthur's businesses, for a while. Sign nothing. Make no promises. Make no decisions.'

'I'd like to make reparation for the wrongs Arthur did. I suppose you'll say that I can't do that, that I might end up a bankrupt if I tried, that all sorts of people would descend on me, demanding money, and it would clean me out.'

Here was a nice ethical dilemma. Would it be right for Felicity to divest herself of everything, in order to return money to people who'd been foolishly trusting, or looking for a quick buck . . . like the Meadows-Fitches? But then, what about some of the other people he'd fleeced? Some

— maybe most — had been after a quick buck, and you could say that it served them right if they lost their money.

On the other hand, while Mrs Anderson had come out of her dealings with Sir Arthur all right, many others hadn't. But would Felicity really want to make reparations in a month's or a year's time when she was on her beam ends?

'Suppose you ask Thomas about that? Anyway, wouldn't it be a good idea to appoint someone to act for you in business matters? There must be someone in your circle whom you trust.'

'You. Kate. Thomas. Bill.'

Ellie lifted her hands in dismay. 'You've only known us for a short time.'

'I've watched you deal with all sorts of problems. Thomas is a shining sort of person, isn't he? And Bill is so straight. The way he talked to me, I could tell I could rely on him absolutely, but that he wouldn't mince his words if I did something stupid. I really liked Kate, too; Arthur said she's looking for a part-time job. She could deal with the City sharks for me, couldn't she?'

A part-time job with Felicity might well solve Kate's financial problems. 'Ask her.'

'Then there's your aunt. I think she likes me. I could trust her, in a way, too. I think she'd tell me if there were a conflict of interest.'

Silence. Ellie studied Felicity's profile, and Felicity studied the coffee dregs in her cup. 'Hey,' said Felicity, 'I've just realized. I've inherited the right to half this house when you die.'

Ellie smiled. 'So you have. Diana tore up the cheque. I wonder what the legal position is now?'

'Arthur shouldn't have tried to buy it in the first place. I'll give you the paper to burn. I'm not sure Diana had the right to sell it, anyway. I'll have to ask Bill. Do you think he'd take me on as a client, properly?'

'Try him.'

'I will.' Felicity thought of something amusing. 'Diana's going to be so mad when she finds out.'

'Yes, Lady Kingsley, she will.' Ellie grinned too.

Felicity stirred, looking around her. 'I have to register the death, make arrangements for the funeral. I have to go back to the house, shoot Marco out if he's still there, liaise with the police. The phone will be ringing night and day — his business "friends", the newspapers — and I shan't know what to say. I can't bear the thought of sleeping there, ever again. I hate the place, and I want to sell it as soon as I can.'

'But Felicity . . .'

'Oh, I know lots of people would think it was heaven to own such a huge house, but it's meant nothing but drudgery and unhappiness to me. I'd much prefer something like this of yours, Ellie. So, could you bear it if I come back to sleep here at night?'

'Yes, of course. But, Felicity, you shouldn't be by yourself. Haven't you any friends or family who could help?'

'Mummy's friends? Or Arthur's? Arthur didn't like me to have friends, and neither did Mummy. I have to start afresh. Ellie, it's a lot to ask, I know, but I need to clear out Arthur's things, and I need company. Will you come with me? I can cook for you and you can show me how to make puff pastry and . . . why am I crying again?'

'Because,' said Ellie. 'Just because. By the way, it's too much trouble to make puff pastry. Buy it frozen and cheat.'

* * *

Felicity went to bed early that evening, and Kate came over to catch up on what had happened with Ellie. Kate agreed to help Felicity sort out her affairs, and then they got on to the subject of the poisoning of the dog, which was where everything had started. 'Everyone kept telling me how good I was with people,' said Ellie. 'I shouldn't have listened. I didn't know enough about poisoners to realize where I ought to have been looking, and I didn't recognize the signs when I saw them. It's been a salutary experience and in future I must be more careful.'

'You think you know who it was?'

Ellie nodded. She gave a name and her reasons for thinking she'd identified the culprit. 'There's no proof, though.'

Kate thought about it, and agreed. 'So what are you going to wear for the funeral of the late unlamented?'

* * *

A fortnight later, Felicity was ferrying Ellie over to the private hospital in which Aunt Drusilla lay, recovering from her hip operation.

The funeral was over and done with. Some of Arthur's colleagues had talked of a service of remembrance, but Felicity had vetoed it.

Marco was in a bail hostel, awaiting trial on charges of criminal damage, and the police were trying to extradite Martinez from Morocco to face charges of attempted murder on Julian Talbot, who was fast recovering. Diana had sold another flat and so was reasonably secure financially, though not on speaking terms with her mother for the moment.

Felicity's complicated affairs were being sorted out slowly but thoroughly by Kate, and Bill Weatherspoon had agreed to help too. Miss Quicke had suggested that Felicity go into deep mourning and cry whenever she was pressed to sign something she didn't fully understand. Felicity had followed these instructions to the letter. Chris Talbot had found Felicity a buyer for her big house, but she still slept at Ellie's every night.

Ellie was planning to have her own house completely redecorated, and had ordered a new kitchen, which Felicity had helped her choose.

Felicity was looking better groomed and beginning to smile now and again. She continued, dutifully, to visit her mother, but not as often as she had.

She'd even talked about getting another dog soon. 'If only we'd been able to find out who killed Rex. Poison's such a mean, cowardly trick.'

Ellie nodded. 'Surely that's all in the past now.'

'I tell myself that, but somehow it keeps nagging at me. You don't talk about it any more. Do you think you know who it was?'

'I didn't for a long time and I'm only guessing now. Kate gave me a lot of stuff on poisoners. It took me a while to read all through it and, well, it did make me think about one person in particular. I'm not saying it *was* her. There were so many people your husband wronged, but with a few exceptions they're all men, or people who hadn't the opportunity to deliver the pizza to your doorstep.'

'Who was it?'

Ellie was in a mood to tease. 'Well, it wasn't your father; not his style.'

Felicity was horrified. 'Of course not!' Chris Talbot had at long last persuaded her to meet him for dinner. They were not yet on easy terms, but perhaps they soon would be. Felicity had even wondered aloud if Julian would like to spend part of his convalescence down at the manor.

'No, not your father,' Ellie agreed. 'I did wonder about Martinez or Marco for a while, but poison would never have been Marco's weapon of choice, and Martinez had more to gain by keeping your husband alive than killing him. It wasn't you—'

Felicity gasped, 'What?'

'—because you'd never have risked the dog eating any of it,' said Ellie, smiling at her. 'But your mother . . .'

'Nonsense! I was sitting with her at the home when the pizza was delivered to the house.'

'I know, but I did wonder if she could have got the commodore to deliver it for her. But no,' said Ellie. 'She wouldn't risk your eating poison, because you're her meal ticket. So it wasn't her. It wasn't your husband's housekeeper at the manor, either, because she's had plenty of opportunities to poison him down at the manor, and hasn't done so.'

'I don't know why I haven't given her the sack,' said Felicity.

'Because you're sorry for her,' said Ellie, 'and because you need someone to look after the place until you decide whether or not you want to keep it. There were one or two other candidates. Mrs Meadows-Fitch: well, we know she took her own revenge, as did Paddy, the odd-job man — when is he coming to repaint your garage doors, by the way? Then there was the architect's wife, Mrs Anderson. She took a more than adequate revenge on your husband, and anyway, she's not the type.'

'I don't know anyone who is,' said Felicity.

Ellie looked at her watch. 'Look, we're a bit early. Aunt Drusilla won't want to see us till after her afternoon nap. Why don't we drive round by the park? There's this woman whom your husband was persecuting, a dried-up, secretive, poor sort of creature. The sort that might let an insult fester, brood upon it. My guess is that she fits the bill.

'Mrs Alexis is the only one I talked to who was a loner, played down her hurt, and hasn't, apparently, taken any revenge. I thought at first she was too repressed to strike back, but now, I'm beginning to wonder.'

Felicity drove them round by the park and stopped outside Mrs Alexis's house. There was a For Sale notice at the gate, windows hung wide open, the front door was off its hinges, and two workmen were piling lengths of old carpet and lino into a skip at the roadside. Their foreman was standing in the front doorway, fingering a mobile.

Felicity was thoughtful. 'Kate was talking to me about this house only the other day. It was rented out for years to someone who was always behindhand with the rent. There were several court orders to try to get her out, but she always managed to pay up at the last minute. Now she's gone, the builders are going to modernize it, to attract a buyer. It's a wonderful location, and there's even a garage, but just look what someone's done to the garden!'

Ellie frowned. Was this the truth? It might be. She approached the foreman. 'Has Mrs Alexis gone, then?'

'Got eyes, haven't you?'

Ellie nodded. Felicity went to look through the window at the front, and then disappeared into the house. Ellie followed her in and out of rooms, which seemed to be larger, brighter and more welcoming than she remembered. Felicity was inspecting the house in mounting excitement, making notes on a memo pad.

The foreman found them upstairs. 'Do you want to buy it, then?'

'I own it,' said Felicity, with a touch of impatience.

Ellie asked the foreman, 'Do you know where Mrs Alexis has gone?'

'Bit of a mystery, that,' said the foreman. 'No forwarding address.'

'There'd have been a removal van?'

'Self-drive. Hired for the day. So the neighbours said. They didn't know she could drive, but apparently she could. Went off without saying goodbye. Sounds like she won't be missed.'

Felicity led the way downstairs. 'Ellie, this is just the sort of house I want for myself. It needs completely gutting, of course, and a larger kitchen built out at the back. The garden's nothing much at the moment, but it would give me a blank canvas, and the park's just opposite for walking a dog when I get one.'

Ellie turned to stare at the house. What Felicity said made sense. Yes, Ellie could see Felicity happily living here, perhaps with a part-time job to keep her occupied, not because she would need it; Kate would see to that.

Felicity was already on her mobile, making arrangements to have the house taken off the market. 'I'll see if Roy can meet me here tomorrow to do some drawings for a new kitchen and shower room. Also that garage will have to be rebuilt; it looks as if it's falling down.' Felicity was beginning to find her feet.

Ellie said, 'It doesn't worry you that the house was occupied for so many years by such a sad creature as Mrs Alexis?'

'I didn't feel any of that. The house is just a shell. I felt it welcomed me. What made you think she poisoned Rex?'

'I don't think she meant to do that, but she's the sort of person who might have wanted to give your husband a bellyache. She wouldn't have known about the dog.'

'We should tell the police.'

'Would they be interested? Rex's death was an accident, and your husband didn't die of poison. Surely the woman has been punished enough, by losing her home? And we've no proof.'

Felicity thought about it. 'It's hard to stop being angry. I was so angry about Rex, but maybe that was because I couldn't afford to be angry with Arthur then. I think about poor Rex now, and I still want to cry. But if Mrs Alexis wasn't able to keep up with the rent, and Arthur was urging her to get out, I suppose I can see how she could get so desperate that she might want to hurt him. The police could trace her, if they really wanted to. Couldn't they?'

'Probably. But the accidental killing of a dog wouldn't be a high priority.'

Felicity nodded agreement. 'Right. Let's get on with our lives then, shall we? Do you think your aunt will like these lilies I've bought for her?'

'She'll probably say she's seen better in a crematorium. She'll add that she's not dead yet, and has no intention of dying just to please us!'

Felicity laughed. 'I do enjoy visiting your aunt. I've never met anyone like her. I've been wondering, though. How do you think she'd get on with my father?'

Ellie started to laugh. 'A clash of giants. I suspect they'd recognize a worthy adversary, be terribly polite to one another, and afterwards, each would warn you against the other. They're both way above my head.'

'Not with people, they're not,' said Felicity. 'You're the glue that sticks us all together.'

'Oh, nonsense,' said Ellie, and blushed.

THE END

THE JOFFE BOOKS STORY

We began in 2014 when Jasper agreed to publish his mum's much-rejected romance novel and it became a bestseller.

Since then we've grown into the largest independent publisher in the UK. We're extremely proud to publish some of the very best writers in the world, including Joy Ellis, Faith Martin, Caro Ramsay, Helen Forrester, Simon Brett and Robert Goddard. Everyone at Joffe Books loves reading and we never forget that it all begins with the magic of an author telling a story.

We are proud to publish talented first-time authors, as well as established writers whose books we love introducing to a new generation of readers.

We have been shortlisted for Independent Publisher of the Year at the British Book Awards three times, in 2020, 2021 and 2022, and for the Diversity and Inclusivity Award at the Independent Publishing Awards in 2022.

We built this company with your help, and we love to hear from you, so please email us about absolutely anything bookish at feedback@joffebooks.com

If you want to receive free books every Friday and hear about all our new releases, join our mailing list: www.joffebooks.com/contact

And when you tell your friends about us, just remember: it's pronounced Joffe as in coffee or toffee!

ALSO BY VERONICA HELEY

THE ELLIE QUICKE MYSTERIES

Book 1: MURDER AT THE ALTAR
Book 2: MURDER BY POISON PEN
Book 3: MURDER OF INNOCENCE
Book 4: MURDER BY ACCIDENT
Book 5: MURDER IN THE GARDEN
Book 6: MURDER BY COMMITTEE

THE BEA ABBOT AGENCY MYSTERIES

Book 1: A FALSE CHARITY
Book 2: A FALSE PICTURE
Book 3: A FALSE STEP
Book 4: A FALSE PRETENCE
Book 5: FALSE MONEY
Book 6: A FALSE REPORT
Book 7: A FALSE ALARM
Book 8: A FALSE DIAMOND
Book 9: A FALSE IMPRESSION
Book 10: A FALSE WALL
Book 11: A FALSE FIRE
Book 12: A FALSE PRIDE
Book 13: A FALSE ACCOUNT
Book 14: A FALSE CONCLUSION
Book 15: A FALSE FACE

Printed in Great Britain
by Amazon

46129604R10157